A DRESS
the COLOR of the SKY

By Jennifer Irwin

Published by Glass Spider Publishing
www.glassspiderpublishing.com
ISBN 978-0-9990096-5-9
Library of Congress Control Number: 2017953150
Cover design by Dana M. Boone
Edited by Vince Font

Franklin's Tower
Words by Robert Hunter
Music by Jerry Garcia and Bill Kreutzmann
Copyright (c) 1975 ICE NINE PUBLISHING CO., INC.
Copyright Renewed
All Rights Administered by UNIVERSAL MUSIC CORP.
All Rights Reserved Used by Permission
Reprinted by Permission of Hal Leonard LLC

Publisher's Note: We endeavor to provide you with a book that is of the highest professional quality and free of printing errors. If the copy of the book you have purchased contains any printing errors, please contact us at info@glassspiderpublishing.com to arrange for a free replacement of this product.

DEDICATION

For my mother, Ellie, my guardian angel. And to all the women who are chasing a dream.

ACKNOWLEDGMENTS

I could never have written this book without the help of so many amazing people. To Charlie, my partner in crime, for the many times you felt as though you'd lost me to the pages of a book. Thank you for reading, editing, coaching, encouraging, and cheering me on. For picking up the slack at home when I had to keep working through dinner and dishes.

To Chase Irwin, Campbell Irwin, Bailey Irwin, and Mason Hargraves, who tirelessly listened to me talk about the book, read excerpts, and put up with my need for everyone to be quiet. Thank you for continually encouraging me and for telling all your friends and their moms about the book (regardless of the embarrassing subject matter!). When each of you said you were proud of me, it inspired me to keep going. To Chase, who took my teary phone call in the middle of the night and talked me off of the cliff. To Campbell, for advising me on the appropriate language and phrases used by people in recovery. To Bailey, for your unfailing belief in my ability to write this book and the magical way you always knew when I needed a pep talk.

To Edward Young, who helped me build a foundation to work from. Thanks for the brilliant protagonist name, the perfect title, and for all your coaching with storytelling.

To Christine Brown, who stepped up early on to help me with grammar and editing.

To Annette Stevens, who read an early version of my manuscript and asked to purchase the film rights. Thank you for your input, critiques, comments, edits, and constant support. You never stopped rooting for me and the success of the book. Your faith in me, my writing, and the story kept me going through even the darkest of days.

To my amazing friends who read early versions of my manuscript and took the time to provide a critique and/or write a review: Jan Hargraves, Alie Keese, Chris Drum, Erika Couture, Lisa Matricardi, Becky Irwin, Cami Evans, Annette Stevens, Connie Smith, Sarah Adler, Dario Ghio, Andrea Kahrs, Mark West, Breezey Snyder, Melissa Riede, Emma Wells, Tina Dellis, Erika Garcia, Stacy Heim, Karen Stuckman, Rachel Larkin, Carolyn Kavanagh, Ann Hall, Kara Davis, Jen Sanders, Lauren Roman, Jane Pratt, Stephanie Kuehn, Don Edwards, Andrea Truslow, Bella Cosetta, Patricia Fairweather Romero, Madison Stevens, Susan Whitman, and Peggy Fuller. Your reviews provided a foundation for me to begin marketing the book. Every review encouraged me keep going and believe I was writing something special.

To the friends who tirelessly liked my social media posts, gave me positive comments, and encouragement throughout the writing process: Jan Hargraves, Alie Keese, Anita Lugliani, Andrea Kahrs, Chris Drum, Katrina Goldberg, Tracy Chrystall, Kara Herbrandson, Cami Evans, Annette Stevens, Madison Stevens, Andrea Truslow, and Nancy Sullivan.

To my brother, Jay Kuhn, an absolute angel. Thank you for your love and support and for caring for Dad in his dying days.

To my writing coach, Angie Fenimore, who helped me "untangle the necklace."

To Something or Other Publishing, for teaching me the importance of marketing and how to build a solid social media platform.

To Anita Lugliani, for taking over my book marketing when I needed to focus on writing.

To my agent, Karen Gantz, who encouraged me to publish small press.

To my attorney, Charlie Hargraves, who negotiated all of my contracts and fought for my rights at every turn. Lord only knows where'd I'd be without your guidance and scrutinizing eye.

To Pia Mellody, founder of The Meadows and author of *Eight Emotions*, the feelings chart I referred to in the book. Pia's theories on the effects of childhood trauma have become the foundation for the Meadows' programs, and are a major reason for their success. I used The Meadows formula as a reference for outlining the therapeutic treatments in my book.

To my editor, Vince Font, you are simply a pleasure to work with. You polished my manuscript with detail and a keen eye for smoothing out the rough edges. Thank you for putting my book at the top of your priority list and working tirelessly to meet the tight deadline we set for publication.

To my publisher, Glass Spider Publishing, you said "yes" to all of my requests, even when I asked for something you hadn't done before. I felt you wanted the success of my book as much as I did, which gave me an incredible sense of peace.

And finally, to Prudence Aldrich, my alter ego; thank you for being my voice to tell this story.

$\mathcal{P}$ROLOGUE

$\mathcal{D}$r. Sheryl O'Brien, PhD, was one of those women whose sexual orientation you couldn't guess. No telling if she leaned bi, gay, or if she was into men. Sex consumed me—I pictured people doing it. To imagine Sheryl's face contorting in orgasm proved impossible, and *that* bothered me.

No other option than to slump on the shrink sofa, wedge a throw pillow behind my back, and hunker down. The hem of my jeans hiked up. I tugged them and wished for one brand in size twenty-six, long enough for my legs while pretending too short was *très chic*. One more thing I was pretending.

"How are things going with Nick?" A dramatic press back in her chair. "Last time we spoke, you were considering a trial separation."

"He moved to a swanky apartment. No idea where he's coming up with the money." A ringlet dangled over my eye. I studied its vibrant copper tone. "Not sure where I fall in the lineup between me and the other woman. I obsess over everything about them." The neutral shade of my pedicure brought me momentary pleasure. I rubbed my earlobe and pondered the unfamiliar calm deep inside me since he left.

"Elaborate."

"How she orgasms, moves, her preferred positions, the list never ends. He might be happier without me." I yanked a tissue from the box and wound it around my fingers. "I want him back and need to get my shit together."

"Do you think he needs to work on himself?"

"No, I deserve this." The Kleenex hit the decorative wastebasket on the first throw. "In a strange way, he's more communicative now."

"Nick may appear as though he is trying to change, and he will—a shade here, a shade there. The old behavior will return in times of stress. The concern is to find the source of what drives your compulsions."

A pry into my soul like a storm about to rip through the landscape.

My shrink pulled a book from the shelf. "Read this. The similarities between a sociopath and your husband may upset you."

"Do you think?" The eerie, hollow-eyed face on the cover creeped me out. A combination of Freddy Krueger and the Phantom of the Opera.

"He exhibits sociopathic characteristics."

"Well, I am the one who failed at the most important commitment of my life." The inner demon flogged. *Slut. Whore.* "My financial struggles and the marriage beat me down." A plethora of self-loathing doused the velour cushions. "I don't deserve blessings. I'm quite adept at sabotaging."

"This goes back to your life before age eighteen." She dropped the bomb without pause. "Consider an inpatient program."

"The problem is, I have a son and no time or money." The velocity of my voice increased with the level of anxiety. "Which is why I bang the architect. He pays me." Parched, I grabbed my water and took a swig.

Quiet, easygoing Sheryl. "This will not be resolved until you face the demons, your past. It's time to immerse yourself in recovery and stop denying these self-destructive patterns. Your current survival mechanism doesn't serve you now."

Most women associated intimacy with love. Why couldn't I be like other women? Careful. Dignified. Normal.

"Talk to Nick. Something tells me he will come up with the funds."

"Fine."

The mere thought of that conversation scared the bejesus out of me.

CHAPTER ONE

A moment of awkward silence dangled between us. Mr. 17A and I wedged between the vanity and stainless-steel toilet. My legs knocked against the edge of the sink. All eye contact avoided. The familiar *ding* directed us back to our seats.

"Must be about to land." My too-snug J Brands proved a struggle in the small space. I jabbed his ribs while inching them up. He planted an awkward peck on my cheek and took in my reflection. His dark hair matched the whiskers peeking through a morning shave.

"Beautiful." He smiled with a downtrodden vibe. "Best if I go out first. Wait a minute before you follow."

Am I his first mile-high experience?

He winked, pushed open the bathroom door, and left. I re-latched and cupped my hands to my face.

Obsession and Head & Shoulders. Put-together exterior, yet hiding flaws and secrets.

A lingering handwash. With damp fingers, I loosened my curls.

I counted the seats in my head. The attendant blocked me, and I squeezed through. My new friend shifted to the window.

"You're back." Relieved and surprised, he lifted the armrest, breaking all remaining barriers.

"Drinks?" The impatient flight attendant clutched the airline-branded napkins. I wondered if she suspected, or if she had ever banged a guy mid-flight.

"Chardonnay." The order couldn't come fast enough.

"Vodka tonic." I watched him struggle to liberate his briefcase from underneath the seat in front of him.

"My treat." The unpleasant idea of trading intercourse for a five-dollar drink was enough motivation.

There were multiple credit cards in my wallet, but I wanted to avoid any with Nick's name. With the other woman in his bed, he had no business knowing about me buying cocktails for two. I removed the card without disturbing the platinum band resting inside.

"Prudence," she said. "Uncommon name."

Approved. Phew.

A lime skewered, unscrewed bottle, wine emptied.

"Are you traveling for work?" I asked. "Perhaps you wear business casual for shits and giggles."

An analysis of his everything.

"In sales, travel a ton. Most flights aren't this exciting." A dried-up citrus wedge floated on top. "Cheers." Two strangers clinked plastic. "How about you?"

"On an extended trip." I hoped he wouldn't ask any more questions. The Cartier Tank adorned my wrist. It made me connect to my mother as if her energy radiated through the timepiece. Most of what she left me fell in the category of statement pieces. My taste tended toward delicate and didn't scream, "I'm wearing jewelry!"

"So, you're on vacation?"

"Well, no, I used to be married to an alcoholic." A half-truth. Nick was a bad drinker, but we were still wedded. "My son is fourteen."

Tell the mouth to stop moving.

"I'm on a much-needed holiday to engage in some soul-searching."

Not sure what kind of soul-searching goes on in a drug treatment facility.

"I live in LA," I blathered on. "Never been to Arizona."

Way too much about me for the hot guy in the window seat.

"What do you do?" he asked. Green eyes glowed over the cocktail rim.

"Interior designer." Fabric samples by the thousands, measurements, over-demanding clients, hammering nails; I feigned the assumed glamour.

"Not surprised, you come across as rather stylish."

Stylish and sad. I downed the last drop of chardonnay. Desperate for more, I pressed the instant call button. The same annoyed woman sauntered over.

"Yes?" Her breast grazed my hair as she turned off the light.

"Two more, please." I waited for a safe distance between us.

"These are on me." An American Express Black Card passed my face. No luck deciphering the name.

"The way I pounded down the booze, one might consider me a drunk."

"Not at all." He sipped. The knob in his throat lowered. "Believe me, life can be stressful." A bad-boy grin flashed at me. "I'd love your number so we can hang out while you're healing."

I was high on his attention, my drug of choice.

He placed a napkin and pen on the middle tray. "Old school," he said. "No one writes down their digits anymore."

Out of habit, I wrote the first three of my number and the last four of Christian's. I'd learned the hard way to bang them and leave.

Rubber-gloved hands collected our trash—a grim reminder of my failure to insist he use a condom. "Place your seat in the upright position for landing."

I was thankful Mr. 17A brought a carry-on so I could avoid awkward post-coital baggage claim conversation. The illuminated overhead light went black, and I undid my seatbelt. Regret hit, and the cabin temperature elevated.

My heart pounded as I walked into the airport in search of the driver or a Serenity Hills sign. The outer world disappeared. A sense of isolation and self-hatred overcame me. Naked and vulnerable, I needed protection.

Wait, this is anonymous. How will I find him?

A tall Native American man with chiseled features surveyed people in arrivals. My eyes pulled off his ponytail tie and loosened the long, dark locks.

"Ms. Aldrich?"

"Yes."

"The name's Jimmy, your driver. Got any luggage?"

"Yes, checked one."

I spotted my suitcase on the carousel and breathed easier knowing I was reunited with my beloved possessions. The way he swept up my bag, one would never guess the massive number of items inside: piles of clothes, Spring-edition fashion magazines, and enough sandals to last a lifetime. Outside the exit, a wall of blazing heat and blinding sunlight slammed into me. A full sunglass scramble.

"Beautiful day." Sweat invaded his face as he heaved my bag into the back. A "heavy" bag tag was strapped to the handle, screaming "over packer!" A badge of honor for a clothes horse like me. The packing for rehab I'd chalked off as more than challenging.

Out of instinct, I reached for the front passenger door. Jimmy scurried around and opened the back door for me. Perhaps some addicts tried to jump him for money or grab the wheel to careen into a liquor store. Once in the car, I clasped my hands together like a good girl.

"First time visiting Arizona?" Bloodshot eyes, his life story, passed to me without words.

"Yeah." The seat held the agonies of those who had ventured before me. "You must have some epic tales."

"Got a few." I caught a whiff of his musky manhood, a long, deodorant-free day.

"Ever been propositioned by one of your rides to bed down and ask for nothing in return?" My shrink advised me to hesitate before I moved my mouth and landed in hot water or a stranger's bed. "All the built-up stress would lighten if we hooked up before you delivered me. Swing by your place?"

"Believe me, I am flattered, but I can't. I'd lose my job."

"Got to give a girl credit for trying." It took me five minutes to find the hand cream in my purse.

He scanned the radio stations, fiddling, dissatisfied with the choices. "Those are saguaro." The stagnant air filled with his voice as he pointed ahead. "A sacred plant. Kill one, you risk going to jail. The oldest ones have the most arms."

Towering cacti dotted the parched desert. Men reached out to me, bristling with thorns. A sudden urge to examine them and touch their spines. On the radio, Marcy Playground belted out "Sex and Candy." After one verse, he flipped the channel.

I dumped my bag on the back seat and opened my compact. A hateful woman stared back at me. After applying lipstick, I rubbed some on my cheekbones. He observed my every move. "May as well make a decent first impression." I blended the color while we bonded through the rearview.

Clean, rocky, Zen-like landscaping flashed past. *A rehabilitation experience on Mars.* My palms sweated under the lotion.

"Here we are."

He opened the back door. Frozen, immobilized, terrified, a weathered hand guided me. No chance for an embrace. My last intimate contact for five weeks. In my final moment of freedom, I dipped ahead and swayed my hips.

"Best of luck."

My safety net vanished as I crossed through the double doors. An orderly took my everything.

"I am so pissed," I seethed under my breath. "My cosmetic bag is on the floor at home."

Nick's impatience had rattled me. He ticked off the minutes until my departure. The last-ditch chance to salvage our marriage and rescue myself.

"It's better you left the cosmetics behind."

I bet he flung steel at the gym after work. A real meathead bodybuilder type.

The mask to hide behind. My only camouflage, powder and a half-used Chanel lipstick in Rouge Coco Legende. A poster on the wall read, "Fake it 'til you make it."

Story of my life.

The meathead orderly rifled through my things. A procedure as personal and violating as a cavity search at the county jail.

A stern woman in white hovered over me. A full-blown Nurse Ratched.

No sightings of a medical worker in white since kindergarten. These people must see it all.

A sexy guy with sun-bleached hair walked through the door and didn't even glance my way.

I must not be attractive enough for a thirty-something beach hottie.

"For the last hour, I'm all edgy and anxious," he said to the nurse. "Can I be issued my next dose early? Suffering going on here." Our arms bumped. "Are you checking in?"

"Yup." *A savant.*

"The first day's the hardest. I'm Toby."

We touched hands, as sensuous as one could be at an addiction facility. He was a total street rat, but I still wanted him, or for him to want me.

He deciphered no extra meds would be administered. "This is fucking bullshit." The final burst as he exited.

"There's some paperwork for you to fill out," the Ratched impersonator said.

The office was tiny, with a chicken wire glass cut-out. I sat in the only available chair and wondered what genius had decided on menopause mauve. A photo of a chubby baby was propped on her shelf. "Your daughter?"

"No, my two-year-old granddaughter."

"Hard to remember my son as a baby. He's fourteen now."

The office shrunk in around me. Sweat beaded above my lip. The thought of being away from him for so long; panic over the amount of damage I had caused an innocent child. If I cried, I'd ruin the last of my makeup. Anyway, those floodgates were locked up for bigger reasons than cosmetics.

"Bring letters here, and we'll mail them for you."

A terrible mother.

"Can you tell me why you checked in?"

"Now?"

"Do the best you can."

"Some kind of situation with too many guys. No official diagnosis." The blatant fib embedded in my mind until I believed it myself.

"Any more information you would like to tell me?"

"Nope."

"The program requires you to agree to an abstinence contract." A stack of pages, the edges aligned, cleaned up and smoothed out. "This agreement represents your commitment to abstaining from engaging in sexual relations with men or women during your five-week stay. This includes sexual thoughts, conversations, provocative outfits, and masturbation. Violations must be reported. Any questions?"

My vagina tingled.

No sexual thoughts? Really?

"Sign at the X."

A bank of phones mapped the hallway.

"Each of the three units contains a timer, and you are allotted ten minutes once a day. On your second week, you may make your first call. Violations will cause loss of phone privileges."

A woman shouted in the receiver, hung up, and stormed out. Nurse Ratched determined if the behavior necessitated an intervention. Full attention once again on my admission forms with a bland, expressionless face like gloppy oatmeal. "Complete immersion achieves the best results."

"Can I call two people a day, or only one?"

"One." She tucked a card with my name on it into the plastic sleeve at the end of a purple lanyard. "Wear this at all times in public spaces. No one enters buildings or attends meetings without a badge."

With a tilt of my head, she crowned me the Purple Lanyard Princess. "Here's a notebook, writing utensil, and water bottle. More supplies can be purchased at the bookstore."

"How do you decide who gets which color lanyard?" I asked, letting curiosity get the best of me.

"The counseling groups are broken down by color. We place patients in a group based on their addiction, as well as other factors. You have been assigned the Purple Group, which is comprised of people with similar issues and life challenges. This helps the groups stay cohesive, and the patients grow from sharing each other's stories."

My survival kit.

There were bundles of lanyards in crayon colors and rolls of stickers scattered inside the drawer; no laughing, no care-taking, no talking. She peeled a neon fuchsia sticker from a roll lost in the back. *Females Only.* "This informs the others you can only speak to women."

Meathead dipped his upper body into the cubicle. "All clear," he said. "I disposed of the magazines."

Fuckable.

He transferred my clothes from the floor to my bag, one item at a time.

He must get a thrill out of handling women's panties.

"Please place your valuables in here." She held out a bin for me to drop my life in.

"Inside this phone," I said, "a world of secrets."

Need the cell to contact my men.

She wasn't listening. I snagged my measly cosmetic bag from my purse before dropping it in.

"Around the corner is the restroom. Leave a urine sample."

Unwrap cleansing cloth. Wipe front to back. Catch midstream. Do not fill container.

No urge, I forced out a few drops. After I made the delivery, I cursed myself for not following the wiping rules: *Cover up the evidence of my tryst on the plane.*

A hand reached in like Thing from *The Addams Family*, stealing the opportunity to toss and start over.

This kind of regimen last occurred at Edith Woodson.

Nurse Ratched escorted me to a square riser, something Santa might sit on at the mall, situated adjacent to the entry. A railing surrounded it to support the fresh-off-the-wagon drunks. Another patient moved out of the way to allow the debutante to take the stage.

The focal point of the stage was a framed poster on the wall. It read *Eight Basic Emotions.* Below that, eight words appeared in bold caps: *ANGER, FEAR, PAIN, JOY, PASSION, LOVE, SHAME, GUILT.* Next to each were three corresponding words in smaller type, like subcategories. My eyes gravitated to the last word on the chart: *GUILT,* followed by the words *regretful, contrite,* and *remorseful.*

"You will use this chart to describe how you feel during your five-week stay," Nurse Ratched said. The Spanx hidden underneath her uniform accentuated a bulge-free body. She held a pad and blue roller ball, as if waiting to deliver a baby. "The words on this chart are comprised of every feeling you have within you, so it should be easy to acknowledge your current mood by referring to the chart. Part of the treatment program is to help you get in touch with and identify how you are feeling." She gazed at her clipboard. "We notate your answers to monitor any extreme mood changes, for safety reasons."

I tried to guess the correct answer. "Fear, shame, and guilt."

A creamy brunette in civilian clothes walked over. "This is Deirdre," Nurse Ratched said. "She is in her second week and will show you the facility." The white suit disappeared with my phone and my life.

"Ready?"

Young, firm body. I gave her a once-over and, per the norm, pictured her naked: perky breasts, toned abs, straddling some guy, arching her back, moaning.

"This is extra awesome because we're in therapy group together," she said. Our purple lanyards appeared the same but for a certain colorful something. "Let's do a run around the campus and after, I'll take you to your room."

She bounced. A classic mini-cheerleader jump.

The walkway hugged the building. Deirdre's butt bobbed in front of me.

I bet boys like to tap that ass.

The Arizona oven overwhelmed me, and I couldn't catch my breath. While I panted in the heat behind her, Deirdre stopped to open the door. I bumped into her, figuring everyone in the dining room had witnessed my lack of coordination.

A Wrangler-jeaned rancher addict sauntered out of the dining room just as I was getting myself off her heels. "Ladies." The plaid top-stitched shirt, mother of pearl buttons, and obligatory scuffed boots complemented his country drawl.

"Bo, this is Prue." My guide whipped around her hair.

"Hey. I'll be around. Not going anywhere anytime soon," he said.

Bo reminds me of that half-Hawaiian farrier I banged. What happened to him?

"Sorry," he added, "I'm having a bad day."

"This is where we dine," Deirdre said. "Meals are a huge deal here. No sugar or caffeine is served, but the cookies are delicious." I glazed over her words while she barked out meal times. "Herbal tea or lemon water available all day."

Let me sleep until I'm cured.

"Can you repeat what you said?"

"We help each other, you don't need to remember." Not at all how I'd pictured a druggie.

My over-imaginative mind told a story about every passerby. We moseyed to a conference room where a woman was in the hot seat spilling her guts. I felt like a voyeur.

"This room is used for morning meetings, music therapy, movie night and AA groups."

A scratched and scruffy black upright sat against the far wall.

"Can we use the piano?"

Mrs. Sutton would be so disappointed in me.

"As long as no one is occupying the room." She stared, perhaps in disbelief that I played. "Alright, we're off."

A cactus garden graced the hillside between the upper building and swimming pool. White pebbles covered the ground between the succulents. We paused at the gate. I pulled a leaf from a branch, crushed the greenery in my hand, and inhaled lemon and ginger.

"Separate swim time slots for men and women. Ours is from one until three."

When is men's?

"The workout room is coed." She stared at my neon-pink *Females Only* sticker.

"Awesome," I said, a little too enthusiastically.

The place to scope out men.

"Now, I'll take you to your room and come back for you in ten."

My new home: three beds, desks, and wardrobes—two of everything, occupied. One person created a nook with furniture. Another sat against the window and behind a desk with privacy and a view. The empty bed sat out in the open, vulnerable.

At hotels, I tended to unpack right away.

The best option, pretend to be on an exotic vacation. The orderly messed up my bag.

I found Mom's shawl balled up next to the stuffed pony Nick gave me on the way to the airport. I swaddled it in cashmere and placed it on my bed. A symbol showing deep down inside, he might care about me.

My fingers moved along the hangers, plotting the first impression.

Chic yet effortless, understated sexy.

A bias-cut sundress and Joie sandals. My newly acquired items in hand, Deirdre knocked to escort me to my first group meeting.

New-age music issued from a speaker in room 103. Inside, there were eight chairs arranged in a semicircle. Deirdre snagged one of the two that were unoccupied. She closed her eyes and placed her hands on her lap, palms up. Before I could calculate the male-to-female ratio and assess whether any of the guys were hot, the man seated next to the desk swiveled around. His hair was clipped in a three-two, longer on top and shorter on the sides. He had a boxer's face that looked out of place with his soft hazel eyes—in a fight for his life, a tangled brawl in a dark, seedy bar. The rugged features contrasted his sterile, Friday-casual trousers and striped oxford. His bicep twitched as he motioned for me to sit.

I felt attracted to him and feared the truths he might find within me. On the way to my chair, I cursed myself for dressing like a goddamned runway model. A nervous laugh wanted to spill out. My mind jumped from thought to thought, a virtual taillight blinker until the music stopped.

"Welcome, I'm Mike, sober five years. We'll start with introductions from the end."

"The name is Owen, *alkie-hol-ic*, druggie, suicide survivor, and codependent." Owen's lanky frame stretched out in the chair. He carried a boyish charm, with wiry features and brown, soulful eyes that matched the color of his mocha skin. A sharpened number nine fiddled between my thumb and index finger. It plunged eraser first and bounced to the middle of the room. I hustled over to pick it up.

"Please go back to your room and change," Mike said.

Frozen, with no place to hide. All eyes on me.

"As you bent over, you revealed your breasts," he said.

Silence caved in around me. The running started when the door clicked behind me.

My legs moved at a breakneck pace while I tried to remember the location of my room, my mind already strategizing a clothing overhaul. Sweat dripped down my back and into my butt crack.

No point in worrying about the past.

I tugged a high-necked, navy blue J Crew tee over my head and covered it in deodorant on both sides. The bathroom light flickered. I adjusted the backs on my diamond-stud earrings and worked at not berating myself.

When I got back to the mind-shrinking room, a curvy, jet-black-haired girl was sitting cross-legged on the floor with a long document of some kind.

"Let me interrupt Gloria for an introduction," Mike said. He gripped the carpet with his soft-soled, cap toe lace ups and rolled his chair a bit closer to me. I was astounded by how easily he commanded the group with his mere presence. Like balls of putty in his hand. I knew I wouldn't be as malleable as the rest. He tipped his head in my direction while the others waited for me to spew my horrors.

"I'm Prue." The words reverberated in my head. I looked yearningly at the girl on the floor. My eyes begged her to start talking and get me out of the hot seat.

Gloria started back up where she left off. "My boyfriend, Tom, has a wife. So, I guess that makes me an adulteress or something. There's a lot of love between us. That's all I can tell you."

This stinks as bad as day-old fish, and I pity her.

"He lies to me, makes promises, and breaks them," she said.

Like my father.

"Take a moment," Mike said. "This is a safe place to discuss these things."

Dodged a bullet.

"At fifteen, I left home, and other than a stint waitressing, I've worked as a stripper ever since. My obsession with bad boys started the day I lost my virginity from a guy, not my dad. I don't count that." She carried the world between her shoulders, and hidden under all her

25

black eyeliner resided a remarkable softness. "Abusive, hot-tempered men are my thing." She had youthful skin, more sorority girl than pole dancer. "I gave him everything and can't live without him. My heart believes he will keep his promise and leave his wife."

Sitting through the personal disclosures of my group felt like forcing down a garlic milkshake while swimming in everyone's filth.

"Love addiction will be a topic of discussion later this week," Mike said. He conducted with the jerky movements required to maintain our attention. "Tell us why you're here, Prue."

My past held me captive. It began when we left my father.

CHAPTER TWO

"We're moving far away to live with my mother." A half taped-up box teetered on the hood. My mother fished around in her purse for the keys. "The ducks can't go with us. The only option is to take them to the park and let them go into the wild."

Henry bawled so hard he couldn't be much help catching our pets.

With the duck cornered, I clamped my hands over her wings. "Shhh," I said.

Henry unfolded the blanket and swaddled Quacks. He kissed her smooth, milky-white head.

"Go to the car," I said. "I'll catch Waddles, too." At eight, I made it a point to protect my big brother.

Waddles ran in circles while I sat cross-legged at the edge of the fenced-in area, reaching my arm out, trying to lure her in with a scrap of bread. A film of dust settled on my tortoise shell glasses. I cleaned them with my shirt. The moment she snatched the treat, I scooped up the quacking, flailing bird.

"Never forget, I love you."

With the bird clutched in my arms, I settled into the car.

Mom shoved another box in the back. "Come on, now. Someday we'll get another pet, perhaps a horse."

Snot bubbled from Henry's nostrils.

"For sure?" I asked, not letting her promise go unnoticed.

"Someday, when things are better." She tossed a few tissues between us on the backseat. "Time to go."

I placed Waddles' feathered body back into the water. My sleeve swiped across my face. Her orange webbed feet swam out of sight. An ache in my heart at the thought I might never lay eyes on my ducks—or my father—again.

"From one coast to the other." Mom clutched the wheel. "Pedal to the metal."

I sat wedged between the window and everything we could cram into the Buick. A thousand miles of desert, the flat Midwest, and the lush green foliage of Virginia blew by. Henry's golden hair shimmered in the sunlight. People said we resembled salt and pepper shakers. With light hair and blue eyes, he counterbalanced my dark features. Although he was older by two years, he tended toward caution. Most every thought in my head, I blurted out of my mouth. Both of us, toothpicks.

My mother had decided on my name when my father failed to show up for the birth. Prudence: good judgment and sensibility. The eternal optimist, she packed up her Jackie O. fashion and tracked us back to our ancient roots—back to the refuge of Goose Neck Harbor, where generations of our Featheringill ancestors rested in the church graveyard. Our family tribe cast ashore eons ago to man whaling ships overflowing with blubber. We lived by our blue blood heritage and talent for looking the part.

My grandmother's home overlooked the water and merged with the sea by a winding path parted by a floor of pachysandra, a green ground cover bearing clusters of tiny, white flowers. Long Island's summer snow.

Back to a new world for me.

We pulled up to my grandmother's house at dusk, one week after we left California. One week after we said goodbye to my father. Her weathered house stood at the peak of a steep hill. The back door opened and arms waved toward us like someone who'd just won at bingo. The driver's side window cranked down. "My looney mother, nervous breakdown and all." Mom spoke under her breath, but I heard every word.

My grandmother was a classic beauty, even if she wasn't as chic as the other aristocratic grandmothers out and about town. She mirrored an aging movie star, with kelly green trousers hemmed at her ankles and a begonia silk scarf waving in the breeze. Crusted remnants of frosted peach Revlon adorned her full lips. Cropped steel-gray hair, worn in an organized yet disheveled manner, portrayed her pizzazz. The fashion show stopped at her feet: sturdy socks and sensible walking boots caked with dried mud.

"Beagling attire," Mom said.

"Welcome!" The three of us sprung out of the car, tired and filled with hope. Her gnarled hands ran down my braids. She repositioned a stray hair behind my ear. "Did you know your grandfather wore tortoise shell eyeglasses?"

"So does my dad."

I sensed Mom's discontent as I spoke of my father. My heart seized Gram's adoration and soaked in the sense of belonging.

The old house had seen better days. The front door, floured with dust and cobwebs, was crowned by a plaque: *A Historic Home, 1803.*

Dingy, checkerboard linoleum made up the mudroom floor. Gram shooed us into the house like a brood of chickens. Through the pantry, into the kitchen, the open cabinets were loaded with family china and tattered cookbooks. Intense musk filled my nose like an old basement with aromatic hints of wet dog. A lighting fixture was suspended from the ceiling, the cover long gone, one lonely bulb trying to illuminate the dark room and the glossed ivory walls, yellowed from decades of preparing meals.

My mom sighed, one hand on her trim hips. "This place is still filthy." Jet-black hair pulled up in a ponytail. Part of me wondered if she might pull out a broom and start sweeping the room into shape. To prevent giving her the option of requesting my help, I whirled past and into the adjoining room. My brother tagged along. I always took charge.

An ebony table stretched across the room, and I counted sixteen worn needlepoint-covered chairs. The head chair was adorned like a throne. Gram reached her leg underneath it, and a bell shrilled in the kitchen. "The buzzer called for the maid, back when we had full-time help." Tarnished candelabras decked the table. Dusty candles leaned every which way.

Gilded frames housed dark portraits of expressionless Featheringills captured in cracked oil paint, staring back at me. The paintings were mounted with brass lamps. Useless cords dangled below.

I curled up on the window seat and squished my face against the old, wavy-paned glass.

This is home for a while.

∞

Henry spotted the lake the moment we pulled into the church parking lot. "Can we go?" He focused on the end goal.

"After the service, if you both sit without any problems," my mother said, and Henry acknowledged the bribe. "It's important we show gratitude for all our blessings."

We chose a pew next to an enormous stained-glass window. Water glistened through blue-and-white images of Mary holding the baby Jesus.

After services, Henry sprinted to the pond while Mom chatted with the pastor. A peacefulness coated my body and I said a prayer, grateful to start over.

Please bless Dad.

My mother and I held hands as we traversed the side of the church and walked down to the lake.

Henry crouched, unaware of his untucked tee and khakis twisted around his waist. He opened his cupped hands, and a frog leaped out.

A formation of elegant birds with elongated necks glided overhead. "Those are Canadian geese," Mom said. The creatures honked to each other in a symphony, improvising the score. "Their arrival lets us know spring is here."

If they traveled all the way from California, Quacks and Waddles might find us, too.

The dark-green water reflected the surrounding trees. A breeze rippled across the surface. "When the leaves turn, the vibrant colors spread across in the water like a Monet painting. Quite magnificent." The buttons on her blouse pulled as she took a deep, long breath. Her walnut eyes smiled. "The air is soft as silk."

Into the promise of happiness, synchronizing the rhythm of our lives to the turning of the leaves and the rise and fall of the tides.

One of the founding members of the Sound Club happened to be my grandfather. This granted the Featheringills and their progeny lifetime memberships. It was a simple white clapboard building encircled by a wraparound porch. Rows of trophies boasting the winners of tennis tournaments, regattas, and swim records crowded the room—the heated matches between members wearing the required all-white tennis attire on the red clay courts like a ballet of butterflies dancing on a stage.

The place opened every summer on Memorial Day and closed on Labor Day, all but the boathouse. The kids' camp included swimming, sailing, and tennis. At meets, we competed with the two upscale clubs in town as intimidating parents yelled at their preppy blue blood offspring to kick harder—jewels around the mothers' necks, wrists, and hands.

The hard, wooden Adirondack chair in the grown-ups-only section sucked me in. A waitress served us a plate of cookies and iced tea with a lemon wedge. My pig brother chugged the last few drops of his drink and parked his eyes my way. I relinquished my glass to him. Too much excitement about the goings-on to bother wasting time nibbling sweets.

The two of us sat on display for Gram's friends, and I wanted to make a stellar impression.

"Are these your grandchildren? Aren't they adorable," commented everyone who strolled by.

She clutched a string of pearls to her chest as she bent over. "My dear friend's granddaughter is your age and a real firecracker." A striking, proper-looking woman walked over. Next to her, a teensy girl with cobalt eyes.

"This is Lily," she said.

"Do you want to go explore?" Lily turned to lead the way, then paused. "Your brother can come too if he wants."

On Saturday night, we attended the clambake and ran wild in a game of capture the flag. The sunset glowed across the sand spit, illuminating fiery tones of red and apricot. Boats sailed across the water.

With scabbed knees, Lily's scrawny legs jumped high off the ground. "Let's go on my Blue Jay!"

I recalled something Mom told me: "A ship in the harbor is safe, but that is not what ships are built for."

The boat was tied up at the farthest dock. With a salty life preserver snapped around my waist, I struggled to keep my footing on the tippy floating wood and prayed not to slip. My surefooted friend zipped along in front of me with fine balance and agility, as if walking on solid ground. Barnacles and seaweed clung to pilings in the murky water, and colorful grease slicks swirled on the surface. Small fish circled the green slime, pecking for food.

"Don't want to slip." Splintered slats turned to ivory as my feet hit the notes.

"Fallen in. Trust me; gross." She grimaced. "Once we cruise further out, the water is ideal for swimming."

"How about we go riding sometime?" A familiar territory, and one which I adored.

"Never cared for horses." Lily scrunched her nose and stuck out her tongue.

After I climbed aboard the small vessel, she untied the lines and gave the side a push. For a second, I thought I might be solo for my first sailboat outing. In the final moment, she leaped on board.

"Hoist with this line," she commanded while steering.

Hand over hand I pulled, as the white triangle ran up the halyard.

"Tie the line at the base of the mast."

She left the tiller unmanned while she unwound my handiwork. "Make loops on the cleat, like this."

The steering arm moved on its own until she took back control, heaved right, and averted a mooring collision. A mix of joy and satisfaction beamed across her face.

"Now hoist up the other line." All instructions registered. "The jib is small but mighty, and helps us gather more speed."

Within moments, we soared past the jetty and into deeper waters. The ocean took us on an adventure beyond my wildest imagination.

"What a strong crew member!" Lily said. "Want to team up for the end of summer regatta?" The breeze tussled her ponytail. A halo of hair whipped around her face.

"Do you think I'll be ready?" The life jacket rode up and wedged itself under my jaw.

"If we practice every day, you will be."

A sense of togetherness warmed inside. If she believed, I did too.

∞

My new best friend biked to the house at dawn the next morning. "Put on some clothes."

I pulled shorts and a top from the floor with my toes. Red apples chomped down while peddling to the dock before the sun lit up the bay.

"Today, I'm going to teach you how to load a spinnaker."

"What?"

"A thing for the end of a race." She clutched something silky and colorful. A bucket hung from her fingers. "This gets stuffed on land." She draped the fabric on the ground. "See, there are three corners with rivets. Pull up like this, gather together, and shove it in the bucket. Keep an eye out for twists and leave the metal pieces hanging over the edge." She tipped the bucket over, and the material tumbled out. "Now you try."

The day of the race, I was determined to do everything the way my friend told me. With her life jacket buckled, Lily smeared white sunblock across her face. "Ready?"

"Yes!"

We prepared for the start horn. Lily clapped her hands in excitement. A green vessel sailed by with two identical girls inside, one a few inches taller than the other. "Those are the DuPont sisters, and I want to beat them."

"If we believe we can, we will."

The checklist rallied in my head. This needed to be the best race of the summer. A horn sounded.

"Let out the jib a smidgen."

We inched ahead on the second tack, and my captain squealed. Only two vessels in front of us. The leaders rounded the last mark and released their spinnakers. Blue, green, and red-patterned silks colored the skyline. Each one vibrantly paraded its identity, like family crests passed down for generations. She yelled for me to pop the sail. With the halyards hooked, I hoisted it up—our competitors a distant memory. The darned thing fluttered and twisted and flopped around like a wet blanket.

My shoulders scrunched to my ears. "Sorry, I must have stuffed it wrong. I'm a loser."

The sisters veered past a buoy, their colorful spinnaker puffed out like a chicken's chest. The boat sailed close enough for us to witness them smacking a high-five.

"Those girls think they're so awesome." Defeated. "Take the helm."

Lily eased out the mainsail. The vessel surged forward, levitating on the water. I gripped the tiller and avoided careening into objects.

"Pull to the right," she said.

The smallest wind gatherer leashed in. A blast sounded as the dreaded sisters moved over the finish, their voices echoing across the water. "Yes! Wahoo!"

Lily took back the captain's position, and I sat in my spot by the mast. The sound blew: fourth place.

"Sorry."

I failed her and myself.

"I've made the same mistake a million times." She encouraged me to do better, to be better. "Next summer, we can try again."

Best friends again, we skipped to the locker room and put on our swimsuits. One jump into the blue water and the spinnaker fiasco washed away.

My beanpole brother strode up to the edge of the shallow end. "I'm bored. Want to go find crabs?"

We wrapped towels around us under our armpits and followed Henry to the sand.

A dark, crusty-shelled horseshoe crab maneuvered its way down the shore like a cast iron skillet. "Pick them up by the tail." Henry turned over the prehistoric creature, and we admired the gills. Five pairs of crawly legs moved around in the sand.

While the sun went down, we played on the swing set. A black convertible pulled into the lot. "Happy to take you home," Lily's mom said.

"No thank you," Henry said. "Our mom is on her way."

Their red taillights turned to dust down the road.

No one left but Cap Reed, the old, curmudgeonly live-in caretaker who manned the boathouse. His soles squeaked as he walked past us, a captain's hat propped on his head.

"Your mother *still* isn't here?" he grunted as he clipped by.

We pumped our legs hard to swing high enough to see over the fence and into the parking lot. A plot began as to where we would spend the night, until a car careened around the bend.

"On a phone call for too long," Mom said.

The two of us climbed into the beater, salty, sandy, and ready for a bath.

⚬⚬⚬

After two years, Mom found a rental. We sat in the car staring at the small, white clapboard shed we would now be calling home. "Not a forever place, but a start," Mom said in an encouraging tone, perhaps to convince herself more than us.

Screws fell right out when Henry pulled the screen door. He poked the skeleton key into the hole. A corner of the peeling linoleum tripped me in the dim room. The light fixture speckled with the sacrificed lives of moths and bugs.

"Are you sure this isn't someone's tool shed?" Henry opened a cabinet. "Eww, a mousetrap!"

"Of course, I will wipe everything down." Mom scooted Henry along and closed the cabinet door.

The lean-to sat three feet off the street that split the town from north to south. Floors creaked and moaned. My body tilted to the right, only because the house made me.

A mysterious slatted door next to the steep, narrow stairs got me curious. Inside the door, I pulled a string below a bulb. An ominous stairway leading down to a dirt floor lit up. "Yikes, creepy."

"Don't go down there," Mom said. "Leave the door latched."

I ran upstairs and pretended to be a real live Alice in Wonderland within the attic rooms.

Mom yelled up. "Share the room on the left."

A suitcase smacked my butt. My dumb brother threw his bag on the only bed. "Dibs."

"Where am I going to stay?" A crack in the floor caught my eye. Piles of corncobs in earth tones shone through the subfloor. "Tons of corn!"

"A long time ago, they used it for insulation." She dropped a suitcase and two soft bags filled with linens.

"Is this place an old pigpen?" I knelt and squinted between the planks.

"Stop looking at the corn. You're making me nuts."

A two-paned window the size of a record album sat mid-wall on the other side of the room. Streaked with dirt, I pulled my sleeve and cleaned while humming my favorite song.

Mrs. Brown, you've got a lovely daughter . . .

"There's a swamp of some kind on the edge of the field."

"Riddled with snapping turtles." Mom's words grabbed my attention. "And you're sleeping right here." She peeled a pale-blue coverlet out of her bag. "This, I made for you."

Once I had assessed the girly fabric and handiwork, I surrounded myself with her love.

"A custom-made bed," she said. One of the bags held my keyboard. "Sit on your bed and practice. Someday, I'll be able to afford a real piano and lessons."

Like in the movies.

Mom woke up at five to catch the six-thirty train. Gram came over and made us breakfast before scooting us to the bus stop. A brisk smooch as Mom darted out the door. Perfume lingered behind her, and then the place reverted back to its strange musty odors. With Mom at work, when school dismissed, we were conveniently left to our summer mischief.

The day Gram took a part-time job, Mom hired a teenager to babysit.

"This is Millicent." Mom's arms swept up like Miss America. Henry and I scowled. We didn't need a sitter. After all, my brother was starting sixth grade soon.

"Why can't Henry babysit me?" I stomped for effect.

"She can monitor things in case of an emergency."

Blubber bulged and dimpled in her sleeveless V-neck. "Well, aren't you a doll," Millicent said. When she leaned down, I sneaked a peek at her boobies.

Most of the morning, we perfected our fort while she kept busy doing *whatever* in the house. After Lil arrived, we got hunger pangs and marched up to the house for provisions. Most of all, I craved a fresh package of Twizzlers. The back door squeaked open. "Hel-lo?" No response. "Millicent, we came in for a snack!"

We discovered her sprawled out and asleep. "Maybe we should find a mirror and check if she's breathing," Lily said.

Beer cans were toppled over and strewn about the floor. Among the wads of tissue and her stinky feet, we discovered two unopened beers. We snatched them and ran to our favorite climbing tree at the end of the property.

A scruffy Henry crawled out from the brambles. "Whoa, where'd you get that?"

"From Millicent." Lily popped open the can and sucked the foam out. With a full mouth, she passed it to me. I took one swig and spit out the bitter grossness. Some came out of my nose.

"This is worse than the stench of cigarettes and poo," I said.

Henry took an adolescent boy's aren't-I-cool sip while we monitored.

"We both drank some," Lily said. Even though my brother had chipmunked his. "Which means you will be alone with Millicent if we die." She cracked up and almost peed herself. After a healthy gulp, I cringed.

After Millicent and Lily went home, we sat outside. As the sun fell in the sky, the chirping crickets joined us. A symphony performed at twilight and an owl hooted in the night air.

"The pizza is in the car. I need a massage," Mom said. High heels ditched on her way through the door, I massaged her tired feet until her face relaxed.

Neither of us said a word to Mom about Millicent and the beer. She kept out of our hair, and we didn't bother her when she drank too much.

A blanket, stolen from the house, cushioned well beneath the brambles of our fort. Henry went to the house for sodas and snacks. "Fatty is snoring," he said when he came back. A little spit dribbled down his lip. "Guess what I found in the yard?"

I shrugged.

"A beehive."

"Neat." When he hurled a pinecone at the bees, my interest peaked.

A banana bike skidded on the driveway. "What are you doing?" Lily asked. She hurled her bike down, creating a dust cloud.

"Trying to knock down a bee's house so we can analyze the contents," I said. Better if I gave it a scientific touch.

"Let me try."

Lily's arm wound up and aimed at the dangling cluster, knocking the sack clear to the ground. A swarm lifted like an ominous black ball and moved toward us. We started running, with Henry in the lead about to blast through the door. He banged and jiggled the lock.

My legs burned all over with pinprick stabs. I stomped around wildly, to no avail. The buzzing came from all directions. Lily flailed and hopped around in a panic.

"On your face!" I yelled. The smack far too tardy, the bee's stinger lodged in Lily's cheek.

"Open up, please!" Henry begged.

Millicent glared at us through the window with no apparent intention of unlocking the bolt. Henry's face swelled with welts. With one last pound, we hightailed it down to snapping turtle alley. When the swarm cleared, fatty finally granted us entry.

Crusted with chalky calamine lotion, we huddled together until Lily's mother came for her.

When Mom walked through the door, her mouth fell open. "What on earth?" Too swollen, we kept our mouths shut. "What happened to my children?"

"Threw something at a hive." Millicent weaved, defiant . . . drunk.

"Yeah, we did, and she wouldn't let us in," Henry said, risking a scolding.

"Why?"

"Because I'm allergic to bees."

Millicent got fired, and Mom took a job at a boutique in the village. After school, we bounced back and forth between the shops where Mom and Gram worked. Gram's was filled with horsey things, and Mom's with clothes and the opportunity to play store clerk.

One afternoon, the door chimed. A gust came through. "May I help you?" Mom asked in a high voice, like when she talked to Dad.

Through the evening gowns, I caught a glimpse of pale ankles between too-short tan pants and worn-out topsiders. "Yes, I need a birthday gift for my cousin Marilyn." A close inspection of the jewelry case caused his dark-frames to move down his nose. The fringe of his thinning hairline flaked with dandruff.

"Well, those earrings tend to appeal to the elderly ladies. Are you looking for something for a mature woman?" Mom asked.

On his blue alligator polo, I noticed a stain where the belly button might be.

Mom fondled her hair. "Is Marilyn's last name Carmichael?"

"Yes!" the man said.

"We're friends from high school."

"Now she has kids in junior high."

"Been ages," Mom said.

"A few years ago, she went through a divorce."

"Gone through the nightmare myself."

"My name is Richard."

"And I'm Anna."

The man hung in her hand way too long.

"This is my daughter, Prue."

I emerged from out of my hiding place, a sequined beret on my head.

"Well, hello." A strangle of nicotine and aftershave billowed in the air. "Add the hat to my tab." He signed the charge slip with nicotine-stained fingers. "Would you like to go out sometime?"

"For sure."

I retreated into the clothing rack. A vague foreboding crept up my spine.

Richard arrived for their first date, and I ran to the door. He wore the same ratty boat moccasins, red slacks, and navy belt stamped with whales. On his sloping shoulders, a sweater completed his ridiculous ensemble. My mother floated over.

"Hello, gorgeous." He whipped red carnations out from behind his back. "These are for you."

"How thoughtful." She turned the flowers over to me. "Put these in water. Do not wait up, I will be home well after your bedtime."

Richard became a permanent fixture in the corncrib. And in Mom's bed.

Chapter Three

My next stop: the resident psychiatrist. The receptionist gave a half-smile; her hair mimicked the lead singer from Flock of Seagulls. A tattered *Psychology Today* magazine on the end table tempted me, but not enough to move my body to retrieve it. Hair twirling left me unsatisfied, so I rubbed my earlobe. The purple rope dangled around my neck.

I look like a fucking Easter egg.

"Are you Prudence A?"

The only person in the waiting room (other than the stringy-haired girl slinking out of the doctor's office) happened to be me. "Yes."

My heart raced as if someone might push me off a cliff. The name tag clung to my left breast like a man's hand. The second I stepped foot in his office, I assessed his shoes. Ferragamos. A diploma from Harvard and a Cedars-Sinai Psychiatric Residency certificate hung on the wall. Dr. Howard Livingston.

"Tell me how you are today," he said.

One sentence needed to eke out before I blathered like an incoherent mess. "Have you ever stepped in dog doo? The poop embeds in your shoe grooves and stinks. You try to scrape the crap out with a stick or a hose, and it won't go away." I paused for effect. "The shit is me."

"Why do you think you assimilate yourself with feces?"

Hard to believe he was asking me such a dumb question. "Because I am a disgusting human with no redeeming qualities."

He scribbled on a yellow legal pad with a Mont Blanc. At least my horrors were written with a fine instrument. He pointed to the be-all-end-all wall chart.

Guilt plagued me. *Shame* called me by name. *Love and passion.* I craved yet felt undeserving of these beautiful words. *Pain* represented my existence on Earth.

His fingers smashed together. "You won't be able to use the fitness center for now."

Oh, God, I will turn obese.

"Are you for real?" My face flushed, the heat rose. "Why not?"

"The fact of the matter is, you are quite lean yet you believe you are overweight," Dr. Livingston said.

Panic-stricken. How can he do this to me? Dimpled cheese is forming on my extremities.

"Other than not being able to exercise, how are you?"

I sipped water, swallowed. A question I loathed. My mother taught me the correct response was always: *fine.* "Whatever came my way, I deserved."

The protective skin covers me and keeps everyone and everything from getting in.

A tissue box moved across his desk. Just in case, I supposed. He flipped to a new page on his pad.

"The little girl is all grown up. You can take off your boxing gloves." My heels ground in at his words. "After a long review of your psychological evaluation, I would say you included more detail than most." Thick fingers fumbled through the stack, and he pulled my freak test out of my file. "Can you describe your drawing for me?"

"I put the men in bubbles above us because they aren't included in my family's inner circle."

"Tell me about your mother." The stern face softened. I didn't need his sympathy.

"My mother is dead. Don't make me dig her up and bash on her."

"Would you say she protected you?"

"Did she protect me? I believe she did her best."

"Are you angry?"

"The only thing I'm still chapped about is she tossed out everything from my childhood."

"Why do you think she threw out your belongings without your permission?"

"Her work was completed. She had finished raising us."

"And?"

"Nothing else for me to say."

"Do you want to talk about Nick?"

"Is a magic spell hidden in your folder to fix everything?" The futility of this conversation was wearing me down.

"Well, we can't control others, can we? He is not here, you are."

The story of my life.

Dr. Livingston marched me in the direction of the bookstore for a few reads. The reflection of a beautiful girl followed me.

That can't be me. I'm a disgusting, filthy pig.

A cup of tea and a secluded corner: the remedy to calm my jangled nerves since fucking someone was out of the question. With reading material in hand, I dipped the bag in hot water.

A man's voice interrupted my trance. "Mind if I sit with you?"

My neon-emblazoned tag lit up underneath my chin. I went back to my book.

"Mitch," he said. "From group today."

"Doesn't mean I can talk to you."

His amber-speckled eyes magnified through wire rims. Gray-tipped flecks in his hair with a stylish cut. The fitted white polo caused me concern. His arms might be thinner.

"I'm gay. I live with my partner. We've been together five years." He pulled a photo from inside his binder showing two dapper men in tuxedos, one much younger. "My man, John."

"Handsome."

"The agony he's endured because of my drinking." Crinkled and well-loved. "Alcoholic. At one time, I enjoyed many cocktails without any trouble. Gastric bypass fucked everything up."

"I'm going to need stomach stapling by the time I leave this place."

"You're an absolute rail," he said. I balked. "Before the surgery, I bordered on obese. John didn't mind, but I did. Post-op, a thimble of vodka and boom! Blacked out."

"Yikes."

"I went missing for two days. John stayed up all night, worried. Finally, he called the police. I woke up in Vegas, blacked out."

"Scary." The envy place sauntered in. *Someone worried about him.*

"With you here, I'm calmer," he said.

"Funny."

Fooled them all.

"All I do is fidget because inside my head is a tornado," I said.

He laughed so hard I thought he might cry. "You're hilarious. This will be a long-lasting friendship."

More than anything, I wanted him to know he could count on me.

"Come," he said. His warm, callous-free hand grasped mine as we ventured to the smoking area. No chance of any line crossing between us with his gender preference, and I was relieved by the attention. "You got any kids?"

"Yes, a son. He's fourteen." A ponytail adjustment allowed him to release my hand. Talking about my child gave me pangs dumped into one gut-wrenching ball. "How about you?"

At a quaint smoking pergola, Parliaments smacked his palm and we sat down.

"Home sweet home." He unwrapped the cellophane. "Want one?"

"Ex-smoker."

An ashtray brimmed with beige and white filters, some rimmed with lipstick, most smoked down to the quick. A lizard darted across the floor, paused near the edge, bobbing. My brain fogged.

His lips pursed over the filter, he shimmied a lighter from his front pocket. "John and I had many heated discussions about kids. Not sure if I want to go on the hunt of finding a donor egg, in vitro and all the stress." A smoky ghost blew toward the pointed ceiling. "John desires a child." Long arms draped over the railing. "You, I'm certain, are a wonderful mom."

"I do the best I can, not perfect. Made plenty of mistakes." My gaze shifted back to the reptile. "For some reason, I'm dizzy like I'm dreaming. It's all so surreal."

"You'll find peace with the rhythm of daily routine."

"To speak the words is a struggle." Weighed down, my neck locked up.

This is too hard.

"So, where do you guys live?"

"In Atlanta. Buckhead. Love the city. How about you?"

"Right now, Los Angeles, but I consider myself a New Yorker. Can't take the NYC out of a girl."

"True." He stamped out his cigarette, stood, and reached out to me. "Mademoiselle."

My new friend turned right, and I strolled left. The thought of going back to my room and dealing with myself seemed less than appealing. I wandered around the campus, pushing away the thought the old Prue might have been looking for trouble. Up ahead, past the grassy area, a guy was stretched out under a tree with a book. My pace slowed as I drew nearer to him.

"Prue, right?"

I nodded.

"Just sitting here chilling. Owen, remember? From group." He patted the ground next to him. "Wow, today with your wardrobe malfunction."

"I'm not here to cause problems." I inched down next to him.

A blob similar to mangled Silly Putty was sprawled across the underside of his wrist. The forearm moved. I tried not to stare.

"Compound fracture from a car accident," he said. "Out of my mind at the time." A matter-of-fact manner, words spewed. "Thankfully, I didn't kill anyone. So, you're addicted to the horizontal bop?"

Wow, he's direct.

"Yes, I am."

Might as well dive in.

"All of us like the old in and out, but I needed drugs more." In slow motion, he slouched down. The same way a person would inquire as to how I liked my coffee.

"Hard to believe how blunt everyone is here," I said.

"What's your DOC is one of the questions we ask here in rehab."

"I don't understand."

"Drug of choice."

"Um, yeah. Been dealing with this for a long time." I distracted myself with peeling apart my split ends.

"At home here, we discuss our darkest deeds in an open, honest way. No point in holding back."

"Don't we all keep a secret or two stowed away?" My secrets and lies outnumbered the truths.

"I've done some jacked-up things to score pills." Both eyes on my breasts. "Most dudes dig a girl like you in the bedroom, though."

"Guess so."

What the hell is wrong with me? Wish the world away.

"Technically, I'm not supposed to talk to you," I said.

"Want to take a walk, hang out?" His body moved like a marionette.

Did I cause this?

"I'm going to head back to my room."

I'm a freak.

CHAPTER FOUR

We dressed up for the plane to LA. Henry hated the hubbub of having his hair slicked down and getting decked out in his white button-down, gray flannels, navy blazer, and stiff loafers. My red Mary Janes pinched, but they represented fancy, like our father. I clung to the idea of waltzing back into his life and still being his little girl. We rode on TWA with wings firmly attached to our chests.

"Can I take your hotdog?" Henry asked.

"Of course."

He slathered the wiener with mustard and hoovered it in three bites. The dress itched. I squirmed and scratched. Not elegant enough for Dad. On occasion, evil ideas about him invaded my head, and I told my brain to stop. The man resembled a mythical creature, bigger than life itself. Yet I didn't understand him.

On the elevator descent, we placed a bet on who would find him. I spotted the polished wingtips first. "There he is!"

He threw his arms around us, opened his wallet, and handed each of us a crisp one hundred-dollar bill. "Friends are friends, and cash is king."

"Do you think Henry will be as tall as you one day?" I asked.

"Sure, he will. Grown a whole three inches since last year. You will for sure pass six-foot-two." He raked a hand through his deep burgundy hair. "My daughter is a stone-cold fox with legit pins."

"Pins?"

"Stems, getaway sticks, gams, legs." Pickup lines oozed from his mouth.

One mention of my bra and I will faint.

"You're so pretty, people might think you're my girlfriend."

I was proud he found me beautiful enough to be his lady. People used the word "dapper" to describe him, but I said "handsome and smart" because he went to Princeton.

"My wife thinks I'm in Fresno on business," he said to the parking booth lady. The Doobie Brothers boomed from his car stereo, singing about rocking down the highway. We glided across the slick leather seats at each turn.

We drove up a winding street to our grandparents' Tudor-style house. A vibrant green, pristinely manicured lawn sprawled out in the front of the house. "You kids are Nana's favorites. The other grandkids are pagans, with Fred Flintstone feet and oversized bones."

"My darlings, come in," Nana said. With a True Blue clamped between apple-red nails, her appearance didn't lend itself to being called "Granny." Her jet-black hair curled in a Jane Russell coif. On the bougainvillea-covered patio, we ate slice-and-bake sugar cookies and drank lemonade from a glass pitcher. A charm bracelet clanged as she poured.

At bedtime, we relaxed upstairs in an enormous room with vaulted ceilings. After Dad showered, he opened the door. His hips shimmied as the towel scraped across his back, and his penis dangled below.

"Would you mind if Alicia spent the night with us?"

Henry and I shared one of the beds. Dad slept on the other.

"Sure," I said, looking away.

"I love my kids." Dad was a night owl and wasn't going to bed anytime soon. He laid down in between Henry and I and snuggled against us. "Delighted you're here."

"We love you too," I said. My brother, too tired to answer, was already fast asleep and snoring.

The next evening, the new girlfriend arrived in an orange mini number with holes encircling her tummy. A lilting Southern drawl made Alicia appear sweeter. They read a book to us before bed, with pictures of animals mounting each other.

"Intercourse is a beautiful and natural thing people do when they love one another," Alicia said.

"Fantastic family time," Dad said.

CHAPTER FIVE

I forced myself to go to lunch. My hot-pink label, as nightmarish as an "A" for adultery tattooed on my forehead, warned off every man in the place.

"Meet your roommates." The girls spoke in unison. My gut sensed danger.

Put-together and young enough to be my daughters.

"I'm Gabriella, and this is Bridgette," the brunette said. "The two of us came in after you fell asleep and didn't want to wake you." She had the enviable kind of skin one gets at the end of a long, beachy summer.

"I'm Prue."

"We pretend to be sisters and do everything together," Gabriella said. Just then, a scruffy dude walked by and she adjusted her blouse. "Hold me a seat," she whispered, as if dropping juicy gossip. "I drool whenever he's near me."

"Not hot," Bridgette said. "My eyes are on someone else." Her short, blonde pixie cut framed almond-shaped eyes and rosebud lips. A diamond ice rink flashed under the glare of the lights. "I'm married. No kids. This is my third treatment for pills and by far the classiest one."

"Oh," I said. "This is my first time."

Why aren't these girls wearing stickers? I'm the anomaly here.

"Well, I'm here on a court order for a minor issue involving too much tequila," Gabriella said. "My hubby better forgive me. We've only been together a year." She traipsed off in the direction of the scruffy guy's table. With no other choice but to follow, I hovered behind the only available chair and contemplated my options.

If I sit with a hot guy, I'm shattering my contract. But if I don't, they'll think I'm a bitch.

I laid down my tray next to the surfer dude I met during check-in and took a seat.

Now I am doubly busted.

His choppy, shoulder-length blond hair had a salty texture. The ends were rat-chewed and split.

In this deciduous climate, the only way to get that beachy look would be Bumble and Bumble sea salt spray.

He wore a white t-shirt with white shorts that landed well below his knees. An inch of skin peeked out between the top of his white tube socks and the bottom edge of his Dickies. The only change since I'd first run into him was the color of the bandana hanging from his back pocket. Both of his arms were covered in tattoos; plumeria flowers, hibiscus, ocean waves, and on the exposed calf skin, the eyeballs of a koi fish.

"Hey, Toby," Bridgette said with a flirtatious back arch. "Missed you in session this morning."

"Slept in. Too much going on in my head. Last night, I wandered around the desert to open my chakras."

I resisted an eye roll. He handed Bridgette a piece of garden bark with scribbled ink lines.

"This reminds me of driftwood washed up on the shore," he said. "Perfect waves remind me of you."

"Beautiful." She examined the art project. "Isn't this neat?"

"Cool," I said.

The lack of male attention gnawed at me.

"How about I make one for you?" His arm grazed mine as he handed me the piece of garden bark. I felt a surge across my pelvis. I turned and went back to the cookies I shouldn't be scarfing since I couldn't work out.

"This is our new roommate," Bridgette said, lifting my name tag and wagging it around. "She's a sex addict and can't talk to you."

I wanted to swat away the flies.

"Well, I'm going to head out," I said. "Got some things to buy."

"Joking," she laughed. "This is rehab, don't take it too seriously!"

As much as I wanted not to, it was hard to pretend my life didn't depend on somehow burying the old me and turning into a new human being in a month. All the paths converged at the place I couldn't go.

A wall of glass accentuated the contented faces of those sweating inside. I heaved open the heavy bookstore door and almost blew out my shoulder. A silver-haired woman behind the register smiled, hands hidden in her work issued apron.

"Can I help you find something?"

"No thanks."

The title of my newly assigned book landed me in a funk. Something about how my mirror was broken. I checked out the spiritual trinkets and pondered the possibility my new roomies might think poorly of me.

I'm not here to make friends. I'm here to reclaim a certain someone.

Back in my room, I assessed my clothes.

What the hell? Why did I bring all these plunging neckline dresses?

My entire wardrobe was not Serenity Hills friendly. I hurled it to the floor. The Mother Teresa high-necked tee would be it for a month.

∞

"Let's start with you," Mike said.

"I'm addicted to men, I guess." Shock radiated through me. "I felt like a bursting dam and needed to come to grips with what happened when I was a kid, deal with my husband's extramarital affair. My heart says he doesn't love me or like me."

The other inmates shifted in their seats while I stared at the taupe carpet and spilled my life in front of them.

Everyone is pondering why I still want him.

"What else?" Our group leader wasn't my kind of man. He lacked the required *GQ* face, yet I still wanted him and fantasized he would bring me to a better place.

"When I ask him if he loves me, he says, 'I fuck you, don't I?'"

Outside the window, a sunny day moved along without me.

"Find the smoking gun, why you're here."

Glass shards flew across the room. I took a sip of water, desperate for the bottle to suck me in. My deplorable actions were not justifiable. It would be a cop-out to blame him.

The self-described title, hateful whore.

"Why I'm here?" Repeated lines, a stall tactic learned from the best, Nick. "The more I hated myself, the less I cared about living."

When we lost all our money and I took in renters, the people I once called friends shot disapproving looks. The shallow questions with emphasis on "are" when asked "How are you?" Did they enjoy seeing me suffer?

"Keep going." His tone lightened. A bright energy line glowed between us.

"A blackness worked its way inside me. At first, I buried the ache with material things, but finances put a halt to shopping. I forgot about the agony of my life when I flirted and obsessed over my appearance."

"Go deeper." Plaid sleeves pushed up his forearms as hard as he pushed me. The disheveled, messy exterior suited him; more genuine.

"A desperate need to be seen, I guess. I showered with the door open while a man painted my bedroom. We engaged in inappropriate conversations." My voice spoke, but someone else made the words come out. "No line in the sand. Yet, I interacted with the outside world as a mom, a wife, and a friend." All details remembered, crystal clear. "After a few days, he stared at me through the steam."

An animal, ready to pounce.

"What did the experience draw up in you?"

Everyone in the room was hanging on my story.

"That I was dissatisfied. In search of new thrills. A momentary high. The beginning of the end."

I'm not another horny suburban housewife with a cheating husband.

"The attention I got from men awakened something in me."

"Let's open for comments," Mike said.

"Wow, that was a moving share," Mitch said. "The black hole. I relate to a lot." He turned the platinum band around his finger.

Did he cheat too?

"Anyone else?" Mike asked.

The outcasts being mediated.

"To pinpoint the moment it all began is impossible," Deirdre said. She sat with straight posture to match her hair. "Men assaulted me on three different occasions, all date rapes. A hell of a lot of self-hatred inside me. I keep trusting men and getting let down."

Find the fucks who raped her and arrest them.

"I can tell you're going to add something unique to the group," she added with an approving nod.

The one-hour session left me more depressed. My protective wall strengthened. Hands, both male, on either side of me. A series of sensations: elation, excitement, and impulsive thoughts about fucking. My mouth moved along while they recited the prayer.

"Can you stay for a few minutes to go over some things?" Mike asked me as the room emptied. A jagged chip on his left front tooth added to his strength and toughness.

"Sure. What's up?" From afar, I envisioned him as taller than me, yet we stood eye to eye.

"On multiple occasions, I've witnessed you engaging in conversations with men, one in particular. This is a breach of the contract you committed to."

"But Mitch is gay."

Why is the guy policing me?

"Doesn't matter. Men fuel the addict and validate your power over them, something you lost as a child."

"He doesn't pose a threat to me crossing the line because he doesn't like women," I protested.

"Try your best not to."

Would he make love with the same easygoing poker face?

"Do you think you can?" he asked.

I nodded while studying his keychain: Jeep, Baldwin brass key. Safeway card. An unidentifiable gym membership. A miniature boxing glove.

"Part of your treatment is learning how to engage with men in a nonsexual way." He handed me a printed list of open job positions — part of the therapy, it seemed, was keeping the inmates too busy to fall back to their dangerous vices. "Do any of these jobs interest you?"

I perused the sheet. "The gym, or a tour person. Not around food or *anywhere* near a bathing suit."

"How about I assign you as a guide?" He smacked the list with his fingernail and I flinched. "Here is a facility map. It's not necessary to show every building, but be welcoming. Exhibit compassion." He glanced at his black G-shock wristwatch. "A man is in admitting now."

"This doesn't constitute a rule break?" I said, and regretted doing so the second the words spilled from my mouth.

"Interact in a professional capacity, first. After, learn to socialize with them."

"Alright." My bag fell down my arm. "Can I ask you something?" Without waiting for a response, I said, "Am I the only woman with my type of problems who's checked in here?"

He smiled, but it wasn't a rude smile. It was more in line with *hell no.* "Nope." He shoved his hands into his pockets, butt against the edge of the desk. "Plenty before you, and will be more after you." A shrug added impact to the message. "Progress, not perfection."

He ushered me back out into the cold, cruel world.

Goosebumps blasted up my arms as I moved from the air-conditioned interior of the main building into the dry heat outside, then back into the climate-controlled check-in area. My nipples went on high alert. "I'm here to give a tour," I said, forearms crossed over my chest.

"Almost ready," Nurse Ratched said.

Her legs swished, the sound of Mom's stockings. The ones she pulled from an egg. My sadness lightened when I spotted matching logo-covered couture luggage being searched by security. The curator of the LV faced the door, pen in hand, signing his life away. He had a chiseled jawline and an aristocratic profile. Lean, though not skinny, with eyes as dark as his hair.

"This is Alistair," Nurse Ratched said.

I sucked my abs in and unleashed the hair from behind my ears.

"This is Prue," she continued. "She will give you an overview of the campus and take you to your room." She marked the clipboard with stealth efficiency. "Your items will be delivered shortly."

His luggage lurked in the corner. He glanced over with admiration.

"Hiya." A glossy, British accent. The smoldering eyes penetrated me, as if casting a spell. His extended arm revealed a monogrammed sleeve and a platinum Patek Philippe I'd seen in a jewelry store window once.

"Are you from London?"

Ask the obvious.

"Yes, Kensington." His thick hair glistened with a light coating of pomade. Double dimples when he smiled. "A ton of jet lag."

I led him outside. Gucci loafers clicked on the sidewalk behind me.

"Bloody hot." He wiped a hand across his brow.

"Oppressive, dry air. Nothing like England's weather. What are you in for?"

"Cocaine," he said. "Wanted to nip it before things turned south."

I nodded in lieu of opening the possibility of discussing my problems.

"This thing clashes with my mojo. Bloody hell." He tugged his newly acquired accessory.

My preferred humor. Sarcastic, self-deprecating.

"What does *Females Only* mean?"

All wonderful things must come to an end.

"Means I'm not permitted to talk to men, so this needs to be our last personal chat."

"*Males only* should be administered to me. Been a horrid player."

The skin on his face turned pale, sickly. I ushered him inside the cafeteria and pulled out a chair for him at the closest table.

"Sorry," he said. "I'm a tad lightheaded."

"It's the climate," I said, taking a seat next to him.

"As of right now, I am officially cut off from civilization." His words stabbed at the harshness of our situation like a dagger. "My business better keep running while I'm gone." He inhaled, exhaled, and concluded with a sigh.

"Let me get you some water." I scurried over to the drink area. A kitchen worker had just restocked the rack with warm glasses. I grabbed one and filled it with ice before adding water.

Well-kept fingernails rumpled his hair. The button-down pulled across his back, outlining defined muscles.

"The first day is hard," I said, setting the glass down in front of him. "And I'm about twenty-four hours in front of you." My angst, tied up with a cherry on top. The caretaker in me desired to make things right, tell him he would be okay.

"I'm downright exhausted." He chugged the water in two gulps. "Cheers," he said.

"Commendable for deciding to be here." I understood the depth of the decision first hand. A sense of closeness vibrated inside of me, along with the thought he might need a proper fucking.

Elbows set up a kickstand for the heaviness in his heart. "Bad things lurked down the pike. If I'd kept up the partying, I was bound to lose everything. After an all-night bender, it was tough to maintain a façade of professionalism; bags under my eyes, cold sweats, a few lines at my desk to get through the day. An imminent implosion if I didn't resort to drastic measures."

My desperation to solve his issues were blocked when I spotted a mole near his cheekbone, the kind of mark most girls dream of having.

"How rude of me, talking about myself," he said. "How are you surviving? Is anyone at home waiting for you? Tell me your story."

People bustled around the table, but we sat in our own world. "Hard to summarize. The highlight is my son, Christian. At the moment, I'm separated."

"Career goals robbed me of settling down."

Kissable lips.

"You have lots of time," I said.

The inner child fantasized.

He might be the one.

"Think so?" he said, studying me, hearing my voice. "A beautiful aura surrounds you. Has anyone ever told you that? Quite comforting to a chap who's freaking out."

The aura had better be a genuine, new-improved me and not the man-eater I wanted to ditch. "Thank you for the nice comment," I said. "Don't worry, we're all freaking on the inside." The chair squeaked as I pushed away from the table. "We better get moving." I stood, and he followed my lead.

Face to face, six-foot-two-ish.

"I guess I can't solve all my problems today." More than polite, he shuffled ahead of me to hold open the door. His dramatic sighs sounded the same as my son when he lost at Monopoly; he flipped from hopeless to hopeful, despondent to determined, in a split second.

We walked side by side to the next tour destination; the dreaded gym. A sullen patient working the desk smirked. Futile inspirational quotes littered the area while a beefcake spotted someone through a bench press. On the far side, an anorexic frenzied the elliptical.

Alistair lifting weights, grunting, sweating, veins bulging. The scent of his body after a workout—or better yet, after he's made love to me.

The lights, the rank air, and the sounds brought back my disappointment. "Basic gym setup," I said, and stepped out before suicidal thoughts set in.

In front of the door to his new home, my desperation rose. "Your luggage should be here any minute." I felt an invisible rubber wedge shoving itself between us. "Your bed, desk, and armoire with drawers."

We were drawn together by a magnetic field. I bent at the waist— less of a rule violation. One-inch proximity to his neck; the scent of summer linen and vanilla.

"The highlight of my day," he whispered, and fine goosebumps flew down my arms.

"Well, I'm off. I'll see you tomorrow in group."

Away I turned, from the ghosts that brought me to this place. From an insatiable desperation to be wanted and my urge to fill the emptiness inside.

Chapter Six

Richard invited us to his cousin's house. I didn't like the way he swooped in on our family like a tornado, yet I can't deny the newness was a bit exciting.

His cousin's name was Marilyn, and she resided in a modern home made of glass. The interior, furnished with chrome tables, steel sculptures, and cold leather seating arrangements, shouted, "Don't touch!"

She had two identical twin boys, Jerry and Anthony. The only physical difference I could see between the two was a scar on Jerry's jawline.

"Want to come upstairs?" Anthony asked.

They led me up to the third floor, into a playroom with shelves brimming with board games and toys galore. A ping-pong table stood in the center of the room. My math calculation estimated three corncribs.

"Do all these belong to you?" I asked, tracing a line across a wall of bins filled with Legos, puzzles, G.I. Joes, and crafts.

"Of course they're ours, you nimrod. Whose else would they be?" Jerry said. He smacked the ping-pong table with a paddle. "Want to do a tournament?"

I tolerated the name-calling in exchange for the opportunity to play with their stuff. "Yes! Hang on, I'll be right back." I ran down to the library and found Henry. "Two against one, and I'll never win without you," I said.

"No," he said, his freckled face buried in his book.

"Well, you're missing out on the most fun in your whole life."

For the next several visits to Marilyn's house, Henry relaxed downstairs while I traded ridicule for playroom access.

"Can I try?" I asked.

The boys sat in beanbag chairs playing Pong on their Atari set.

"What are you wearing?" Jerry said with a smirk, looking me over. "A baby romper?"

I was horrified he might mention the bra straps, which were about as prominent as my budding breasts.

"Or you're just ugly," Anthony added.

With strength and focus, I moved chess pieces around a board.

"Hands off," Jerry ordered.

Frightened, I pulled out a bin of puzzles instead.

"That's off limits too." Anthony took a menacing stride toward me. "Why don't you use crayons? Coloring is about your speed."

When the night came to an end, Richard drove our car. I wasn't sure why we never used one of the heaps junking up our yard. "We had a fabulous time," Mom said.

"Well, I didn't," I said from the back. "Those boys are mean."

"Don't be silly. You are way too sensitive."

A shut-up-or-else look blasted my way.

"Don't make me go again," I pronounced.

"Not another word."

The next weekend, we were back at Marilyn's house. The twins greeted me at the door. "Come upstairs. We got a Lite-Brite and Rock 'Em Sock 'Em Robots."

Richard must have told the boys to be nice.

The colored pieces and the light screen excited me.

"Bring it in the dark," Jerry said, motioning to the walk-in closet.

"I'm fine here."

Anthony pulled the plug from the socket. The lizard tail slithered across the floor. "Come on. Be cool," he said, and they beckoned me with their smiles.

"Scared of the boogeyman?" Jerry chided.

"No."

I followed them into the closet. The toy fell from my hands with a crash. Hands groped my everything. A wet mouth shoved against my face, probing for my lips.

"Stop!" One of my hands wriggled loose, and I flung it around in the darkness. My wrists were pinned behind my back. Hard fingers scrambled at my panties. "Don't!" My words came out with a ragged breath.

The chemical odor of new carpeting invaded my nostrils and crammed into my face. A hand wiggled its way up my body, groping my breast as I fought for the door. I clenched my knees together as my floral cotton underwear were wrestled down. Sharp stabs in my private parts. One leg freed, I kicked into the shadows and landed a direct blow to a chest.

"You're no fun! Come on, Anthony. Let's go."

All hands released me, and I scrambled for the light. The door opened.

"After you, Prue."

Up on my feet, I pulled up my twisted flowered underpants.

"Not only are you retarded and ugly, but you're annoying," Anthony said.

Immobilized while the boys wandered downstairs, I remained locked in the powder room until someone called me.

After we dropped Richard off at home, my mother droned on about Marilyn and her hospitality. No words came. "You're quiet tonight."

"Don't make me go back," I said, tightening my grip on the door handle.

"You will come with us, use your manners, and put a smile on your face."

"Why do I have to entertain the boys?" My dress inched up, revealing a newly acquired bruise. I tugged it back down.

"Henry is shy. Be polite and don't embarrass me."

No explanation. Who would believe me?

The next time we went back, Henry immediately plopped down in his usual spot. A giant basket next to the sofa gave me an idea, and I climbed inside to hide and wait out the evening. "Remember," I said, "I'm not in here."

After a few hours, I really had to pee. I popped my head out to see if the coast was clear. Both arms got stuck. My hiding place heaved and tipped, and I tumbled face first onto the coffee table. The glass top broke with a deafening crash. Still tangled, I let out a cry. Mom barreled around the corner, Richard right behind. Blood streaked my hand after a swipe across my face. The pristine carpet glistened with shattered glass.

My mother screamed at the sight of me. "Let me deal with this," Richard said. "I *almost* graduated from medical school." He carried me to the sink, his hot breath suffocating me. "Stupid brat," he scolded.

My mother stood back while Richard picked a sliver from my skin. "Don't you think we should take her to the hospital?"

"A bandage and she'll be fine." He pinched the slice above my eyebrow and stuck a Band-Aid over the wound. Not a move came from my body.

I was furious with him for hijacking my mother, and at her for being so blind.

"Hold still." He released me from his grip. "All fixed."

Disoriented and dizzy, my knees buckled and I crumbled to the floor.

"Come sit with me," Mom said. Embraced in her love, soothed by the sound of her raspy voice, I rested my head against her chest. I reached up to my earlobe, and she peeled my hand away. "You were born holding onto that ear."

After dessert, Marilyn excused herself from the table. "I'll be right back," she said. When she returned, she was cradling a furry black-and-white bundle no bigger than a toaster. "I found this cute little thing yesterday on my walk, and he followed me home. No collar. None of the neighbors claimed him." The puppy peeked over Marilyn's shoulder and yawned. "Do any of you want him? I'd hate to take him to the pound."

"Can I hold him?" I asked, peeling the pup from her grasp and rocking her.

Henry pulled the puppy from my arms. "I'm taking him," he said, carrying it to his regular spot on the couch.

"Let them keep the dog," Mom said. "My children need to win once in a while."

"Your kids can't even load the dishwasher right," Richard said. "How are they going to care for a pet?"

He had given us strict instructions on how to do the dishes: forks in the basket tines up, knives pointed down; lipstick stains scrubbed from the highballs; cups and glasses on the top rack, loaded back to front; plates went in one way and bowls another. It was all a complex jigsaw puzzle. At first, when we didn't place the dishes the right way, he berated us. Not long after, he resorted to spankings with a belt or a wooden spoon. Once, when he discovered me draining the grease and running a fresh sinkful for the pots, he threatened to put me in charge of dishes and the water bill.

The puppy sat on Henry's lap. Tears welled in his eyes as he stroked its head.

"They can bring the pet home," Mom declared.

Later in the evening, through the thin plaster, I heard the two of them crushing Mom's bed. While I blocked out the noises coming through the walls, I decided on a name for my new pup: Hemingway. From that night on, he slept under the covers in the window seat with me and made the bad go away.

∞

My stepfather fancied old cars, fixed them, and hoarded them. The field in front of our house looked like a used car lot. Mom's complaints went ignored. The man took over our house, our yard, our lives. He stole my father's place, and I worried about what else he might steal.

One day, Mom called a family meeting. I grew excited, anticipating something fun like a vacation or a trip to Disneyland.

"Richard's children are coming to live with us for a while," she said. "The mother doesn't want them."

What sort of mother doesn't want her kids? What kind of father doesn't want his? Mine.

"How many?" Henry sank down in the cushion.

"A boy, sixteen. A girl, fifteen. Let's give them a welcome."

"Where will they sleep?" I asked.

"Yeah," Henry said. "This place is tiny."

"We'll make elastic walls," Mom said.

She prepared beds for them near the kitchen. Their clothes lay strewn on the floor like piles of autumn leaves.

The boy, Glen, was alright. I nicknamed him Oral because of his enlarged teeth and full lips, and because his words were comprised mostly of vowel sounds. The hearing aids lodged in his ears didn't make much difference. Most of the time, he read our lips or ignored us altogether.

Pat, the girl, I didn't much like. The blue metallic eyeshadow she smeared on her eyelids didn't help. Her black, stringy hair turned greasy a second after shampooing. A faint mustache lined her upper lip. A seething jealousy ate at me when Mom took the time to teach her how to shave her legs and bleach the black hair on her face. The violation of my boundaries went unnoticed when Pat bullied her way across every line.

Henry and I were sitting on his bed playing Go Fish when Pat strolled in wearing belled jeans and a too-tight crop top. She sat down on the bed beside us and picked up my electronic keyboard. "What's this?" The instrument teetered on her lap.

"Please don't touch," I said in my nicest voice.

"Oops," Pat said and dropped it. It smashed into a million pieces on the floor. "Sorry." She slinked out the door with a smirk on her face.

I did my best to pretend Pat didn't exist, which proved difficult with her constant, glaring presence in my life. The hardest part was ignoring her stench, like onions and laundry left in the machine too long. That, and she was just plain weird.

I took my baths at night to avoid the long line for the bathroom in the mornings before school. With suds running down my face, I knelt, the handheld ready to rinse, when the wraparound curtain flew open. Shampoo in my eyes, I squinted up at her. Pat stood before me, her eyes locked between my legs. "Let's play rape."

"Go away!" I snapped and yanked the liner closed. She hightailed out, leaving me cold and soapy. "Shut the freaking door!"

The next afternoon, I went to Lily's. "How's it going with the new kids living at your house?" she asked.

"It's a nightmare. The only privacy I can find is when I pee. She barged in on me, mid-shampoo. On the upside, Richard agreed to fund my braces."

"Yikes and yay." My bestie ushered me into her bedroom. "My cousin told me about lying in the bath and letting the water run between your legs. Last night, I tried it."

∞

I scooted toward the spigot in the claw-foot. A rush penetrated my pelvis. For a few moments, I put aside my shattered things and the two strangers and their monster father living in our house. I forgot all about their crap laying everywhere, and our yard smattered with beat-up cars. All of it washed down the drain.

More and more, I stayed at Lily's. One night, the entire bunk bed shook like a California earthquake. I looked over the edge to find her bony legs high in the air and a hand in her PJ's.

"What are you doing?"

"Wait, I'm almost done." She shivered all over. "It's what I told you about with the bathtub, only with my hand."

It would have been an impossible task for me to masturbate at home without alerting Henry, which made me glad for my friend and our bathtub secret.

Lil brought her bike down to hang out at my house. "Are those cars unlocked?" She ran toward an olive-green sedan. The stepmonster had bragged he'd bought the heap of rust for fifty bucks. There it sat, useless, under a grand maple tree. I got in next to Lily and avoided stepping into a stagnant pool of water festering on the passenger floor mat.

The words on the dashboard read *Dodge Dart*.

"More like Dodge *Fart*," I said. Lily laughed and feigned a dramatic drive. "Slow down, we're going to hit a telephone pole!"

"I've got this," she said, and tucked her Band-Aided knee to her chest and pounded the brake pedal. "I just thought of something." She climbed into the back and wiggled below the window. She reached a hand inside her shorts and started rubbing. I joined her. I unbuttoned my cutoffs and found the wetness. Our combined breathing came labored and rapid until the seats shook and the itch was scratched.

"That took a while," she said.

I was flushed from her watching, and from my soaked underwear, too embarrassed to call attention to what had happened.

Mom rented a house a few miles away. The place touted two more bedrooms, but still only one toilet. On the upside, it was closer to Lily's house.

The two-story home sat on a three-stop corner with fir trees hedging in the street side. Ornate trim and diamond-shaped windowpanes promised an upgrade to the corncrib. But a detailed inspection revealed years of wear and tear. Built as a gatehouse to a grand estate, the withered structure would be our home.

The porch steps creaked as I straightened my arms in front of my face to poke through the spider webs. The small living room was painted butter-yellow. "Yellow is a happy color," Mom said with her usual optimism. The house was decorated with thrift shop fare—all but Mom's clothes.

"How come we're poor blue bloods?" I asked, knowing it might make her mad.

"A generation spends, and the next one earns. This era must make the money."

Things, I figured, must be better than having nothing at all.

The kitchen linoleum was dingy and stained, with some squares missing, some torn. The fridge was stored around the corner in the mudroom. The old radiators whooshed and clicked in the room that held a dark, narrow closet. A rickety desk gained my curiosity. I opened the small drawer and examined the left-behinds: rocks, marbles, dice, bottle caps, and a bright-blue hairband. My three Breyer horse figurines triggered a memory, Mom's promise of a pony long forgotten.

Pat stood in my room with a frightening expression on her face. "Let's lock Prue in a dark, scary place!"

I scrambled in an attempt to run, but she pulled me by the arm and shoved me in the closet.

"Open the door, you jerk!"

"Do my chores, and I'll let you out."

"Help!" The darkness captured my crippling fear. "Fine, I will. This is not funny!"

"Funny to me," she said. Wood creaked as she leaned against the door.

The pitch dark tortured me; I prayed for rescue.

"If you drag my sister in again, I swear I'm going to tell Mom," I heard Henry say.

The door was unlatched, and my brother reached in a hand. I gave him an expression of relief. Pat sat at my desk, painting her nails. "Okay," she said.

∞

Within seconds of falling asleep, Pat dropped into a heavy snore. I took the opportunity to explore Mom's vanity. A set of switches operated six bulbs to aid with envisioning your face in the evening, daytime, and in office lighting. My fanny rested on the worn vinyl seat while I stared at myself and flipped the settings. The mahogany box claimed attention, and my favorite of all, jewelry. Elegant pearl earrings screamed to be tried on. I clipped them on my earlobes and turned my head, making glamorous faces. "My darling, I will be delighted to attend the gala."

With everything put back, I went over to her clothes. Rive Gauche billowed, and I stood among her dresses. The station wagon sputtered on the gravel outside, and I dashed for my room. Muffled talk leaked through the paper-thin walls, letting in Richard's growling voice. With my face in my pillow, I hummed a song.

∞

"Come meet our landlords," Mom called in an affected, dulcet tone.

The woman was dressed in tailored slacks, accentuating her slim body. She spoke with on-point pronunciation, like Jackie Kennedy. My grandmother always assessed a person's status—and tendency to be polite—by the state of their shoes. The woman wore the same Belgian loafers as the ladies in town, and the man's shoes were topped with silver bits.

"This is Mr. and Mrs. Sutton," Mom said, and introduced me.

"We are delighted to rent you the gatehouse," Mrs. Sutton said. "Your family can stay as long as you like." Then she turned to me.

"Prudence, your mother told me you play the piano. Would you like to practice on our baby grand?"

"Yes, please," I said.

Their meandering estate stood on the other side of a field full of wildflowers. A circular stone drive and two architectural pillars outlined the heavy front door. In the foyer, an alabaster marble sculpture of a woman draped in billowing fabric towered between a sweeping double staircase.

She took me to a room lined with books from floor to ceiling. A ladder with brass casters assisted with retrieving items from the highest shelves. Sitting kitty-corner was a black Steinway concert grand. With stunning grace, she opened a pair of French doors, pausing to brush a thread from an ice-blue satin settee. A set of wingback chairs completed the seating and flanked the marble mantle, the jeweled crown of the room.

"Come over anytime," she said. "Next week, someone will come and tune. Too many years have slipped by since music resonated through our home."

Outside, a neatly mowed lawn stretched out as far as the distant property line. A pristine white post-and-rail fence ran around the estate grounds. Off to the side stood a crisp, white barn. Horses grazed in the distance.

Something from the movies, or a photograph from one of Mom's magazines.

"What's your favorite kind of book?" Mrs. Sutton asked.

"Fairy tales," I said. "I love happy endings."

She pulled one from the shelf. *Donkeyskin.* We sat on the puffed cushion.

A king and queen had a beautiful daughter, and a palace adorned with all the finest. Majestic horses populated the paddock and stalls. Among them lived a donkey who littered gold. The king's wife fell ill, and on her deathbed, she secured a promise from the king that he would find a new woman who would be more virtuous than she.

When the queen died, the king became wrought with grief, slipping into madness. In his stupor, he believed his daughter to be the greatest beauty in all the land. The distraught princess fell at her father's feet and pleaded for him to forsake his unnatural desires. Seeking help, she went to the Lilac Fairy Godmother.

"Tell your father to make you a dress the color of the sky," the fairy said. "He will never be able to do this, and you will be free from your obligation without displeasing him."

So the king demanded a garment be made by his skillful workmen.

Astonished, the fairy said, "Tell him to make you a dress the color of the moon."

The king presented a dress as stunning as the moon.

Baffled, the fairy said, "Tell him to make you a dress the color of the sun."

The king emptied his crown of its jewels and ordered the most exquisite gown to be made with the gems.

"Tell your father to skin his donkey and present you with the animal's hide," the fairy said.

The king slew the animal and gave the fur to his daughter. Overcome with sadness, she wept.

"Don't cry. This is the happiest day of your life," the fairy said and wrapped the princess in the donkey's skin.

Unnoticed, the princess fled to a faraway kingdom, where she hid her identity. The lowliest of servants, she lived in a humble shack and herded sheep. Alone in her shed, she washed off her filth and donned one of her glorious dresses. The prince in the new kingdom spied her through the keyhole, discovering her truth, and took her as his queen. They lived happily ever after.

"Did you like the story?"

"Yes. At first, I worried the ending might be sad."

"Some of the best endings are sad." She returned the book to its home on the shelf. "Well, you may begin practicing."

My fingers played as if they graced the stage in Carnegie Hall, where Mom used to go to concerts as a child.

"Magnificent!" She clasped her hands. "I'm going to enjoy this glorious afternoon." The sound of footsteps clipped through the marble foyer.

A framed photograph of a smiling girl watched me play and kept me company. A blue hairband pinned back her dark curls. I played all of my memorized songs and a few from the holiday songbook. The mansion echoed with my playing, and as I got smaller, the room became more grandiose. Deep in my heart, I felt I didn't belong, and I yearned to go back to the cozy gatehouse.

I finished playing and wandered outside, pulled by the irresistible allure of fresh hay and manure. A chestnut mare came over. Her muzzle bristled, and I breathed in her nostrils. A burro stuck its head through the middle rung with matted and unkempt fur.

I am a donkey in a world of thoroughbreds.

The barn hand, a spindly man with dark stains on his oversized jeans, approached. He pulled a rag from his back pocket and wiped the horse's mouth and neck. He opened his mouth to speak to me but stopped when Mrs. Sutton appeared.

"I only have time for a short ride, Victor," she said. "My husband and I are attending an event tonight." She sat on a bay gelding with black points. Tan britches stretched over her toned legs. She wore laced-up field boots on her feet and a black cap on her head. She turned to me. "Are you finished practicing?"

"Yes, I enjoyed your beautiful instrument." I was embarrassed I had wandered beyond the parlor without invitation. "I'll be heading home now."

"Ever ridden?"

"Yes. My grandmother manages the shop in town. Sometimes she arranges lessons for me."

"Prepare Balaam for a ride and find a suitable cap," Mrs. Sutton said.

Victor circled the paddock, took the donkey by the forelock, and hooked him on the cross ties. After a few flicks of a brush and a comb through its mane, Victor returned from the tack room with a faded velvet helmet.

"Balaam belonged to my daughter, but now he keeps the other horse's company," Mrs. Sutton said. "A scrappy old boy, aren't you?" she cooed. "At one time, he competed with the best, but now he resembles a mule more than a prized American Shetland."

Victor coaxed me to the mounting block and put both hands on my fanny as I moved to the saddle. My face blushed, and I grasped the reins with purpose.

"Excellent," Mrs. Sutton said. "Stay near me, as some of the trails can turn quite narrow."

Mom came in that evening, and I shared with her my nickname for our new home. "The Gingerbread House," I said.

"A creative mind," she replied.

"The Sutton's home is impressive," I said. "Oh, and she took me riding."

"Never envy others. You don't understand their lives. At one time, their family comprised of three children—two boys and a girl. The daughter was killed at their home in the city. An exquisite and talented child. On the morning she died, she wore a red tea-length coat and took the elevator to the lobby, where a driver waited. The jacket got stuck in the door, and she was dragged to her death."

CHAPTER SEVEN

In the evenings, Mike offered private counseling sessions. Some nights, as many as ten people lined up for one of the five available time slots—each of them yearning for thirty life-changing minutes with the mighty Oz. We exchanged niceties, mayhem, and a few frantic moments before I scored the second-to-last available slot.

Snack time reminded me of the Chinese fire drills we did at red lights when I was a kid.

A food-frenzied clusterfuck.

Not having a kitchen or refrigerator and zero control over when and what I ate left me consuming calories regardless of hunger. Mine became a life lived at the mercy of food service hours.

My worst nightmare.

I chose trail mix, cheese, crackers, and berated myself afterward. The kitchen guy checked me out with a smile and a wink. I stormed out of the dining hall, ran in place for a few minutes, then wandered over to the main meeting room.

My hands had last graced an ivory key in the library at the Sutton's, but seeing the piano in the meeting room that first day stirred a yearning in my heart. I also figured playing might calm my nerves. I cracked open the door and peeked in.

"What's happening?" Mitch asked.

"Wanted to tinker for a while," I said, remembering my vow about not talking to him. He dipped his head toward the piano and shut the door behind him.

The room fell quiet, all but the buzz of the overhead lights. My imagination turned the basic upright into a Steinway. With each hand, I pressed my fingertips on three keys. I lifted my wrists.

Cows need to walk through the barn.

Rusty joints cracked as I rolled through scales, up and down, fumbling, starting again.

Who but my lady, Greensleeves . . .

A black cloak enveloped me. The girl in the red coat sat with me, her energy and warmth radiating like a guardian angel. My arms draped over the keys. I felt love and agony and horror; sadness to the depths of my soul, and happiness beyond measure. Hope and despair and disgust—every single sensation swirled around me. My hand touched the black lacquered bench to ensure she was not beside me. My rigid, stiff joints closed the cover.

The Arizona evening brought new beginnings.

Men, and my attempt at not talking to them, proved impossible for a girl like me. I justified my errors with ease. Owen had checked in the day before my arrival to this heavenly place. We had bonded over our week together in Purple Group—an eternity in rehab. He beckoned me to sit with him in the smoking veranda. A chill flew through me.

The area represented our freedom from the confines of our containment. A place where we let loose, talked about more than our addictions, and laughed at our situations. The united team of addicts keeping our individual identities while overcoming bad habits. All but one: the glowing, smoky, smoldering cigarette. The paper crackled, and a worm of smoke fluttered to the peak of the latticework. Our last resonant rebel call. My friend fished for another. An Irish jig; jumpy, perky, and vibrant. With a small distance between us, I stretched out.

"Damn girl, long legs," Owen said.

"Yeah."

"Orion's Belt."

"The Little Dipper." My head craned around the decorative trim.

Mitch settled next to me, clad in his usual impeccable style. His clothing was wrinkle-free in complementing green tones, his hair coiffed. Solid attention to detail.

"Yikes," I said, "I'm alone with two men."

"No, you're not." A voice grew closer from someplace behind me. "There are girls here to save you." It was Rhoda. She tore the plastic strip from her brand-new pack of cigarettes. Deirdre was with her.

"Move over," Deirdre said. "A Purple Group Festival. Wouldn't Mike be proud?"

"That was a difficult meeting this morning," I said.

"Like eating bad Texas barbecue," Rhoda said. Her blonde locks were stiffened by a coating of hairspray.

"The moment we think we're on solid ground," I said.

Smoke rings popped from Rhoda's mouth. "He forced us to switch seats just to blow our minds. All addicts are creatures of habit, too superstitious to change. It's relapse prevention to maintain a system."

"Prue," Mitch interjected. "You made insightful comments about Alistair."

"Hard to figure out why he asked us to assess our peers." I was unsure of what to do with my hands without a cigarette to fiddle with.

"The guy is delusional to think he can drink and not end up snorting blow," Rhoda said. Another Virginia Slims fired up. "I solved the puzzle! He made us straight *talk* each other." She slapped her denim thigh. "Didn't you give the handsome devil a tour around when he checked in?"

"Yeah, I pined for his luggage." What I wanted to confess would not fare well.

Keep the fantasies where they belong.

"A positive step toward sobriety. You gave a hot guy a tour and refrained from an inappropriate comment." A proud-parent expression beamed from Mitch's face.

"What goes on between my ears is troubling," I said.

"A few dirty scenarios ran through my mind, and I'm a married woman." Rhoda tilted back. "One more." She pursed her lips and released a stream of smoke. "One more, and I'm hitting the hay." Her body folded in defeat.

"All of us are doing better. One day at a time." I pressed my palms together and raised them toward the sky. "Got to call my boy before I chat with our fearless leader."

The out-of-shape fat pig jogged to the nurses' station.

Nurse Ratched read the wall clock. "About to send for you. An hour late."

I scratched my initials on the clipboard and snapped the pen down. "Shame and gratitude."

"Gratitude." She jotted a copious note. "That's a new one."

The far end phone sat available. The other two were occupied by the same sullen people. The timer dinged as the handle moved from its resting place.

"Hello?"

My sweet boy's voice.

"This is your very own mother."

"Hey, Mom. Got a test and Uncle Henry helped me study. Oh, and Dad's here."

"What class?"

Nick next to him, hovering, judging.

The tension seeped through the phone.

"Social studies. Name every state, capital, continent, and ocean," he sighed. "I'm going to do well."

"Sounds hard. What'd you eat for dinner?" The cord twirled around my finger.

"Tacos. Not like yours." A laugh identifiable in a room of giggling boys.

"I miss you lots." My voice cracked.

"Can I ask you something?" he said.

"Yes, anything you want."

"Are you going to go out every night like you did before? Because I don't like being left alone."

My eyes burned. Regret, remorse, and horror flew through my mind.

What if a fire engulfed the house while I gallivanted around?

"Nope, not going out as much." A dagger in my heart.

Irresponsible.

"Yay."

My nugget of love.

He whispered in the background. "Dad wants to say something to you."

"Hey," Nick said. "Give me a sec, I'm stepping outside." A patio chair raked across the slate. "Didn't want to chat in front of Christian. Your brother said he couldn't come to my place due to a stomach ache, so I came over to the house. He seems fine now."

Stressed-out child.

"I didn't expect to talk to you," I said.

"Next time Christian pulls this shit, I'm forcing him because he can't keep manipulating me."

"He is not a manipulative child. He's tormented because his parents are separated. Not to mention, his mother is not home."

"I planned on him meeting Naomi."

"Are you kidding me? Way too much right now."

"News flash. Not your decision to make, Pru-dense." He emphasized the word "dense" in his characteristic pet name for me. "Don't tell me what to do." I heard a cancer stick move from the pack as his lighter wheel turned. My mind swarmed—him mounting her, the sexy way he smoked.

A real Marlboro Man. Rough, dirty, messy.

"I'm shocked." Buried rage ravaged my chest, gaining strength and power. "For God's sake, I'm here trying to fix myself, and all you care about is fucking her." The decibel of my voice increased to semi-shouting.

"Your judgment is not appreciated, I'm doing the best I can. Work is killing me. The business isn't thriving. The two of us are happy right now. Where's the harm? She is my attorney and friend. I still hold a glimmer of hope for us, though." The defensiveness screamed "Guilty!"

Poor, broken Nick. Denied any fun.

My voice leveled down a notch. "Do not underestimate the intelligence of our child. Kids comprehend more than we think. How can you say in the same sentence you want to introduce your mistress to our son and still say you want to give our relationship a shot? Do you ever take my feelings into consideration?"

"Do you bother to think how traumatized I am over you fucking half the town? Every night, I wake up sweating, panic-stricken." His voice thickened like molasses and turned to molten lava.

Touché.

"Fuck off, Nick," I slammed the receiver into the cradle. A nurse approached. "Got an appointment," I said and hustled out.

Deep inside, a tribal scream brewed. Instead of screaming, I counted my steps.

One, two, three, four.

The heart rate slowed, and I tuned in to the critters singing in the night air as I walked to the counseling building. Mike's door opened. Toby walked out, tears streaming down his face. We shared pitying glances. I dropped onto Mike's sofa.

My shaman with the miracle potion.

"Talked with my husband. And no surprise, I'm shaking. The investment in his relationship with the other woman is real, and I obsess day and night. I can't stop picturing them banging."

"Defined as pent-up anger," Mike said. He remained relaxed and easy, unruffled by even the most shocking statements.

"Nick tortures me. He says something kind, and then the switch flips cold. All I want is for him to love me." I sailed over a waterfall; the deluge came gushing out. "The irrational child in me fears if I don't resolve my shit now, *she* will win. He puts me on a tightrope, offers up a gift of hope, and snatches the carrot away. The worst part is how I preoccupy over how he treats her, touches her, kisses her, and how beautiful he claims she is."

"I'm impressed by the details you've gathered about her. Let me try and understand. Your husband says he's willing to work things out, yet he's in love with another woman?"

"Sounds so dumb. We're in some kind of failed trial separation but still having dinner together once in a while. On the dates, I tell myself not to get physical, but we always end up in bed together. Sex is the only power I have left in the relationship. Do you know the scene in *Gone with the Wind* when Rhett Butler wraps his hands around Scarlett's head in an attempt to squeeze her from his mind?" Without waiting for a response, I said, "That speaks to me."

"Humans need water, food, and sleep to live. If Nick leaves you, will you die?"

"Maybe."

"My instructions to you: refrain from talking to him for a week."

Not talk?

"No, I can't."

"You swallowed poison and expected the other person to die."

"Are you saying I drank cyanide and no one died?"

"He fuels your self-loathing, which is not productive right now."

The isolation seared. No amount of ear rubbing, cuticle chewing, or hair twirling could calm me down.

"Time apart can be a positive thing," Mike said. "But everyone needs to make an effort to improve themselves and not engage in intimate relations with others. Nick expresses an interest in saving the marriage, but his actions say otherwise. Don't you agree?"

"So, you think I should tell him not to date the other woman? Do you understand the extent of the violations I committed?"

"You live on love crumbs. A nibble drops, you gobble up the morsel. The crumb sustains you until he gives you another. Don't you believe you deserve the whole loaf?"

Bread makes me fat.

I dropped my head and fought the lump in my throat. "Okay. I won't talk to Nick for a week." I sighed, defeated. "I hope I'll survive."

"You will." Mike stood and opened his door. The next victim waited in the shadows. I scurried out.

Oz did not cure me tonight.

The horrific phone call with Nick replayed in my mind as I stepped out into the darkness. The soft sweep of footsteps interrupted the chaos. From the other side of the grassy area, a shadow approached in the dull light.

"Prue?" His silky voice made its way through the thick night air. We met each other halfway and stood face to face. My entire body shivered.

"Rough night," Alistair said.

My edges softened. "To put it mildly." I ditched my sandals. The grass tickled my toes, and I felt myself grounded by the earth beneath my feet.

"Let's pretend we're anyplace but here," he said. "Perhaps a moonlit concert in a park."

He sat down, barefooted, his flip-flops abandoned. I eased myself beside him. My fingers moved through the blades. He held a thin branch with peeled bark in his hand. "This is not easy," he said. "A sense of hopelessness is setting in."

Our hands touched.

I should not be here. This is bound to backfire.

"You will shine on the other side of this godforsaken fortress." The words flew from my mouth, and I hoped I spoke with honesty. Voices pounded in my head.

Walk away.

A half-moon illuminated his face, his smile. One deliberate finger brushed along my wrist.

Fuck Nick. Fuck rehab.

He pressed his warmth on my mouth. My head rolled with sensations: shock, joy, terror, elation. For one brief moment, I put my troubles behind me. With parted lips, I invited him in. We formed a seamless rhythm, gentle, tender. Each kiss sealed and reopened.

"Sorry, I shouldn't," he said, yet neither of us moved. The soulful eyes edged beyond my hateful self. I kissed him again.

"Don't be," I said, taking in the closeness between us. We sank together and escaped from this place, from all our troubles. Both of us yearned for the same answers, merging with the night.

Then reality struck. My head swarmed. Nick and Naomi in my bed. Christian deserved a better mother. Richard, screaming in my face. Every closet holding me prisoner. My feet scrambled for my shoes, I stood and reached my hand to Alistair. We embraced, our bodies entangled, holding each other for dear life. I froze, entranced by his attention.

"In this dim light, the green of your eyes resembles an emerald," he said. My shoulders softened. "It's as though we grew up together and have been reacquainted from years gone by."

A strong, unafraid face.

"This can't happen," I said, pulling away. "I have no clue what I'm doing or how I will survive. I'm scared of losing my husband and terrified to stay. What about your girlfriend? You live in London." The laundry list of excuses. "This is a fantasy. Nothing more." My body shifted farther from him. I craved space, but a powerful force pulled me back.

"This is not something I've made up in my mind," he said. "No woman has ever captivated me the way you do. This is different, trust me." Our foreheads touched. "Most of all, I don't want to hurt you." He reached behind my neck, his thumbs exploring my cheeks. I permitted him without hesitation. As clarity set in, I had no choice but to let him go.

"Goodnight," I said.

"Night." His hands moved from my face, down my arms, to my fingertips. Alistair walked away, into his loneliness, and left me standing in the dark with my own.

CHAPTER EIGHT

*L*ily and I took the same sixth-period math class. As the clock ticked, she closed her pencil case and pretended to listen.

"Worksheets due and a quiz," the teacher said. The bell shrilled. "Don't forget to bring your calculators tomorrow."

Before the teacher finished her sentence, Lily was already hightailing it out the door. "Hurry up, Prue," she said. Her skinny legs sprinted down the hallway.

"Right behind you!" My backpack swung with every step.

"First one out again," Lily said. We high-fived each other while her mother waited in the turnaround. "Can you come over?"

"Not today. My mom's picking me up."

Lily climbed into the waiting car and waved as they drove away. I sat on the school steps with my book bag resting next to me. The principal appeared after the last bus pulled away.

"Is your mother coming for you?" he asked.

"Yes, she's running a little late."

His facial expression exuded disapproval. "Alright." He glanced at his watch. "I'm sure she'll be here soon," he said and trotted off to his car.

Not a soul was left, so I passed the time singing to myself aloud. I sang about a certain Miss American Pie going bye-bye, and a candy man who can. The songs aggravated my hunger pangs. I fished deep inside my book bag and found a half-unwrapped Twizzler. I brushed away the pencil shavings and tore off a piece. When I finished the licorice, I started getting angry.

Why can't you be on time? Where are you?

The sun dipped below the horizon. I shivered, and my teeth clattered. After a lifetime, our wagon roared into the parking lot.

"I plain-old forgot to get you," Mom said. "Sorry."

I crossed my arms over my chest and stared ahead.

"Don't be chapped. I'm only human."

I was the mortified, forgotten child at birthday parties too. It was as if the whole world kept time to Mom's Cartier Tank. "Thank you for having my daughter," she'd say. "Sorry I'm late."

She had such a charming personality that I would soon forget the unreliable mother and begin each new day with the misplaced faith she would keep her word.

∞

At dinnertime, my stepfather Richard held court at his throne. Mom sat across from him, an oblivious queen as Henry and I played the parts of the jester and the peasant girl. I took a minuscule bite of the bratwurst, chewed the greasy meat, wiped my mouth, and released the lumpy mass into my napkin. In an instant, I fed the sausage to Hemingway.

"Why is that goddamned dog always under foot while we're eating?" Richard glared at me with his red face, his half-chewed food exposed as he spoke. A small chuck flew out and landed on his placemat.

"Let the dog be," Mom said.

The blow seared my hand. My mother winced.

"Hold your silverware like I told you to or I'll smack you again!" he snapped, gripping the knife handle above my throbbing knuckle.

"Please," Mom implored.

"These kids need to learn some goddamned manners."

I dropped my fork and kissed my wound. I looked across the table at Henry. For some reason, he started laughing, which triggered me to start laughing too. A heroic attempt at containing our giggles failed. We couldn't stop.

"Quiet!" Richard shouted, cracking his knuckles.

One glimpse back at darned Henry and I burst out laughing again. I looked down at my plate. It glared back at me with a monstrous amount of Brussels sprouts. "Can I go to the kitchen for another napkin?"

"Yes, you may," Mom said, queen-like.

There were three napkins laid in my lap. I began the process of eating, chewing, and spitting. Much to my dismay, I had miscalculated the ratio of green cabbage balls to napkins.

With a mound of sprouts still intact on his plate, Henry boldly positioned his fork and knife in the I'm-finished position. "Can I please be excused?" he asked.

Richard's evil eyes darted to Henry's food. "I will say this only once, you ungrateful brat." He slammed his hands on the table. My plate jumped. "You're lucky to be given anything, and you will eat every morsel." He stopped rambling and turned his head from Henry's plate to mine, then back again.

I made an assessment of my consumption.

"Both of you can sit here the rest of the night, for all I care."

Mom cleared the table while Richard fired up a cigarette. He pushed back the chair, crossed his hairy legs, and puffed. The smoke poisoned the air. He tapped black ashes onto his uneaten food. Mom replaced the plate with an ashtray. "Thank you, honey," he said.

Henry and I conducted a staring contest. I won. We played again, and again I won. Our warden lit another cigarette. His index finger moved like a baton.

"Pick up your forks and finish," he said. We parked our gazes downward with hands on our laps. A third bourbon chilled in a highball glass. "Take your plates to the kitchen, put Saran Wrap over them, and save them for breakfast."

∞

The next morning, Gram picked us up.

"Richard said to eat leftover Brussels sprouts instead of cereal," I said. The boiled balls oozed under the cellophane shield.

"Why on earth?" She unwound her red Hermes scarf from her neck, removed a wide-brimmed sunhat, and tucked the silk inside. "I wonder about that man," she said, scraping our scraps into the trash.

"What should we eat?" I asked. My stomach rumbled, but not for nasty, day-old vegetables.

"How about I take you to the diner for pancakes before your riding lesson?"

Gram's car was stockpiled with rain slickers, blankets, hoodies, tissues, and snacks in anticipation for what *might* happen. With my velvet helmet in hand, I climbed into the back. Henry sat in front. The musty, flowery car scent comforted me as I nestled in.

She called all the waitresses by name and made eating out an occasion. "Of course, take more syrup." It was as if her sole purpose in life was to make us happy. After breakfast, she delivered me to a private barn for a lesson she had finagled through her connections at the tack shop where she worked. "Tim is marvelous," she told me as I exited the car.

Tim instructed me from a golf cart with a pale-blue hat propped on his head. I figured it was to protect his mottled, pale skin and bald head. A plaid blanket was draped over his knees. He spoke in a way that sounded both kind and firm, which made me want to try harder. Gram sat next to him in the cart.

"Heels down," he said. "Change your trot to a canter."

After the class, I dismounted and crossed the soft, squishy footing of the training ring.

"You're quite graceful," Tim said. "A natural."

"Thank you so much," I said, trying to be proper.

"My granddaughter loved today," Gram said.

In the car, I asked Gram why Tim didn't move from the cart. "He endured a horrific accident years ago while riding," she said. "He severed his spine."

I was glad I decided not to inquire in front of him.

∞

The older we got, the more things we had to do, and the more friends we had to hang with. Our visits to see Dad became more and more disruptive. Mom seemed relieved when she'd drop us at the airport, and I tried not to take it personally.

The August before I started eighth grade, I went into Dad's room to tell him goodnight. He and Alicia laid under the covers. "Goodnight," I said, not committing to a full bedroom entry.

"Guess what I've been doing?" Dad said. He held out two fingers for me to sniff. Alicia giggled, her cheeks flushed. The lavender sheets draped at the edge of her nipples. My instinct told me not to, yet a curiosity ran through me, and I wondered what other women smelled like down there. I lowered my nose to his wet, sticky index and middle fingers; salty and sour, with a bit of rancid body odor mixed in. Her pheromones tickled my insides.

In my bed, I touched myself and fell fast asleep.

The next evening, I requested Dad to come kiss me goodnight rather than me going to his room. He carried the *Physicians' Desk Reference* under his arm, his gait staggered and uneasy.

"About an hour ago, I took a few of these," he said, pointing to something near the middle of the book. It fell from his hands and tumbled to the floor, pages folded and crushed upon landing. He passed out on my bed, breathing heavily but not moving. A spittle of drool dribbled from the corner of his mouth, but I didn't see any foam. I figured it was a good sign.

I picked up the book, hoping it had landed on the page he'd indicated. The truth was, I didn't really know if it was the right page.

Which did he point to? This one, or that one?

Other than books about drugs, Dad enjoyed reading *The Joy of Sex*, which he generously shared with Henry and me. We combed over the black-and-white drawings of naked men and women doing erotic things to each other. At thirteen, a sickening shame counterbalanced my curiosity; the sketches imprinted in my mind for future self-pleasuring. I kept this information to myself and didn't breathe a word of it to Mom.

CHAPTER NINE

My room reeked of perfume. The bathroom counter was covered with makeup brushes, hairspray, and flecks of powdered blush. It was just a matter of time before one of my roommates fucked someone, yet somehow, I was the one who claimed the pink sticker.

These girls are up to something. No one works this hard to be glamorous in rehab without someone specific in mind.

The unbearable thought of my recent relapse confirmed my continued bad behavior. A simple kiss had screwed up my last shot at making things right and sullied Alistair's road to healing.

"Do you want to come to movie night with us?" Gabriella said, scurrying in for a forgotten something. Bridgette propped the door open with her foot. We exchanged smiles.

"No, thanks." I folded my boring clothes and placed them in the drawer.

"You might rethink your decision, because Owen said Alistair is going." Gabriella locked her eyes on my expression.

Did they hear about the kiss?

"Please don't bring any men back to our room," I said, not giving them the satisfaction of any sort of reaction at all.

"Of course not," Bridgette winked.

My respite was that Mike had granted me permission to move in with Deirdre the following day, before the morning meeting. It was the first smart thing I'd done in a long time. She had the same victim thing going on as I did, since we'd both been raped a few times. Most of all,

Deirdre was here to get better, and I had the impression my current roommates weren't. Mike said I needed to learn to trust my gut, and my gut said to get the hell out of the room I shared with Bridgette and Gabriella.

The girls flitted out the door. Trapped in the room, I knelt to pray. *Dear God, please save me.*

I laid my head on the pillow and sank into my sorrow. I couldn't stop the tears.

The sound of running water awakened me. I got up to see what was going on. Someone cowered naked in the tub. "Are you okay?" I asked.

"Toby and I did it," Bridgette said.

My body shivered. I wrapped a shawl around me and listened to her cry.

Fucking never fulfills the high, but the anticipation and preparation does. Once the act begins, the bubble bursts.

I paused in the doorway, far enough to give her space but close enough to provide comfort. She sank down into the tub and turned the faucet with her toes. Black mascara ran down her cheeks.

"I'm so pissed at myself. I'm such an idiot." She moaned and sighed at the same time.

"It was an act of impulse. Believe me, I understand." I held up her towel. "Here, we can talk in the room. If you need me to, I'll stay up with you."

"Why are you being kind to me? I've been a total bitch to you." She pulled the drain and crawled out of the tub, kicking her clothes out of the way. "A dirty whore wore that outfit." Cropped blonde hair spiked around her head as she slipped on a tank and boxers. Gabriella rustled under her covers.

"Now you're senselessly beating yourself up," I said. "Forgive yourself and try to move on." I stretched out my arms and twisted my torso, fending off the uneasy, sickening nausea. It was not for me to own.

"Gabs." Bridgette shook the covers. "Wake up. We screwed."

"Oh, cool," Gabriella said. "Well? Details." She turned on her bedside lamp and propped herself up with pillows. "Wait, are you crying?"

"Yes," Bridgette said. "I fucking cheated again. This time, the hubs might dump me." She dragged a makeup remover cloth under her eyes. "While I leaned against a fence, he fucked me from behind. After he creamed, he got paranoid and wanted to head back. Of course, someone witnessed us emerging from the darkness, so by now the world must know."

"Everyone doesn't," I said. I hoped the rumor wouldn't fly as fast as most did around here.

"Oh, God, my husband is going to find out about this during Family Week," she groaned.

Family Week scared me even before my illustrious kiss. Nick had committed to showing up with Christian. I wasn't sure if he was coming to check out the whole rehab scene or to truly do some work on us. From what I gathered, Family Week provided the opportunity for those most affected by our addictions—our families—to heal. The five long days gave visitors a chance to tell their side of the story and to come to a place of peace. The addicts made amends, one of the twelve steps. According to Mike, everyone put their pain behind them. Even though something told me Nick would never forgive me, I was willing to give it a try.

"I can't believe the dude turned out to suck in the sack," Gabriella laughed. She was the only one.

"Dominic told me this is the last rehab," Bridgette said. "I'd better be good and get clean, or he's done." She turned to me with wild eyes. Her front teeth clipped her fingernails. "What should I do?"

"Well, in my amateur therapist opinion," I said, "you avoid dealing with your pill addiction through attention from men."

The blind leading the blind.

"Why don't you call him and tell him what happened?" I eased onto my bed. "Meet with your counselor tomorrow. Regroup and refocus. It might not be too late."

"I disagree. Don't tell him," Gabriella chimed in. "Go to bed, you'll be fine." Her *best friend* turned off the light and scooted back under the covers. "Now, no more talking. I need my beauty sleep."

"A new day brings a clear head," I said in an attempt to smooth out the last advice she'd received. It was hard to ignore the fact her supposed *sister* exhibited no empathy whatsoever.

"I'm disappointed in myself. Maybe you're right." Bridgette sat next to me and pressed her wet hair on my shoulder. "Thanks, Prue. You're a sweetheart."

"Sweet dreams," I said. Thoughts of my own empty encounters prevented sleep.

My new room radiated positive chi. Good energy flowed through me as I unpacked, grabbing a moment alone before my meeting. For once, I had trusted my gut and put in for a room change before any real trouble culminated.

I searched for a neutral seat at the morning meeting. One not next to Alistair, or any hot guy for that matter. Gloria cradled a doll in her arms—part of her healing program. She waved me over. Pens and scraps of paper were laid out on a table by the door for us to jot down acknowledgments about each other. I made the choice not to write about my ex-roomie banging Toby, and about how I had screwed everything up for Alistair.

"Welcome to the morning meeting," Mike said. "Does anyone have anything to share?"

"I want to say thanks to Deirdre for comforting me yesterday," one woman said.

A few more patients spoke up, some offering positivity, others not so much.

"Tracey gossiped about another patient," someone said.

A claustrophobic state rattled me. The main meeting room was a colorful array of lanyards, each representing what had taken us down.

"Let's not to gossip. Talking about others impedes the treatment process," Mike said.

Next, they handed out sobriety pin awards. Some claimed seven days, some thirty.

How easy is it for someone to score a drink in this place, or for a meth addict to land a rock?

I couldn't escape my drug. Every man represented a line on a mirror, tempting me, enticing me, pulling me in. The words from the wall in Mike's office throbbed against my skull: *You are only as sick as your secrets.*

After announcements, the entire group circled the room. All the lost souls grabbed someone's hand while maneuvering around the scattered chairs. I closed my eyes and let my hands hang, waiting for anyone to grasp it and close the circle chain. I felt fingertips. Our hands interlocked. Alistair squeezed three times.

I love you.

After prayer, his warmth remained and tingled up my arm.

"Hey," Alistair said. "Been thinking about you nonstop."

"You shouldn't be sharing that kind of stuff with me. It's not productive for either of us." I smiled, fearing I'd come across mean-spirited. Deirdre came up and saved me.

"Sorry I couldn't help you move," she said. "Hope you got settled in okay."

"To be out of my old room is a gift from heaven above."

We joined the sea of people heading to their respective group meetings.

"I'm thrilled to share with you." Deirdre wrapped her arm around me, our steps in unison.

I picked up my satchel by the door on our way out of the room. My timeline was rolled up and battened down with a rubber band. I tucked it under my arm like a loaf of French bread.

My monkey brain raced during meditation.

How will I survive this hour?

Alistair was first up on the agenda. In slow motion, he laid out his timeline, the handwriting neat and detailed. Way better than mine. He confessed to an obsession with strippers. Of course, Mike wanted him to go deeper.

"My father ran off when I was about two, leaving my mother to raise me alone," Alistair said. "Oftentimes, I agonized over why he didn't want me." As he spoke, I pondered why Alistair stood out from the others. I tried to pinpoint that rare, special something.

"Don't avoid the subject we spoke about in private yesterday," Mike said.

"Most of the time, I was alone," Alistair said. "My mom took off for days on end and left me with little or no food in the flat. I remember sucking on an old tube of frosting because I couldn't figure out how to use the can opener to eat some beans. On one occasion, I grew weak with worry and hunger. Noises came through the walls from the neighbors. When I heard people singing 'happy birthday,' I dashed into the hallway and knocked on their door. An older woman answered. My unkempt hair, hollow belly, and dark circles alarmed her enough that she offered me a piece of cake."

I want to cradle little Alistair in my arms.

"Elaborate," Mike said.

"My mother abandoned me, and I vowed to never experience the ache again. Not in my heart or my stomach. I suppose this drove me to succeed in my career, to make a better life for myself, and to not open up to women."

All the luxuries of the world couldn't fill the void his mother left behind.

"Now you are getting to the real issue." Mike took us to the battlefield, and we were still alive.

"The cocaine attracted the kind of women who aren't interested in settling down. In a subliminal way, I put off commitment by engaging with immature, unsavory ladies. When I found the marrying kind, I cheated. Sabotaged things."

"Bingo," the great Oz said.

Alistair's troubled upbringing unraveled. A litany of abuses and neglect. The last hurrah: his mother had paid for his first lay. When he finished, Alistair crawled back to his chair. His saddened eyes searched for acceptance. I mouthed, "Stay strong."

"Your turn, Prue," Mike said.

I unfurled my life onto the floor and anchored the curled pages with my flip-flops. The pain began with my father disappearing after my birth and continued with Richard. I omitted the graphic details to avoid triggering other patients regarding their abuse, or exciting one of the weirdos.

I'm afraid of being trapped in the dark. Of not being able to escape.

CHAPTER TEN

Richard called us into the kitchen. "Hurry up. This is urgent!" Henry and I lined up. "Do you know what this is?" Richard asked.

"An ice tray," I said, raising my hand.

"Right now, I'm going to teach you numb-nuts all about ice. Listen, because I don't want any screwups." He led us to the sink. "Fill the trays with water. Tilt from side to side to even out the level. Don't make any too small or too big, because I want perfect cubes." He hovered over Henry, breathing down his neck. "When you empty the tray, make more. And by empty, I mean one or two cubes are left."

A greasy line was smeared across his glasses, and a white pus-ball rested in the corner of his eyes. He watched us with disdain, hoping for a screwup. Henry inched his way to the refrigerator. Water sloshed onto the floor.

"Sorry," Henry said. I flinched in anticipation and sympathy of an ear slap.

"Do it again, you idiot," Richard said.

Henry made a successful journey on his second attempt, then passed the cracked blue tray over to me. I turned on the faucet. Water splattered every place except where I wanted.

"Turn down the pressure, retard." Richard swatted my head. His ring clunked on my skull. Once he was satisfied with our education, he released us.

∞

Later that afternoon, Lily wanted to meet up. Of course, we invited Henry to tag along. No way could I leave him in the house with *that* man.

"I'd go," Henry said, "but my bicycle has a flat."

"Do you want some help?" I asked.

He pumped while I gripped the tire. "That's good."

The back door hurled open. "Stupid brats!" A blue rectangle tapped against Richard's palm. We circled our bikes around. "Which one of you knuckleheads left one cube and put the tray back?" A vein on his temple bulged and pulsed.

We're in for it.

"I didn't have any icy drinks today, Sir," I said. My haphazard braids needed tightening.

"Me neither." Henry squirmed.

"Well, I didn't, and your mother is at work, which means it was one of you two brats. You better come clean." Richard's face reddened. I contemplated making a run for it.

It was too bad Oral had been shipped off to boarding school and Pat had moved back to her mom's. Another set of bodies would take the brunt of this unreasonable person's pent-up rage.

"Get your asses inside the house," he snapped. The beast cracked his knuckles. My eyes snapped shut.

We went inside, and I jammed my back against the kitchen wall, sticking my fingers in my ears. My skin crawled hearing Richard's hand smacking against the flesh of Henry's bare buttocks. When it was over, Henry pulled up his jeans and ran outside.

Richard moved to me next. He yanked down my shorts and leered at me as I covered my privates. His strong hand forced me over his knee. The humiliation of him seeing me naked was far worse than the sting of the strap. The strength within me exhibited not a flinch. When he finished, I strolled out the door.

"Come on Henry, let's go."

Lily wanted to go sailing the next day, so I got up early to finish my list of chores before the sun rose too high. Richard doubled our workload in the summer, but coffee became my responsibility year-round. In the mornings, I moved down the staircase at half speed to not wake anyone. When the teapot was full and heavy, I turned on the burner. It wouldn't light. I lit a match, and it fired up with a *poof*. The Folgers included a complimentary yellow measuring spoon tucked inside the tin. I pulled the Chemex from the cabinet. It looked like an oversized timer with broken wood pieces. A stiff rawhide strip was strapped around it like a belt. Most of the time, I counted out loud and poured the coffee into the paper filter. Richard's voice reverberated in my head.

Six scoops to one pot of coffee. Just don't be a goddamned klutz and break my carafe! Pour the water in a circle to bring the grounds to the middle.

The drips took time. I continued to pour water into the top until the carafe filled up with dark liquid. While the last of it dripped, I lined up two mugs on the counter, one next to the other. I poured the coffee into Mom's cup first, then carried the steaming cups to their bedroom. I set one down on the floor to free up a hand to knock.

"Come in," Mom said. The hot coffee swayed in the mug. "Thank you." Her shiny, jet-black hair was tangled and choppy from sleep. Her lean, freckled arm draped over the coverlet. With every bone in my body, I loved her. My heart grew tingly just thinking about her.

The chore of laundry fell to me, too. After java service, I loaded the washer. The wet clothes stunk to high hell if I left them in too long. I found that out the hard way. When the machine gyrated and purred, I sat on the lid. Most of the time, I daydreamed about Peter Noone of Herman's Hermits swooping in to take me away like Cinderella's Prince Charming. The phone let out a shrill ring. I bounced off the washer and ran before *he* started yelling for someone to answer the damned phone.

"Hey, are we going?" Lily asked.

"As long as I finish my chores, or if *he* leaves."

"Be ready to roll. I'm riding over at eleven. Richard can suck it."

After the wash dried, I rolled the lawnmower out of the garage and kicked the caked-on grass off the wheels. With my foot on the motor, I ripped the cord. Nothing. After three more tries, the engine rumbled to life. I pushed with all my might while Hemingway barked behind my heels. A sharp crack of metal pierced the air. The machine sputtered and stopped.

"Dammit!" This needed inspection. I turned the thing over to check the damage.

Henry came out the door. "You know I'd help you, but Richard's sending me to run errands." The kid looked sick, although our beatings became less severe with both of us as witnesses.

"The blade is bent. Not good." I pinched my earlobe as Mr. Evil barreled out the door. "Sorry, I swear to God on a Bible, I didn't see whatever I ran over!" I figured throwing in religion made my story more believable, even though the man held no faith in the good Lord.

"Out of my sight," Richard said. His hot breath sprayed in my face. Henry stood watching, pondering whether to walk away or follow me into the house. "What are you looking at, dumbass? Didn't I tell you to go to the hardware store?"

Henry skulked away. I hightailed it into the house. Richard stood over the busted mower. I watched him from the window and could feel his disapproval through the glass. He turned toward the house, stopped, put his hand in his pocket, and pulled out his car key. He strode to one of his beaters and climbed in.

Having narrowly escaped another flogging, I sneaked into Mom's room. She was never around anymore. The best way to be close to her was to smell her clothes. Deep down, I missed her. More than that, I needed her. I buried my face in her dresses. The sweet scent of roses mixed with cinnamon wrapped around me like arms in an embrace; crisp taffeta, smooth silk, soft cotton, and brocade. The memories of her old life were held in each garment; barbecues, baby showers, and funerals. The silence surrounded me. I let go of my sadness and allowed myself to feel safe.

The crunch of tires on gravel pulled me out of my trance. I scrambled out of the closet, ran to the door, then stopped cold. The screen door slapped. Shoes stomped in the kitchen. I stretched to peek around the doorjamb. I had no choice but to move back to the closet. My heart raced. A shadow blocked the light pouring in.

Help me, God. Please save me.

I hid in the clothes, still as a corpse. The closet door opened. A long arm reached in and twisted me to the floor.

"Sorry," I said, "I won't go in here again."

My legs tucked to my chest. The lock clicked; a hand unzipped his khakis.

"That's a good girl," Richard said.

My mind floated above Mom's vanity.

CHAPTER ELEVEN

The room felt different. Our chairs, which were always lined rigidly against the wall, had been pulled together to form a circle. A glass bowl filled with rocks rested on the floor.

Where's my chair?

I looked over to Gloria, who was searching for a seat. She clutched her baby doll to her chest, looking like a frustrated mother cleaning up the playroom. She was as distraught by the shake-up as I was.

"Everyone find a seat," Mike said. "We're going to change it up today."

The room filled with a thick heaviness as the patients filed in. We all lived by the comfort of routines. Mike turned on the meditation music as the last few stragglers walked in. Each of them looked around and went on high alert while searching for an open chair.

Mike stepped into the circle and picked up the bowl. "Every rock has a word written on it," he said. "One at a time, you're going to reveal a secret you're holding inside." He ran his hands through the rocks. They clinked around in the glass. "Speaking our secrets out loud releases their power over us." He gazed into the bowl, as if digging up one of his own dirty secrets. "We've all done things we aren't proud of, behavior that doesn't represent us. Don't hold back. This room is a safe place." He bowed his head. "Let's take a moment to meditate and clear our minds."

It took every bit of strength I had inside to silence the voices in my head. The music stopped, and I opened my eyes.

"The final change," Mike said, "is I'm not going to be involved, other than as a support for anyone who needs it. Today is about secrets, and getting them out. After you take your turn, pass the bowl to the person on your left. You'll each share something you needed as a child. Don't think too hard about this. It's not a test. Next, choose a rock with a word representing something you hope for the person next to you. Any questions?"

Toby raised his hand. "I don't have any secrets."

The whole room started laughing.

"We all have secrets," Mike said. "Secrets are poisonous to our bodies. Let's get the toxic waste out. Also, let me give you a gentle reminder. Everything discussed in this room stays here. Let's start with Toby and move clockwise. So, Owen, you'll go next."

"I'm Toby, alcoholic and drug addict."

We repeated his name, even though we all knew each other better than we'd ever know any of our friends back home.

"I'm a pro surfer and have been on the circuit since I was sixteen," Toby continued. "I started drinking and using because there wasn't any adult supervision on tour. By the time I was twenty, I was free falling."

I forced myself to focus on Toby. It helped me refrain from obsessing over what lie I needed to release from the shame-filled black hole poisoning my insides. Colorful tattoos of Toby's storied past covered his arms.

"I overdosed one night," Toby said. "The paramedics broke my front tooth when they shoved the tube down my throat. They were trying to revive me."

I guess everyone has a story.

"Surfing came easy for me," he said. "I'd been number one for a long time, but it meant nothing to me. I had a blackness inside. I didn't care about anything. I had girls throwing themselves at me. It's like I thought I was superhuman. Overdosing was my wake-up call. I could piss everything away. The world title, all my hard work. A few sponsors have already dropped me. I've got to deal with my demons."

Strong, tough, impermeable Toby placed his head in his hands and sobbed. I reached for his heaving back.

Mike slid the tissue box across the circle. "Good work, Toby," he said. "What did you need as a child?"

An unrecognizable expression kidnapped Toby's face. "I just wanted to be a kid." He swished his fingers through the bowl and pulled out a scarlet rock. "Owen, this is for you. Love. I hope you learn to love yourself."

"Thanks, man," Owen said. After he introduced himself, he took a deep breath. "I'm so embarrassed to say this." He paused for what seemed like ages before he spoke again. "I'm in love with my cousin."

I looked around at the others. Their faces radiated with warmth and support.

"We kept our relationship a secret for a long time. A secret from our families, from our friends, and from my wife." Owen rubbed his palms together.

"You're doing a great job, Owen," Mike said encouragingly from the sidelines.

"It was pretty bad when my wife caught us in bed together. We were naked, lying in each other's arms. She put her hand over her mouth and backed out of the room. Shortly after, I tried to kill myself." Then he turned to me. "Prue, I need to come clean. I lied to you. I didn't get in a car accident. The scar on my wrist is from the razor blade."

I ached for him.

"Prudence, is there anything you want to say to Owen?" Mike asked.

"I forgive you," I said.

I do.

"And what did you need as a child?" Mike asked.

"I wanted my dad to be proud of me," Owen said.

The tissue box made its way around the circle. Even the people who I'd never seen cry were wiping away tears. Owen fished around in the bowl for a rock.

"Prue, this is for you."

I took the cool, green stone in my hand.

"Power. I want for you to find your strength. The power to choose happiness, to choose your path, whatever it may be."

I cherished Owen's wish for me, even though I couldn't see a way out.

"Prudence, it's your turn," Mike said.

"I'm Prue, sex addict." I blurted out the next words that came to my mind: "I'm a whore." The words stopped me in my tracks and took my breath from my lungs. "At first, I went after rich guys, whether or not they disgusted me. By the end, I was blatantly exchanging money for sex." My face heated up.

Am I the sickest one here?

"I'm proud of you," Mike said. "Those words are hard to say. What need did you have as a child?"

"I wanted my mother to read me a story."

Mom lays next to me. A book rests on her stomach: The Lorax. *I want to breathe her in and touch her freckled cheek. It doesn't matter whether or not she's had a bad day. I want Mom to be happy in this moment with me. "Unless someone like you cares a whole awful lot, nothing is going to get better. It's not."*

"Good." Mike's voice pulled me back to the room. He eyed the rocks, reminding me of my next task. I picked up the bowl from the center of our circle. The stones slid around, then tumbled back to their resting place when I set it on my lap. I gazed at the rocks, then dug my finger around in search of the one I knew would be perfect.

"Alistair," I said. The shiny blue stone rested between my thumb and index finger. "Trust. I hope you learn to trust your heart." I pressed the rock in Alistair's hand. He pierced my soul with his eyes. When the rock touched his palm, he closed his fingers around it.

"Thank you." His thick lashes framed his glistening eyes. "I will cherish this, and your message." Alistair turned to the group and revealed his secret—a secret that poisoned him the way ours poisoned us.

When it was finished and everyone had shared, Mike held his hands outstretched. "Great work today, everyone."

The group formed a prayer circle. I lingered in my chair, just as I did at the end of every meeting. I couldn't hold Mike's hand, even though I wanted to. It felt too desperate. I put my workbook inside my bag and eased into the circle.

Owen reached a hand toward mine. "Thank you," he whispered, his head already bowed. His hand spread a comforting warmth and energy to mine. Alistair grasped my other hand and gave it a squeeze. Goosebumps covered my arms, and the tiny hairs stood on end.

I wish for a longer prayer, to hold Alistair's hand a moment more.

"Owen and I are going to the nurses' station for afternoon meds," Gloria said. "You want to come?"

"Sure." The goosebumps left as fast as they'd come. I dodged Alistair and hustled out the door.

"We have to hurry because the line gets long this time of day," Gloria said. Her breasts bounced as we dashed along the sunny walkway. "That was a super intense meeting."

"Heavy, but necessary," Owen said. He stopped outside the nurses' station door and turned to us. "Do you guys think I'm weird? You know, because of what I confessed." His red t-shirt outlined his slumped shoulders.

"That's the thing," Gloria said. "We're all fucking weirdos."

CHAPTER TWELVE

Richard pushed the closet door open, and I lifted myself from the floor. His worn boat shoes squeaked along the wood planks.

"Move it before your mother gets home." His voice inflicted fear, poisoning me from the inside out. He unlocked the bedroom door and stomped down the stairs. The screen door slapped shut. My hand reached behind my mother's dresses, and I touched them to my cheek. The distinct sound of Richard's car rolled along the gravel driveway. My stomach heaved and my mouth watered.

I hate you.

In my room, I sat at my desk and wiggled opened the drawer where I kept the trinkets left behind by the previous owner. It smelled musty and sweet, like Gram's house. I shuffled the contents of the drawer around and examined a gray rock encircled with a white ring. Mom had told me these kinds of rocks were good luck. I pulled out three rusty bottle caps and two beautiful marbles. The marbles rolled around the desktop. I found a blue hairband, bent and distorted from years in the drawer, and managed to slide it over my hair.

With the rock in my hand, I rested my head on my forearms and closed my eyes. The hair band seemed familiar, as if I had seen it before. Then it came to me: the framed photo of the girl wearing a blue hair band on Mrs. Sutton's Steinway piano; her daughter. The girl with the red coat.

∞

"What happened to your father?" I asked. The cold weather swirled outside; ice crusted in the corners of the windowpanes. My body shuddered. I zipped up my hoodie and shoved my hands into my pockets.

"I was around thirteen when he died, the same age as you," Mom said. Flecks of unsettled dust floated in the sunlight as she rearranged her magazines.

"Why don't we ever talk about him?" I leaned on the door, watching Mom clean.

"I will tell you when you're older and can better understand. He was not an admirable man." Mom rearranged and fluffed the sofa cushions, then creased the top. "By the way, I'll be commuting on the train again starting Monday. My new title is secretary to the president. Impressive, right?"

"Sure," I lied. Her absence would mean more time alone in the house without protection.

"Come help me pick out an outfit."

He would be in charge. I rubbed my ear. Mom stepped in and out of the dreaded closet, modeling dresses while I laid on her bed and gave my opinions.

"Is this too sexy?" she asked. "It's not appropriate to come across too sexy, but I don't want to dress masculine, either." She checked her backside in the mirror.

"What time will you leave in the morning, and what time will you be home?" I asked. The ear rubbing did nothing to calm my nerves. I twisted a chunk of hair around my finger.

In singsong rhythm, Mom rattled off her justification. "Robert Frost said by working eight hours a day, you may get to be the boss and work twelve hours a day. I am a woman, and may never be the boss."

If being a woman meant working hard all day with a couple of hours left for a disgusting husband, I didn't think I ever wanted to be a woman.

When Mom got up for work, so did I. While she got ready, I did my chores. The minute she pulled out of the driveway, and an hour before school started, I sprinted to the Suttons' house. Victor, Mrs. Sutton's barn hand, always lingered around the stable. He was gross and creepy, but nothing compared to Richard. I kept myself busy carrying hay bales from the storage area to the feed room. From a distance, Victor's dark eyes followed me.

On frigid mornings, I boiled water in Mrs. Sutton's kitchen to melt the ice in the horses' buckets. The regal woman sat at the table in an ivory satin robe with toast, fruit, and a gold-rimmed coffee cup adorned with pink peonies.

"Morning, Mrs. Sutton." The kettle banged the side of the sink. I straightened my posture and tucked in my shirt tail. With the burner lit under the kettle, I waited while my stomach gurgled.

"Your mother isn't worried about where you are, is she? I wouldn't want her to think we've adopted you." She smiled and chewed with her mouth closed.

Adopt me. And Henry, too.

"My mother is at work," I said. The buttered toast and strawberry jam made my mouth water.

"Are you hungry?" Mrs. Sutton asked.

I nodded.

"How can you expect to do well in school without breakfast?" She stood, walked to the toaster, and dropped in two slices of bread. When the color turned golden, she slathered them with peanut butter and wrapped them in a paper towel.

∞

I sat on the fence rail with my breakfast. Balaam licked the peanut butter off my fingers when I gave him the crusts. After eating, I continued to lift the hay bales and transfer them to the feed room.

Victor approached from behind without a sound. His voice was thick and hot in my ear. "Your ass is making me crazy."

I dropped the hay bale, falling on top of it as he pinned me down.

"No, please!" I begged. My cheek was grinding into the straw. He yanked my hair and pulled my head back.

"Shut your fucking mouth." The stench of alcohol on his breath fogged my face. His metal belt chimed as he unzipped his pants. Sharp hay pieces poked my chin.

"Get off of her!" Mrs. Sutton shouted.

Victor released his hold.

"Your services are no longer needed here," she said.

Victor uttered not a word as he slunk away. My knees weakened. I sat down and placed my head in my hands.

"Now, pull yourself together," Mrs. Sutton said. "Let us not speak of this again."

My lower lip quivered. I tasted a tinge of metal from biting my cheek.

"You aren't a little girl anymore," Mrs. Sutton said. "Be careful what you wear on a womanly figure, or you might attract the wrong kind of attention."

"Yes, ma'am." I followed her into the tack room, straightening my shirt and closing one more button.

"Tim Caldwell will be giving you riding lessons on Saturday mornings," she said. "Be sure to tell your mother." As if nothing happened, she hooked silver pulls through two loops and slid on her field boots. "Pay attention at school today."

"Thank you, Mrs. Sutton."

I wonder if Mrs. Sutton will save me from Richard, too.

∞

It took me a full hour to walk to my scheduled riding lesson in the stables located at the bottom of a long, winding road. Tim waited in his golf cart with a red plaid blanket draped across his lap. Gram met me there and settled next to him on the cart. After the lesson, a few horses arrived on trailers. Majestic animals were unloaded by a groomsman wearing a polo shirt with a barn name emblazoned across the chest. Each trailer carried an attached dressing room brimming with elegant riding clothes. Grooms passed polished reins to aristocratic riders who scowled at Balaam and me on their way to their lessons. I was relieved Tim treated me as an equal to the other riders.

"You got talent, kid," Tim said. "Keep it up."

Some things, money can't buy.

For my fourteenth birthday, Mrs. Sutton gave me a framed a photo of Tim atop the back of a stately bay horse. The picture was taken before he lost the use of his legs. In my heart, I loved Tim but never said the words out loud. At the end of every lesson, his wife would transfer him from the cart to his wheelchair. I'd turn away because I didn't want to see him struggle.

Some days, Balaam didn't want a lesson and would buck me off halfway to Tim's barn. The stirrups would tear off during Balaam's trot home, and I'd search for them on foot. The naughty pony waited at the barn gate, nostrils flared.

"You stinker."

The last lesson of the school year, there was no sign of Tim or his cart. I knocked on his door, and his wife greeted me.

"Tim will not be instructing you today," she informed me.

Shortly after, Tim passed away. I tucked his photo under my pillow and cried myself to sleep.

Lily didn't want to go to boarding school, but I did. My applications were filled out. I applied to three all-girls and one coed, then prayed for a fat scholarship. Greasy Richard insisted I stay home, since our bank account put us at next to dirt poor. He stopped paying the bill for my braces, and a few brackets had loosened, cutting the insides of my mouth.

"Mom, I need to go to the orthodontist," I said. "My braces are bothering me."

"Come here." She dug around the inside of my cheeks. I felt the ghost of her probing fingers in my mouth. "We can't come up with the rest of the money to pay the orthodontist." She strolled to the bottom of the stairs and called for my brother. "Take your sister to the garage and pull off her braces with the pliers on the workbench."

"Are you serious?" I asked, as respectfully as possible under the circumstances. "Isn't there anything you can do to get the bill paid?"

"You aren't making this easy on me," Mom said. "I told you, we don't have the money. If we leave the brackets on, your teeth will decay."

I'm a trapped animal with no way out.

"Sorry," Henry said, squirming and pinching his face in pain. He clamped the pliers on a bracket, wiggled it, and pried my braces off. That amateur orthodontist visit still didn't save enough for boarding school.

∞

Cute boys distracted me, yet I remained committed to my academics. It was my ticket out of Goose Neck Harbor and from under Richard's thumb. But once I got boys on my radar, I obsessed over them. My current distraction was a boy named Binky Heffernan, who had moved into town from Seattle in the midsummer. There was only one word to describe him: dreamy.

Lily and I shared a locker all through junior high. It was a tight squeeze. She piled her books on the terrazzo floor while I pulled out my algebra and history books, then stacked hers back inside. We both jockeyed for the illegal mirror glued to the inside of our locker.

"Binky likes you," Lily said. "How can you be so clueless? He lingers around our locker like a lost puppy."

"I don't think he likes me in *that* way." I smeared Dr. Pepper Bonne Bell lip smackers over my lips.

"Trust me, dreamy blue eyes is into you." She spanked my rear. "You could snap a quarter off your butt and send it to China," she said. "Keeping it real, just keeping it real." She closed the locker door while I was still in mid-lip application.

"Hey, Prue," someone said from behind. It was Binky. "Want to hang out or go to a movie this weekend?"

"Of course she wants to go to the movies with you," Lily said. "Don't you?" She could barely hold back her laughter.

Lily might be trying to kill me.

My cheeks flushed. "Sure, sounds fun," I said.

"Catch you later." He whipped his head around, his blonde hair swirling as he turned.

Lily smiled at me as she juggled three books and a binder in her arms. She propped a pencil between two fingers. "If you don't want Binky, I'll take him."

My acceptance letters arrived. I got into every school I applied to, but only with partial scholarships. Once I was home and sitting at my desk, I sneaked the letters out of my backpack and read them again.

I'm out of here.

I kept the letters stashed in my school locker, afraid Richard would once again try to ruin my life. In class, I slipped Lily a note.

Stay by the phone tonight in case I need to cry. Giving my mom the acceptance letters.

Lily's eyes widened. She scribbled on the wedge of paper and passed it back across the aisle to me.

You got this, Chickie! If she says no, you have Binky and me. Wink! Wink!

There was no sign of Richard hitting the highballs when I got home from school. Mom's car veered into the gravel driveway, and I shot down the stairs to meet her by the door.

"What are you so excited about?" she asked.

I waved the letters in the air and danced around in a circle.

"Help me with these groceries," she said.

"I got in! I got in!" I exclaimed.

"Congratulations."

I swapped the letters for the groceries. Mom scanned the pages, flipping through them, squinting.

"Don't get your hopes up," she said.

She poured herself a cocktail and settled in the living room with my letters in hand. An hour later, she knocked on my bedroom door.

"I went over the numbers. You didn't earn enough scholarship. I'm sorry," she said. "Looks like it's public school for you. Look on the bright side. You'll be with Lily."

I buried my face in my pillow and screamed.

The next morning, I dragged through my usual routine. Mrs. Sutton, in full riding attire, waded through the wet grass with a bowl of oatmeal for me.

"Any news from the schools yet?" she asked.

"Yes, but I didn't receive enough scholarship money. Looks like I'll be in Goose Neck Harbor for high school," I said, gratefully eating my breakfast.

"What a shame," she said. "You're such a bright girl with so much promise."

No promise goes unbroken.

I handed the bowl back to her and rubbed Balaam's muzzle. "Thank you for breakfast, Mrs. Sutton. I'm off to school."

"Study hard," she said.

Lily did her best to cheer me up. In math class, the office lady's voice came over the intercom: "Prudence Aldrich, please report to the principal's office." I dashed out of the classroom and down to the office.

The receptionist held the phone receiver out to me.

"Hello?" I said.

"It's Mom. Pack your bags. You're headed to Edith Woodson Academy. A girl with a full scholarship got sick, and you were next in line."

CHAPTER THIRTEEN

I got comfortable on the floor and tucked my bare feet underneath me.

I'm not ready for this. I'll never be ready.

I pressed my hands on the paper timeline to smooth out the wrinkles, wishing I could smooth the wrinkles from my past.

"My life changed when my mother met my stepfather, Richard," I said. My chest tightened just saying his name out loud. "He changed everything."

It felt like a dream. As if someone else spoke for me.

"Two boys molested me in a closet. It happened a lot, and I was afraid to tell my mom because I didn't think she would believe me. There was no safe place in my house. My stepsister asked me to play 'rape' when I was taking a shower. She'd lock me in the closet to mess with me."

My body trembled. I reached for my hoodie and pulled it on like a coat of armor.

"Closets scare me. I can't sleep with a closet door ajar. It has to be latched closed."

Mike nodded. "You're safe here," he said.

"Richard sprung for the deposit for my braces, but then he stopped paying the orthodontist. The metal brackets loosened and cut my mouth, and my teeth were starting to decay. My mother told my brother to remove them with pliers." I smiled to exhibit my straight teeth. "I heard my mom and stepdad having sex almost every night for several years."

I shifted on the floor, reversing the crisscross position of my legs. Rhoda touched my knee. "You're a beautiful soul," she said.

My lungs had stopped breathing. I exhaled. "My mom worked long hours."

I willed the floor to take me. Mike cupped my shoulder. Energy vibrated through his hand. I nodded.

"I went in her closet to smell her clothes. I guess it somehow made me feel closer to her." I tugged on my top, self-conscious and horrified. "The same closet where my stepfather forced me to give him oral sex."

Shame oozed from my skin and onto the floor, pooling around everyone's feet.

"My stepfather called me names like stupid, retard, idiot, loser, fat, ugly, disgusting pig. He tortured us with food, slapped us across the face, whipped us with belts. I have a few scars." The sweatshirt shielded me. "My real dad never hit us, but he was a sexual deviant and a drug addict. He used cocaine, popped pills, and was an alcoholic. He would pass out on my bed. Sometimes he'd leave us alone to go out to drink and party. The local bartender would call to say he had passed out and we needed to pick him up. My brother was timid, so I would go alone. I had to sober him up because I couldn't lift him. My father shared pornographic books with us, nude photos of his girlfriends, sex toys, inappropriate stuff."

My finger moved along the timeline as I detailed the rest of my trauma up to my eighteenth birthday.

Little things add up to a lot.

"You exposed your soul, and we're all grateful," Mike said. He turned to the group. "Comments?"

I rolled up my paper. Shame seeped down to my core.

Rhoda spoke through her tears. "I can't bear to hear the things you have endured." She wiped her eyes. "I'm awestruck by your strength."

"Now that you see the trauma on one piece of paper, what does it tell you?" Mike asked.

"I'm a victim of abuse, still alive and desperate to put it behind me," I said.

"I want you to know you are a precious and valuable person," Mike said. "Thank you for sharing with us."

Relief.

Alistair raised his hand. Mike tipped his head, signaling for him to speak.

"Wow," Alistair said. "Heavy stuff. One never knows what people have been through. You come across so normal, and yet you have lived a life of horror and torture." He shook off the tears, his skin flushed. "It's uncanny how much I relate to your story. There are similarities between us, our childhoods." He swept his fingers through his thick, dark hair. "Especially the way we compensate for our tragedies with other things."

"Insightful," Mike said. He rolled up his sleeves and leaned forward. "Can you elaborate?"

We all knew it wasn't a question; it was a command.

"Bloody hell." Alistair rubbed his thumb and index finger along his stubble, looking like a guy straight out of *GQ* magazine. "Well, this isn't easy to say with tact, but I will try." He sorted his thoughts while I soaked him in. "We both came from humble beginnings, but try to cover it up."

"Excellent." Mike perused the group. Some of us, it seemed, were caught up with the stories in our heads. Others wanted to engage with the group to avoid their own personal hell. A silence filled the room, and out of the corner of my eye, I saw a hand raise. "Mitch?"

"Yeah, I see where Alistair is going with this," Mitch said. "At first glance, I'd guess Prue and Alistair were born with silver spoons. I'm not saying they act snobby. More British royalty and American blue blood."

The room filled with laughs and side comments. Mike waited for everyone to quiet down. "Humans have the propensity to compensate in a variety of ways for our perceived weaknesses," he said, leaning against his desk and crossing his arms over his chest.

Superman.

"Deirdre," Mike said. "Can you come up with an example of a behavior you exhibit to compensate for a perceived weakness?"

"I think so," she said. "I try to appear friendly and happy-go-lucky, when in reality I suffer from social anxiety and depression. I compensate by acting one way, when inside I'm feeling another." Deirdre pulled at the fringe on the end of her spiral notebook, and white flecks speckled the carpet.

"Great work today," Mike said. "Lots of real progress happening in here." He glanced at a sheet of paper on his desk. "We got a little sidetracked, but I think it was helpful. Let's form a circle."

After prayer, Mike pulled me aside. He had a pained expression on his face, and I feared my stories had upset him. "You deserve love," he said. "You are worthy of love. Believe it."

I wanted desperately to believe this shaman.

CHAPTER FOURTEEN

The Edith Woodson scholarship came in after the semester began, so I missed orientation and freshman friend-making. My assigned room had been used to store brooms before I moved in. A guy from security volunteered to help me carry two suitcases and three bags up to my shoebox. Not a soul came out to greet me. Small packs of girls strolled by, giggling at inside jokes. I felt like an outsider.

Gray stone buildings complemented elaborate lead-paned windows. The larger ones burst with colorful stained glass. Ominous gargoyles crouched on every architectural point, their eyes following my every move.

The traditions ran deep at Woodson. In May, girls pranced around a pole adorned with ribbons. At Christmastime, they performed Revels with racks of authentic, preserved costumes. A lawn slated for seniors tempted underclassmen to roam and find out what *might* happen if they stepped a foot on it. Mandatory "chapel" on Wednesdays and Sundays provided a place for me to say my prayers of gratitude.

My new school exuded academic excellence and elegance. My financial situation, I kept to myself. On the first day of class, some fool stockpiled my room from floor to ceiling with balled-up newspaper. In a split second, I weighed my options: cry, or act as if I didn't care. The eyes of the girls who had committed the crime bored into my back. I dove in and threw the wads around the hall. Girls swarmed out of their rooms like roaches in the light.

"Hi, I'm Sarah," one of the girls said. She motioned to two girls standing behind her. "These are my roommates, Jenny and Carolyn."

"Welcome to Woodson," Jenny said. "You passed."

∽

My wardrobe was comprised of clothes collected at weekend student-run sales. With a knack for fashion, a high-end brand name on a tag gave me a solid camouflage.

I took a convenient shortcut through one of the tunnels on a torrentially rainy day. Back in the old days, the long, brightly-lit tunnels kept the girls safe from worldly influence while moving from one building to the next. In modern times, the tunnel served to shelter us from the inclement weather. As I moved through the tunnel, I caught up with a petite brunette I recognized from one of my lectures. A chic, chin-length bob framed her heart-shaped face.

"My hair would be a frizz if I went out there," I said, raising my voice over the echo of our loafers on the white subway tiles.

"Me too," she said.

A bad hair day for her seems impossible.

"Aren't you in sociology?" she asked. "By the way, I'm Alie."

"Yes," I said. "I'm Prue."

A stamped gold brick hung from a delicate chain around her neck— a small-scale replica of something I imagined the Federal Reserve stashed in their basement.

"A gift from my father," Alie said, fingering the nugget. "My mini-Fort Knox." Beyond coveting her necklace, I yearned for her caring parent.

"What dorm are you in?" I asked.

"A single on Kellas One. My parents wanted me in my own room to focus on academics. I've been a bit lonely."

More than anything, I wanted to dislike this coiffed rich girl. But her transparent, open-hearted kindness won me over.

"I got here a few weeks late and sleep in a two-foot cell," I said.

"The girls said you took the newspaper incident like a champ. I would've bawled like a baby."

"Your top is awesome," I said. I was proud she'd gotten wind of my cool reaction.

"Borrow anything you want anytime."

We arrived at the end of the tunnel and passed through a heavy door, then up a flight of stairs that led us to the humanities building. Alie waved as she turned left and I walked up two grand stairs to my Shakespeare classroom. The picturesque lead-paned window of the English department staged the rain while it clapped on the slate roof.

For Thanksgiving, Henry and I visited Dad in Manhattan Beach, a suburb on the outskirts of Los Angeles. The balmy temperatures turned out to be less of a shock than what Dad cooked up the first night. He piled a white mound of powder on the kitchen counter and cut it up with the edge of a credit card. With great detail, he chopped it up and snorted it with a rolled hundred-dollar bill. The groovy house bustled with his high energy as he greeted his guests.

"This is my new girl, Bunny," Dad said. "Bet you can't guess who she plays the violin for." He spoke without waiting for our answer: "Van Morrison."

Bunny was a blonde version of Dad's previous squeeze. She had a small chest and a bigger backside—just the way he liked them. Dad claimed women with small boobs tried harder in bed.

"What happened to Alicia?" I asked as Bunny dove to the drugs and out of earshot.

"We're still friends," Dad said. The house line rang. "Grab the phone, son."

"Hey, Mom," Henry said. "We just walked in the door." He dropped onto the leather sofa.

"Is everything okay?" I asked. My patience was growing thin.

"Hang on a sec," Henry said. A smile stretched across his face. "It's over. Mom left Richard."

Without a beat, I yanked the receiver from his hand. "Did you leave him?" My whole body tensed.

"Aren't you happy?" Mom asked. "Look, I've got to run. Enjoy the time with your father. Love you."

She spoke as if she was reporting the details of her last workout at the gym. The room started spinning. My own horror movie had come to an end. "The nightmare is over," I said. The things Henry and I had endured but never spoke of. We knew.

"Your mother left the asshole?" Dad said. He kicked out the rhumba and pulled me with him.

∞

Dad threw a blowout party on the last night before I headed back to school. While I bartended, DJ Henry selected the music. Dad twitched with dramatic, jerky moves. He jammed a key fob into my palm.

"Take the Beemer to connect with my supplier and pick up some blow."

I dropped the keys onto the counter like a hot potato. "You realize I only have my permit."

"And do you realize I can't leave my friends?" Dad asked. There was no chance to argue. He guided me out the door. "Go to the Albertsons down the road. Drive to the side with the dumpsters. Wait for a black Mercedes and give him this." He passed me a wad of cash.

"This is not a grand idea," I said.

His lips moved around his words, jumbled and erratic like a foreign film with subtitles. "You are the best, baby. You'll never guess where he went to college. Harvard!" He closed the door as I stepped out onto the front porch.

I'm pretty sure Alie's dad wouldn't send her out to buy cocaine.

The car lurched as I deciphered how to turn off the blinkers, wipers, and hazards. I was terrified of a sideswipe, so I drove down the center of the road until a hotrod blared his horn. It took me forever to drive a full three blocks. When I got there, the shoppers were long gone. I rounded the corner of the building and found the vehicle. Every nerve in my body went on full-tilt overdrive. I opened the window and reached out with the money clutched in my clammy hand. The Harvard-grad-turned-drug-dealer took the money and handed me a soft, plastic packet.

After the delivery, I was fed up and retreated to my bed. I woke up to the sound of breaking glass. After a few more odd noises, I made the executive decision to survey the commotion. The new girlfriend, Bunny, stood in the living room with a fiery stare. A crazed, gut-wrenching sound came from her mouth as she overturned the coffee table. In the kitchen, plates sailed to the floor, transforming into glass piles. The cart where Dad kept his expensive liqueurs in crystal decanters was toppled on its side. Multicolored puddles seeped into the white shag. The stench of crème de menthe masked the odor of bodies mixed with stale food. Henry stood behind me, frozen, his mouth agape.

Must I do everything?

"Please stop trashing the house," I said, as maturely as possible for a teenager.

Her face dark red, Bunny tore a macramé planter from its hook. The soil flew through the air. A beast emerged from within me. I wrestled her quivering body down. All the fight escaped her, except for her grinding jaw.

"The bastard left and went to his whore's house!" she screamed.

The thrashing stopped, and she went limp, curling into a half-fetal position. I clutched a clump of her hair in my hand. I opened my palm, and her tresses tumbled down.

"Which whore?" I asked.

"That slut, Alecia."

Henry took the sobbing woman to the garage to find the BMW gone. Dad's extra car was a poop-brown Karmann Ghia. The three of us climbed inside. Henry got behind the wheel while Bunny gave directions. I sat in the back, fuming and stewing over my idiot father. We arrived at Alecia's house within minutes.

"Can you please deal with it?" Henry begged me.

Like a baby clawing its way out of the birth canal, I crawled from the car and stomped to the front door.

Alicia answered. She was dressed in a red silk kimono. Dad peered over her shoulder. His eyes were dark and fierce, and his limbs shook like birch trees in a gale. He had a black down parka wrapped around him. From the coat down, he was buck naked.

"The house is trashed," I said. "After we take your girlfriend home, we're going to Nana's."

"Why did you let her trash my place?" Dad's jaw moved wildly, and blood ran from his nostril.

My anger overtook my polite side. "The fact is," I said. "You are nothing but a sperm to me. You are not my father."

The next morning, we left Nana's house and shuttled back to Dad's to return the car. "We need to leave for the airport, and you're too jacked-up to take us," Henry told Dad. "I'm calling a cab."

It was a thrill to witness the forthright Henry. Dad hovered over two paper squares loaded with coke. He took a few sniffs and tucked one into each of our school backpacks.

A parting sentiment.

∞

In my opinion, Daisy Giordano won the imaginary "most beautiful sophomore at Woodson" contest. The pink strips of her toe shoes fluttered around the polished dance studio floor as she slipped into her sneakers.

"Come smoke with me," she said.

A walk to the smoking benches with Daisy belonged on stage at the Met.

"Those legs," Daisy said. The girl on the other side of me lit my cig while Daisy stroked my thigh. "Amazing."

"Thanks," I said, thick smoke rings disappearing with the wind.

"We need to hang out more," Daisy said.

To avoid more strokes, I turned away. "Do you like our ballet teacher?" My muscles stiffened when her head dropped on my shoulder.

She crushed the beige filter under her Tretorn. "Let's get out of here."

Hand in hand, we wandered through the long, wood-paneled hallway to her suite.

"The whole class says you're an exquisite dancer," I said. In my dreams, I danced half as well.

"Do you know how beautiful and talented you are?" Daisy said. She stopped and stared at me, perhaps waiting for a reaction.

Is she being real with me?

"My passion is riding," I said.

"That makes you even sexier."

"My bio professor assigned a note recap, which is going to take most of the night," I said, inching away. But there was no way to escape. She dragged me to her room.

"What kind of music do you like?" Daisy asked, leaning in close. In the background, Billy Joel was belting out a song about chandeliers. The music spilled from speakers hanging from the ceiling corners.

I was a rabbit in an open field; prey for the hawk.

The needle on the album jumped. Daisy reached into my leotard and massaged my breast. A warm sensation surged through my pelvis.

"Come here, sexy girl," she said.

Her luscious lips engulfed mine with smoky, sticky breath. My legs spread as she groped wherever she wanted.

The thought of getting busted gnawed at me.

Immediate expulsion.

Daisy untied her wrap and pressed her firm eraser nipples to my mouth, pleasuring me as gracefully as she moved. A few fingers explored the parts only I had roamed. My back arched. I pulled her in for more. She buried her face between my legs and moved her body around. Unadulterated pleasure came in waves. My tongue searched, unsure of where to venture. She moaned and grabbed my hair, showing me, placing me. The moment I climaxed, remorse pressed down.

Like a kitty, she curled up next to me and purred. I wiped my wet, sticky face on her sheet.

"Homework looms," I said. "Gotta run." My twisted, inside-out clothes slowed me down.

"So soon?" She stretched and yawned.

My legs lagged like lead pipes. I spotted Alie vacuuming at the end of my corridor. I was thrilled we had finagled a room change before winter break so we could be together. Most everything light enough to lift was cluttered in the hall. Bent over, she feverishly dragged a nozzle across the carpet. Alie couldn't start her homework without the room being spotless. An upbeat Harold Melvin & the Blue Notes song played from the shit box stereo Dad mailed after a year of reporting it was "on the way."

The vacuum dropped to the floor, and Alie turned down the music. "Where have you been?"

"Well, I just fooled around with Daisy."

Her hand flew over her mouth. The pave diamond band she wore on her middle finger twinkled as she tugged me into the room. "Spare no details," she said. "Daisy is hot, but what the hell?"

"No way can I go to ballet again," I said.

"This story calls for a drink," Alie said.

We kept a bottle of Bacardi 151 and glasses hidden on the ledge of our balcony. Alie reached out for our provisions. The liquid burned on the way down our throats.

Someplace inside my bag, the "present" from Dad lay hidden. I reached inside and pulled it out. "Do you want to try this?" I asked. The alcohol swirled in my head.

"Is that what I think it is?" She took the folded-up paper square from my hand and examined its contents.

"A gift from my dad."

Not exactly what Alie's father would bequeath her.

I unwrapped the paper and dumped the coke onto my desk. With the edge of my student ID, I made one long row. I sniffed up half a line with a rolled-up dollar bill. My nostril blasted with fire and my eyes watered. A numbness coated the back of my throat. In true ladylike manner, Alie snorted the rest. The rush came down hard, and I feared my heart would jump right out of my chest.

What if the housemother knocks? What if I like this stuff too much?

For the first time, I understood my name, and why Mom had left Dad. The thought I might turn out like him killed me.

"Let's dump the rest," I said.

I flushed the evidence down the toilet. As I glanced at my reflection in the bathroom mirror, I wished I could wash away where I came from too.

Alie and I roomed together again junior year. At spring semester, the school exchanged twenty girls for an equal number of boys from a nearby academy. When the strapping juniors arrived, Woodson changed. Those girls who had worn dirty hair and nightgowns tucked in their jeans to class traded up for full-blown outfits and makeup. Instead of a tying my hair up in a ponytail, I shampooed and let my curls air dry.

One of the boys, Finnegan Fuller, captain of the lacrosse team and junior class president, garnered the most attention.

One day, I was seated at my favorite study table in the far corner on the upper floor of the library when someone pulled out a chair and dropped their books onto the table. The audacity of anyone sitting in my special study place, which was typically unoccupied year-round, was beyond intolerable. I glared over the top of my book to see who had dared invade my space, ready to lay them out with the stink eye.

"Prue, right? Not sure if you remember me," he said. "I'm Finn. We met at the welcome reception." He flashed a straight-toothed preppie smile.

"Everyone knows who you are," I said.

To my relief, he laughed, and I did too. In an unfamiliar balance of thrill and comfort, we whispered about life, music, and other things until the librarian finally escorted us out.

Finn's cords hung just so, the lax hoodie stopped above his high and tight derrière, his hair delivered an effortless swing and, the look was made complete with faded L.L. Bean blucher moccasins.

Something told me I might never be the same.

∽⦡⦡∽

The complementary school shuttle took me to the metro to catch the train to New York City for spring break. My thoughts were preoccupied with Finn, and going to formal with him.

I maneuvered my cumbersome bag through the crowd at Penn Station and cursed myself for overpacking. I found Lily through a sea of people, waving out her car window.

"You are the only person who can sit on the street at Penn Station in an illegal zone and not be harassed by police officers," I said, heaving my bag into the bed of her truck.

"The cops can suck it." She hit the blinker and barreled out between two cabs.

"Whose pickup is this?" I asked.

"I got it from my parents for my birthday."

"Sweet."

The pale leather seats warmed the interior. A tonally matching starfish hung from her rearview. The Cure streamed from the custom system as she made her way out of the city and onto the expressway.

"What's new at school?" I asked, checking my face in the light-up mirror. "Any gossip?"

"Nothing new. Football players are annoying, cheerleaders are stupid." She laughed. "There's a get-together later tonight at Binky's. Out-of-town parental units. Thought we might make a ruckus." She wore the expression of someone who'd swallowed a parakeet. "Hope you're not going to be mad, but me and Binky are kind of a couple. You know, dating." For the first time since becoming friends, I saw Lily blush.

"Why would I be upset?" I said. "I'm happy for you! And yes to the party."

An unspoken rule tied us together. Nothing and no one came between us.

"I'm staying with Gram this week," I said. "My mother's been in full dating mode since the divorce. Some dude is sleeping at the house for the weekend. Needless to say, I'm not interested in meeting yet another one of her boyfriends."

"Wouldn't it be crazy if we ended up at the same college?" Lily said.

"It would be awesome! Hey, drop me at Mrs. Sutton's. She wants to give me something. What time are you getting me? Make it after supper so Gram doesn't think I'm ditching her."

"Be ready at eight, and wear something slutty."

"I'll be wearing my chastity belt," I said.

"See ya later, Chickie."

Balaam stood at the fence, whinnying. "Did you miss me?" I patted his velvet muzzle, then made my way to the grand front door.

"How are you enjoying the school?" Mrs. Sutton asked. Her crisp white shirt was tucked into a pair of houndstooth slacks. "Some of my happiest years were spent there. My mother loved it too." She guided me down the marble corridor. "I'm so pleased the scholarship came through."

It was then I realized my ticket to Woodson hadn't come as a result of a scholarship student getting sick. Mrs. Sutton had rescued me once again.

In the parlor, a bowl of potpourri left a hint of roses in the air. "I took the liberty of ordering you something for prom," she said. A pale lavender Bergdorf Goodman box teetered on a wing chair.

"This is too much," I said, thrilled by the gift.

"Go ahead, open it."

"What a magnificent shade of blue," I said, lifting the dress from the box. I held it up to my chest.

The tissue paper fluttered to the floor. Mrs. Sutton directed me to try it on. The dress was the same color as the Tiffany boxes Alie received from her family for gifts on holidays.

"Oh, my, it's perfect." Mrs. Sutton paused and hooked the clasp. The front door opened and Mr. Sutton braced himself in the frame, scraping off his boots.

"Wow!" he said. "Quite elegant." He stepped across the oriental in his socks and kissed his wife. "Give a twirl."

"Would you like to join me for an afternoon trail ride, Edward?" Mrs. Sutton brushed specks of dried mud from his polo.

"Not enough time before my meeting," he said. "Nice to see you, Prue." In an aristocratic manner, he traipsed up the staircase.

Mrs. Sutton turned her attention back to me. She held my hand as if posing for a curtsy. "We can shop for a few other things one afternoon in the city before you go back."

"Finn is going to *die*!"

"Be careful who you give your heart to." The conversation took a turn. "Remember, a successful man is one who makes more money than his wife can spend. A successful woman is one who can find such a man." With the box in my hand, she led me to the door. "Never forget, you deserve the world."

I waited at the end of the driveway. Statuesque oak trees lined the lane, creating a vibrant, fresh green canopy overhead. Each home carried a name and an accompanying placard at the entrance. The placard before me read *Harewood – Mr. and Mrs. Edward Sutton.* My Gingerbread House sat off in the distance. As I stared at it, a sense of smallness overcame me. It was as though my existence held no meaning.

A taupe Corolla pulled up; the brakes screeched. "My beautiful granddaughter," Gram said.

Saved from the abyss of less-than.

As she maneuvered the dusk-lit roads, she reached for my hand. My hollow insides refilled.

∞

My head pounded from way too much beer. I hunkered deeper under the blanket.

"Let's go car shopping!" Gram stood over me, a snappy scarf tied around her neck. Her lime-green pants blinded me.

"What?"

"Your friends can't chauffeur you around for the rest of your life." A fresh coating of coral lipstick glossed over her words.

At the car dealership, she opened her checkbook and purchased the Civic in full. Then she took something out of her handbag and snapped the item to my new keychain.

"This is pepper spray, for protection."

I sat in the driver's seat and inhaled the new-car scent with utter joy.

The Gingerbread House was my first new-car destination. With Mom not around, I walked up the creaky stairs and stood in her room. Nothing was left but her things. In shock and relief, I sat down at the vanity, curious as to what new jewels lived in the mahogany box. Under the faux pearl bauble, at the bottom, I discovered a notecard.

Anna, my darling,
You are a stunning beauty who has turned my world upside down. The most sensual woman and best lover I have ever known.
See you tonight at our special place.
—Edward xxx

I felt a sudden rush of nausea. My hand trembled as I replaced the pearls and closed the lid. To erase the picture of Mom doing the nasty with Mr. Sutton, I surrounded myself in her clothes.

∞

We took Finn's beater to the Thunderbird, a grotty motel in the neighboring town. He checked us in with his fake ID while I sat in the car until he gave the thumbs-up.

Inside the motel room, Finn fumbled a box of condoms from his pocket and set them on the bedside table. "Just in case," he said. He removed the jet-black tuxedo jacket from his athletic physique and draped it on a grungy, floral brocade chair. With one tug of his bowtie, he unfurled the black strip. One arm swept around my waist, and he drew a heart at the crease of my cleavage. "It's fine if you don't want to."

Not the scene I had envisioned in my mind: the two of us entangled on a breezy, sunbaked island; a hand caressing my face; his lips kissing my neck. This moment, I had replayed a million times.

"I'm going to use the restroom," I said. To confirm my intended whereabouts, I pointed to the door. I ran the faucet and stared at myself in the mirror, searching for the last trace of innocence left inside of me—the part of me I would surrender to him.

I gathered up my shimmering Tiffany blue satin and rolled my undies down to the icy tile floor. With them wadded up, I unlatched the clutch Mrs. Sutton gave me and shoved them inside. I kept the water running so he wouldn't hear my tinkle sound. I repositioned my breasts to puff them out. Finn waited for me, shirtless. A glimpse of his pecs left me giddy. I stood at the end of the bed and unzipped my dress. He smiled, clasped his hands behind his head, and watched the show. "You're beautiful," he said.

The straps fell, and I left the gown in a heap on the orange rug, mortified by the thought of bending over to retrieve it from the floor.

"Adorable." Finn opened his arms. "Come here." I laid my head on his chest and listened to his pounding heart. An erection raged against my leg. "I love you," he said. Silence engulfed the room. The three simple words bounced off me without sinking in.

More than anything, I wanted to say it back to him, but the words wouldn't come. I figured my heart was irreparably broken, and not even Finn could fix it.

∞

Alie couldn't study unless her pencils were lined up to perfect points, and I couldn't study without the purr of the electric sharpening machine.

"Are you bummed we opted not to go to the mixer?" she asked. "School is ruining our lives." Her sinewy body leaned out the window and bathed in the faint sound of music wafting through the crisp air. "The dances are so lame." She sighed.

"Studying with you beats dancing with some guy from Albany Academy for Boys," I said.

My time with Finn left me with beautiful memories, but I craved freedom. The breakup left him heartbroken . . . for about ten minutes. Yale gleamed in my sights.

"All our hard work will pay off," I said.

"My brother advised me not to *peak* in high school, because the real fun happens in college." The reading lamp illuminated Alie's flawless skin.

"Keep the faith." I savored the safe haven of my dorm room, Alie, and our understanding of each other's dreams.

A housemother peeked in. "You have a visitor, Prue."

"Who?" I asked.

"No idea, but you need to go sign *him* in."

"*Him?*" Alie raised her eyebrows.

I snatched my book bag, just in case I needed my ID or something. We both ran down to see who it could be. Henry was leaning against the wall. Lily stood next to him.

"Yay!" I said. We jumped and squealed and hugged. An awkward moment lingered as my two besties stood face to face.

Lil made the first move. "Prue has told me so much about you." She wrapped her arms around Alie in a warm embrace.

"Same here," Alie said.

Phew.

"Did you come all the way from school?" I asked.

"Lily got a recruitment from the sailing coach and wanted to tour Trinity," Henry said. "After she saw the school, we came up with this scheme to surprise you." He swooned at Alie; I caught him in the act.

"Can you go eat with us?" Lily asked. "Starving." She rubbed her belly.

"The only snafu might be the guard," I said. I inched over to the office, where the dorm rent-a-cop sat and watched the various security cameras. "Can we get a pass, please?" I asked him. With my newfound feminine power, I grinned and twirled a strand of hair.

The man ravaged me with his eyes. "Sure, I can't say no to you."

$$\infty$$

I sat in the front seat to give directions. Lily drove, and Henry and Alie shimmied together in the back. Within minutes, they were giggling like twelve-year-olds at a cotillion.

"Grub is on me," Lily said. "My mom gave me her Visa. Pray my dad doesn't notice *this* is gone." She reached under her seat and pulled out a bottle of champagne.

"Very strategic," I said. Nothing surprised me with her.

At the make-out spot overlooking the city, we piled out and sat on the hood of Lily's pickup. Henry popped the champagne cork and took a swig before it bubbled. Lily passed around paper cups.

"Guess who brought dessert," I said, pulling a fresh pack of Twizzlers from my bag.

"That's my Chickie!" Lily took a cup from Henry.

The Grateful Dead spilled from her cassette player. In that moment, I allowed myself to feel genuine happiness.

In another time's forgotten space
Your eyes looked through your mother's face
Wildflower seed on the sand and stone
May the four winds blow you safely home
Roll away, the dew.

The mail room was a battlefield. Girls screamed, sobbed, or succumbed to lying on the floor. My feelings fell to the realm of neutrality: admittance to Trinity College, with the full cost of tuition on them. But there was one more place to hear from: my dream school, Yale.

The envelope waited on the other side of the tiny glass mailbox door. Some colleges sent manila envelopes for the yes's and the no's in standard white, but not Yale. All notifications came in the same goldenrod package, whether accepted or rejected. The mailbox dial could be turned with a blindfold. I flipped up the metal toggles.

Lux et Veritas. Light and truth.

The first word I read was *Congratulations!*

Across the room, Alie opened an envelope. She spun around, locked on me, and leapt over like a gazelle. "I got into Columbia!" she screamed.

We applauded each other's success and dedication. I held up my letter, and she squealed.

"Not sure how I'm going to come up with the funds," I said. Reality struck with the thought of Mom and her reaction.

"What do you mean?" Alie asked.

She couldn't relate to my money struggles. I couldn't fault her for it.

"I'm worried about what my mom will say."

"Everything is going to work out," Alie said.

Things always did for her.

"See you in the room," I said. "I have to call her."

"Fingers crossed!"

I slipped into the phone booth and dialed. "Guess what!" I said when she picked up, as if I didn't expect the whole world to come crashing down on my head. "I got into Yale."

"That's fantastic, honey. How much money did they award you?" Mom asked, but my silence told the story. "Be realistic. Henry told me Trinity offered you a full grant."

"But I got into an Ivy League."

"What on earth are you thinking?"

"I'll work to come up with it." My hand numbed around the phone.

"Fine, but don't raise your hopes up."

Yale slipped through my fingers.

My first summer after Woodson, I went to the Adirondacks with Alie, who sunned and organized our social calendar. She resided at her family's summer home, and I rented a second-floor room from an old couple named Mr. and Mrs. Strickland. My door lacked a bolt, but the only other available room was located in the broiling attic. I snagged a spacious room with a private bathroom and dirt-cheap rent. No dishwasher or air conditioning in the old house, but the place seemed alright.

The four other tenants kept to themselves, and the elderly couple went to bed early. Radio silence at nine was enforced, and I never interacted with my landlords except in passing. If I didn't time my departures and arrivals, the old bat would drone on about her only son, Doug, who had enlisted in the Army. On more than one occasion, she made me late for work. Her cherished son's photos were displayed on the walls; from a grinning baby in Peter Pan collars to a stern-faced soldier with an assault rifle.

A local restaurant hired me on the prerequisite to being attractive and fit in a microscopic outfit. The fat, mean supervisor told me every day for a week straight how waitresses worked in teams of two, and I'd better find a teammate or he'd fire me. Alie held no plans of working for my creep of a boss or wearing a mini-sailor number. The hem of the outfit, a nano-second below my ass, forced me to crouch when gathering anything off the floor. On a daily basis, I bugged her about coming on board.

"One of your hot little friends better show up for an interview, or I'll give your job to someone else!" my supervisor commanded.

This required urgent response. I called Alie from the hostess stand.

"Please come work with me," I begged. "The entire kitchen staff is made up of buff frat boys."

"For you and Yale, I will," Alie said. "But if the slimy boss hits on me, I'm gonna smack him."

"He's a harmless pig. I will protect you."

I didn't want my old lady landlord to judge my work attire, so I always left the house in street clothes, my uniform stuffed into my satchel. It was the best and only way to escape her sneering jabs.

On Alie's first day, we got high in the back lot. We repeated the tradition throughout the summer. Most days, she made us mixed cocktails at the bar which, we pretended were Diet Cokes. Her livelihood didn't depend on the money.

The word *klutz* was an understatement when describing my waitressing skills. Of course, Alie demonstrated a promising career in service. One night, with a slight buzz, I fell while holding a tray of steamed lobsters. Four clawed beasts and a gallon of drawn butter went flying. My uniform rode up, exposing much more than my thong. The customers left a hefty tip, and the busboys applauded. My first standing ovation.

That night, I went home hot and humiliated. To make matters worse, I'd failed to crack the window before leaving for work, and my room was sweltering. I wrenched the window open and hurled my soiled clothes in the corner. Stripped down to my panties, I counted my tips. One hundred and twenty-three dollars, which I placed in the jar I kept inside the drawer behind Gram's mace. I had almost a grand, but not enough for Yale. I dragged the bedsheet over my chest and prayed it would all work out.

After a few minutes, I heard the doorknob turning. Startled, I squinted into the darkness to make out the shape in the shadows. A figure stumbled into my room and took a swooning lurch. The sour odor of fermented fruit wafted at me.

"Shhh!" the man said.

I pulled the sheet up to my chin. "Someone's in here!" I said through the darkness. "The renter. You must be in the wrong room."

"Don't you think I know?" he said. "I live here." He staggered forward and sat down on the edge of my bed. His weight pulled the coverlet from my body. "I wanted to be friendly and introduce myself. I'm Doug." His words slurred as he set a bottle of Jack Daniels onto the bedside table.

I moved to the other side of the bed. "I don't mean to be rude or anything, but you need to leave."

On all fours, he crept over to me, laid on his side, and ran his fingertip up my arm. Terror brewed inside me while an inner voice told me I deserved everything, all of it.

"Aren't you going to be nice?" Doug's oversized forehead shined in the moonlight. His hair was chunked from sweat. "I'm your landlord."

"You should not be in here."

I considered my next moves. How far was I to the door? How fast were his drunk reflexes? And if I got out the door, where would I go?

Bourbon breath blew into my face. "You're pretty," he said.

I scrambled for the door. He smashed my mouth and pinned me down with the weight of his body. A cry made its way through, muffled and weak. "Shut up!" he snapped. I tried to bite his hand. "Bitch." His breath burned my face. "Tell my parents, and I'll say you're a liar."

He ripped my underwear. I struggled. For a second, I broke free and lunged for my nightstand. With brute strength, he threw me on my back and held me down with his knees. "You're going to like this," he growled as he unbuckled his pants. Pain dug into my hips, cutting off the circulation in my legs.

"Please don't!" I said. My voice softened. I hoped a change in tone would help him see his actions.

It didn't work.

∞

The sun beamed into my room. Birds tweeted in the tree branches. My body ached. I stood in the shower and washed my bruises, hoping the poison would flow down the drain. A layer of foundation blocked the ripe purple tones bursting through my skin.

"What happened?" Alie asked. There was no tricking my friend.

"The Stricklands' son came into my room last night."

"Do not live there anymore, stay with me." Her concern mended my shattered spirit.

"He leaves on Sunday and won't be home again until Christmas, long after I'm gone."

"I'm distraught over this," she said. "Honestly, my parents won't mind."

"I can't impose on your family. The other room locks, and I'm going to ask to switch. I appreciate the kind gesture, though."

After work, I asked to move upstairs. The landlady didn't ask me why, nor did I tell her.

That night, Doug knocked for what seemed like an hour before finally giving up.

After the incident, I started sexually engaging with different men. At my favorite bar, I flirted with a loud-mouthed guy who bragged about his family owning Tabasco Island. With a few drinks in me, I snuck him into the house. In the morning, he darted out the back door. Mrs. Strickland strutted into the kitchen, where I was making toast.

"Out!" she blasted. "I heard everything! Every last bit of it! And I don't want you in my house. You're a tramp. Girls like you make me sick."

With no place to go, I called Alie. "Well," I said, "I got booted out. I'm taking you up on your offer."

"They evict you while their rapist son goes unpunished?" Alie exclaimed. "Glad you're moving in, because I'm freaking out about you living there and now I can sleep."

Alie pretended to be her mom and called the restaurant. "Prue and Alie contracted the stomach virus," she told the restaurant manager. "They will be out for a few days." It was pure agony not to bust out in laughter.

The pillow-topped bed in my room had the softest linens. A royal-blue stripe encircled the coverlet; the family monogram was embroidered in the middle. The pillows were plush with goose down. For once, I knew what it must be like to be a guest in the finest hotel in the world.

Even though Alie had her own room, she bunked with me. The maid brought us iced tea, grilled cheese sandwiches, and homemade chocolate chip cookies. We watched romantic comedies and perused interior design magazines. In the afternoon, we lounged by the pool and drank wine from tall silver flutes.

"I want you to stay here until school starts," Alie said. Her body was draped across a pool chaise. "Don't even try to find another place, and I won't take no for an answer."

There was no standing up to Alie.

Over the month of August, Lily scored a cabin at the lake close by. She hitched a trailer to her truck and towed her new boat everywhere— the ultimate badass with hair streaked from sun and salt. We put together a kegger to celebrate her summer sailing wins. Word got around to our friends from Woodson, who attended schools like Smith, Wellesley, and Mount Holyoke, along with a few hotties from Dartmouth, Trinity, and Harvard.

With such amazing women in my life, I started to believe I might not be that bad.

CHAPTER FIFTEEN

Mike's words of encouragement rolled through my head on the way to art therapy.

I am worthy of love. I am worthy of love.

I struggled to remember the exact moment the self-hatred had poisoned my body. The moment I was no longer worthy of love. Then, it hit me. The last time I'd felt loveable and powerful like a superhero was the day I'd caught Waddles for Henry. The day my family fell apart.

"You must be thinking about something serious," Mitch said as he came up the path from someplace behind me. I turned. Sweat beaded on his forehead.

Oppressive, film noir heat. *Double Indemnity* heat.

"I called your name and you didn't flinch," he said. Regardless of the sweat, Mitch had a fresh, clean scent and soft, touchable skin.

"Did you just shave?" I asked, grazing my fingertips over my face. "Your skin is glowing."

He halted mid-step. "Yes, and stop avoiding my question."

The beating sun felt unbearable. "I was trying to recall the last time I loved myself," I said. "Does that sound weird?"

"No, actually, it sounds lovely." There was nothing more he could say. Mitch had solid instincts telling him when to speak and when to remain silent.

The blast of the art room air conditioning gave us instant relief. The door clicked shut behind us. Large sheets of paper covered most of the carpet. Petite Mrs. Yamamoto was tearing more from the huge roll in the adjacent art supply room.

"What's this all about?" Mitch asked.

"Stand beside one of the sheets of paper lying on the floor," Mrs. Yamamoto said from the supply room. After she had placed the last piece on the floor, she juggled a pile of crayon boxes and dropped one next to each paper. Then she turned and addressed the room. "Alright, I need everyone's attention, please." A pale-green art apron was cinched around her wasp of a waist, and a wandering piece of straight black hair fell over her face. She tucked it behind her ear. "This exercise requires a partner. One of you will lie on the paper, and your partner will trace your body. Then you will switch."

Chaos hit while everyone jockeyed for partners.

I locked eyes with Rhoda and mouthed, "Trace me." She waved me over. People crowded the floor as I stepped over and around the bodies. They looked like a crime scene forensics team made up of crayon-wielding kindergarteners.

"Hey, darling," Rhoda said in a lilting Southern drawl. "Lay your cute little body down and I'll trace you. What color do you want for your outline?"

"I'm so happy you're tracing me," I said. "The last thing I need is a guy running their hand around my body." I stretched out onto the paper and lay my arms in a flattering pose in an effort to downplay the shapeless blob I envisioned my body to be. "Trace me in purple. The color of royalty."

Rhoda lifted a purple crayon from the box. "Wait, I need to smell it first." She took a long, slow sniff. "Smells like my childhood and being a mom, all jumbled together." She crouched beside me and started at the crown of my head, moving clockwise around my body.

"It tickles," I said.

She traced each of my fingers. Her eyes magnified through her reading glasses. When she finished, I peeled my lard-ass off the floor. Rhoda laid down onto her paper like she was curtsying at a debutante.

"What color do you want me to trace you with?" I asked.

"Blue." She touched her heart. "It stands for loyalty in the Texas flag. Loyalty means everything to me."

I gripped a dark-blue crayon between my fingers and traced her body.

"Loyalty means a lot to me too." The conundrum for me was deciphering the difference between loyalty and faithfulness.

"Attention, please," Mrs. Yamamoto said in the firmest voice her tiny frame could muster. "Now that everyone has traced their bodies, I'm going to instruct you on what to do next."

She crossed the room and stood next to my oversized paper. "Here, you see the outline of a human body. The body is made up of more than bones and tendons, organs and veins. Your body reacts to the feelings and thoughts your mind sends to it." She crouched next to my giant purple monolith. "The body feels pain, love, anger, shame, passion, joy, fear, and guilt in different places."

She pointed to the *Eight Basic Emotions* poster on the wall. Mike told us all of our feelings were contained in these eight words, and each had three gifts they brought us. He said my horrific shame brought me the gift of humility.

"Choose a crayon to represent words from the chart." Mrs. Yamamoto held a bright-green crayon between her fingers. "For example, I might say I feel love through my chest, down my arms, and in my stomach. Then, I would color these areas, mark green on the paper, and put the word 'love' next to it as a key."

The crayon flew through the air, reminding me of Picasso and his light drawings.

"Show me where on your body you radiate these emotions by coloring on your outline. Try to avoid the obvious. Think deep." She pressed a button on the boom box. Ethereal yet haunting music filled the room.

With closed eyes, I took a long, slow, deep breath. My body heated as I thought about passion soaring above me, flowing from my head to my toes. I scribbled pink across my chest, into my heart, and around my head. Pink represented more than physical passion. I was passionate about fashion and interior design. A part of me wanted to scribble pink in the area where my vagina was, but I figured it wouldn't be appropriate.

I spoke the same words at every damned feelings check: "Guilt, shame, fear, and pain." I lived by these words. Shame and guilt were the knife I stabbed myself with. *I am bad and do bad things.* Fear loomed behind me; my dark, evil shadow. I was fearful Nick would leave me, that I would never love myself and never be normal.

The comforting, waxy scent of the crayon eased my mind.

There were good parts of shame. It helped us to grow and change. I believed the day would come when I could live without shame. Just one day. I bowed my head over the crayon box. An intense tightness filled my throat. Blue shame covered my chest, stomach, and plagued my arms. The shame Richard and the twins put on me was scrawled down the page, into my vagina and around my pelvis. I crawled up my paper body and scribbled blue around my lips and throat.

Mrs. Yamamoto put her hand on my shoulder.

Please stay with me. Please keep your hand there, always.

"Superb," she said. "Find buried feelings, or ones holding you down or building you up."

Tell me I'm a real person, and I'll love myself someday.

Her hand moved from my shoulder, yet her warmth remained. Little Prudence wanted to lie on her mother's lap, hear the sound of her breath and the inflections of her voice as she stroked Prue's hair.

Get your head back in the project. Green for guilt. Guilt swarmed my body like the bees that had attacked me as a child. I scrawled green around my forehead for the guilty thoughts riddling my brain, and in my stomach where it ached. Guilt for hurting Christian and for doing awful things. The crayon moved through my pelvis, down my arms, and colored my hands.

147

Love and hate. Yin and yang. One day, I loved Nick. The next day, I hated him. I swirled my most hated color around my paper chest and neck, turning them a muddy brown. Teal hate shaded my eyes, vagina, and mouth.

Red for love. Love tingled and hurt. Red warmed my heart. I placed my favorite doodle where the vital heart organ might be. Red was sketched down the arms I envisioned holding my beautiful child, and the fingers worshipping his plump cheeks. My forehead, eyes, and mouth were scribbled with crimson love. Then I stretched to my paper feet and turned them red.

Thank you, Lord, for my ability to run away.

My chaotic mind made it difficult to focus.

Bo was drawing intricate cords around his outline. It seemed as though he needed me. I stepped over to be with him. A Crayola trembled in his hand.

"My brother and a neighbor tied me up and raped me in the attic," he said. "My grandmother didn't protect me because she couldn't climb the stairs." He spoke with a quivering lip. "I begged my mom not to go to work."

My stomach soured and my mouth filled with the telltale saliva. Panicked, I darted around for a place to throw up. A hand touched my arm. It was Mrs. Yamamoto, guiding me back to my own work of disaster. Serenity Hills had taught us Bo's pain was his, and mine was mine.

After pulling my hair up into a ponytail, I completed the assignment with the final words. Our small but mighty leader stood by the door with a tape dispenser.

"Excellent work today," Mrs. Yamamoto said. "See you next week. Please take your masterpieces with you."

With the muddled sketch rolled into a tube, I anchored it with the small piece of tape. There was an hour to spare before my meeting. I pulled up a stool at the art table and took out a sheet of paper. Art brought me to a peaceful place. I propped my elbow on the Formica and tapped the colored pencil.

Draw something happy. Little Prue in britches and a riding hat. A cinnamon braid draped over her shoulder. With the reins in her hands, she stands before her chestnut pony, Balaam. A bright sun shines in the sky. Tufts of green grass lay beneath her feet.

The sign on the wall read *Art with no signature will be removed within twenty-four hours. Artwork with the artist's name will remain hanging during the entirety of your stay.* I scribbled my name at the bottom and hung it on the wall.

Gloria leaned into the doorway. "Hey." Her voice was fragile, like delicate wind chimes that might shatter with the first gust. "Want to come smoke with me before the meeting?"

"Of course." I entwined my arm with hers, and we walked outside.

Alistair sauntered by. He looked away as he passed. He dragged behind him a massive red vinyl-covered foam block tied to a chain.

Well, that might be worse than a pink sticker.

The block followed him across the ground like a bouncing puppy. His cheeks were mottled and rosy.

"What the hell?" I whispered.

"Rumor has it he has to drag the block around because he thinks he can continue to drink alcohol and abstain from snorting blow," Gloria said under her breath. "His girlfriend doesn't have a clue he's in rehab."

Why did I kiss him?

Gloria handed me her baby doll so she could rummage through her bag for smokes.

"How come I don't have a baby to carry around?" I asked. Anguish crept into my heart.

"You must have been nurtured as a kid," Gloria said. "I've got to care for my baby better than how I was taken care of. But bringing her to the smoking area might not constitute good mothering skills."

A pack of Newport menthols slid from her pocket. She tapped the box on her palm. I was entranced by her smooth, subconscious moves. She lifted a cigarette from the pack and pursed it between her lips. Like a living piece of complex music, she flicked the lighter, sat down, and crossed her legs in one elegant sequence. No breaks; one seamless overture.

The routines of addiction will transport us all to the same comfortable place.

We sat in silence while she burned through the cigarette. When she was done, she tamped it out and reached for the doll. "You know, Mike told me my childhood was robbed from me. Who even knew where the fuck my mom was most of the time? He said my maturity is stunted because of it." She smoothed her baby's dress, pulling it down over its chubby thighs. "Every single night, I slept in the cold, hard bathtub."

The storm brewing beneath Gloria's outer shell was beginning to converge. I figured a listening ear was the kindest gift I could give her. It was the most I could do, and it was at the very limit of what I could handle. Gloria's downpour might disrupt the hurricane rising inside of me.

Darkness covered Gloria. She stared off into the distance. "My father molested me in the same tub I slept in."

"Do you want me to take her?" I said, reaching out for the baby I yearned to hold.

"She's not real. Just a doll." Gloria folded around the baby. She lit another cigarette. "Believe me, if I could erase it from my mind, I would. But it rolls on repeat. Can't turn off the fucking noise."

"I can relate," I said. It was a constant battle to block greasy Richard from seeping into my brain. "Yeah, I'm trying to do the same." Delicate fairy ashes dotted our shoulders. "At what moment did you realize you needed help?" I crisscrossed my legs underneath me.

Protection.

"Tom checked me in and paid for this Disney ride. Too much Xanax, bars, you know, to numb the pain." A fat smoke stream blew straight to the top of the veranda. "One night I took too many, and he couldn't wake me up. I guess he loves me."

She's doing a whole lot of guessing. Dear God, please help Gloria.

Her enviable thick, dark lashes were smeared with mascara and day-old black liner. "I'm cross-addicted. News to me," she said.

"I've got a few more diagnoses as well: body dysmorphia, codependency, and love avoidance." I recited my laundry list of addictions with ease.

"Awesome." Gloria grinned. "I'm not the only train wreck in this place."

"We're all train wrecks," I said. It was the truth. Rather than make eye contact with me, Gloria preoccupied herself with the fake baby, planting sweet kisses on its face.

"No one gets out of here with just one diagnosis." She shifted and dropped the baby. "Whoops." She dragged it back onto her lap.

"Dammit, I want my marriage to work," I said.

The sense I had somehow failed at life drifted back.

Smoke billowed out of Gloria's mouth as she started to speak. "By the time you leave, you might not want your man back. You'll see him in a clearer light. Who knows what he'll seem like under noonday sun."

I winced at the burning image of naked Naomi straddling Nick, groaning in pleasure, his hand fondling her ass, his mouth over her nipple.

Handsome, put-together Mitch strolled to the veranda. With a fresh smoke dangling from Gloria's mouth, she handed her baby off to me. I rocked the doll, inspecting its rubber earlobes. Heartbreak rushed in. A haunting, buried memory of my arms holding my precious, lifeless child.

"Mind if I pull up a bench?" Mitch said, taking a seat next to me. "I see you're tending to the little one." He popped a cigarette from his pack. "Pall Malls are doctor recommended." He laughed and flicked the wheel of his lighter.

Comfortable silence became the norm. We all had some kind of living hell residing in our brains.

∽

We hustled to the AA meeting with the baby in tow. I wandered away from my friends to focus on the message. One of the younger and more attractive patients volunteered to open.

"Ryan, alcoholic," he said. His legs were spread. His Adonis-like body was draped in a rumpled t-shirt. It was work not to stare.

"Hi, Ryan," we said in unison.

"Binge-drinking was my biggest problem," Ryan said. "I had frequent blackouts. Crazy, embarrassing behavior. It was ugly. Tremors took over anytime I tried to stop. My coach kicked me off the football team. Who knows if he's even going to give me another chance." He shook his head in his own living hell. "Some of the incidences jeopardized the school's reputation. I was flunking my classes." His crisp, confident demeanor faded with each word. "My parents want me sober. I want to be sober."

"Thank you, Ryan," the leader said.

I figured I was old enough to be his mother. Tall and sweet Ryan, with his boyish charm, had led a privileged life. A cheerleader waited for him back home. To an outsider, he seemed to have it all. Growing up with no money in an affluent neighborhood made me gifted at smelling a child of privilege a mile away.

I wish I could be the petite cheerleader who caught Ryan's eye and heart.

Addiction doesn't discriminate. Every addict was the same. Poor, rich, fat, thin, gay, straight, old, or young. We were here because we needed help. Gold Rolex watches and striking features warranted no extra attention at Serenity Hills.

"One more thing," Ryan said. "After Serenity Hills, I'm going to have a little wine with dinner. Be normal."

Everyone in the room squirmed and shifted, taking long, loud breaths.

"Want to find out if you're an alcoholic?" Rhoda said. "Walk into a bar, have two drinks, and see if you can walk away." Her sharp Texas twang added impact to her delivery. "If you can't, you're an alcoholic."

Perhaps I raised my hand because I wanted to help myself, or maybe because Ryan's story left an ache in my heart. The leader acknowledged me with a nod.

"Thank you, Rhoda." Shivers erupted inside my body. The shaking moved up my spine and down my arms. My intertwined hands heated up my lap.

"Stay strong," Rhoda whispered.

Just the encouragement I needed.

"I'm Prue. I'm married to an alcoholic. I'm also the child of an alcoholic." I clenched my jaw.

"Welcome, Prue," they spoke in clear, concise unison.

The Sahara Desert couldn't be as dry as my mouth.

"I'm grateful to be here. AA meetings help me understand the disease of alcoholism." My gaze moved from the floor to the circle of eyes. "I knew my boyfriend was an alcoholic when he proposed. After a particular incident, he quit and stayed sober for a while. I learned here that sober people who don't attend meetings are dry drunks. Sober Nick had some of drunk Nick's intolerable traits. Once he started drinking again, it escalated and adversely affected my son and me."

The words tumbled to the floor and flowed under the chairs.

"I tried giving him rules. Like no shots. No hard liquor. For a short time, I had a handle on his drinking." It sounded dumb when I said it out loud. "Nick's not a mean drunk, but more a sloppy, lovey-dovey kind of drunk. The polar opposite of his normal personality."

The well-built dam strengthened. I was not ready for it to break.

"I guess his addiction isn't my problem, but it's frustrating to know I can't help him." I balanced a pencil between my fingers. Anything to distract the anger from surfacing. "Thanks for letting me share."

153

After prayer, Mitch and Rhoda cruised over.

"That was a touching share," Mitch said. He held out his hand and lifted me from the chair. "We all know how much you love your hubby and wish you could help him."

"It's such a shame he isn't willing to get help." Rhoda shook her head. "No point in taking that on. You're fighting a battle you can't win." Under the fluorescent lighting, her skin resembled powdered crepe paper.

"True," I said. The carpet pattern played tricks on my eyes. "I still love him, though."

"Well, we can't solve our problems all in one night." Rhoda's purse rested on the crook of her elbow. It was emblazoned with a crystal-encrusted cowboy boot.

"Let's head over to snack." Mitch rubbed his belly. "I'm in anguish over the shit I put John through. A thimble of food might calm my nerves." His eating disorder had begun when his father called gay men "homos, queers, and faggots." The seething hatred his father carried for gays confirmed his truth could not be told. Acceptance was not an option.

"My load lightened a little after sharing. Baby steps," I said, walking my fingers through the air. "I'm skipping snack to score an appointment with Mike. I'll catch up with you guys later."

"Meet us in the smoking area after your meeting." Rhoda blew me a kiss on her way down the path.

After flicking off the meeting room lights, I made my way to Mike's office. The whole place reminded me of the Island of Misfit Toys.

We're all misfits. Every single one of us.

After landing the first spot on the list, I wondered what to talk about in my meeting. An aching homesickness weighed me down. Homesick for Goose Neck Harbor and the soft, dewy air. I strolled to the nurses' station.

"Only an hour late," Nurse Ratched said, glaring at the clock. I scribbled my initials on the chart and stepped onto the platform.

"Guilt, shame, fear and . . ." I paused. "Love, since I'm about to call Christian."

CHAPTER SIXTEEN

y the fall of my freshman year, I decided to suck it up and attend Trinity with a positive attitude. There were, after all, two silver linings: Lily and I were going to be roommates, and Henry would also be attending. He got in with a half-tuition scholarship. Mom told him she'd handle the rest with some cockamamie "elastic walls" kind of plan, like the time Mom tried to cram Richard's kids into the corncrib. Sometimes, it seemed as though her view on life was a little too rosy and erred on the side of unrealistic. All Henry wanted was to graduate and land a high-paying job on Wall Street.

Lily left a few weeks early to train with the sailing team. When the time came, Henry and I loaded the car and headed to Connecticut. After a long wait, we stood at the front of the class registration line. "Last name?" the clerk barked.

"Aldrich, Prudence." I handed her my class selection.

The clerk dragged her finger down my course selections and scratched a black line through my name. "You're set. Next!"

"Aldrich, Henry." He held a course selection sheet in his hand.

The clerk moved her finger down the list. "Your tuition isn't paid. Next!"

"Excuse me, it should have been paid," I argued.

"Not paid. Students can't register until tuition is paid in full."

Henry snapped his papers back up. "Mom isn't going to have the money. She always pays my tuition late. Dammit."

"I'll call her," I said. I ignored the student center chaos and hunted for a phone.

Even now, Mom's still running our lives. We can't catch a fucking break.

Mom picked up on the first ring. "Get Henry back in line," she ordered. "The bill will be paid by the time you hit the registration desk. Got to run. Love you." She hung up before I could ask any questions. Henry wondered where Mom was coming up with that kind of money, but I had an idea.

It makes me sick to think of Mom and Mr. Sutton in bed together.

By the time we got back to the registration table, the money had dropped. We unloaded my stuff from the car first. With boxes and suitcases balanced in our arms, I hunted for my room. Lily must have been watching from the window because she leaped out into the hallway and shouted, "You're here!" Her skinny legs danced. She curtsied as we walked inside.

"Oh, wow! Lap of luxury." The decor was more than perfect. A high ponytail showed off Lily's flawless, golden skin. Our dorm room seemed lifted from a page in *House Beautiful*. "You went all out." The bed linens must have been a thousand-count cotton; I swept my hand across the sheet.

"Do you guys want a gin and tonic?" Lily asked, gesturing to the makeshift bar set up on a mini-fridge with lemons and limes decoratively arranged in a bowl. We even had a blender. A gray shag carpet covered the floor. Sheer, pale-gray curtains hung from rods with nickel-plated rings. Both bedside tables had glass lamps topped with steel-gray shades. One bed sat under the window, and the other along the wall. Both beds had matching comforters and fluffy down pillows topped in gray-toned decorative floral cases.

"Beyond ready for a drink," I said, and dropped into a pile of plush pillows.

Lily mixed the cocktails. "Want one, Henry?"

"No, thanks, I'm taking off. Come down to Phi Delt sometime. Epic parties."

Once Henry was gone, Lily closed our door and leaned her back against it. "A gorgeous guy walked down the hall before sailing practice this morning." She melted to the floor. "Let's go see if we can find him."

We cruised up the stairwell and peered around the corner. He stood in his doorway talking to another guy. A random girl down the hallway spotted us lurking.

"Lance," she said, unprompted. "He's a sophomore."

I grabbed Lily's arm. "I have an idea." After digging through my suitcase, I found a few Woodson hand-me-downs and threw them into an empty box. I tore a sheet of paper from my notebook and wrote:

Dear Lance,
I would take my clothes off for you.
Love,
A Secret Admirer

"Brilliant." Lily clapped as I stuck the note into the box and closed the lid.

I ran the box up the stairwell and slid it across the hallway. It hit Lance's door with a thud. We hauled ass back to our room, both of us giddy with laughter. A few moments later, Lance stood in my doorway. He was as tall as a tree; a lean, built body; dark, gorgeous eyes; chiseled jaw; thick, dark hair. He looked like a movie star.

"I'm Lance." He held the box in his arms.

"Hi, Lance. I'm Prue."

"Someone tossed a box of clothes against my door and left this note. You wouldn't happen to know anything about it, would you?"

"Nope." Unable to contain myself, I started laughing.

"Well," he said, "I'm going to let you in on a little secret. I pulled the pants out of the box and saw the tiny waist and legs to forever, and I said to myself, 'I want to meet this girl.' Plus, I think the whole secret admirer note is clever." He lifted my jeans out of the box and pointed to a tag sewn inside with my name on it.

"No way!" I gasped. My hand flew over my mouth.

Lance handed me the box of clothes. "Welcome to Trinity. I like your style."

Lily swooped in with the ice bucket. "I'm Lily. Can I tempt you with a cocktail?"

Lance and I became a couple. It was that easy. Nothing had ever been so easy, but getting Lance must have been some kind of fate. A group of us started hanging out together. Life with Lance was, for a while, enchanting. But sometimes, drunk Lance would lock me out of my room and speak to me only in Spanish.

"Lance, let me in! The door is locked."

"*Mañana.*"

∽

Lily and I rushed for membership in a sorority. Confident in our acceptance into Tri Delt, I was shocked when the list was posted without my name. Back in my room, I cried. After my solo pity party, I called Mom.

"Tri Delt nixed me. I'm a loser. For some stupid reason, I thought they liked me."

"Pull it together," she said. "We're talking about a sorority. In a few years, this will be meaningless to you. Focus on school. Don't you need to maintain a B average to keep your scholarship? This might be a positive thing." I wondered why I never felt better after talking to Mom.

Just then, Lily grabbed me coming out of the phone booth. "Everyone has been looking for you!" she exclaimed. "There was a mistake. They misspelled your name. We're sisters!"

"Wait. I'm in?"

"You're in!"

The hours I'd spent thinking I was rejected made me empathize with all the girls who hadn't. At that moment, I vowed not to let sorority activities rule my life, and to continue hanging out with my new friends who had not chosen the Greek life (or the Greek life hadn't chosen them). All the while, I tried to convince myself I was worthy of belonging to a sorority.

∞

"Phone message for you," the student at the front desk said, never taking her eyes off her book. "Aren't you supposed to work a shift tonight?" Gum snapped as she spoke.

"Thanks, and yeah, I work the phones in an hour." The message said Alie had called. Dinner could wait. I stepped around the corner to the phone booths. The minute Alie answered, I jumped into my questions: "How's Columbia? Do you like your roommate? I miss you!"

"Thanks for calling me back so fast," she said. "I'm dying to hear if you and Lily got into a sorority! My roommate is from Wisconsin, so we don't have much in common, but she's neat, and you know how much I love that."

"Wisconsin. Did she bring lots of cheese?" I asked, and Alie laughed. I told her Lily and I had been accepted by Tri Delt and recounted the torturous hours I'd spent believing I'd been rejected.

"I'm still unsure about joining," Alie said, and I knew her well enough to know she was weighing the time commitment against her academic workload. "How's the guy you met the first day? Lance, right?"

"Not too serious," I lied. We bantered for a few minutes about a hot guy in one of her classes, and how she was still working up the guts to say hello to him. I sensed a sad tone in her voice and asked about any promising new friendships.

"I'm a little lonely," she said. "The girls here aren't super friendly."

When we said our goodbyes, her voice cracked, and I realized she missed me more than I had thought. I wished I could beam us back to boarding school so we could take a shot on our balcony.

Lance and I slept together, ate every meal together, even did most of our homework together. But something was missing. Malcolm, a nerdy guy in my geology class, caught my attention, so I jockeyed to be his lab partner. He had unruly, dirty-blond hair, a lean frame, and was hilariously funny.

"Put your lab glasses on," Malcolm said one day in class, chipping away at a geode. "We wouldn't want anything to happen to those bedroom eyes." White tape was wrapped on the bridge of his protective glasses, and he wore a tie-dyed lab coat.

"Your coat turned out fantastic," I said, admiring his artistic creation. "Who knew you had so much talent?"

"I'll tie-dye yours so we can be twinsies." He sorted rocks and crystals to make it appear as though we were doing lab work when what we were really doing was spending time together.

"Will you tie-dye mine and help me study for the midterm?" I asked. A hair wandered into my face, and I brushed it away.

"Am I dreaming?" he asked, exaggeratedly bracing himself on the lab table.

"Very funny." The plastic lab glasses added a comedic element to our conversation.

"Well, girls like you don't talk to guys like me. But yes, it's a deal."

We left the science building and walked across the quad together. Cold air gusts swirled the leaves across the brick path like mini tornadoes. With my lab coat wedged under my armpit, I zipped up my parka. "The tie-dying stuff is in my room," he said, his pale cheeks mottled red from the brisk air.

Leaves tumbled as he scuffled his worn boots through the leaf piles. I heaved up my backpack and shoved my popsicle hands into my pockets.

"Once we do this," he said, "you're officially a hippie." He propped open the main door to Crawford Hall with his foot and fumbled with a lanyard full of keys.

"I'm ready to be converted to hippie-dom," I said and followed him to his dorm room.

"My humble abode," he said.

I dropped my backpack to the floor and shimmied out of my coat. "Let's study first, since I need an A in this class. At the moment, I'm scraping a low B."

Malcolm plopped his backpack on his desk. A few pencils tumbled to the floor. After analyzing every detail of his room, I maneuvered to his bed, the only available seat. A Bob Marley mosaic poster was taped above his headboard; van Gogh's "Starry Night" hung over his desk. Behind the door, John Belushi wore a sweatshirt with the word "College" emblazoned across the front. Body odor, dirty clothes, and Right Guard summed up the room scent.

"After you admire my posters, we should start studying." He pulled a massive geology textbook from his backpack and tenuously sat down next to me. "Better grab your book."

"Yes, sir!" I dragged my bag along the floor and unzipped it as Malcolm's eyes burned through my back. I sat beside him. The text book teetered on my lap. "Where should we start?"

Silence hung between us. We gazed into each other's eyes; marbles, blue with gray and gold specs. He leaned in with inviting lips, puffy and soft. I closed my eyes as the hair-tie slipped from my hair.

Malcolm knew things. I was the student. The book dropped to the floor. He touched and kissed me in new places: my belly, the small of my back, behind each knee. He undressed me, my body his, responding in new, unfamiliar ways. He pulled my wet panties to the side. His tongue moved in unison with his fingers. My hips lifted closer. I moaned and let go of control.

"Good girl," he whispered. "It turns me on to please you."

The new, uninhibited me rolled on the condom. I straddled him, exposed, vulnerable. My head lay on his hairless chest, and I sucked on his pale nipples. He moved and shifted, lifting me; his thumb reached around. I was putty, ready to be molded into whatever he desired.

No guy had desired me and told me I was beautiful more than Malcolm. He was nothing like Lance.

"Let's not to tell anyone about this," I said when it was over. A pang of guilt hit me, but I brushed it off as I slipped into my shirt.

He lay his chin in his hands. "I wish things could be different, but I get it."

"That was a lot of fun."

No amount of digging guilt kept me from going back.

∞

Lance had nowhere to go for spring break, so I invited him to Goose Neck Harbor. "My mom is living with her boyfriend in his condo," I warned him. "I have no idea what to expect."

We pulled into the shabby condo parking lot. I took a long, deep breath. Nervous, uneasy feelings scrimmaged in my stomach. There was no place to call home anymore.

"Hi, kids." Mom waved from the condo's second-floor balcony.

"Hey, Mom." The unfamiliar place she called home even had a weird odor. "This is Lance."

Henry squeezed by us, planting a breezy kiss on Mom's cheek.

"Thank you for having me . . . um . . . Mrs. . . . um . . . Aldrich," Lance said.

"Please, call me Anna. I'm going to put Lance and Henry in the guestroom. Prudence, you'll sleep on the sofa in Rob's office." She wedged her fists into her hips.

"Awesome." After a massive sigh, I dropped my bag on the hideous maroon couch.

"Henry, take the car to the store and pick up a few things." A list and the keys were shoved into his hands. You don't say no to Mom.

"I'll go with you," Lance said, gunning for the door. I caught his eye and mouthed the word "sorry."

Mom shuffled around the kitchen as I sat at the tiny table and took in the scenery. "What do you think of Lance?" I asked, wondering if I really cared what she thought.

"He's too good-looking." She poured us each a glass of chardonnay. "I don't trust him. He reminds me of an empty suit."

"Give him a chance. Aren't you being a little judgmental?"

"I didn't say I didn't like him. I said I didn't trust him. The guy is too good-looking for his own good." She draped a dishtowel over her shoulder. "You're too focused on outer appearances."

"Lance has a kind soul," I said, but there was one thing bothering me. Before I could stop myself, I blurted the words out: "I'm not that into sex." A spoon spun between my fingers.

"You're with the wrong man." She slammed her hand against the table, and the spoon sailed to the floor.

She was right. My sex life with Lance was bland at best, but he had the body and style I was drawn to. After I cheated on him with Malcolm, I was invigorated and guilty as hell. I *did* like sex. Just not with Lance. He only satisfied a small part of my soul. But still, I couldn't break it off with him.

After graduation, I rented an apartment in an Upper East Side brownstone. Lance moved in with me after I landed a job working for an interior design firm, Patrick Dunn Interiors, who also happened to be a friend of Mom's. Lance floundered at his job search, never quite finding his niche. Resentment crept in, along with the gargantuan boulder on my shoulders. Stuck.

My office was in a beautiful SoHo loft where clients reviewed design boards and fabric swatches. New Yorkers rode the subway. It was the smallest city in the world, and I was always running into people I knew. On my way home from work one evening, I spotted my sorority sister, Cami, and shoved my way through the subway to stand next to her.

"Hey, Prue." She took me in from top to bottom.

"Are you working downtown, too?" I asked, grabbing a handle as the subway lurched forward.

"In the investment banking training program at Morgan Stanley." She swooped her arm up and down. "Thus, the bland suit. Are you still dating Lance?"

"Yeah." I wished I felt happier about my answer. "We live together." It seemed obvious she wanted to tell me something. "Why do you ask?"

"Well, Garrison's sister was visiting for a few weeks." Her feet spread as the subway turned a sharp corner. "You might have known her. Ansley, a few grades below us."

"How could you *not* remember her?" I had admired Ansley through my classroom window. She was the kind of girl who rocked a mini-kilt, tights, and L.L. Bean boots like there was no tomorrow, skirt pleats flipping and swinging with every step. Whatever she had, I wanted it too. "Only the prettiest girl at Trinity."

"Hate to be the bearer of bad news," Cami said, "but Lance was over every day when she was in town. I saw him come out of her bedroom. Ansley was wrapped in a sheet and, as far as I could tell, nothing else. Garrison told me she and Lance have a real thing going on." It was possible she enjoyed delivering this news to me. "Sorry, but I thought you'd want to know. I would, if it were me."

"Thanks for telling me." Even though I had no right to be angry, I seethed inside. I deserved every bad thing that happened to me.

"Well, this is my stop," Cami said as the subway halted and the doors clicked open. "Let's have lunch sometime." She waved as my train pulled away.

I tossed Lance out of my apartment that night. Within a year, he married Ansley.

To preoccupy my mind, I took a design class at NYU while I worked for Patrick Dunn. A nine-to-five desk job felt confining and not creative. Mom slapped me with the label "not driven by money." I wasn't sure what she meant. I also wasn't sure what drove me.

My class consisted of all women, so when I walked into class and discovered a gorgeous guy had come to present his innovative ideas on marketing for designers, I cursed myself for not sitting in the front row.

Thatcher Miller, III, wheeled in the television platform and popped in a cassette. Worn-in khakis accented his round, firm ass. The pants clung enough to see perfection and were baggy enough to tell he didn't care. A single bead hung around his neck from a piece of rawhide, and a Tibetan prayer bracelet encircled his wrist. Beat-up Timberland boots gave him a dose of toughness to contrast his soulful energy.

A fast-paced commercial unfolded on the screen depicting a young, hip decorator who had contributed to the Kips Bay Decorator Show House. Thatcher talked about being a contributing designer for the Show House, and the invaluable exposure for the price.

"This program gets your name out there as a legitimate designer to a plethora of influential people," he said, then tied it all up with a charitable bow: "The proceeds support the YMCA."

When class was over, I loaded my notebooks and pens into my bag, pulled them out, rearranged the contents of my satchel, and then replaced everything. After the auditorium emptied out, I swished on lip gloss and strolled over to him. Thatcher was still gathering his materials.

"Can I help you put anything away?" I asked, tilting my head to loosen a few curls. "Your presentation was interesting. I'm considering submitting a design to the Show House. I'm Prue, by the way."

He gave me a firm handshake. A complicated mix of professionalism and sensuality coursed through him. "Thatcher," he said. "Fantastic. Would you mind holding my bag while I put the TV back in the supply closet?"

With his bag on one shoulder and mine on the other, I followed.

"Thanks," he said, taking the bag from my arm. "I'm famished. Want to grab some sushi? I know a place a few blocks away. It's a real hole-in-the-wall, but the sushi is amazing."

"Sounds great." I turned away so he wouldn't see me blush. He put on a leather motorcycle jacket and helped me with my coat. His musky scent pulled me in.

"You weren't kidding when you said it was a hole-in-the-wall," I said when we arrived. The narrow restaurant had us maneuvering around small tables. We grabbed two seats at the end of the sushi bar.

"This place is small, but I dig the ambiance." He had deep-blue eyes lined with thick, cow-like lashes that grew straight down. "They don't have a menu. Just the chalkboard with specials. The chef makes me whatever he wants. My apartment's a block away, so I eat here a lot."

He spoke as if he were detailing tax return minutia. I was enthralled. He rolled his hand through his coarse, blond hair and ordered a bottle of sake and rolls.

"Where'd you go to school?" I asked.

"Brown," he said. "Majored in philosophy."

I was desperate to tell him about Yale, but there was no point in telling him I'd been accepted only to have to back out due to lack of money. It would sound dumb.

"Cheers." We clinked glasses. The sake burned going down and heated my face. I emptied the tiny cup in one sip, which Thatcher promptly refilled. Rugged, artsy, and aristocratic, he fit into all my favorite categories like a dream.

"Other than volunteering for the Show House, what do you do for a real job?" I asked. The sushi arrived, and I poured soy sauce into my dish and dropped in a lump of wasabi.

"I'm a copywriter at Ogilvy and Mather. On small accounts, but I love it."

Time stood still as we talked, drank, and ate. By the time we got up to leave, I noticed most of the patrons had already left. After paying the tab, Thatcher picked up my bag and crossed it over his body. "Let's go," he said and led me out into the snowy night. Flakes dropped on our faces and clothes, melting on impact. He ran ahead, gaining enough speed to skitch down the slippery sidewalk.

"Sidewalk surfing would land me right on my ass," I laughed. The wind whipped around, and I wrapped my head in a scarf, fearful my hair would frizz to oblivion. Icy vapor clouds billowed around us with each exhale, but I felt nothing but warmth. Thatcher pulled me toward him and gave me a soft kiss.

"Want to see my place?" he said with perfect puppy dog eyes.

I shivered in a nervous, happy, what-the-fuck-am-I-doing kind of way. He hooked his arm in mine and led me down two stairs to a ground-floor apartment in a funky pre-war building. After unlocking two deadbolts, Thatcher opened his apartment.

"Make yourself comfortable," he said. I dropped into a worn leather club chair. He threw his jacket to the floor and fiddled with a stereo system stacked against a decaying brick wall. A moment later, it kicked to life playing the Stones' "Let's Spend the Night Together." He winked.

I scanned framed photos while Thatcher poured cocktails. "Who's that?" I asked, homing in on the one of a striking girl with long, brown hair in a grassy field making a peace sign.

"Oh, that's my girlfriend, Liz." Deadpan. No hint as to why another woman could be allowed in his sanctuary. "She's studying in Florence." My stomach flipped. "Why don't you take your coat off and stay a while?"

Halfway to my earlobe, I stopped myself. "I should be going." I feigned a half-assed glance at my watch. My gut told me to get the hell out of there.

Strong and sturdy, Thatcher came up behind and enveloped me, rocking my body with his to the music. My coat slipped down my shoulders as his hands glided back up my arms, moving as smoothly as a painter's brush. He pressed his face into my hair, breathing hot, seething passion. He folded his body around mine and unbuttoned my blouse. "Stay," he pleaded.

Drugged, swimming in his sensuality and his desire for me, he guided me into his bedroom. That night, even though my head shouted for me to run, I gave Thatcher my heart. In the morning, he hailed me a cab and handed the driver a twenty. "Get her home safely," he said.

"Thank you," I said, twisting my head out the window. "That's not necessary."

He leaned into the back of the cab. "See me tonight. A few of my friends and I are going to listen to jazz downtown. Come with me." Thatcher knocked on the door, signaling for the driver to proceed. My head dropped into my hands. I was elated, frightened, and ready to walk off a cliff.

We spent most every night together. I even ditched Mom to sleep with Thatcher when she came to the city to see me. Of course, Mom said he was trouble—a heartbreak waiting to happen. When Thatcher prepped me for a week-long visit with Liz, I got the feeling she was right.

"You'd like Liz," he said. "You two are very similar."

Fantasies about Liz riddled my mind. How does she dress, talk, make love? When the other woman arrived, Thatcher went on radio silence. The moment she boarded the plane back to Italy, he phoned me. "Let's have sushi tonight."

He introduced me to his mother. I wondered whether she thought I was a cheating tramp or if she felt sorry for me. Thatcher grew up in an Upper East Side brownstone with normal parents who had friends with summer homes.

We went on a weekend getaway and drove out to Goose Neck. Thatcher led the way on his motorcycle. He would continue on to his parent's country home in Millbrook the following day. Rather than camp out on Rob's living room floor, I arranged for us to stay at Lily's house. With the car windows rolled down, the wind whipped through my hair and sunshine warmed my arm. On a straightaway, he hit seventy while I followed behind, clutching the steering wheel in disbelief. He stood on the seat, turned, and blew me a kiss.

That evening, we made love on the kitchen island and under the dining room table. We raided the wine cellar and cracked open a bottle of merlot, enjoying it in the bathtub. After our activities, Thatcher fell fast asleep. I stared at his beautiful face. It took me a while to relax; he had a grip on me. Fear wound me up and pounded my brain. In the morning, I reached over for him and touched a smooth, cold sheet.

I pulled open the curtain and looked out the window. Thatcher stood naked at the edge of the swimming pool. Strong legs led to an ass one would find in a fireman fundraiser calendar—round, smooth, toned. He jumped into the pool and cranked out a few laps. Then he pulled his glistening body out of the water. After shaking off the excess water, he slid into his khakis and sat on a rock to lace up his boots. Never in my life had I wanted anyone as much as I wanted Thatcher. But when Liz came home for good, I never heard from him again.

A discussion with Mom was not an option. I heard her I-told-you-so across the miles.

The answering machine in my apartment blinked on and off: seventeen messages. Exhaustion plagued my body from head to toe after doing a huge installation at an apartment on Park Avenue. The client would be coming back from vacation today, and I wanted everything perfect. I dropped the fabric sample books, my tote bag, and groceries, then pressed play.

"It's Henry. Call me."

"Where are you? Please call me the second you get this."

"Dammit, why aren't you home on a Sunday? Call me."

No point in hearing the rest, I dialed Henry. It was hard to decipher his words through the tears. Then I heard, "Mom was in an accident. Oh God, Prue. M-M-Mom's dead."

I sank to the floor.

Mr. Condo had wrapped his cherry-red Porsche around a tree, and Mom had sailed through the windshield. Draped over the hood, she took her final breath.

Gram drove into the city since I was too distraught to take the train. The elevator doors opened, and I walked into the lobby. There she was, waiting for me.

"Oh, Prue."

We embraced for a long time. Then Gram pulled away and wiped my cheeks with her soft, wrinkled fingers. Even with her freshened lipstick, I couldn't be fooled. Her eyes were as puffy as mine.

Our hands intertwined during the drive to Goose Neck. "Your mother had a will." The silence was broken. "She left you and your brother quite a nest egg."

Thoughts of Mr. Sutton crept into my brain, but I flushed them away. No point in worrying about where Mom got the money. There were other things to think about.

Lily was sitting on the front porch when we pulled up the driveway. Gram lifted the emergency brake, and the car lurched. Even with a red nose, Lily was beautiful. "Oh, Prue. I'm so sorry." Lily broke the wall around my heart. With my face buried in my hands, I allowed myself to wallow in sadness for a brief moment.

Lily organized a reception at her parents' home. A small, beautiful service was held at the church in Goose Neck Harbor while the Canada geese squawked overhead. Henry and I tossed rose petals on the box carrying our mother's ashes. Then we turned and walked away from the life we had known.

CHAPTER SEVENTEEN

Nightmares of men screwing me while I laid there detached from my body plagued my sleep. I reached between my legs to relax.

No one will find out.

I yearned for the relief, then decided to behave. The bathroom light buzzed as I stared into the mirror.

Who is this woman?

The eye bags added five years. I ran the water, but it was never cold enough to reduce the swelling. I pumped the last of the dried-out mascara sample from the bag I carried in my purse—the same mascara I used after my trysts. The camouflage was gone. My behavior was as worn out as my heart. After brushing my teeth, I ran my hands through my hair and pulled it into a messy ponytail. I applied lip gloss, blush, and a touch of mascara.

Don't want to be sent to back to my room to wash my face.

"We have a lot to do today," Mike said, perusing a document. His dark jeans and fresh sneakers presented a more casual image. He wore it well, but I didn't say anything. "Bo left off yesterday. He needs to complete his timeline. After Bo, you're up, Owen." Mike rolled his chair in line with the rest of ours.

Bo's Wranglers were worn and faded from working on the ranch. In my mind, he seemed taller than when I'd first met him; his confidence made him grow. He leaned in, and his t-shirt inched up, exposing a farmer's tan. He was just the kind of guy I had always wanted to be with but never was.

"I've done a lot of thinking since I spoke yesterday," Bo said. "There are a few things I'm holding inside and having a hard time getting out." I wanted to suck his voice into a can and listen to it day and night. It was thick, Southern, and soulful, mingled with dark demons. He gazed at his feet, pressing his fingertips together. The room fell silent like snow falling on a winter night. "This shit poisons my inside and gives it power over me. Just like holding in the abuse from my brother."

The silence left a thickness in the room. We all had been drinking poison and expecting someone else to die.

"I'm proud of you for taking this step," Mike said, breaking the beautiful silence.

"I visited the same strip club three nights a week for about a year after my wife left me," Bo said. "I spent a lot of money. Trust me." He stretched out and crossed his cowboy boot-covered ankles. "You know, drink a few beers, snort a few lines, but I was there for Violet."

Bo had darkness inside of him. Dirty, filthy darkness. I knew I had it, too.

"She worked there as a dancer."

In case we couldn't figure that out.

"I figured getting lap dances helped her out financially. The girl had me mesmerized. Still does. Violet has a little problem with meth. At first, I lingered around the club for a few hours but always went home alone. All the while, I couldn't wipe Violet from my mind. She started texting me, asking if she could come over and bring a few of her friends."

The room grew fidgety, shifting seats and clearing throats. We all saw this hell coming.

"So, these tweakers are at my house wigging out. Violet stayed calm. She'd say, 'Chill, Bo. We're just partying,' trying to appease me. She did a little meth but seemed to be functioning. She said it helped her stay thin. After everyone cleared out, Violet and I slept all day. The start of the work week, I was useless. A wreck. It cycled like this for a while.

Then I said 'enough.'" Bo shook his head. "I couldn't stop thinking about Violet."

"What happened next?" Mike asked. He expected us all to dig deep, to find our own answers.

"She robbed me. She flat-out robbed me."

"And . . .?" Mike encouraged.

"She showed up at my house tweaked out of her mind, banging on my door and screaming, 'Bo, let me in, you son of a bitch!' I let her inside to quiet her down, and she went nuts, slapping and punching me. The neighbor called the police. Things took such a turn."

The wheels on Mike's chair squeaked as he leaned in closer to us. "Let's discuss. Deirdre, you start."

"Thank you for sharing, Bo," Deirdre said. "Sorry for all your suffering, from your brutal childhood to your divorce and now this. I'm sure Violet has a lot of redeeming qualities that draw you in. I can relate." She turned to me. My turn.

"Thanks for the share, Bo," I said. My sick mind wished I could be his Violet. "It's easy to be sucked into the storm of someone else's life. In some weird way, it numbs our own pain, and we believe we can save them."

"Excellent insight," Mike said, and his praise made my inner student happy. "What would we say Bo's addictions are? Anyone?"

Gloria raised her hand. "Love addiction?"

Poor thing knows all about that.

"Good. Anything else?"

"Codependent," Owen added.

"Yes. We're still missing one," Mike said.

I raised my hand. "Addicted to strip clubs?"

"Bingo!" He flashed me a smile.

After circling for the Serenity Prayer, we moved like a herd to our first music therapy session in the same building. The music therapist had textbook-perfect long, gray hair and a goatee; a lingering relic from the sixties. The room had colorful pillows on the floor with a variety of drums in front of each pillow. The hippie was sitting in a chair strumming his guitar as we walked in.

"Welcome, welcome." He spoke with a far-too-groovy smile on his face. A purple satin pillow on the far side of the circle was both welcoming and had no guys sitting nearby. I squished into it and crossed my legs like a good kindergartner. Gloria sat on my right and Deirdre to my left. I ended up across from Alistair. He made funny expressions at me.

"Stop!" I scolded playfully.

"Well, hello everyone!" Mr. Groovy said. "What a lovely group of friends we have gathered in this room." He propped his guitar on its stand, kicked off Birkenstocks, and shifted to a pillow, down to our level. "My name is Josiah, and this is music therapy." His head bobbed in sync with his words. It took every bit of strength I had not to burst out laughing.

"Music has magical, mystical healing powers and can affect our mood in a positive or negative way." Swollen lips turned his goatee into a powdered donut. "Let's start by going around the room and introducing ourselves. I am a recovered addict and have been sober for six years."

He settled his hands in his lap palms, facing up, while we introduced ourselves. I performed an internal attitude check since I was getting a little too cynical. No matter how many times I had heard everyone's introductions, they still intrigued me. Finally, it was my turn.

"Prue." Panic, fidget, dry mouth. "I'm a . . . um . . . sex addict."

"Superb," Josiah said. "Thank you all for those warm introductions. Let's play *imagine*. I want each of you to think of music that's made you cry, and music that's elevated your mood."

Joni Mitchell makes me sad. Harold Melvin & the Blue Notes makes me happy because it reminds me of Alie.

"It doesn't matter if you are an experienced musician or have never played an instrument in your life. Talent is not needed here." His head

175

bobbing was beginning to annoy me. Gloria peeled her black nail polish, leaving a peppering of flecks on the floor around her. "Let's all pick up our drums and get mad!"

Josiah pounded a mallet on a standing jembe and encouraged us all to join in with dramatic sweeps of his other arm. The first person to start beating her bongo was Gloria and her now-disastrous manicure. I joined in with my mallet and small jembe. Alistair had an excellent set of maracas he was shaking. Mitch mirrored Gloria's bongo pounding. The room filled with a horrific noise that made me quite mad. The only person in rhythm was Owen.

"Stop!" Josiah shouted. The room fell quiet. "Comments?"

Gloria raised her hand. "I like getting my aggressions out on the bongos."

"Me too," Mitch chimed in. The bongo complemented his khaki-colored shirt and tan skin.

"I felt rather stupid," Alistair intoned, clutching his lavender maracas.

Josiah released the maracas from Alistair's grasp and replaced them with a ukulele. "Perhaps maracas are the wrong instrument for you," he said.

Alistair held the little guitar and strummed. "Much better," he said. Josiah seemed quite pleased. I tried not to obsess over cute Alistair with a ukulele in his arms.

"Now let's get happy!" Josiah rose up and raised his arms. He strapped his guitar around his shoulder and strummed as he marched around the room. The group pied-pipered behind him. Owen dropped his bongos, picked up the lavender maracas, and took up the rear with some exotic dance moves. At that moment, I was happy, and it seemed everyone else was too.

CHAPTER EIGHTEEN

Dad offered to drag me along on his vacation to Belize with Virginia, his new flame. Her physique matched his requirements, but she was disheveled and careless in her attire and hygiene. She schlepped around her degree in clinical psychology like it was enough to keep my drug-addicted dad in check. I had to live with the unanswered questions and unresolved ache buried in my heart and my mother's grave. With Mom gone and Thatcher out of the picture, I needed a getaway.

We spent the first few days at a sprawling resort on Ambergris Caye. I buried myself in a pile of books, poolside. At night, after hitting the lobby bar for a few drinks, I laid in my hotel room bed and cried.

Early one morning, Dad startled me with a frantic pounding on my door. "We're heading out to an outer island in one hour!" he said. "The diving is better and more remote. I can't deal with the riff-raff at this place."

When Dad gave his all-systems-go signal, he meant it. I packed up my suitcase and schlepped it to a vehicle waiting outside the hotel lobby. Once at the airport, a pilot greeted us on the tarmac. I kept my focus on the rickety looking prop plane we were supposed to be boarding. The pilot lifted my suitcase and asked me my approximate weight, which I promptly lied about.

"Take a seat in the rear of the aircraft," he said. We were off and flying in minutes.

On the descent, I peeked out the small window as we inched closer and closer to a grass landing strip. There was no tarmac or terminal in sight, only an old hangar far down the runway.

A stocky girl named Kristin greeted us with a beat-to-hell pickup truck. The happy couple took the front seat, relegating me to the flatbed with our bags. After Mr. Toad's Wild Ride, we pulled into the Marlin resort. Marcus, the manager, greeted us with too much enthusiasm. He gave us the lowdown on diving, fishing, and amenities—or lack thereof. He introduced "Mama," who was in charge of housekeeping, the kitchen, and the bar. Then he introduced us to our fishing guide.

My jaw promptly dropped. Before me stood a tall, muscular man with salty, golden skin and sun-streaked hair. His angular, chiseled jawline gave him a masculine edge that balanced his strong, aquiline nose. I figured underneath his dark wraparound sunglasses were some seriously dreamy blue eyes.

"This is Nick," Marcus said, but I couldn't hear anything else he said. I'd fallen into a Nick coma. Nick dipped his head instead of speaking, then sauntered toward the employee quarters while Mama led us to our cabanas.

"Not too shabby," Dad said, throwing up his arms and turning in a complete circle. Virginia had disappeared somewhere between the pickup truck and the row of cabanas.

"Yup, it's cool. I might want to try out fishing while I'm here. Where's Virginia?"

Unpacking her giant suitcase full of lingerie and vibrators, I bet. Why can't you date someone normal?

"Your cabana is next door, sir," Mama said. Dad patted me on the back a little too hard. "Alright. Well, I'm off. Let's catch up in the dining room in a few so we can map out our dive program for the week."

After Dad left, I unpacked my suitcase and perused my wardrobe. I wanted to make the perfect impression on Nick, who I assumed would show up in the dining room at some point to eat dinner. After changing, I put creamy peach blush on my cheeks and some sparkly gloss on my lips. It was only a few steps from my cabana to the dining room. I opened the door, and the tight spring slapped the screen behind me.

Nick was sitting at the bar in a faded green polo. His hair was combed in a clean side part. I barely recognized him. He glanced over, unshaken by the racket I'd made. His eyes were just as I had imagined: mesmerizing dark-blue pools. He smiled, revealing a gap between his front teeth. The plier incident years before had nearly stolen my dream of having a million-dollar smile, triggering my obsession with perfect teeth. Veneers, purchased on the strength of mommy guilt (and more than likely with someone else's money) brought my smile up to par. I figured the rest of him was so perfect, I could give him a pass on his imperfect smile.

A backgammon game was in play between Nick and Marcus, the only two workers of any interest. What Nick seemed to lack in sophistication he made up with a mysterious air. He peeled the label off a beer and tossed it on the floor while Marcus warmed up the dice.

It was a good hair day for me, which elevated my sense of confidence. My outfit had received many past compliments. Mrs. Sutton's words of wisdom—"Stick with a winner"—sounded in my head. My winning island outfit was cutoffs, with threads hanging haphazardly around my toned thighs. A pink-striped grosgrain belt added a preppy vibe, while the easy peasant top clarified my free spirit and sheer lace bra.

"Hello," Nick said, digging coconut from his back teeth.

"G'day," Marcus said. "We met earlier." Somehow, I had missed his lovely Australian accent and friendly face with long, pointed features. His dark hair, with bleached ends and bloodshot eyes, were the telltale sign of island life.

"Someone needs a cocktail." Nick patted the stool next to him. I couldn't help but wonder what made him think I needed a drink.

Nick flashed a naughty, boyish smile. "Make her a Turtle Island Flow," he said to Mama, who had switched hats and was now playing the role of bartender. Her voluminous rear barely fit behind the counter. Bottles grazed her dark, fleshy body with every move, yet she never knocked a single one over. She prepared the colorful cocktail, filling it to the brim. "This one's on me," Nick said as Mama eased the glass down.

I slurped the first sip. "Yum." I set the glass down, my every motion performed with the audience in mind, then asked, "What brought you to such a remote place?" I directed my question at Nick and Marcus; the backgammon game paused while I commanded their full attention.

"My family invested in the resort," Marcus said. "I'm staying for a few years to keep an eye on things." There was a pack of Marlboros and an orange plastic lighter neatly stacked beside his beer.

"I got a DUI last year," Nick said, "then to top it off I was suspended from college for bad grades. My parents forced me to come here, make some money, pay off my legal fees. I give fishing lessons." His monotonous tone cushioned my shock over his story. Not the catch I'd imagined. "How about you?" He took a swig of his drink; his Adam's apple lifted and lowered.

"My mother recently passed away. I needed to take some time off."
Everything in the city reminds me of Mom. The sounds, the restaurants where we dined, the Wolford stocking store on Madison. Every little thing.

Nick touched my hand. "I'm sorry about your mom." The warmth of the Turtle Flow squelched my sadness.

Dad and Virginia wandered in looking like disheveled lovebirds. Virginia always had a freshly-laid aura.

"You hungry?" Dad asked, massaging my shoulders. Nick and Marcus took the cue and returned to their backgammon game. After dinner, I signed up for a fishing lesson.

At sunrise, I stood by the clubhouse. Nick walked through the palm trees with a pair of dark sunglasses perched on his aquiline nose. Blond wisps of hair peeked out from under his salt-stained cap, and flip-flops snapped sand over his tanned calves. He radiated bad-boy cool.

Without even a good morning, he handed me a bucket and a pole. "I'm going to grab some coffee. You want some?" he asked.

I was thankful for this new distraction from my life.

⚮

"The sport of fishing is about patience and silence," Nick told me. I would otherwise have found a dude wearing his hat backward to be juvenile, but this time I accepted the style choice.

Patience and silence are easy, but catching this cabana boy requires determination.

He gripped the rod between his knees and pierced a snail through the hook while I cringed. The snail swung side to side as he passed me the rod. I held the line holding the dangling snail steady. Nick pointed out to the water.

"See the ripple," he whispered. "The fish are working under the surface. Cast the line right into the middle." I swung the line back and hooked it on a tree.

"Whoops!" I yanked the line, releasing it from the branch, then cast out into the ripples. Nick circled behind, wrapping himself around me. Our warm flesh pressed together, and his hands covered mine as he tugged the rod.

"The fish need to believe the bait is alive," he said. Goosebumps swarmed my arms. "We got a bite!" The fish flopped around as I reeled in the line. Nick gripped the slippery scales and cut the line with his teeth. I inched closer to watch him wiggle out the barb. With the fish in both hands, he dipped it into the water and it darted away.

That evening we sat on the beach, taking in the moonlight. The water ebbed and flowed while crabs scampered across the sand. Nick ran his fingers through my beachy waves. Our lips drew closer, both of us moving in, wanting to take the next step. Warm beer, salt, and cigarettes merged in our mouths, tongues searching for truth and love. I sat lost in time with this passionate mystery man.

The next afternoon, Nick and I met up outside the clubhouse. Marcus showed up with a twelve-pack in hand. Almost casually, Marcus divulged the fact that Nick's girlfriend, Whitney, had left the day I arrived. His words were like a knife in my gut. A sharp shut-the-hell-up look flashed across Nick's face.

"You didn't think to mention a girlfriend," I said.

"He doesn't know shit about me," Nick said. "Whitney and I broke up when she was here. We don't want the same things." My broken puppy dog eyes locked on his. "I didn't ask you if you were dating anyone, and you didn't ask me."

I brushed off the nagging voice in my head that told me I wasn't getting the whole story.

We spent our days fishing, lounging, and being mutually inseparable. An insatiable attraction left us both perpetually hungry for more. Every inch of the property provided sexual opportunity: the phone booth, the shower, the deserted beach, the end of the dock, and both of our rooms during all hours of the day and night. I wrote off the Whitney incident. Nick wasn't Thatcher.

I've got my own secrets, and he'd dump me if he knew half of them.

Dad flew back to California, but I called in sick and stayed an extra week. Nick led me out into the starry night and took me in his arms. "I love you," he whispered. "I'm happy you stayed."

They were the words I needed to hear. My body rose up toward the moon, and when I landed again, I was light as a feather. A giddiness filled my insides, and I tingled all over.

"I love you too," I said.

The words echoed in my head. I worked hard to convince myself what I was feeling had to be love. A dark cloud attempted to creep its way into my head and heart. I pushed it away with all my might.

Promptly upon returning to New York, I quit my job, staying only long enough to pack my things. With the promise of a new life, I moved into a bungalow in Belize.

Mama admired my cabana cleaning techniques. "Girl, you're good. We need to keep you here permanently." I scrubbed, rearranged furniture, added shells to bedside tables, and draped colorful sarongs over chairs. The job brought comfort and kept me exhausted.

Every morning, Nick woke up quiet and sullen. He held himself in the shower, rocking side to side under the warm running water. Late afternoon beers turned into drunken stupors, landing him in jail after a brawl with a local. A second arrest came after he totaled the resort's truck, drunk out of his mind, and being belligerent to the responding police officer. I found myself putting my needs and desires aside to please him.

One afternoon, I came back to our bungalow to find my clothes strewn across the sand and in the bushes. A knot swelled in my gut as I opened the front door, expecting the worst. Ankle-deep water splashed with every step. A hole was punched through the door. Nick, the culprit, lay on the other side. I turned the handle. The door was locked, and the bathroom sink had been ripped from the wall. I stared at the ceiling, waiting to call Lily.

"Nick's an alcoholic," she said. "Just like your dad, just like Richard. Leave, before something bad happens."

Nick emerged from the bedroom, stinking of liquor. "I'm sorry."

"I'll call you back," I said and hung up. I looked at Nick. "It's over."

He fell to his knees and sobbed. "I'll quit drinking," he promised. Even through my anger, I felt sorry for him.

After avoiding Lily's calls, a four-page letter arrived, bashing Nick and urging me to leave him. Lily ended the diatribe with one final piece of advice: *Please don't do this. Come home.*

But I didn't feel as if I had a home to return to anymore.

The next day, I walked into the cottage. Nick was sitting with Lily's letter. It was a solid violation, but he acted as if going through my mail was normal. Something snapped inside of me. I packed my belongings and inscribed each box in black marker with Lily's address. My only option was to stay with her until I could get back on my feet. I berated myself for being such a loser.

Nick walked in, lost and desperate. He knelt and slipped his grandmother's cocktail ring on my finger. He promised sobriety, professional success, and that his wealthy and influential parents would adore me. We packed everything up to move in with his parents in Los Angeles, where Nick would go back to school.

We waited outside LAX with our bags. "We're looking for a black Suburban," Nick said. "There they are." A sleek, plastic-surgery-perfect blonde with Wayfarer Ray Bans perched on her regal nose waved through the tinted window as they pulled to the curb.

"A pleasure to meet you. I'm Mary." The slight woman wore a crisp and fresh ivory linen pantsuit. "This is William, Nick's father." William, a heavyset man with sunburned skin and sweat-stained armpits, prattled away on his cell phone while Nick loaded up our luggage. I worried I had underdressed. I felt like a small child buckled in the back. Nick flashed me a faint smile.

"Nick has told me so much about you," Mary said. I pondered whether to call her Mom, Mary, Mrs. Davenport, or ma'am.

"All set," William said into his phone. "I'll call you tomorrow." He motioned for us to be quiet. "Yep. Sounds good." He tossed the black brick into the console and craned his neck around. "Well, hello, Prudence."

"Please, call me Prue," I said. "Thank you for picking us up, Mr. Davenport."

"Call me William. I hear you're from New York."

"Yes, I am, out on the island."

"Nick!" William exclaimed. "Why didn't tell us what a looker she is?" He winked at Nick.

"Thank you."

"Ignore him." Mary squeezed William's thigh. "He's just a dirty old man. Right, Nick?"

"That he is, Mom." He rolled his eyes.

"Nick tells us you plan on keeping your last name after the wedding. A little independence is a good thing in a woman," William said. At a loss for words, I smiled and stared out the window.

"Whitney is in town and will be at the party tonight," Mary said. "You're both invited."

I wondered if she had purposefully changed the subject to something a bit less controversial, or if she intended to add a note of discomfort to the conversation. With zero festive clothes in my suitcase, I contemplated jumping out of the car.

"Has Nick told you about his ex-girlfriend, Whitney?" Mary turned and smiled at me. The car behind her honked when the light turned green.

"No, not that I recall," I lied.

"Well, Whitney's parents are like family. They dated all through high school. She's quite intelligent. She just graduated from USC."

"An excellent school," I said.

I got into Yale.

"You're going to love her. I'll make a point to introduce you."

Lovely.

We pulled into Bel Air Estates. The houses sported immaculate lawns and entrances, some with long driveways, fences, and gates blocking the front doors.

"Here we are," Mary said. "Home sweet home."

The house had an East Coast vibe: white clapboard, with shiny black shutters flanking the windows. We hauled our suitcases up a brick path to the white front door. Inside, Oriental rugs decorated the floors along with antiques and chintz-covered cushions.

"Your home is beautiful," I said, mirroring Mrs. Sutton's elegance and impeccable manners.

"We love it." Mary opened the French doors to a lush, tropical backyard. She picked up a cushion from a mound of patio pillows and feigned an attempt to sweep the dust. "Be a dear and put these cushions on the chairs for cocktails before the party tonight."

She left before I had a chance to reply. I began arranging the cushions on the patio furniture. Mary reappeared with paper towels, glass cleaner, and a broom. Through the French doors on the far end of the patio, Nick socialized in the library with his father. He glanced out at me, the cleaning lady.

Mary disappeared again and returned dressed in cocktail attire. She exuded energy, like a spinning top. "Got to earn your keep around here." It was hard to tell if she was joking. "Our handyman is on holiday. He does most of the chores." She ran her hand along a glass table, clearing off hibiscus flowers that fell from the canopy of greenery clinging to the house. After examining her fingers, she clapped her hands to together. "Let me show you to your room."

I followed my future mother-in-law up the stairs. Twin beds flanked the room on opposite walls. Nick's trophies, football photos, and awards were proudly displayed. "I'm going to let you stay in the same room because you are engaged," she said and left.

I looked at my hand. The engagement ring sparkled, a reminder of the commitment I had made.

I'm an unhappy bride-to-be.

I sat on the bed and something crinkled under the mattress. I ran my fingers along the edge and pulled out an issue of *Playboy*.

Nick masturbating, stroking, grimacing.

My suitcase and clothes reeked of sex and the ocean, but there was no way in hell I was going to ask Mary if I could use the washing machine. The only appropriate thing I had were slim white pants and a sheer, white blouse. I flicked on the bathroom light and dug around the bottom of my makeup bag for costume diamond-stud earrings. Mom had said every woman should own a pair of faux diamond earrings.

Buy big ones, no one can tell if they're real or fake.

I applied a thick coat of sparkly lip gloss, flicked off the light, and headed downstairs.

"You look nice," Mary said. It was hard to decipher if she meant it or not. "Chardonnay? We're having martinis, but I understand you prefer wine."

The sun fell behind the Los Angeles basin, leaving a burst of color behind.

Dear God, please bless me with strength and grace. Please let Nick's parents like me.

After drinks, the four of us walked to an estate at the end of the street. "There are a lot of people here who I want to introduce you to," Mary said. Nick signaled me to go with her. "Prudence, these are the Ericksons. Their son is one of Nick's best friends."

With a forced smile, I cruised around with Mary for as long as I could take it. She introduced me to everyone, telling them where I was from and how the lovebirds had met.

"I'm going to go use the restroom," I said, relieved to make my getaway. I found Nick sitting by the pool, leaning in and chatting with a stunning redhead. His blazer was draped over her creamy skin. Nausea rose up as I approached. He sensed my presence and reeled around.

"Prue, I was just coming for you."

No, you weren't.

The bombshell clutched Nick's jacket and reached out her hand. "I'm Whitney. I have heard so much about you." She glistened in a gold, strapless jumpsuit with sky-high, strappy sandals. She was gorgeous, and I hated her.

"A pleasure to meet you, too." The fakest I had ever been. The words flew too easily out of my mouth.

"Congratulations. Let me see the ring." She held my hand. I needed a manicure.

My ring would look better on her.

"Nick," I said, "I'm sorry, but I'm exhausted. I'm going back to your parents' house. Lovely to meet you, Whitney." I trembled as I walked back to the house alone.

Dammit, why can't I be the one wearing Nick's jacket?

I climbed the elegant stairs of my new home. A dark pit tugged at my heart.

What have I gotten myself into?

CHAPTER NINETEEN

I longed to hear Lily's voice.

"Hello?"

"Lil, it's Prue."

"Hey, Chickie, how are you? How's the loony bin treating you?"

"Ha," I said. "I'm calling to say hi, and for advice. Some rock solid, honest Lily advice." One flip-flop dropped to the floor, and I propped my food on my knee like a stork.

"You know I love to give advice. I am super proud of you, though."

"After I tell you what happened, you might not be so proud." My body draped over the counter, my foot searching for the lost sandal. "There's something I need to confess."

"Whatever it is, you know I'll never judge you. Hang on, let me close my door." She set the phone down and clicked her door shut. Through the miles, I pictured the bedroom she shared with Binky, her now-husband; piles of down pillows, a puffy duvet in citron, and always fresh flowers and a glass of water on her bedside table. I forced away the pangs of jealousy and felt genuine happiness for her. Lily had found her soulmate and never looked back. They lived a seamless existence in Goose Neck Harbor, a block from where we grew up. Her son, Charlie, was born three months before Christian. After enduring two miscarriages, her daughter, Madi, was born. "Ready," she said.

"I screwed up and kissed a guy. A huge moment of weakness. What if I messed up the guy's rehab, got him kicked out? Dammit, I'm pissed at myself because I was doing so well. What the hell happened." I grunted.

"Hopefully, he's hot." This would be Lily's cue to make a dramatic expression as she said the word *hot*. "You fell. Acknowledge your mistake. Better to be honest than live with a lie."

My hand cupped the receiver, and I lowered my voice to a whisper. "Can you hear me?"

"Yeah, if I plug a finger in my other ear."

"This guy is different. Even after hearing my story, he still cares about me. I'm drawn to him. Not in a lust way . . . well, a little . . . but as a person, too. The messy part is I still love Nick. The kiss complicated everything."

"Remember the time you stuffed the spinnaker wrong, and the DuPont girls won the regatta? We knew there would be another chance; another day where the spinnaker would fly perfectly. There were many of those days." She paused, and I forced myself not to fill the silence with words. "You shouldn't pursue a relationship while you're in rehab. Don't get me wrong, I'm not saying you should stay with the asshole, but this is not the time or place for romance."

"What should I do about my indiscretion? The kiss?" I already knew the answer.

"Confess to your counselor. And you should tell Nick, too. What's the worst thing that could happen? I doubt they'll kick you out. Far more horrific things occur in rehab. You crossed a line. Don't you feel better after telling me?"

"A little." The thought of telling Nick sent panic waves through my body. "I'm scared I'll lose him. He can't take any more of my antics."

"Nick can suck it. What's he going to do—dump you?" She laughed. "That might be a good thing. It's no secret what I think about the asshole. You had a minor slipup. Don't beat yourself up too much, Chickie. I love you no matter what."

The timer on the phone dinged. "I gotta go," I said. "Love you. You're the best friend a girl could have." She might not have heard the last part, because the phone went dead.

"That's all we have time for today," Mike said. "We'll start with Owen tomorrow. Let's gather for the prayer."

Bo's calloused hand reached for mine. I pictured Violet and made up stories about her in my head. I lingered until the room cleared and approached Mike.

"Can I talk to you?"

I could tell he sensed my desperation. "Sure." His navy polo complemented his soft blue eyes. The things I felt for him were hidden deep inside, and I never allowed them to come to the surface.

A hummingbird dipped into a blossom outside the window, its wings seemingly motionless. "I'm struggling with my assignment, my body, my head. I'm drained." I tugged a loose thread from the hem of my shirt and rolled it between my fingers. "Tons of shame and guilt buries me alive. Self-hatred, hopelessness—like I'm not any better, and Nick's never going to forgive me." I rearranged my notes, rekindling my desire to do well and achieve an A.

Mike wheeled his chair out from under his desk and sat down. "I've got an hour free right now." He settled back in an easy, unassuming way. "Begin at the top. Tell me what happened, without being graphic."

The calendar on Mike's desk said it was Friday, but for me, the days ran together like watercolors. His weekend began while I stayed behind in my own living hell. I imagined his life outside of this place, this asylum, where the misfits pretended to evolve: restaurants, friends, a bike ride, no too hot; his Arizona social life. My wonderment took me back to him, having sex in his kitchen with a woman in nothing but his button-down. He pulls it out, rock hard, turns her around . . .

"The memories come to me in the shower, in lectures, and during meetings in bursts." Where to begin? I flipped the pages of my pad. "I'll start with Darren. We met after Nick and I separated. Nick was living in his bachelor pad and seeing Naomi."

More anger crept in every time I said her name.

"Darren claimed he loved me, but he only loved himself. We parked at the mall. I gave him blowjobs in his Mercedes."

The film played in my head. What was I thinking? My armpits started to sweat.

"I jockeyed for an invite to Thanksgiving, but he blew me off. The following week, he came over to hang out."

Could my stories be the worst? The more I revealed, the more I had to believe they were.

"Darren reported his Thanksgiving turned out awesome. A group of friends went to his house. I found out why he didn't invite me. The loser was engaged."

"How did that make you feel?" Mike asked.

I thought about it. "Betrayed? Deceived? The guy was full of shit, but I brushed it off because I had more to worry about. Nick had run our business into the ground. Finances were getting stressful. I stretched to make rent, to put gas in my car and to pay for food. The last time I saw Darren, I asked for twenty bucks to put gas in my car. After I begged, he gave me ten."

"Good. Now you're getting somewhere. It was the money that was significant to you." He eased a Chapstick from his pocket and swiped it over his lips.

"Two things, actually," I said. "I could get money from men and didn't want to date a cheapskate. This sounds bad, but I'm worth more than ten bucks."

"Anything else?"

"I'm not just a whore, like a slut. I'm a prostitute." The words provided mild relief. *Truth time.* "I need to confess something. Rather, I want to." My name tag turned and stuck out like an erect penis. The pink sticker curled on one edge. I resisted a full peel.

"Whatever it is," Mike said, "we'll pull through."

"The other night." My lips warmed and swelled. I reached up and touched them. "There was an incident." No reaction. "Late, after a rough phone call with Nick and an appointment with you. Alistair and I . . . we kissed . . . a romantic moment." A wall of words, my defenses spilled out of my mouth nearly drowning me. "Sorry."

Mike sighed, but the look on his face was far from judgmental. "This is a huge step. You stopped yourself at the kiss. Once you confess, the power is taken away. I'll speak with Alistair. Can you recommit to your abstinence?"

"Yes, I want to and will." Mike had inviting lips. Kissable, rosy, puffed, soft. He patiently waited while I stalled. "One more thing."

The room exuded bland: the boring carpet, the ugly chair fabric, the basic blinds lifted above the window. There was no sign of Mike anywhere. Perhaps he hung boxing gloves on a wall at home underneath a photo of him in the ring, an arm victoriously held up, the winner—shelves filled with books on addiction, jazz music playing from a real album, a dog curled up on a well-worn sofa. There was passion in him; his eyes told the story.

"The connection between us is like a magnet," I said.

I sound so high school. Grow up, Prudence.

"People in treatment form close bonds due to being in a raw, vulnerable state," Mike said. "The program recommends waiting a year before getting involved in a relationship. I suggest you seek closure with your husband before starting something new." He crossed his arms over his strong chest and relaxed in his chair. "You aren't supposed to be talking to men at all. Time to start following the rules. Rules are set for a reason."

"You're right. I try to, but I'm torn between being unfriendly and thinking I'm a freak because no one else has a pink sticker." The glaring neon reminder dangled around my neck. "Alistair is a distraction from my fear of investing in saving my marriage. Nick's not investing in me. Whatever it is between Alistair and me more than likely won't become anything. I'm trying to be honest. Honest with myself and with everyone else." Heat rose through my cheeks and up to my scalp. "I guess I'm embarrassed by the whole thing."

"Rather than use the word 'trying,' tell yourself 'you will.' Your subconscious listens to everything you tell yourself. I'm not saying you can never date Alistair. But you can't get involved with him here. You need closure with Nick, and you should wait a year."

People were gathering in the hallway. Mike closed the door, and I forced myself not to admire his ass—to regress, slide, and slip. My inevitable downward spiral.

"Let's talk about Nick," he said.

My heart pounded as I sucked the last few drops from my water bottle. "Fine."

"You admitted your role in the breakdown of your marriage. Do you think Nick will be prepared to discuss his role when he comes for Family Week?"

"No." I stretched across Mike's desk for a purple stress ball resting next to his phone. My knuckles whitened with every squeeze. "He might feel he's being attacked. The trouble is, Nick doesn't like to admit he's done anything wrong. I just kissed a guy and admitted I like him. I'm the fuckup." The ball dropped to the floor.

"Focus on your progress, on what you can control," Mike said. "Holding Nick accountable for his role in the breakdown of your relationship is in no way attacking him. How can you amend your behavior unless he is willing to do the same?"

He clenched his jaw. The inner boxer strengthened, ready for a fight. Then it hit me.

Mike is my protector.

CHAPTER TWENTY

Nick and I wed at the Sound Club the week after my father overdosed. Dad's heart, weakened from decades of drug abuse, had been a ticking time bomb. Someone found him, a woman he'd dated. When Dad failed to return her messages, she stopped by his place. The phone call from Henry came the night of my bachelorette party. I begged him to spare me the details, and he did. Instead of hopping in the planned limousine for a night on the town, Lily, Alie, and I stayed in and ordered Chinese. Lily pulled out old photos, and we reminisced with childhood stories. She possessed the only pictures documenting my life. In the third photo album, we came across a photo of Dad and me. That's when I broke down.

Gram walked me down the aisle. Lily, Alie, Henry, and the Suttons were all there. After the ceremony, Gram and I stood on the grand porch as the rain danced on the dark, gray bay. The clubhouse door flew open, and Lily and Alie came outside to join us. Music filled the air, then silenced as the doors drifted closed.

"Make new mistakes instead of the mistakes I made," Gram said. "I love you, darling. You are a kind and intelligent woman." She pulled a monogrammed linen handkerchief from her pocketbook to dab the tears welling in her eyes. "Weddings make me think of Emily Dickinson and my days at Amherst. 'I'm nobody! Who are you? Are you nobody too? Then there's a pair of us—don't tell. They'd banish us, you know.' For a spinster, Emily Dickinson sure knew a lot about marriage, didn't she?"

Gram edged closer to me. Her faraway eyes looked out beyond the blue-gray sea. "My words of wisdom," she said. "Keep your identity. Don't merge it with his, because if it all falls apart, you still have your beautiful self." She kissed me on the cheek, snapped open her umbrella, and walked to the parking lot in the teeming rain.

"Rain on your wedding day is supposed to be good luck," Lily said. "You'll need it."

We found a small house to buy. Nick said he'd rather put an ice pick through his forehead than ask his parents to write us a check, so I dipped into my inheritance for the down payment. I'd forgotten Mrs. Sutton's advice to marry a man who loved me enough to care for me.

Our new home was just far enough away from his parents' so they couldn't stop by unannounced. Nick landed a job waiting tables at night while attending school in the day. I insisted he finish college. Patrick Dunn Interiors hired me full time in their new Los Angeles office. I was lucky to be making the amount of money they were willing to pay. I hoped my luck wouldn't run out.

The girl with no luck is counting on it.

The once dowdy area we moved into was being overhauled by double-income families who took pride in the aesthetics of their homes, so I had that going for me.

Every morning, I checked my temperature to track my menstrual cycle. "You're too worried about it, Prue. Let it happen," Nick said. Little did he know, I had stopped birth control when we left Belize.

"Your uterine lining is thickened, making it impossible for an egg to implant," my doctor told me. "The egg fertilizes and has no place to rest. I'm going to schedule a D&C, and we'll take it from there."

A month after the surgery, we started trying again. The package on the ovulation kit said a green line confirmed ovulation. I stepped outside into the bright sunlight to make sure I wasn't seeing things. To seal the deal with Nick, I positioned myself under the Christmas tree, naked, with a bow stuck to my ass.

"I could get used to this," Nick said.

That night, I felt the egg fertilize and implant. After numerous dreams about my baby, I bought a three-pack of early detection pregnancy tests. One day after my period was due, I peed on the stick. Then waited. The bathroom lighting played tricks on my eyes. Disheartened, I tossed it.

I forced myself to let go and stop obsessing, which was exactly when I got the long-awaited plus sign. The pregnancy was uneventful—no morning sickness, just extreme horniness. I masturbated multiple times a day, never feeling relief. After we brought Christian home, I was laid up with a severe headache. After a few days of total agony, I dialed my doctor just before his office closed.

"Sounds like fluid is leaking out of your spine," he said. "This can happen after an epidural. Your symptoms are classic. I'll meet you at the hospital."

Even pressing the speed-dial button to call Nick made my head hurt. "The doctor said I need to have an emergency procedure to get rid of these headaches. Can you take me to the hospital and see if your parents can babysit?"

"I just got to work, and the restaurant is slammed," Nick said. "I can't leave these tips. My parents can take you. They live for this stuff. I'll call them now. Gotta run."

The thought of Nick's parents driving me only worsened the pain. I phoned Frank, our neighbor. No answer.

"Dammit!"

My throbbing skull refused to lift off the sofa, and the baby was screaming. After phoning a babysitting service, a woman arrived and took Christian upstairs. An hour later, William pulled into the driveway and blasted his horn. The moment I rose from the sofa, my head pulsed with pain. William laid on the horn again. My brain exploded with each heartbeat as I twisted the handle and pulled on the front door. He sat in the driveway in his shiny SUV, talking on his cell phone and waving his arms, clearly in the throes of some critical business deal. I crawled across the driveway and pried open the back door.

"Hang on a minute." William put the phone down and wrenched his fat neck around to gawk at me sprawled across his back seat. "Why don't you sit up here with me?" he said, oblivious to my pain.

"Actually, I can't lift my head. I think I'll stay here."

We charged to the emergency room. My father-in-law strutted in behind me. A nurse shuffled me into a stall, pulled the curtain, and told me to put on a gown.

"Do you need help undressing?" William asked, lurking on the other side of the curtain.

"I think I can manage," I said. The physical pain was one thing, but the embarrassment of William seeing me naked took it to a whole new level. He turned away while I stripped. Unable to tie the gown, I wrapped it around my body and lay down on the gurney. A young intern came in, picked up my chart, and walked away. William realized nothing was happening and returned to his phone call.

"Sir, no cell phones allowed," the nurse ordered.

"Oh, sorry."

The nurse prepped my back as I folded myself over, exposing my butt crack to William and anyone else within the line of sight.

"There will be a pinch and some burning," she said. "I'm going to draw blood from your arm, and then the doctor will inject the blood into your spine. You should have immediate relief."

William decided to make himself comfortable for the show. He took a seat, coughed, and fidgeted throughout the entire procedure.

"Rest for a few days," the doctor told me when it was all done. "No heavy lifting, no baths, no exercise." He directed his attention to William, who by now was preoccupying himself with some missed calls. "Why don't you pull up the car? The nurse will wheel Prudence to the door."

We drove back to my house in silence.

"Thank you for taking me on such short notice," I said and slid out of the passenger's seat.

"No problem." He waited in the car as I let myself out.

∞

Two months after Christian's birth, I heard moaning coming from my bedroom. I picked up the baby to go check on Nick, who lay curled in a tight ball on the edge of the bed. I assumed he had a stomachache, so I kept my distance in case it was contagious.

I peered into the bedroom. Nick's head was resting on his knees. His shoulders were pulled up to his ears. Something wasn't right, and it didn't appear to be his stomach. My first thought was he might be having a nervous breakdown.

"What's wrong?" I asked. "Are you okay?"

Nick swayed back and forth, never looking up. "I'm scared I'm going to kill you," he said.

My adrenaline pumped. I wondered if I should go to him or back away. "Nick," I said, "you're scaring me." Christian wiggled in my arms as I stepped backward to ensure the front door was within sight.

"I feel like I'm going to kill the baby, too." Nick's voice sounded unfamiliar; fearful and frail.

I shifted Christian from my hip to my chest and clutched him with both arms. "How are you going to kill us?" I asked. Panic crept in and crawled through my body.

"I'm going to stab you."

Nick was trembling like the San Andreas fault. My instincts kicked in; I had no choice. I headed for the front door. I flipped the deadbolt and hurled it open, only to realize I had no car keys. My heart was pounding. Christian began to cry. Frantic, I ran across the street to the neighbor's house and punched the doorbell.

I asked to use the phone and frantically called Nick's mother. When I told her what was happening, she ordered me to stay where I was and not to discuss it with anyone. After what felt like an eternity, her car careened into my driveway. Minutes later, she came back outside, gently leading Nick to her car. I waited to leave the neighbor's house until they drove away.

Mary lined up a therapist for Nick. He lived with his parents until it all blew over. After a week, Mary called with a request. "Nick would love to come see Christian," she told me. "Can he visit this afternoon?"

My heart wanted to see Nick, but my brain told me to run and hide. "I don't know," I said. "I'm not sure."

In true Mary fashion, she maneuvered around the conversation until I relented and set a time for a visit. Mary dropped Nick off, drove away, and never returned.

The therapist told me Nick wouldn't hurt us because "it was all in his head." I wasn't sure what that meant, but I was fairly certain it was intended to soothe my worries. Our day-to-day life resumed, moving along as if nothing had happened. But every time Nick went anywhere near the knife drawer, a surge of panic would rush through me.

∞

The brunt of the housework fell on my shoulders. Nick stopped alcohol and spent his free time lounging around smoking weed. The faster I worked, the slower he moved. I remained determined to get him interested in life again. One Saturday afternoon, I encouraged him to help me paint the fireplace.

"Couples fun," I said.

Nick lit up a bowl, took a long, deep puff, and held the smoke in until he started hacking. He painted with meticulous detail while Bob Marley encouraged him from the stereo. My paintbrush moved in a quicker, more efficient manner. Not many words passed between us, but when he reached for me in bed in the evening, I couldn't resist.

Sam King took over the design firm when Patrick Dunn went into semi-retirement. My new boss happened to be both attractive and impeccably dressed. Fresh off the divorce train, Sam tended to be flirtatious. The attention thrilled me; the guilt nagged at me. I figured honesty might help bridge a variety of gaps and create solidarity between Nick and I, so I told him.

"I need to tell you something," I said. "My new boss, Sam." Nick nodded, half-watching the television. "Well, he's *hitting* on me. For some reason, I like the attention, and I wish I didn't."

Nick popped up from the couch and stood over me. "What the hell, Prudence? Did you *fuck* him?"

"No! Nothing happened. I was just sharing my feelings, hoping we could talk about it together. It bothers me that I'm sort of tempted."

"Why do you have to act like such a whore?" Nick snapped. Spit droplets hit my face as the words flew from his mouth. "I should've listened to my mother and married Whitney. Jesus Christ, I don't need this shit."

"Forget it," I said.

❧

A thick tension filled the house. I had to make things right. After asking around for recommendations from friends, I set up an appointment with a marriage counselor. Nick grudgingly agreed to go with me, stating, "Shrinks are a waste of time."

The therapist's presence gave me the courage to open up old wounds. "Nick," I said, "why does Stacy Bender keep texting you?" I turned to the therapist. "Nick had a one-night stand with Stacy in high school. We see her at social gatherings. She enjoys bringing up their illustrious night together at parties and carries on about the size of his penis."

Nick exhaled and rolled his eyes. "This whole thing is fucked up."

"Can you please respond to Prudence's question?" the therapist said, folding her hands. She was expressionless, emotionless, and shot-up with Botox.

"She's texting me because we had lunch, as friends, to talk about her marital problems. She showed me her new house. She came onto me, and I told her no, I'm married, and she's married. Not going to happen." Nick turned to me. "I already told you this." He faced the counselor with his patented wounded-animal face. "I'm not sure why she keeps bringing this up."

"Nick, don't you think it would be wise to stop communication with Stacy since she attempted to have an affair with you?" the therapist said.

"Stacy was hurting. It was a moment. She didn't mean it." Nick turned red, aggravated and angry. "Prue, let it go. You're acting like a jealous loser."

Nick could have at least erased his text history.

He's guilty.

CHAPTER TWENTY-ONE

"Let's take a break," Mike said. "I need to make a few phone calls. My afternoon private canceled, so I can give you a little more time." Rumor had it Bridgette checked herself out and vacated a slot. I was sad for her, but I couldn't say I didn't see it coming. "Why don't you go outside, grab something to drink, and I'll meet you back here in thirty."

"Good plan," I said. "Thanks again for your time, it means a lot to me." His buzzing phone relieved me of deliberating whether or not to hug him.

With no place to go, I sauntered out to the smoking area. One lonely figure was slouched on the bench with a cigarette, dressed all in black. It took my eyes a moment to adjust; it was Gloria.

"Hey," I said, giving her plenty of warning before sneaking up on her, but she remained still.

"You're saving me from my thoughts," Gloria said.

"So I see." I slumped down across from her.

"I'm losing my mind." She sucked in a deep drag, hollowing out her cheeks. The cigarette filter was tattooed with dark lipstick.

"Me too," I said.

"Really? You mean it?" She crushed her cigarette into the standing ashtray and lit another.

"I spent the past hour with Mike, rehashing my disgusting behavior," I said.

A wrist full of rubber bracelets slid down Gloria's pale, thin arm. "I'm homesick, but not sure where home is. Homesick for something."

My first instinct was to dole out advice, but who was I to talk? We both sang the same tune.

"We're going to make it and come out on top," Gloria said. She raised her face to the sky. "God has a plan. He knows." I envied her sliver of positivity. "I future-trip and think about setting up a house with Tom, having little dark-haired babies, driving in a carpool, and eating family dinners together. Do you think it's possible?" Her eyes searched mine for answers.

"Anything is possible." I shimmied closer to her. Gloria held her cigarette out like the Statue of Liberty wielding her torch and clutched my knee with her other hand. "I'm heading back into my meeting with Mike," I said. "I'll come visit later if you're up for it."

"Yeah, for sure." She smiled, and her eyes smiled too.

∞

I leaned against the wall outside Mike's office door.
Lord, please give me the strength to get through this.
I sighed and tapped on the door.

"Come on in." He motioned for me to sit back down in the same hot seat. "Where were we?"

"I guess I'll start listing my memories." I pinched my ear.

Mike rolled the stress ball in my direction. "Hold this for strength." His boxer eyes softened.

With the stress ball firmly in hand, I began my confession. "This one came to me while I was walking over here," I said. "I picked up a guy at a hotel bar on a business trip. Even though I had zero attraction to him, I still did it because it made me forget my problems. After sex, I lost interest."

"A Band-Aid on your wounds," Mike said. He could see beauty in the monster sitting across from him. "Then what happened? Remember, no explicit details."

"Sex with this particular guy could have been described as work." My eyes scanned the books on Mike's shelf in a vain search for something to describe what sex with an old guy was like. "He was a lot older than my usual conquest. Gray hair, and all the issues described in Viagra advertisements." A nervous laugh spilled from my mouth. "After we had sex, he took a shower and wore the hotel bathrobe to chat with me for a moment. You know, acting like he cared. After he left, I picked up the robe from the bathroom floor. There, smeared on the inside, was a gnarly poop stain."

Stoic, unfazed Mike looked at me. "What do you think is significant about the stain?"

I turned it over in my mind, searching for all I had buried. "Like I'm a piece of shit." The image of the large, brown smear burned into my brain. "I felt sick for him, and horrified for myself."

"Good," Mike said. Kindness resided in his entire face.

I am unworthy.

"Gustavo and I met at a client's party after Nick moved out," I said. "We flirted, made eye contact, you know—the things that spark a man's interest. He asked for my number. He called me, and our conversation flowed. I was giddy. His voice sounded natural and sweet, with an underlying confidence. The first date turned into a yearlong affair."

"What qualities drew you to Gustavo?" Mike picked up a yellow legal pad from his desk and jotted my name at the top. Below that, he drew a series of lines, adding men like a company org chart.

"He was affectionate, adoring, full of joy, but way too young for me," I said. "And we both knew it. We dove in regardless."

Mike continued to scribble with his fat, blue roller ball. My favorite pen. The ink smeared on your fingers when you used it, but the thick lines made it worth the trouble. I counted the creases in Mike's forehead like the rings of a tree—symbols of a life well lived.

"Gustavo assumed we were exclusive," I continued, guffawing internally at the thought of anyone trusting me. "I threw my phone number at guys, even when we were on a date." A storm of shame rumbled inside me. "I was disrespectful to him."

"This is hard," Mike said. "So, you dated Gustavo and slept with other men? Correct?"

"Yes."

I'm the worst of the worst.

"There was the fireman I met at the grocery store," I said, "the crane operator at a baseball game, the pilot at the beach, and the politician at a restaurant." A thrill rose in me as I recounted the men I had picked up. I caught myself and reeled it in. "Sorry, I'm getting sidetracked." My foot burned with pins and needles. I repositioned my legs. "I started realizing I had a problem when I was with three different men in one day. Something about me was off, not normal." I laughed nervously. "Most women bond with their partner during sex. Not me. The men grew attached, and I got sort of high from them begging for more time, more sex, more of anything they could steal from me."

Nervous energy had me all jacked-up. I figured a few laps around the quad would calm me down, but then I'd be too sweaty.

"How many times did you engage in three encounters in one day?" Mike asked. He sounded so clinical he may as well have been asking my shoe size.

"More than twenty times," I said.

And if it were my shoe size, it would be eight.

"I had to give them nicknames to keep track," I added.

"How did giving them nicknames help you keep them straight? They all had names. Couldn't you just call them by their given names?" Mike wrote something down and turned his eyes back to me. Notes and more notes. Where would these notes find their resting place?

"The one-night stands were frequent. I couldn't remember their names." Dirty, bad feelings seeped in. I rubbed my earlobe, wondering how Mike could see anything inside of me, how he could see me as anything more than broken and filthy.

"Can you say anything more about nicknames?" he asked.

"What do you mean?"

"Do you have nicknames for your son?"

"Yes, but I consider those endearing."

"Dig deeper. Does anyone have nicknames for you?"

"Well, Nick calls me Pru-dense, in a derogatory way, which is kind of like a nickname."

"Why do you think Nick says your name in a derogatory way?"

It took me a moment to gather my thoughts. "When he speaks my name, a sense of worthlessness comes over me. It feels as though he wants to crush my spirit." And then I figured it out. Nick pushed me away with his little pet name. "He dehumanizes me with it. My stepdad called me stupid, retard, waste of space. He had to dehumanize me to beat me, to molest me."

"Excellent." This was exciting to Mike. He was solving a complicated jigsaw puzzle: me. "Nicknames serve to set someone apart, or even identify them as belonging to a community." He took a sip of coffee. The mug bore the Serenity Hills logo, but I could tell it was Starbucks. A rich java scent, not the decaf crap they served us. "Think about when you call someone honey or sweetheart. You invite them into your inner circle, your heart." He tipped back in his chair while I pondered the idea. "Can you see how referring to someone as honey can either invite them in or, in some cases, push them out?"

"Not really," I said. "Pet names are used because you like or love someone." Mike couldn't give me the answers, but dammit, I wanted him to.

"Let me put it this way. Did anyone ever call you by a pet name that separated you from the group, pushed you away, or belittled you?"

I thought about it. I felt as if I were verging on a breakthrough.

"Little P," I said, clapping my hands.

Broke and desperate.

Those two harmless words held the power to transport me back to where I had been before I checked into Serenity.

"The first guy I exchanged money for sex with called me Little P." The name stirred a tension inside me. Not quite nervous tension—more like nausea. "Roger came on the scene a few months after Nick moved out. Gustavo and I were still seeing each other. It was around the time Nick stopped paying my rent. Our business was floundering, and Nick was skimming profits for himself. I trusted Nick." My throat tightened as if there were two hands wrapped around my neck. Sweat covered my face. "I can't breathe."

"Try and relax," Mike said. "Take some deep breaths. Inhale. One, two, three, four. And exhale. One, two, three, four." The sound of the ocean and soft, tinkling wind chimes filled the room. "Focus on your breathing. Let thoughts pass without judgment."

I'm on the Sound Club porch with Gram. She smiles but doesn't speak. Somehow, I understand what she wants to tell me. I'm going to make it through.

"Thank you." I opened my eyes, lightheaded and weak. I dragged my clammy hands down my jeans.

"Take a break tonight," Mike said. He shifted his attention to a sheet of paper on his desk. "Tonight is movie night. Go. I'm ordering you."

I resisted the agonizing desire to give him a hug as I gathered my things and shoved them in my bag. "I'll follow orders and go to movie night."

With my pillow in hand, I picked up Gloria on the way. I had avoided coed social activities, but Mike had given me his blessing to enter a dark room half-filled with men.

"Knock, knock," I said, pushing Gloria's door open.

"Fun!" she said. "We're both in black leggings. Brilliant minds think alike!" She tucked her pillow under her arm. "Any idea what movie they're showing?"

"The calendar said they're playing *Pretty Woman*, but it also said *subject to change*, so who knows? It's one of my all-time favorites."

"What's not to love about that movie?" She wiggled her curvy hips. Moves like that would get me arrested. We both avoided stating the obvious.

A film about a woman like us, desperate for money, vulnerable and broken.

Gloria wore a white draped top with her leggings. The outfit showed off her round, firm rear and enviably small waist. I tugged at my plaid button-down, regretting my outfit choice.

The auditorium chairs rested around the perimeter. The room resembled an elementary school slumber party. Everyone was in comfy sweats or pajama pants and hoodies. Gloria edged her way along the back wall, searching for a suitable spot.

My first movie without Twizzlers. Downright wrong.

Gloria chose us a piece of real estate and dropped her pillow. "The perfect spot," she said.

I inched down next to her and exchanged niceties with those sitting in our immediate area. An aide passed us each a small bag of popcorn—a consolation prize compared to Twizzlers. A foot bumped my butt, and I shifted around to see who was going to apologize.

"Hey, guys," Bo said, sitting on the floor behind Gloria. She leaned back on his Wranglers and untucked shirt with mother of pearl snaps.

"Bo," Gloria swooned. "You make the perfect pillow."

Bo waved at someone near the door. I was too focused on my popcorn to bother looking. The lights dimmed, and the screen lit up.

"Hiya," someone said. I twisted around to see Alistair had wedged himself in behind me. "Never seen this movie." He whispered so close to my ear that goosebumps flew down my arm as fast as a California wildfire.

I should tell him to move.

"Shhh," the person next to him said.

"Someone is getting a little agro," Alistair whispered.

I stifled a laugh and propped my arms behind my back. Alistair rested his hand against mine, skin to skin. Positive energy vibrated through me as Julia Roberts worked her magic on the screen.

Happiness.

∞

After the movie, Gloria and I went back to her room and rehashed our favorite scenes. "When she goes back to Rodeo Drive and asks the sales clerk if she remembered her?" She waved her toothbrush around. "Big mistake. Huge."

I laid on my side at the end of her bed, absorbing the elation a simple night at the movies brought her. "*Pretty Woman* never grows old," I said. For me, it was about happy endings and hope. "I'm heading to bed."

On my way out, I dipped into the bathroom to kiss her cheek. There was no point in telling her I was stopping by the front desk to pick up my mail. Gloria hadn't received a single letter since checking in, and it seemed cruel to remind her.

Nurse Ratched must have seen me coming, because she held out the envelope. "I see you got the message you have mail. It's past curfew. Get to bed." She always said the meanest things with a smile on her face.

"Sorry," I said, realizing I needed to stop fucking apologizing for myself. "There was no way could I sleep knowing I had mail."

I snatched the letter and bolted out the door. I recognized Henry's chicken scrawl on the envelope. I crept quietly into my room. Deirdre was already in bed, purring like a kitten. Settled deep under my covers, I opened the envelope. It was a greeting card with the image of a cat dangling from a branch and the words *Hang in there!* just below it. I opened the card and read.

P,

These things aren't easy for me to talk about, but here goes. I'm proud of you for taking a step toward healing and facing all the shit from our childhood. In all truth, I'm not as brave as you, and I hope you clear out the past for both of us. We're alive, still standing, and we have each other, which is why I'm writing you. Christian shared a bit about how hard things have been for you financially. Damn, Prue, I'm sick over it and am committed to helping you get back on your feet. We can hash out a plan, but know I will cover your basic expenses so you can focus on healing. We're family. It's what we do.

    Henry

CHAPTER TWENTY-TWO

Nick and I tried five marriage counselors. At every session, Nick closed up. We visited a therapist Nick met through work. She charged a fortune, but I was desperate and willing to give her a try. She lived in Oregon and rented a suite at a swanky hotel in Beverly Hills to see clients. Nick and I stood outside the door of her suite. I was feeling bitter, almost as though I'd paid for the luxurious hotel room myself. Nick pressed the buzzer.

She embraced him like an old friend and stuck her hand out to me. "Hello, I'm Marguerite."

"Hi," I said, as kindly as I could manage. Everything about the situation set off my internal alarms. From the moment Marguerite greeted us at the door, it became clear to me the playing field was not a level one. It was skewed in Nick's direction.

We moved to the living area of the suite. I chose a creamy faux-Barbara Barry, and Nick got comfortable on the sofa.

"Would you mind telling me your credentials?" I asked Marguerite. "Nick knows you, I don't."

"Are you aware how rude and aggressive you sound?" Marguerite said. She kicked her sleek black boots onto the coffee table, effectively blocking my view of her and leaving me staring at her scuffed shoe bottoms for the rest of the session. It was a strategic move. "You're also walled up and not being open."

I'm walled up? You just created a proverbial wall with those boots! What is this bitch's deal? Nick's the one with intimacy issues, not me.

When she was done with me, she turned her attention to Nick. She worked incredibly fast. In a matter of minutes, she broke him down and turned him into a bawling baby. The transformation both shocked and disturbed me. Nick tucked his legs underneath himself and scrunched his shoulders. It occurred to me Marguerite had done this to him before. He was as malleable as a piece of clay in her hands.

"How old are you now, Nick?" she asked.

"I'm seven," Nick said in a child's voice.

"How do you feel as you enter your childhood home?" Marguerite leaned in toward Nick to better cast her spell.

Nick wept in an unfamiliar way. Not light tears, but snotty, shoulder-heaving sobs. "I'm not wanted," he cried. "No one notices me. No one cares. Not my mom or my dad. I am a nothing and a nobody, a piece of furniture."

This woman had taken my tall, broad-shouldered husband and broken him into a million pieces, with me as the audience. After she was through shattering Nick, she suggested a vacation. A couple's getaway. Even though Marguerite gave off bad mojo, I had to try to save my marriage.

Nick decided to accompany me on a business trip to Hawaii. The firm was doing an installation for a demanding, high-end client. Extra cash to throw at a vacation was nonexistent, so I figured squeezing in some "us" time during a business trip was better than nothing at all. Things didn't exactly go as planned. The whole time, Nick sat in the hotel room, bored to death, while I worked my ass off. A receipt from the hotel arrived a few weeks later and caught my attention; I called the hotel to dispute the charges.

"No, it's accurate," the hotel employee said. "Someone in the room consumed every bottle of liquor in the minibar, every single day."

I questioned Nick, hoping for a plausible explanation. "Did you drink anything from the minibar in Hawaii?"

"What? No!" he replied.

Really?

I stewed about it until our next session with Marguerite, presenting the bill during our therapy session. I asked the question again: "Nick, did you drink all the booze from the minibar in Hawaii?"

"Yeah, so what?" he said. "A nip here, a nip there. No problem."

I twisted on the Barbara Barryesque chair toward Marguerite for validation. "He lied to me about this when I asked him before," I said.

"Well, give him credit for coming clean now," she said. "It's not easy to do."

My attempts at monitoring Nick's consumption was futile. Anytime I took my eyes off him, he'd take down a few shots, and then I found myself dealing with a drunken, barely-able-to-stand Nick. In a panic, I'd whisk him away before people noticed.

One evening, we attended a party at the home of a business associate of Nick's. The veranda, pool house, and entertaining spaces were bustling with attractive, affluent couples who were loose with their alcohol, their drugs, and their hands. Nick's business associate, Jackson, cornered me. I kept Nick in my sights while trying to be polite and engaging.

"Am I boring you?" Jackson said, locking his eyes on mine.

"No, no. I'm sorry." I knew I had to pretend I wanted to be there.

"Let's get something to warm you up." He took my elbow and escorted me to the bar. "How 'bout a martini?" Jackson leered down my dress as he slipped his hand from my arm to the small of my back.

Oh God, creeper alert!

I stretched my neck around, scanning the room.

"Are you looking for Nick?" Jackson asked, and I nodded and sipped my drink. "He's out in the pool house with my wife. Let's go see what kind of fun they're having."

Should I be relieved or worried?

Jackson escorted me across the pool deck. A sparkling, gold evening gown was wadded up in a puddle of pool water. There was a couple standing in the shallow end. The apparent owner of the evening gown had her legs draped around a naked man, her breasts bobbing in the water. Jackson laughed. "Are they fucking?" He stared at their rhythmic motions while I stood speechless.

We rounded the corner to the green-and-white canopied pool house and discovered Jackson's wife straddling Nick, her braless nipples pressed against his face. One of Nick's hands was pushing its way under her dress. The other hand cradled her ass.

I weighed my options.

I can either lose it or I can follow Nick's lead.

I untied my halter dress. Jackson pulled my straps down and cupped my breasts.

"Beautiful, perfect nipples," he cooed.

Anger, disgust, and lust washed through me all at once—sacred things tarnished. I didn't care. I leaned into Jackson and kissed him.

"Prue," Nick said, suddenly standing next to me. "It's time to go." He whisked me off to the car and berated me all the way home. "You're nothing but a fucking whore."

∞

"Have you been putting anything foreign in your vagina?" my gynecologist asked. "There is a peculiar abrasion encircling your vagina."

I pressed the blue paper down from my knees. "My husband likes sex toys," I said, horrified yet unwilling to lie to my doctor. "Oversized dildos and things."

"You shouldn't place things in your vagina just to please your husband," he said over his spectacles, gazing between my legs. "Only do what feels pleasurable. I suggest you avoid things that hurt you. Both partners need to agree before introducing toys into a relationship . . . like oversized dildos."

Please, never say the word "dildo" again.

∞

The company promoted Nick to regional sales manager, which came with a relocation to Charleston. I stayed in Los Angeles with Christian, worked at the design firm, and prepared the house to sell. Nick moved to Charleston alone and flew back to LA once a month. I hoped a few conjugal visits would keep him faithful. This time, my pregnancy was a surprise. After the house sold, I quit my job, packed everything up, and moved across the country with Christian.

We rented a cottage on a quiet cul-de-sac. Even though I tried to keep a positive attitude, I worried the Southern girls might hate me. It was the beginning of a wonderful new chapter of my life, and I wanted things to go smoothly.

On the day we moved in, I handled the task of supervising the movers. From across the street, I saw a woman playing with her kids. She had blonde, shoulder-length hair with bangs framing her round face. From afar, she appeared to have a stocky, muscular build, but it could have been the loose top and Bermuda shorts. Determined to make a good first impression, I took Christian's hand and joined them.

"Hi, I'm Prue, and this is Christian," I said, giving his hand a loving squeeze.

"I'm Meredith," she said. "These are my kids." I envied her Prada sunglasses while she listed their names and ages, who played piano, and who played football. Her youngest was a curly-top blonde who was competing in the Little Miss Charleston Pageant. According to Meredith, she was a real contender. I expected Meredith to give me their social security numbers and Southern lineage. "Oh, and I'm not fat," she added, gesturing to her belly. "I'm pregnant." It seemed she was ready to open up her underwear drawer.

"I'm pregnant too," I said.

"You're *pregnant*?" She gave me the up-and-down, her mouth agape.

"Yes, I'm due in October."

"I'm due in October too!"

Meredith was out 'til Tuesday, and I was just beginning to sport a baby bump. The blessing of being tall, I supposed.

The neighborhood turned out to be wonderful, and I cherished the life of a stay-at-home mom. Every evening, my street filled up with kids and moms. The sound of children playing on the lawns and under the walnut trees dripping with Spanish Moss in front of our homes gave me comfort. Neighbors swapped sugar and babysitting duties, polite hellos and gossip. I soon found my feet and fell in love with the Southern charm. Meredith and I tolerated the heat and our pregnancies together on one another's front porches.

One night, Meredith said to me, "Do you realize I've never met Nick or laid eyes on that ghost of a husband of yours?"

The realization embarrassed me, and I vowed to make it right. "Let's do a barbeque at my house on Saturday night so you can all meet him!" I suggested. But when I presented the idea to Nick later in the evening, he balked. As usual.

"I can't make you any promises," he said. "My worst nightmare is dealing with those people at our house after a long day at work. It's bad enough I have to work on the weekends."

"I'll do all the cooking and cleaning. It'll be fun! You're going to love our neighbors." I was trying my hardest.

That Saturday night, the house filled up with parents and kids. The men all lounged in folding chairs, swigging their beers, while the women gabbed about their gardens and who was on what wait-list for the country clubs. Every neighbor came, except for one: Rachel, who was married to Carter.

Carter was a nice guy—I liked the fact he never gave off a creeper vibe. He spoke with a Southern lilt, was an attentive, involved father, and had a wicked sense of humor. He had a pleasant, doughy face and the "dad body" most of the guys claimed after we all gave birth. Meredith told me he did something with computers and worked out of the house, but the real breadwinner was his wife, Rachel, who was the head of human resources at Boeing.

Rachel worked constantly. That fact, along with her large rack and tiny waist, set her apart from the rest of us moms. The other women steered clear of her. To his credit, Carter made himself fit in without his wife, but the longer the evening wore on, I began to empathize with him. I knew what it was like to have a spouse who wasn't interested in having real friends.

An hour into the evening, Nick still hadn't shown up. I asked Meredith's husband, Woody, to handle the barbeque until Nick arrived. It was a good thing I did. Nick didn't come home until after eight.

When Woody tried to relinquish the barbeque, Nick simply patted him on the back and said, "You got this, bud. I need a drink."

After downing a few beers, Nick loosened up. I could tell he had started drinking from the obnoxious bellow of his voice above the friendly chatter, and a characteristic drooping of his eyelids.

When dinner was over, all of the moms went home to put their kids to sleep while the guys headed to Carter's garage to play pool.

I drifted in and out of sleep all night, re-shifting pillows, trying to settle into a comfortable position. Nick didn't find his way home until four in the morning. I smelled the liquor before he stumbled into bed, jabbing my side with his elbow. After writhing around, he ripped the covers off me and started snoring.

At least he's getting to know the neighbors.

Meredith waited until Monday to call me. "Did you hear what happened on Saturday night?"

"No," I said, praying Nick hadn't done something to strain my new friendships.

"Well, I don't want to upset you, but I heard Rachel was all over him. Woody said she was sitting on his lap, playing with his hair."

What the fuck!

"I can't believe Rachel was hanging out with our husbands," I said.

"Men will be men, but Rachel isn't someone you want your husband to be friendly with."

What could I say?

"Prue, are you there?"

"I'm here. Thank you for telling me, Meredith." Belly rubbing, and the hope a new baby brought, calmed my nerves.

"I wonder if did the right thing by telling you."

"You did," I said. "Let's talk tomorrow."

I asked Nick about it when he came home from work. In typical Nick style, he blew me off. "Prue, you're paranoid. Nothing happened. I was just having fun with the guys."

"Sounds like you had fun with Rachel," I said, steaming, trying not to blow.

"Isn't this what you asked me to do? You're the one who wanted to have the damned barbeque, for Christ's sake."

I buried my pain, put a smile on my face, and got on with my day.

The heat in Charleston in late September was unbearable. My swollen belly and ankles made me feel like a roasted pig. One morning, I went to haul the garbage cans to the curb and found a slathering of maggots crawling all over the cans. Perplexed by how to get rid of them without spreading them all over myself and the yard, I called Meredith, hoping for a Southern remedy.

"They won't take your trash with maggots," she told me.

"Dear God."

"Can't you ask Nick to clean it up?"

"Yeah, right." I rubbed my ear.

I covered my face with a bandana and put on an apron, plastic gloves, and rain boots. I was ready for battle. My skin crawled as I hosed off the outside of the cans, keeping the water pressure low so as not to spray them around. Every bag was covered top to bottom with writhing maggots. With careful precision, I laid the bags in the ivy bed and sprayed them off. I hosed out the inside of the cans, but the water pressure was too high, and a hurricane of maggots and water splattered my face, my hair, and my clothes. Feeling like a circus freak in my anti-maggot attire, I screamed and stomped in the muddy driveway. I dragged the cans to the curb and vomited into the gutter.

"Better you than me," Nick said later that night when I recounted my nightmare.

I was still exhausted from the maggot incident the next morning. After making Nick's breakfast and sending him off to work, I laid back down on the bed. With a hand on either side of my belly, I focused, hoping for a kick, a flutter, something. Nothing.

I called Nick first and got his voicemail, so I called Meredith. "Do you think it's normal for the baby not to move for hours? The baby usually moves a lot."

"You should go in and get checked," she said. "I would. Why don't you send Christian over? I'll say a prayer for you."

Please, let my baby be alright.

I called my doctor, and they told me to come in right away. I tried reaching Nick but got his voicemail again. I left him another message, this time asking him to meet me at the doctor's office.

The expression on the face of the ultrasound tech as she rolled the wand around my belly, searching for the familiar staccato rhythm of a beating heart, did nothing to ease my worries.

"What are you seeing?" I asked, unable to make sense of the images on the screen.

"The doctor will be right in," was all she said.

Several minutes later, the doctor slipped on a pair of gloves and took the tech's seat. He moved the wand around my belly. "How long since any movement?" he asked.

"A few hours, I think."

He set the wand down and stood. "Why don't you dress, and we'll talk in my office." I was left alone in the semi-dark room to put myself back together.

"These things happen," the doctor told me, touching my knee. "I'm so sorry."

I was numb.

"You're going to have to deliver the baby at the hospital," he continued. "We'll make it as comfortable for you as possible."

My precious daughter was delivered in a dim hospital room on the maternity wing. Her limp, lifeless body was laid on my chest. They let me admire her beautiful face for a long time before whisking her away. My gut-wrenching sobs contrasted the joyful sounds of happy families visiting newborn babies only a few doors away. Nick arrived, and there was nothing he could say.

We had my daughter's tiny body cremated, and I tucked her ashes into my mother's mahogany jewelry box.

∞

Nick received another promotion. Once again, we left our home and moved back to Los Angeles. I tapped into my savings to buy a house in a neighborhood with good schools. I wasn't enamored with the house, but it was a solid, long-term investment. After the closing, I had nightmares of a dam breaking and the house sinking into the ocean. It was the most money I had ever spent on anything.

"The company gave me some bad news today," Nick told me only weeks after our move. "There's been a restructuring, and my division is closing. The company will find a place for me. A coworker warned me not to move my family, because things were going down. I guess I should have listened."

I guess you should have shared that information with me.

Nick kept busy, firing employees before Christmas and closing the doors of every single retail outlet in his division. All I could do was focus on getting Christian settled and try not to worry about the huge mortgage.

"The company found me a position in the San Fernando Valley," he said. "You won't see much of me. It's more than two hours from the house. Oh, and my pay is being cut in half."

After a year of Nick commuting to the Valley, he was fired again. I found out when he strolled into the house carrying two big boxes.

"What happened?" I asked, lifting a box from his hands and putting it on the floor. "You said they pegged you for a promotion."

"It didn't work out, alright? They fucked me over and picked someone else. I bleed this company. How could they do this so me?"

"You will find another job. A better one."

Mom's elastic walls theory extends to an elastic bank account too, I guess.

We survived on my inheritance until Nick landed another job. I went back to work part-time at the design firm to help pay for Christian's clothes and activities. Nothing ever happened between me and my boss, Sam, beyond mild office flirtation, but I fantasized about it and hated myself for it.

The Christmas after I started working again, two clients texted me saying they wanted to stop by the house to drop off a gift. The clients were two UCLA students who'd hired me to decorate their condo.

When Brittany and Faye arrived, they handed me an enormous gift basket filled with chocolates, champagne, scented candles, and bath salts. I invited them inside. Everything was fine until Nick sauntered into the room.

"This is Brittany and Faye," I said, "the clients I told you about."

He didn't even pause to say hello. Instead, he settled onto the family room sofa and turned on the television. I was mortified.

"Is he mad?" Faye asked under her breath.

"No," I said, "ignore him. He's always like that."

"We should go," Brittany said. "Walk us out."

Embarrassed, I couldn't muster up an appropriate response. Brittany waited until we were out in the driveway and out of earshot from Nick. "He's nothing like I imagined," she said. "It's hard to see you with someone so . . . cold."

"I hope I'm not overstepping here," Faye added, "but he makes me very uncomfortable."

"Everyone says the same thing about Nick."

∞

The next job Nick landed was another two-hour commute away. Christian didn't even notice when his father came and went. At least Nick was making decent money. A year into the job, he felt confident he'd be the next vice president, but within a week he received a termination notice.

My bank account balance drifted lower and lower every month. Nick accepted a job in Arizona and lived there for six months until he found work closer to home. By then, he had managed to alienate every friend I had.

On top of his complete oblivion to our looming financial demise, other things were going wrong. I had to replace the dishwasher. The bathroom sink wouldn't drain, and the bathtub kept backing up. Nick was useless, even when I begged.

"I don't know anything about plumbing," he said. "Handle it. I'm up to my elbows with work."

I did the only thing I could and called a professional. As I stood behind the plumber while he snaked the shower, I noticed how his muscles bulged as he twisted the cable into the drain. When he finished, I followed him to his truck with my checkbook in hand.

I could tell he was a cheap beer kind of guy. Not bottled beer, but the kind of cans you buy at a corner gas station. He rolled down his window and rested his arm on the door, showing off a half-sleeve tattoo of an ocean wave and hibiscus flowers. A bottle of Silver Oak merlot lay next to him on the front seat.

"I didn't figure you for a wine connoisseur," I said, leaning in and giving him a clear cleavage shot.

"You miss out when you don't go beneath the surface."

Or you cause yourself all kinds of trouble.

"What kind of wine do you like?" he asked.

"All kinds, but most of the time, I drink chardonnay."

"Why don't you come to my place tonight? Got some Rombauer waiting for just the right occasion."

"I can't tonight."

This is a bad idea.

"Daytime is better for me," I added.

"How about lunch at my place tomorrow?" He wrapped his hand around the wine bottle.

"You cook?"

"I do, but I wasn't talking about food." He cocked a five o'clock shadow smile.

I felt high from his attention. My feet lifted off the ground, floating. Lunch with "the plumber" became a regular escape. He mounted me without foreplay, erect and rock hard. He pumped while switching positions every minute. I obliged. He swirled his hips, mimicking the sex toys Nick brought home. No orgasms for me. Orgasms would require him knowing a woman's anatomy, the clitoris, and its location. The devastating truth: I wasn't the lucky girl who orgasmed on top with a simple hula-hoop motion.

Every inch of me thrived on the plumber's attention. The sex relieved my sadness, even without the orgasm. A part of me craved him, or at least something about him. I desired whatever he was providing me that Nick didn't. The plumber always fell into a post-sex coma afterward, and I would slip out from under his arm, scoop my panties off the floor, and get dressed. He didn't care about me. We both wanted to fuck, but it ended as fast as it began.

A few weeks later, Nick and I went out to dinner. I sipped wine and pretended to be happy, but nearly gasped when I looked to the end of the sushi bar and saw my plumber. An attractive brunette sat next to him. We made eye contact; I refocused my attention.

I wonder if Nick loves me.

CHAPTER TWENTY-THREE

My session with Mike was like giving birth. After, I felt relieved and drained. I went back to my room and slipped on a boring one-piece and a modest coverup. My heart ached for Christian. I scribbled him a note and stopped at the nurses' station on my way to the pool to mail the letter and do a check.

"Guilt, shame, and pain," I said. The words depicted life inside my head, every single freaking day.

"Anything else?" Nurse Ratched said.

"Hopeful," I said.

She smiled. "Please stick to words from the chart. Enjoy your swim."

Gloria and a few others cheered as I unlatched the pool gate.

Damn, there's a lot of love here.

"Get your sweet booty on one of these rafts," Gloria said.

The warm, amniotic water refreshed me like a rite of passage. I sank into the raft and closed my eyes. Somehow, I was peaceful for the first time in ages. It tingled through my arms and across my chest.

Gloria paddled over. "Hey sister, how are you surviving today?"

"I'm doing alright. Trying not to get caught up with the anticipation of Family Week."

"Think good thoughts. If you and Nick are meant to be, then it will happen." Her words reminded me I could only control so much fate. "Can I ask you something?" she said, lifting her hand in a salute to shade her eyes from the sun. "Has a therapist ever told you they were afraid for your life?"

"Interesting," I said. "My therapist said it so many times it was annoying."

I compared Gloria's body to mine, the soft curves my body lacked. A simple tattoo in varying shades of charcoal of winged, fallen angels ran down her spine, tracing a line from heaven to hell.

"Well," Gloria said. "I heard it too. I'm grateful to be here." Her comment awakened me from coveting her perfect body.

"Why were your counselors afraid you might die?" I asked, not certain she wanted to talk about it.

"From turning tricks with the wrong guy and having him kill me or give me AIDS, or from all the drugs I consumed to ease the pain from having sex for money." She adjusted her swimsuit over her perfect butt-cheeks. "I'm so damn happy my HIV test came back negative. Fuck, I was so nervous, not knowing if I had it."

I nodded. The guys I screwed might've been more upper-class than hers, but I had put myself in some scary situations with unsavory characters.

Gloria licked her swollen lips and wiped black hair from her brow with a dripping hand. "I would have killed myself if I didn't stop doing all those crazy things for money. I'm beginning to think Tom will never leave his wife, no matter how much I want to believe he will." Her eyes turned glassy, as though holding back deep feelings that wanted to come out. "We're both survivors, Prue. We don't need to survive anymore. Now, we can live." She threw her hands up, splashing water around. I wanted her kind of joy, just a small piece for myself. "Whatever you're thinking about, erase it right out of your mind."

"I'm thinking about Family Week and Nick. He won't take me back after I come clean to him." The sun beat against the backs of my knees.

"You are one brave girl to face what you've done and find out if he has the heart to forgive you. I sure hope he does. He'd be an idiot not to." Gloria seemed so childlike at times, and as wise as an old owl at others. "What was your breaking point? How did you know you needed help, if you don't mind me asking?"

No wonder men love her. She's so damned cute.

"I don't mind you asking at all," I said. "You mean my rock-bottom?" I stalled, wondering which one to tell. "My first instinct is to say it was getting raped twice, but I guess that didn't break me." This was something I had not told a soul.

"Oh, God, Prue. I'm sorry."

"It made me tougher."

I told Gloria everything. Nick had left me and was fucking Naomi. He'd cut me off, and I needed money fast. For a time, I dated guys who had money, not caring whether I felt any attraction to them. While on a date, I'd wait for an opportune moment to discuss my financial stress—tug on their heartstrings. More often than not, they'd offer to help. As time went on, I became more brazen and laid things out in a clearer, more concise manner. I had something they wanted. They had something I wanted. I viewed it as a business transaction.

The night played in my brain like a 3D movie. My bills were piling in equal amounts to the stress of trying to stay afloat. Every single month, I'd be hit with multiple overdraft charges. My income only scratched the surface of covering my expenses. With my bank account overdrawn by nearly a thousand dollars, I had no wiggle room. It meant everything to me to keep Christian in his school, to stay in the neighborhood and provide him some semblance of order in the chaos of my life.

After Christian and I had dinner, I sat in my room and scrolled through my phone in search of someone who might help me. I passed a stockbroker's name I'd had coffee with once. He had given me a few hundred dollars for no reason. I also knew he pined for me, something I could leverage to my benefit, so I texted him. He messaged back and said he wanted to see me. Since he was married, he asked me to meet him on a trail near his house. I agreed and told Christian I was going out for an hour or so.

My nerves were in overdrive and evenly aligned with my desperation. I parked my car where he had told me to and got out. He was there, on the trail with his dog. We embraced, and he told me how great it was to see me. He signaled to me what he wanted, and I dropped to my knees. The rocks and twigs on the trail dug into my skin. After he finished, I headed back toward my car, too awkward to ask him for the pay. Halfway down the path, he told me to come back. I did. He jammed a wad of cash into my hand and thanked me. When I got to my car, I counted the bills: fifteen hundred dollars.

"I clutched the money in my hand and sobbed," I told Gloria. "I was overjoyed to have cash, but disgusted for myself and my son."

"Why for your son?" she asked.

"Because his mother is a whore. I pray to God he never finds out what I had to do to keep our water and electricity on. I hope he doesn't find out who I am. Well . . . who I *was*."

"It's not who you are," Gloria said. "Remember what Mike said. It's what you've *done*, not who you *are*. I must have been listening well that day." She turned her face toward the sun and smiled.

"Alright, ladies, everyone out of the pool," the supervisor said. I paddled my raft to the edge, stepped off, and dragged it out of the water. Gloria followed.

"Thank you for trusting me," she said, throwing her arms around my neck. "I love my Prue."

The dining room was the usual chaotic mess. Rhoda waved me over to her table and pointed to an empty chair. I maneuvered through the room with my tray. The glass filled with lemon water slid into the plate but didn't spill—a reminder of my epic waitressing skills. It took every bit of strength I had not to eat a cookie off the plate Deirdre set in the middle of the table for sharing.

"Salad bars freak me out," I said, focusing on the jelly-filled treat with a dusting of simulated powdered sugar on top. Gloria popped one into her mouth. White flecks dropped onto her t-shirt.

"Dang, these are good," she said. "Why do salad bars freak you out?"

"It has something to do with germs, and lots of people poking around the lettuce." I bit into a piece of dry chicken and washed it down with lemon water.

"There are a lot of people breathing around the salad bar," Rhoda said. "Now I'm freaked out, too." She examined the cherry tomato skewered on the end of her fork. "I miss having my own kitchen and cooking." She flicked the tomato from her fork. I worried I might have ruined everyone's salad bar experience for the rest of their lives.

"What I wouldn't give for a stack of Denny's pancakes," Gloria said. "Oh, God. Don't get me started. Now I want bacon."

"I want sushi," I said. "And sticky rice with a fat piece of toro on top." My mouth watered as I said it, and then I felt disgusted. I stealthily changed the subject. "I'm going to the CODA meeting. Anyone interested in joining me?"

Alistair and Bo were sitting two tables over. Alistair caught me glancing over, lifted his glass, and mouthed, "Cheers!"

Busted.

"Let's all go," Gloria said. She cleared her tray and wandered over to Bo and Alistair. Her hair was in a half topknot with silky tendrils falling around her shoulders.

I couldn't score that kind of tousled-hair perfection if my life depended on it.

"We're walking over now," Rhoda announced in Gloria's general direction. Bo and Alistair shoved their trays into the cleanup bin and followed us out the door.

The meeting room had already been set up, the chairs forming an imperfect circle. I picked a seat adjacent to the leader where I could see the door. Everyone else scattered around, mixing in with patients from other color groups. We all tended to separate when we were getting ready to spill our guts.

"Thank you, everyone, for coming," the group leader said. "This is the Codependents Anonymous meeting for people who share a common desire to develop functional and healthy relationships. The topic for today's meeting is: 'I have difficulty identifying what I am feeling.' I'll start with a reading, and then we can go around the room to discuss how this topic might apply to you."

Feelings? What feelings?

While the leader shared, my mind raced. I willed it to stop, but once my monkey brain kicked in, there was no turning back.

How do I feel about my mother? Nick? The damage I caused Christian? All the men I slept with?

"My name is Gloria, and I'm codependent."

"Hi, Gloria," the group said in unison.

Gloria stretched her arms out in front of her and interlocked her fingers. "Oh man, this is hard. I have difficulty identifying my relationship with Tom. I love him." Her voice lifted to a high note when she said his name. "Deep inside, I wonder if I'm pissed off because he promised me he was going to leave his wife and he hasn't yet." She dug her toes back into her silver sandals. "We barely see each other. So why waste it whining about his wife and being mad at him? I guess that's all I have."

Alistair raised his hand, and the leader nodded in his direction. "My name is Alistair. I'm codependent."

"Hi, Alistair," the group spoke, again in perfect unison.

Alistair's face brightened when we said his name. "Thank you for sharing, Gloria." He swiped his knees and gazed at the floor. "It's been difficult to identify how I feel about my girlfriend, Eleanor. I thought I loved her but, after some soul-searching, I believe I said it to please her, when in fact the feelings weren't there." He shoved his fingers into his hairline, lifting it into a pompadour. "Someone here, a patient, opened up a new sensation in my heart. One I feared didn't exist due to my horrific childhood." His voice cracked. "I can't say who it is, which is sad in itself, but this is so important to me."

I froze, staring down at the carpet.

Alistair pressed his palms to his chest. "My heart works. I can identify this feeling is love." He dabbed his eyes, and Mama Rhoda passed him a tissue from her cowboy boot purse.

How can Alistair love me when I can't even love myself? I'm a piece of shit.

CHAPTER TWENTY-FOUR

The summer before Christian started middle school, I took him for a month-long summer vacation to Alie's camp in the Adirondacks. The place looked like a page right out of a Ralph Lauren catalog. Woodchip paths connected each cottage to the main house, which rested on the majestic lake. The lawn was covered in a minefield of wickets for our nightly, heated games of croquet. We roamed around with our mallets, the adults drinking wine from plastic goblets and the kids drinking lemonade from plastic cups. Alie's husband seemed to me to be wrapped up in goodness.

Why can't I attract a good man?

No one questioned the absence of my husband, which I appreciated. Even so, a needling desperation rumbled under the surface. My inner demons screamed for male attention.

We spent the mornings horseback riding, memories of Mrs. Sutton and Balaam—all the things that made my heart soft—playing through my head. We lounged on the dock in Adirondack chairs, swimming when the heat became too much. I took in the perfect peacefulness, broken only by the occasional plaintive cries of black-crowned herons.

One afternoon, Christian was poking along the beach, searching for skipping stones. "Want to go out in a canoe with me?" I asked. The sun dipped in the sky, falling to the edge of the lake. The setting sun cast twinkling lights on the lake like a million jewels.

"Like you even have to ask me if I want to go on a canoe ride!" Christian exclaimed.

"Yay! Let's go."

Alie called out to us from the boathouse. "I'm setting up *hors d'oeuvres*. I'll have a glass of wine waiting for you."

Christian slid the shellacked canoe into the lake and gripped the dock tight while I stepped in. "You sit in the front," he said. He steered us out into the middle of the lake, and we glided over the glassy water.

"I'm proud of you." I smiled at the memory of Lily toting her tiller everywhere.

"Mom, you need to leave Dad. Dad doesn't love you. He doesn't know how to love. You should leave while you're still pretty and young."

I was as floored by Christian's depth as I was by the startling revelation. He was right. "I love your father, but he doesn't love me, and it makes me sad. He loves you, though."

"I know he does," Christian said. We pulled the canoe back into the dock and lifted it out of the water.

I heard Alie's voice coming from the screened-in porch above the boathouse. "I have chardonnay and Manchego cheese up here. Don't make me eat this by myself, or no one's getting dinner." Citronella candles glowed around the dock during the mosquitos' celebrated hour, leaving a wafting lemony scent.

"This is my absolute favorite time of day," I said. "The sun setting on the lake is magical."

Christian's words burned in my heart. I knew he was right, but I couldn't change anything.

"A slice of heaven, isn't it?" Alie said. Cigarette smoke plumed through the screened-in canopy. "I'm smoking a daddy and trying not to get caught. Hence, the citronellas." Alie's carbon flaw.

I moved a porch chair to sit next to her. She leaned into the screen, a cigarette in one hand and a wineglass in the other.

"I wonder what Nick is doing," I said. "Probably cheating." Not like I was any better.

"My mother had a saying. Men only have two emotions: hungry and horny. A guy without an erection needs a sandwich."

We both cracked up, celebrating friendship and the beautiful lake.

The next morning, I dropped Christian off for his tennis lesson at the Adirondack Club. "Have fun, play well," I said, only half paying attention. A blonde tennis pro two courts over with a thick Italian accent was giving instruction to an overly sunned, soft-featured woman. With four yellow balls in one hand, he fed them to her on the other side of the court.

"Yes! Excellent," he said. "High to low, and follow through with your racket."

Alie had told me about the new tennis pro. "He's Italian and graduating from college this year. His presence has caused a real ruckus among the tennis ladies. Wait until you see him."

"Mom, don't forget to get me like you did yesterday," Christian said. His oversized racket dangled in his hand, nearly dragging on the ground. I touched his face.

"I won't forget, and I already apologized about yesterday. I'll sit right here while you have your lesson."

Got to do better.

Halfway through his lesson, I strolled over to the tennis office. "I'd like to sign up for a private lesson with Giovanni," I told the lady behind the counter. "I heard he's a talented teacher."

I'm such a good liar.

She perused the large white calendar on the top of the counter. "Giovanni has an opening on Saturday at two. Does that work for you?"

"Yes, perfect."

∞

With my tennis bag slung over my shoulder and my club-required, all-white tennis dress, I walked to the far court where Giovanni waited. The bottom of my pleated minidress swung up and down with each step. I slid my hand over my ass to make sure the pleats were even before turning the gate latch.

"You must be Prudence. I am Giovanni. It is my pleasure to meet you." He extended his muscular arm to shake my hand.

"I guarantee this will be the worst tennis lesson of your career," I said. "I'm very rusty."

"Alright. Let's play some tennis." He moved around the court with athleticism. I focused on his instructions until my lesson ended.

"I had your son in camp today, no?"

I pulled off my hat and adjusted my ponytail. "Yes, you did. Christian."

"A good boy. You are married?"

"Separated." I wanted to believe my lies and hoped he would too.

"Tonight, there's a party in Centerville. You should come." He bounced a ball on his racket.

I stifled the reasonable, levelheaded Prudence for the irresponsible, reckless one. "Sounds awesome."

After a few tennis lessons, flirting, making out, and going to a party together, Giovanni and I arranged to meet at a ramshackle motel in the center of town.

Who would stay here? Cheaters sneaking around in broad daylight.

Giovanni lived with a local family who also happened to be members of the club. Sex at his place was impossible. I parked around back like the seedy, lowlife cheater I was. I popped a piece of gum in my mouth. The buildup in my head matched my nerves. I walked around the motel, searching for room 113. I reached up to knock on the door, and before I did, Giovanni opened it.

"Hey, gorgeous." he said.

"Dammit, you scared me." Shirtless, Giovanni waved for me to come in. "Thank you," I said.

His six-pack abs ended at a V, where the boxer line peeked an inch above his torn, faded jeans.

"You want a drink?" he said. "I brought some beers."

"Sure."

Giovanni pulled two sweaty Heineken bottles from his backpack, popped them open, and handed one to me.

"Cheers," he said.

Reality set in, then the guilt came. Giovanni leaned in and kissed me. He reached under my t-shirt and unhooked my bra. He tugged my shirt, pulling my bra with it, and stepped back to admire my breasts.

"*Bellissima*," he said.

I unzipped my shorts and slid them down my legs. Giovanni pushed me down onto the bed. I laid there with my hands behind my head, watching him take off his jeans. Out popped the smallest penis I had ever seen.

He stroked it, admiring me from above. "I wish it were bigger," he said.

"Why would you say that?"

"I see the guys in the locker room."

I moved to the edge of the bed and took him into my mouth. He lifted me onto the pillows.

"You like my cock? My cock likes you." Beads of sweat covered his face, making his blonde curls stick to his forehead. "Get on all fours so that I can admire your hot ass."

I flipped over, preferring minimal eye contact. "Oh, yeah, give it to me harder."

"Ride me on top. I want you to come." Giovanni moved his hand around, trying to please me. I moaned the way I knew I was supposed to.

We screwed five times. I rolled away, dragging the sheet with me to the bathroom. I needed to hide my nakedness, my vulnerability. I avoided my reflection in the mirror.

Our behavior turned more brazen with each encounter. Sex in the pool cabana. Sex in gas station bathrooms. Parked behind the main clubhouse in the car. I was the creepy housewife doing the much younger fantasy-worthy tennis pro. He snuck me into his room, and we did it right under the noses of the prominent members of this exclusive enclave.

Who are the people who live here? Do they have moral values and regular family dinners? Do they say "I love you" to each other? Would they accept someone like me?

After the summer had ended, and I went back to my regular life, I decided to visit Giovanni at college. Nick thought I was at a furniture show. My lies grew and became more frequent. I had trouble keeping track. Giovanni escorted me to a frat party. I tried to blend in with the college students. He passed out in the living room. I fell asleep in an upstairs bedroom, exhausted and ashamed. When the bedroom door opened, I assumed it was Giovanni.

"Shhh," he said. He had same thick Italian accent Giovanni had. "It's Diego, Giovanni's roommate." A dark, sensuous man stood over me. "Beautiful. Giovanni's a fool. He should be here with you. I cannot resist you."

He sat on the bed and peeled the covers off my body. "Your nipples, wow." His warm mouth covered my areola, then moved up my neck until our lips met. I feigned shock, but as he pressed his lips against mine, I spread my legs to let him inside.

Diego fucked me all night. At dawn, he snuck out, leaving his spicy scent behind.

My first double. And I'm not talking about tennis.

Nick got an idea. "Let's sell our house, liquidate our savings, and buy a business. I can't work for the man anymore."

I had no choice but to trust him. It took a year of Nick not working for him to find the right business venture. In that time, he would loaf around the house for half the day. I couldn't stand him. I wanted to slip away, to disappear. At first, I would tell a flimsy lie, pretend to be going to the gym so I could meet with a hookup. I'd fuck some guy in the afternoon and then come home at night and fuck Nick. My body was cloaked with shame, and I was disgusted with myself.

One night, on the way to another one of my hookups, an Aimee Mann song came over the radio and socked me in the gut with images of a girl in need of a tourniquet.

Me, hanging from my closet door, dying a slow, painful death.

I took a part-time job at a design center. One of my coworkers, Marie, invited me on a trip to Mexico with a group of women from the office. I pledged to behave.

First, I have to ask Nick for permission.

"I guess you can go," Nick said. "I'll be here slaving. You earned it. Go take a weekend with your friends."

His sarcasm poisoned every inch of me. Nick's lack of trust had the opposite effect of his intention; it drove me further away.

My assigned roommate made the decision to switch rooms so she could be with another equal-opportunity snorer. I was left to spread out in my room alone. After we had settled in, we met up at the cantina for margaritas. It was a fun evening, but too short. When the rest of the girls retreated to their rooms, I stayed and cozied up to a forty-something divorcee leaning against the bar. My usual type—toned and fit, with a pile of bad boy on the side. It didn't take long for us to get naked. Doggie-style lacked intimacy, so I let him pummel me from behind.

"You're a naughty hot bitch, aren't you?" He yanked my hair and spanked my ass. The slap brought me rushing back to reality, and I scooted him out of my room. Spanking was not my thing. I went to bed ashamed and disgusted.

I called Christian in the morning before the day revved up.

"You forgot about the end-of-the-year baseball party, and I missed it," Christian said. "I wanted to pick up my trophy."

The sense of failure I thrived on set in, and I gave myself a proper flogging. "I'm so sorry," I said. "I'll pick it up at the coach's house when I get home."

"Whatever."

I'm no better than my mother. I forget everything important.

Instead of letting my failed mothering skills ruin my vacation, I brushed it under the rug just like I did everything else.

Marie cornered me at breakfast. "Did I see a man leave your room last night?"

"No, that was one of the guys from the room next door to mine," I lied.

Not like she isn't up to the same thing.

I avoided the spanker when I saw him at the pool. We laid on chaises most of the afternoon. The other girls left to take in some shopping; Marie and I stayed behind. Across the pool, a couple of guys were eyeing us and chatting among themselves.

"I don't know about you, but I'm going to have some fun," Marie said. She walked over to them, talked for a minute, and left with one of them. The one with the cheesy board shorts and tank top strolled over. Too many margaritas went down too easily.

"My hotel is down the road," he said, scribbling the name on a napkin. "Here's the info. See me tonight. Let's have some fun."

Buzzed from the liquor and excitement, I spent time getting dolled up, then snuck out of my room and into a cab. The fun pool day ran through my mind as I walked down the strange hotel hallway. It took him a while to answer my knock.

"Hey," I said.

"No way," he said, clearly surprised I'd taken him up on the offer. He stumbled backward, motioning for me to come in. "Can I offer you a drink?"

The hairs on my arms stood on end.

I'm not safe.

He grabbed me, pushed me up against the wall, and ripped my dress off. He yanked my underwear to the side while I locked my legs together. Outweighed and outsized, my fight was futile, but I never gave up. Pain tore through my vagina. He pushed himself deep inside, every thrust slamming me against the wall with his full body weight. My wrists throbbed to his heartbeat.

"Such a sweet, tight little pussy." A sharp pain stabbed my nipple. "You love it."

Rancid, hot alcohol breath covered my face. His red eyes, violent and dark, stared down at me. He drew in close enough for me to bite him, but before I could, he released my arm and slapped me across the face. I tasted copper.

"Stop, stop, stop!" I screamed.

"Shut the fuck up! Isn't this what you came here for you hot little slut?"

"Leave me alone!" I spat, aiming for his face.

"Bitch, you want this, and you came for it, and I'm going to give it to you good and hard."

He shoved his hand in my mouth. I bit down, pushed, and kneed him in the groin. He fell over, and I scrambled for my dress and purse. Two hands gripped my ankles, and my legs flew out from under me. He dragged me across the floor.

"Shut your fucking mouth." He shoved his dick in, thrust three times, and moaned. Salty sweat dripped on my face. He crawled off and stood over me. "Hope you're on birth control, sexy girl."

Without looking at him, I stepped into my dress, grabbed my purse, and walked out. Once the door closed, I ran. My dress slipped off, and I tied it in a knot as I sprinted away. Scrambled and disoriented, I nearly ran over a hotel employee.

"Señorita, can I help you?"

"No, gracias," I said, frantically pushing the down button on the elevator.

One, two, three, four, five, six . . . please, God, please!

The unavoidable elevator mirror displayed my bloody, swollen mouth, and cherry-red cheek. My wrists throbbed and pulsated. The body and soul broke apart. I floated above. My hand wiped the blood and dragged it across my dress.

"You need a taxi, *señorita*?"

"*Si.*"

CHAPTER TWENTY-FIVE

The line for the phone was three patients long. I settled into the only available chair. Once seated, I succumbed to fidgeting, foot flipping, knee crossing, and ear rubbing. The girl next to me glanced over. I smiled; she smirked. The old me would have been bothered by the brush-off, but this time Mike's words crept into my head. Other people's reaction to me might not be *about* me. With my notes folded across my lap, I prepared for my conversation with Nick. Even going in prepared, the thought unnerved me. I tried convincing myself I wasn't in a life-or-death situation.

I lifted the gray receiver—my lifeline, my love, my warmth, my connection to the outside world. Nick's cell phone cycled through three rings before I heard his voice on the other line.

"Hello?"

"Hey. Just calling to check in and say hi. How's everything going?"

Nick performed a throat-clear. "Just trying to survive in a hostile environment."

I ignored the sarcasm. "Things are going well here, learning a lot and getting through some hard childhood stuff." My heart thumped through my shirt. "How are you? I miss you and Christian."

"I've been dealing with my anger."

The room turned into a sauna. "I can't blame you for feeling angry. All I can say is I'm sorry, and I'll keep saying it until you believe me."

"I can't do this anymore," he said. "I don't even know if I love you. Too much has happened to try and fix it." I heard the sound of papers shuffling on his desk. "I've been staying with Naomi. We have strong feelings for each other."

"What do you mean?"

He cleared his throat again. "I'm in love with her."

"Well, I'm in love you." The vulnerable Prudence searched for a place to hide. "I wish things could have been different, but they aren't. We can start over. The past is the past, Nick. I want a future with you. How is that possible with this other woman in the picture?"

"What are you saying? You want me to leave her?" he asked.

"I'm doing a lot of work. I'm ready to be the wife and partner you need and want."

Do I even know what he wants?

"You can't fathom how this has been for me," Nick said. "My feelings for you are cloudy, at best."

"How can you say that? You said you were willing to work on our marriage. Isn't that why I came here? How can we work on our relationship when you're seeing someone else?"

"I need to see how things unfold with Naomi and me."

Panic surged through me. My hand went numb.

How do I respond? How do I get through this?

Gloria's words crept into my mind: "You're a beautiful soul."

"Let's get through Family Week and see how it goes," I said. "I'm not going to beg you to leave Naomi."

Lecture lessons being put to the test. The irrational Prue wanted to scream and smash the phone into the counter, but she didn't.

"I promised Christian we'd go to Family Week," he said. "I don't want to go, but I'm doing it for him."

"How's Christian?" A scrambling topic change.

"He's been with your brother. Shit is coming down at work. I need to keep it together." He covered the receiver to speak to someone. "I gotta go."

The phone remained in my hand until the bell on the timer rang. It was my phone time, and I was going to use it until the end. "Goodbye," I said into the receiver, even though he had long hung up. "I love you."

∞

The new girl traipsed across the meeting room, dragging her elegant fingers through her thick, dark curls. She was exotic looking and radiated sensual energy. Every man locked eyes on her, following her movements as she glided to the only empty chair.

Mike should pass the goddamned tissue box around the room to clean up the drool.

I didn't hate her at first sight. The truth was, I wanted to be her.

"This is Kim," Mike said. "Why don't you introduce yourself and tell us why you're here?"

"I'm a sex addict." She fingered her name tag, the pink sticker clashing with her bias-cut floral dress. "I'm married. Two kids, a boy and a girl. Not sure how I ended up like this, because I don't have a big childhood trauma story." Kim turned her prowess—her sensuality, her crafty charm—toward Mike.

Is she seeking his approval, or permission to stop talking?

"Excellent, Kim. Go ahead." A pang of jealousy turned my stomach. I hated the thought of sharing Mike with another sex addict, much less a beautiful, sensual sex addict.

"I slept with the contractors, gardeners, electricians, plumbers, you name it. Any man who worked at my house." She coughed, a telltale stall tactic. I studied her fine features. "Then I started sleeping with my friends' husbands." The more she spoke, the more authentic she became. "My husband Brett and I went to dinner with a few couples, friends of ours. I followed Brett's friend to the men's room, desperate for sex. I propositioned him while Brett waited at the table without a clue. Of course, Brett's friend told him, and well, here I am."

She could be me. Hallelujah, I'm not the only one!

Desperate and excited to talk to her, I couldn't focus during the meeting. At prayer time, I jockeyed for a position next to her.

"I'm Prue."

"Well, that was rough. Embarrassing, to say the least." A curl dangled over her cheek, and she tucked it behind her ear.

"The first day is the hardest," I said. "We're like family here. No judgment." It was then that I made the decision to be genuine with this beautiful creature. "Do you want company while you unpack and settle into your room?" I held up my pink name tag. "We have something in common."

"Yeah, sounds awesome."

Kim's room was two doors away from mine. Nothing at Serenity Hills happened by accident. "Hope you won't be sick of me because my room is next door."

"No, I'm happy you're close by."

We walked into her room that resembled tornado wreckage. "I'm not the best at organizing," she said and shrugged in a sweet, childlike manner. "My daughter loves keeping things neat and tidy. Must have inherited that from Brett."

I stepped over a mound of clothes piled on the floor. "Your daughter and I have something in common, because I love organizing too." I lifted a dress from the floor and placed it on a hanger. "Why don't you put underwear and things like that in the drawer, and I'll hang stuff up."

"Thanks for helping me. I'm not myself." Kim heaved a wad of colored panties into a drawer. "Do you have kids? I hate not seeing my kids." She rummaged through a satchel and pulled out a picture frame. "Here they are." She started crying. The hanger slipped from my hands. I felt like crying too.

We paused to admire her photo. "Your twin," I said.

Snot mixed with her tears, and she grabbed a tissue from the bathroom and blew her nose. "Sorry," she said. "I'm overwhelmed. My son is the mirror image of Brett." She buried her blotchy face in her hands. "I feel so shitty, like the worst parent in the world."

"Believe me, self-flogging is not productive. Feel proud you made the decision to change, to get help. Your kids love you. Nothing can change that."

I was better at helping others than I was at helping myself.

"You're right. Got to pull out of this funk. How about you? Do you have kids? How are you keeping it together?" The black mascara pooling under her eyes did nothing to lessen her innate beauty.

"One son, Christian. He's fourteen. My husband and I are separated. Basically, my life is a disaster." There had to be some humor hidden in our stories, and I wanted to find it. "I try not to go to the dark place, because I'm afraid I'll never get out." My cloak of shame wasn't going anywhere fast. "I'm doing my very best to change and do better, and you are too." I picked up a colorful dress from the pile. "This is cute."

"Borrow anything you want," Kim said. "Do you want your husband back? Brett is my rock. Without his support, I couldn't survive. There must be something in my childhood to make this happen." She filled the rest of the drawer with delicate bras and tiny string bikinis.

"It all goes back to childhood," I said. Difficult subjects were more easily embarked upon when doing something with my hands. I shrugged off the dark feelings brewing inside of me. "I've been coming to grips with being molested. My husband isn't understanding, like yours. It's hard to tell if he loves me, which is a whole different set of problems."

I had to keep it light, for fear I might crumble.

"I'm sorry." She dragged a finger under her eyes, then dropped a pile of jeans into the next drawer. "What's my excuse? I don't have a story, other than I was my mother's keeper. My mom is unstable, bipolar I guess. I had a lot dumped on my shoulders."

"That could be your answer." I hung the last of her dresses and looked them over again. Half of Kim's wardrobe would be deemed non-approved rehab attire, but I refrained from dropping that bombshell. "Your childhood was stolen from you, like mine was, only in a different way."

"Just talking to you makes me feel a lot better," she said. "You're right. I can't solve all this in one day." She pressed the framed photo of her kids to her lips and kissed it. It was then I knew we were soul sisters.

CHAPTER TWENTY-SIX

No sooner had I returned to my hotel room in Mexico than I received an urgent message from the front desk to call Candlelight Elder Home in New York—the retirement facility Gram had been staying at for the last two years.

Dear Lord, please keep Gram out of pain.

"This is Prudence Aldrich," I said into the receiver. My mouth throbbed. I ignored the ghostly sensation of the rapist's hands clenched around my wrists. "I received an urgent message."

I was put on hold. A few minutes passed, then someone picked up. "This is Margie." It was the gaudy, over-smiling, fake manager. "I'm sorry to have to tell you this over the phone, but your grandmother passed away peacefully in her sleep last night. Listen, honey, you or your brother need to come and fill out some paperwork."

I went into robot mode. "I'm going to catch the next flight I can out of Mexico and should be there by tomorrow afternoon."

Pack your bags, change your flight, get to the airport, get to Gram.

After calling the airline to change my ticket, I tossed my folded clothes into my suitcase. I pulled all of my sundresses off their hangers and laid them in the bag—all but one, the bloodstained dress on the closet floor. I ran the shower as hot as I could stand it. My breasts throbbed, toothmarks outlining my areolas. I scrubbed my skin raw.

Henry was waiting in the lobby when I arrived at Candlelight. Anguish covered his face. I wrapped my arms around him.

"We have no family left," he whispered. "We're all alone."

"The business purchase papers are getting inked today. I'm excited about this, Prudence." Nick never got excited. I was still stewing over his decision to not include me in the signing of the business papers. I was livid when I found out our partner's wife had been there and they'd all gone out to celebrate afterward.

When Nick staggered in a few hours later, I played possum. The stench of liquor and fermented fruit wafted from his pores. My resentment overshadowed the shock that Nick would have the audacity to shut me out of the purchase made with our pooled funds.

I'm not part of his team.

Amorous, drunk Nick pressed his hard penis into my back. He spat on his finger and reached around my waist to touch my clit.

In the morning, Nick still reeked of alcohol. He refused to admit to a hangover. I settled in the club chair next to our bed with a book until he woke up.

He crawled out of bed to pee, leaving the bathroom door open. "I'm a business owner, baby." A frothy urine odor filled the room.

"Don't you mean *we*?" I wasn't down for a fight, but I couldn't let his comment slip through.

"Whatever, Pru-dense, you know what I mean. Why do you always have to dig at everything I say? It's annoying."

You mean I'm *annoying.*

I might have confessed as a way of pushing him away. Or maybe to ease my conscience, or free myself of the dark secrets.

"There's something I have to tell you." I tucked my knees up under me in the chair next to our bed. The bed where Nick took me every night. The bed where I deprived myself of my needs. "I was molested, sexually assaulted."

It happened. I felt myself floating above the room. Memories I had blocked until I couldn't anymore.

"I'm having nightmares and flashbacks. I read some articles that said I disrespect my body because I don't see myself as having any value." My head hung down. "Something is terribly wrong with me."

The veins in Nick's arms popped through the skin, but I knew there was no turning back.

"I cheated," I said. "I feel like I'm going insane. I don't know who I am anymore."

"Who was it?" His eyes bugged out. "Your bastard stepfather? Sick motherfucker." Nick paced at the foot of the bed, then punched the door. "I can't deal with the cheating. This better not be some glamorous way for you to get out of your cheating and bad behavior. What are you saying? You're a sex addict?"

"No, I'm sick. My past haunts me. I can't stop thinking about what happened. I'm sorry, Nick. I love you."

"What a fucking sick bastard." Nick walked around like a caged animal.

"We should separate," I said. "We aren't happy, and I can't blame you for wanting to move out. I can't imagine how I would react if you told me all of this crap."

He stopped pacing and looked at me. "The truth is, I met someone. The attorney who worked on the deal. I'm relieved you said it first."

I wanted to do something dramatic, like scream or punch him or faint, but I couldn't move.

"I'll sleep in the guest bedroom," I said.

A fiery sensation burned my scalp. I couldn't live without Nick, but I couldn't stay with him, either. My mind rationalized Nick's bad behavior, and the way he treated me, was because I deserved it. The sane side of me knew this was not a healthy relationship. It was sick and manipulative and twisted.

The guest room echoed with silence. I scanned my Blackberry for someone to call.

Lily. She'll answer, day or night.

"Hey, Chickie!" Hearing her voice was like sweet relief, if only for a moment. "Damn, girl, did you forget I'm on East Coast time? Lucky for you, I'm awake reading to fight my insomnia. Fun, fun."

"Sorry." I clutched the phone, yearning to be next to her.

"No worries, I'm messing with you," Lily said. "Are you guys coming east this summer? I want to see you and Christian. We can go out on the boat. Hang at the club." The ocean spoke to Lily. It called her name. The unworthiness of her friendship pained me.

Good and Evil.

Tears erupted from my throat.

"What's wrong?" she said.

"I told Nick about everything. That I cheated." My Blackberry was my only safety net. "About Richard, the bad stuff. I'm so scared." And then, the irony of the situation. "To top off my perfect night, Nick told me he fucking *met* someone. He's having an affair with the attorney who did the business purchase deal. Now I know why he didn't invite me to the signing."

"Get the fuck out. What a complete dick!" Lily said. "Bring Christian here and clear your head. I have miles I can give you. Prue, you're going to be all right. Nick isn't the one for you. You haven't been happy for a long time."

"I guess," I said between sniffles. "I married Nick even though I knew it was a mistake. I love him, Lil. I love him." I touched my ear.

"I never liked Nick, and I don't think he's right for you. He brings you down. I want you to be happy. Life is short," Lily said. "You are going to survive. You're a girl who got a little out of control, and if Nick can't see past your behavior and acknowledge the trauma you had as a kid, well, then screw him."

"What's wrong with me?" I asked. My body shivered all over. I sank deeper under the comforter.

"Nothing is wrong with you, Prue. You picked the wrong guy. Stay strong. You've got to fight. You invested a ton of money in the business deal. You can't crumble now. Don't forget who you are. You're a tough girl from Goose Neck Harbor. I'm here for you. Call me anytime, day or night."

"Thanks, Lil."

"I love you, Prue," Lily said. "Try to get some sleep. It's all going to work out."

With all my savings tied up in the business, I assumed Nick would pay for my living expenses, but I was too afraid to ask. My job at the design firm was only part-time, and my income varied. I tried not to count on it for anything more than extra cash.

"Can you help me find furniture for my place?" Nick asked three days before he moved out. "I'm too busy." A fresh aftershave odor lingered as he passed through the kitchen.

"Sure," I said, but I didn't mean it. My stomach turned thinking about Nick and the attorney, Naomi, fucking at his apartment. Nick had created an emotional void from the beginning. Now he was walking away. The pain bore a deep hole in my heart. Lucky for me, I was adept at pretending the agony didn't exist. "Are we going to try to have dinner once a week? I hope this is a trial separation with the goal of getting back together." I stirred the boiling pasta water.

"I don't know, Prue. Don't ask too much of me. I'm being pulled in a million directions. Just get me furniture, please." Nick scooped up his keys.

"Where are you headed?" I asked. He had on his uniform: faded jeans, Gucci loafers, and an untucked button-down shirt with a groovy paisley pattern. I was pretty sure I knew the answer.

"A meeting," he said, then walked out the door.

A text popped up on my phone screen just before I finished making dinner. It was Faye. "Brittany and I are grabbing a drink. Want to join us?"

"Yes! Where?" I texted back.

"Our usual spot. Meet us in an hour."

I slapped Christian's food on a plate and set it on the table. "Christian! Dinner! I'm going to go out to meet Brittany and Faye. I won't be out late." I played with my earlobe as I waited for his answer.

"What time will you be home?" he asked, giving me sad, puppy dog eyes. Pasta sauce smeared his lips as he ate. "I hate being alone." His fork rested in his hand. "I want you to have fun, but can you text me when you're on your way home?"

"Of course. I'll text you when I get there, too." I walked around the table and kissed his head. "Thank you. This has been hard on both of us with Dad moving out." Our dusty-brown mutt, Lou, rested on Christian's feet. "I won't be out later than ten. I'll be home in time to tuck you in. Watch him, Lou."

I weighed my guilt against the anxiousness burning inside me. I had to go out. Outfit ideas ran through my head. "I'm going to go get ready," I said. "Put your dish in the sink when you're finished eating, then you can watch TV."

Am I single? Separated? Does it even matter?

Nick sent an email rather than delivering the grim news to my face. Rent was all on me. I clicked my email shut.

"Motherfucker."

I ground my teeth and started to sweat. Henry would help, but my pride got in the way. Inside me lived a survivalist. I scratched down the names of people who might want to rent a room. I divided my rent by the number of bedrooms and put the word out. Between my income and bringing in renters, I could make it for a little while, at least.

The rooms rented quickly. One room was occupied by two women who used the room on alternating weekends, so I was able to charge more. Not an ideal situation, but I had no choice.

"Christian, I saw pornography in the computer history. I'm very disappointed." I perched my hands on my hips as I stood in his bedroom doorway.

"Mom, I swear on the Bible," he said, setting a fantasy novel face-down on his bed.

"Well, I want you to write a one-page essay about the effects of porn on a teenage boy's mind. There's no one else it could have been." I sat down on his bed. "Christian, those women are mothers, like me. They're desperate for money." I walked out of his room and closed the door.

That night, while I made dinner, the personal trainer who rented a room from me lingered in the kitchen.

"You didn't by any chance use my computer, did you?" I asked.

"Um, yeah. Why?"

"Someone was looking at porn. I assumed it was Christian." I rested the casserole on a hot plate.

"It was me," he said, never taking his eyes from his phone. "Sorry. I didn't think it was a problem. No one was here."

That night, he texted me from his room. "Can I come over and play?"

Chapter Twenty-Seven

Kim's indoctrination into the group was much the same as mine. Within moments of her entering, Mike sent her back to her room to change her clothes. She traipsed out the door, her badge with the hot-pink sticker swinging for everyone to see. I twisted my watch around my wrist. It took every bit of restraint to not ask Mike to help her find something appropriate to wear. After group, I asked her to hang with me at the art studio.

"Sure, I love drawing," Kim said. Her delicate toenails were painted two shades lighter than her hot-pink sticker. "I can't believe Mike thought what I was wearing was inappropriate." She had changed into a maxi-skirt and a cap-sleeved scoop neck top. The outfit covered as much as possible while silhouetting her sensual curves.

"Yeah, it happens sometimes," I said. "Don't worry too much about it." I opened the art room door, allowing Kim to go first so I could examine her every move. She pulled up a stool and rolled a stack of delicate silver rings around her index finger.

"Are you cool with colored pencils?" I asked. "They have markers and crayons, too, but I like the way they blend."

"Perfect." She slid off her flip-flops, chose a cobalt-blue pencil, and examined it. "Reminds me of my childhood." She rubbed it on her palm. "You know, you're sexy. Has anyone ever told you that? I mean, a woman?"

"Yes." Heat rose into my cheeks.

Why am I embarrassed to be seen as sexy?

"Sex oozes from every inch of you, too," I said.

"So I've heard." She shook her head and half-smiled. "I miss running so much. I run ten miles every day. I feel trapped here. Edgy, like a cat in water." She colored circles on her paper.

"I understand. I haven't even been able to use the gym, and insanity is setting in." An anxious feeling engulfed my body. "The high you get when you run. Your body is craving exercise. At least mine is." I wanted to cry.

"That's not the only thing my body is craving," she said, lifting her shoulders to her cheeks in a cute, sexy way I didn't think was possible.

The studio door opened. I couldn't see who it was, but I knew who it was even before he appeared—the vanilla, the pheromones.

"Hey Prue," Alistair said. "Just swinging through to touch up a project. Lovely day today. Not so hot, and a little breeze. Quite tolerable." He stood before our art table, unobtrusive, genuinely interested. "I would love to see the finished piece. Please show me. I admire artistic talent, as I have absolutely none."

"I'd take a mind for numbers over artistic talent any day," I said. "You met Kim, right? She's new in our group."

"Yes, I did." Alistair went to the sink and washed a paintbrush. The change I saw in him since his first day here was dramatic. I saw myself in the way he'd managed to peel off a layer of aristocratic bullshit. A broken child, alone, unloved and desperate to make everyone happy. I no longer saw his shoes, watch, clothes; I saw *him*. A malleable soul. The desperation to change had resided in him for years. He had found his inner child and cared for him with all his heart. He cut through the shallow, superficial, materialistic shell I had built.

Kim poked me. "Hot!" she whispered, then turned to Alistair. "Where are you from?" She ran her fingers through her soft, springy curls.

"London." He juggled a brush, a small paint palate, and his paper to the table. The brush dropped to the floor.

"I got it," Kim said, floating to the paintbrush and picking it up with a straight-legged bend-over.

"Thank you," Alistair said. "Where do you call home?"

"I'm from Palm Beach." She slid a red pencil along the edge of her lips. "I love your accent. Just *be-you-ti-full.*"

The room fell silent while we drew. The air was charged with excitement, nerves, butterflies, and fantasies beyond any I had allowed into my protected chambers—our private story; kissing, touching, breathing each other in. The desire burned in less obvious places: my brain, and my most protected frontier. A branch scraped the window. I forced Nick's image to burn Alistair's out. A reminder to keep my head in reality and focus on my goals.

I scribbled my name underneath my drawing and tacked it to the wall. "*Voila!* My masterpiece."

Alistair admired my work. "May I have it?" He remained still until I granted permission. Then he unhooked my drawing and gathered his things. "I'm going to go too. This has to dry before I can do anything else." He laid his paper over the drying rack while I waited at the door.

"You coming, Kim?" I said.

"I'm going to finish my sketch and visit the bookstore." She spun her pencil like a baton. "Am I missing out on something fun?"

"Unlikely," Alistair said. "Gentle reminder, this is rehab." He punctuated his statement with a laugh to ensure his dry British humor was appropriately received.

"Meet me in the smoking area after the bookstore," I yelled on my way out the door. Once we were outside, I turned to Alistair. "How come you never come to the smoking area?"

"For one, I don't smoke. But to be perfectly honest, you frequent the smoking area, and I'm attempting to get my head on straight. You turn me into complete mush."

"Dammit. None of it is productive to our recovery." I wanted to be repulsed, or broken and belittled, as every man before him had done, even Nick.

Alistair calmly brushed my arm. "Let's head to the bench under the tree and talk," he said. "I'm delighted not to be dragging the bloody block around." He showed no stress or cracks in his desire to make things right.

"I bet," I said, positioning myself a full body length away. Secret eyes observed the rule-breaking whore. Alistair stretched out his athletic legs. He flicked a bug from his trousers. I pushed through, even though my gut screamed for me to dive in. "I'm sorry for putting your program in jeopardy. I'm sorry for kissing you."

The sun shone through the tree to Alistair's dimples. "Thank you," he said. "I enjoyed it." He gazed at me with deep-brown, soulful eyes. "I might have even enjoyed it too much, but you're right. We crossed the line." He scooted a rock along the dirt with his foot. "You are a memorable woman. I've never met anyone like you. Nick is a lucky man." He gazed at the succulent garden. "You have captured a part of my heart I never knew existed." His cheeks turned red and blotchy.

"Alistair, please." I shaded my eyes from the sun. "I have a lot of things to figure out, and we shouldn't even be talking." I wanted to hug him, but a hug would take away from my apology. "I'll always consider you my friend. I'm grateful to know you." I turned and walked down the path alone. A lump filled my throat.

What have I done?

"I hope we talk again someday," he said in his smooth British accent.

"Yes, I hope so. But this is the last time we'll talk while I'm here." I turned around, zipped my lips, and threw away the key.

I strolled past the bookstore, hoping Kim would be there. Through the window, I saw her perusing a stack of prayer beads. I knocked on the glass, and she waved me in.

This time, I opened the door carefully, not wanting another repeat of the shoulder incident. "Hey," I said. "Did you find anything good?"

"I got my two daily reading books, a workbook for group, and books Dr. Livingston told me to buy." She shrugged. "I'm going to do whatever they say. I want to get better."

"That's the right attitude."

We walked to Kim's room, dropped her things off, then headed to the pool to attend the females-only Sex and Love Addicts Anonymous meeting. Gloria and Deirdre were already sitting at the table when we opened the pool gate.

"Hi, girls," Gloria said. She looked like a high school student with damp hair and a freshly washed face.

"Hey." I dropped my bag and pulled up a chair. A guilty feeling dug into my chest and wrapped around my shoulders. I shrugged and turned my head from side to side.

"You okay?" Deirdre asked. She reached over and touched my arm.

"Yeah." I interlocked my hands and rested my elbows on the metal table. "I'm feeling confused and scared about Nick, I guess." I knew I hadn't told the whole truth. "There's also something magnetic between Alistair and me. We just talked, and I told him I couldn't do that anymore. It's messing with my head."

A heavyset, middle-aged counselor swung the pool gate open. A thick, black three-ring binder was nestled in her arms. Her dirty-blonde, frosted hair was loosely pulled up in a good old banana clip. She strolled to the table in an ill-fitting floral dress, too tight in the top, too loose at the bottom.

"My name is Karen," she said. "I'm a sex and love addict." She sat down and rested her weight on the tabletop; the whole table canted awkwardly.

Who on earth would fuck her?

"Hi, Karen." We tried to speak in unison, but it never sounded right with such a small group.

She opened the binder to the first plastic slip-sheeted page. She read aloud the twelve steps of Love Addicts Anonymous: "'This program is for those who suffer from a compulsion to engage in or avoid sex, love, or emotional attachment.'"

These behaviors, a glaring reminded as to why I checked myself in this place.

"Today, we are going to focus on boundaries. I will read from the sex addict meditation book, then open the meeting for discussion."

When she was finished reading, I jumped in. "Prue, sex addict." Everyone leaned in. "When Karen read the behaviors experienced by SLAA members, it spoke to me. I'm afraid I'm not getting better." I tugged my ear, and it filled with heat.

"Remember," Karen said, "progress, not perfection." The other girls nodded. Perhaps no one felt like they were getting better.

"I still have unhealthy boundaries with Nick. I can't tell if I want him, or if I'm afraid to be alone. Stepping back from Nick has shown me how abusive our relationship has been. Why would I want to go back to the abuse?" I directed my question to the group, hoping they'd have the answers, but knowing it was my problem to solve. "Thank you for letting me share."

Gloria swung at a bug buzzing around her makeup-free face.

Kim cleared her throat and sat upright. "My name is Kim, I'm a sex addict." Bronze lip gloss sparkled on her kissable lips. "Thank you for sharing, Prue. It makes me sad to picture you in a destructive relationship, especially with someone who doesn't appreciate your inner beauty." She paused, as if struggling for the words. "If you go back to Nick for the wrong reasons, you might end up where you were before."

My stomach heaved. I wanted to run from myself. Panic screamed in my head. I forced myself to stay and not give in to my old behavior.

Deirdre was next. Her hair fascinated me it was the straightest hair I had ever seen. I wanted to run my hands through it. She tucked one side of the straight edge behind her ear. "If your gut is telling you something," she told me, "then you should listen to it. Maybe getting back with Nick isn't the best choice for you." She looked around the table. "I guess that's all I have to say."

"Thank you, Deirdre," Karen said. "Anyone have something to share about boundaries, unhealthy or otherwise?"

No one spoke. We knew it was futile. Karen wanted us to follow her agenda, but we needed counseling in the form of female comradery: good old-fashioned girl talk.

CHAPTER TWENTY-EIGHT

Without Nick's help, making rent proved impossible. No job also meant no money for a divorce lawyer. After a short job hunt, a showroom at the design center hired me part-time. The separation agreement allotted a child visitation every other weekend, which diminished over time due to Nick being too busy to see his son. The bills piled in equal amounts to my stress. Credit card statements listing expensive dinners and swanky hotels arrived in the mail. My obsession with Naomi counterbalanced the desperation for Nick's attention and curiosity about them as a couple.

What does she do in bed?

The logical distraction was juggling a multitude of men on my Blackberry to mend my broken ego. Determined to strike a balance between motherhood and dating any guy who asked, I failed at both.

During my first week on the job at the Janus et Cie showroom, I was approached by a big-boned man with a receding hairline and soft features. His name was Roger.

"Any chance you can provide input?" he asked, scanning my chest. "In the hunt for pool furniture, that is."

He asked me out. Free food provided a welcomed respite from my hellacious life. Melt-in-your-mouth chicken piccata eased the nail-scraping annoyance of his booming voice and the unsightliness of his over-bleached, baggy jeans that only added to his bulky frame. He was a borderline fatty with cartoonish features and dark-gray hair.

Roger escorted me out of the restaurant so I could admire his fire-engine red Ferrari. "Go ahead, take it for a spin," he said, handing me the keys. I climbed in, and he sat in the passenger's seat. The tiny racing seat caused the oversized girl a struggle, and my knee smacked against the steering wheel. "I'm calling you Little P," he said, laughing. My foot punched the gas. "Little P drives like a *man!*"

"A compliment." The Goose Neck Harbor conservative in me hated flashy cars, but I acted impressed.

"Want to get together on Saturday?" Roger asked as I unfurled myself from the vehicle. He wound around and kissed my face like a best friend. I agreed.

On Saturday, he arrived in a matte-black Mercedes G-Wagon. "I'm taking you to a fancy restaurant in Beverly Hills," he declared.

Compared to him, I resemble a hillbilly.

Once settled into the car, I waited for the obligatory compliment. "We're going to Mastros," he said instead. "Ever been?"

An inner voice berated me for expecting the compliment that never came. The lobster dinner helped, until Roger belted out how I lacked the beauty he found attractive. "A certain tilt of the hips, back arch, and tiny waist is what I need to get turned on."

Daggers flew from my eyes as I sipped the Kistler chardonnay. He slathered a roll with butter.

"My rule is, I only kiss women I'm dating. And we aren't dating."

"So, we are friends," I said, gripping a napkin between my hands.

"Let's not define this relationship. You are a cool girl, and I need a playmate."

After dinner, the heavy G-Wagon door sealed us in supple leather and window tinting. Roger patted his crotch. "Been a stressful day. I could use some relief."

A sense of obligation plagued my wine-fogged mind. The zipper toggle moved. He shimmied down his pants, exposing a totem pole. My head whacked the steering wheel as my mind wandered to a different place.

"Awesome," he said, hiking up his pants. "Now the fun begins. I'm heading to meet my brother at a strip club."

I guess I'm along for this sick ride.

"Does your brother hire the strippers for . . . you know . . . stuff?" The words tumbled out, and I sank with regret.

"Everyone pays, whether it be directly or indirectly. Everyone pays."

The truth.

A dozen blowjobs later, I revealed the gravity of my financial issues. We sipped wine and admired the city lights from his patio. "My ex-husband stopped support, and I'm freaking out. I sublet every available room in my house and still can't cover my bills."

Open body language; not disinterested.

"He sent me a brutal email," I said. "He told me he's going to stop support, then said he was sure I'd be able to figure it out."

"What an asshole. Doesn't the idiot know you shouldn't move kids during a separation? How about I cover your rent and in turn, you can be my travel buddy?"

I squealed with delight.

He disappeared inside, returning with an envelope. "Never leave a paper trail."

Roger led a double life, like me. The presentable side: a father, businessman, and socialite. The other side included hookers, strippers, and me.

"We'll need to coordinate our child visitation schedules so we can go away together," he said.

To get Nick to cooperate. Futile.

"It's time for me to baptize myself in the Hawaiian waters, and you are joining me," Roger said.

With my money woes behind me, I feigned excitement and panicked internally about squeezing my sausage butt into a bikini. My heart convinced my head Roger would fall in love with me.

The two-story suite at the Royal Hawaiian overlooked the ocean. "Use the downstairs powder room," he said, "and I'll take the upstairs."

Where will I sleep? Will we screw?

Roger beckoned for me as I was unpacking my clothes. "Little P, can you come up here, please?"

The journey up the winding stairs allowed time for my obsessive thoughts to jangle my nerves. Dark, hairy legs stretched out on the coverlet, the curtains drawn. Roger's hand was splayed over his crotch. The bright floral fabric distracted me as I unzipped his cargo shorts. A mound of hair emerged like Poppin' Fresh Dough. My gag reflex calmed, knowing his jade stalk would never reach my tonsils. By the time I counted to a hundred, he had released.

"Let's grab a sunset cocktail and a pu-pu platter." He zipped up his shorts.

Adept at shoving things under the rug.

The sun burst over the sea in vibrant orange hues. The air reminded me of Goose Neck and walks with Mom around the church pond. One Mai Tai later, the sadness diminished. The complementary flower tucked behind my ear also helped. An eager couple next to us said hello. I smiled, a colorful beverage strapped to my lips.

"Are you on your honeymoon?" the woman asked. "Because we are."

The couple looked melted together, no longer individuals but one human. Their rings sparkled. No pits and scratches from years of sacrifice and compromise. Part of me wanted to crush their spirit with words of warning posed as wisdom. The bartender passed by and I motioned for a freshie, hoping to avoid a response.

Roger guffawed and laughed with grandiose gestures. "Nope, just friends," he said, emphasizing the word *friends* just a little too much. Rather than interact with the blow-job king, I engaged in a barrage of questions to the bride about her wedding, begging her to spare no details.

Roger let me restyle him when he carted me to New York. Barney's was first. Parked in the dressing room, I critiqued while he modeled outfits. Several hours and a few thousand dollars later, we made a move to Bergdorf Goodman.

"I'm going to buy you a present." Roger strolled to the Gucci counter and picked out a handbag. "This is for you," he said, handing the package to me. "Ask the salesgirl if she will join us for dinner."

Am I his hooker, assistant, or pimp?

Against my better judgment, I asked. The clerk displayed an expression of horror and disgust before declining. I felt a small amount of tickling pleasure when I reported her decline to his tantalizing offer.

"It's her loss," he said, ushering me out of the store.

We enjoyed a nightcap at the Four Seasons so I could hear more epic stories about how Mr. Got-Rocks made his millions. "Let's head up to our room," he finally said. The lummox prepared for bed while I admired the massive Central Park rectangle flanked by luxury apartment buildings.

Who lives on Fifth Avenue? How do they earn their money?

"What a view."

Ripped from my dreams, Roger guided me to bed. We slipped into the smooth cotton sheets, and he backed his hairy ass into me. "Spoon me, Little P. I'm the needy one, not you."

Christian attended an all-expenses paid sleepaway camp so I could accompany Roger to London. Liquid blisters bulged on both heels as he ushered me through the airport in stiletto-heeled boots, a gift from him. I struggled to squeeze my bag between two poles near the escalator. He stood on the landing and laughed.

"Motherfucker," I said under my breath.

We checked into the Ritz-Carlton, which exuded elegance. Even so, my excitement bordered on zero.

"Wear something sexy," he said. "I'm taking you to a unique place."

Our driver delivered us to an unmarked building on a London side street. "Here we are," Roger said.

A heavy door opened to a long hallway, where a man greeted us. Wood paneling and green paisley wallpaper gave the place a masculine edge. Stunning women in colorful gowns milled around.

Am I supposed to participate, or watch?

A bosomy blonde from the Czech Republic lurked nearby.

Now I know what he meant when he said he needed a certain tilt of the hips.

My evening bag refused to clasp with Roger's bulky cell phone shoved inside. "Handle this," he commanded, wild-eyed from over stimulation.

The blonde joined us in our suite for a drink. Captain Dapper entertained her with his worldly stories. I tucked myself into bed and fell asleep.

"Did she sleep over?" I asked.

"No. She's joining us for breakfast, and then we're going to Harrods."

My master ran a tight schedule and claimed the bathroom first. No time to shower, I slathered deodorant under my arms and threw on a navy Ralph Lauren frock.

"Damn, she got me hot!" he shouted from the shower.

"Tell me more," I said, cramming gold hoops in my ears. A total disaster, I whipped my hair up in a messy ponytail.

He came out of the bathroom with a towel wrapped snugly around his waist, fat billowing over, and gave me a once-over. "Awesome, you're ready," he said. "Did I buy that for you? Fits well."

At long last, a compliment.

Three downed mimosas later, our breakfast guest arrived. Once she slid into the booth, I studied her face. Broad daylight told a different story: a case of chickenpox had left a smattering of pits in varying sizes around her face; the forehead, quite larger than I remembered; stringy hair.

Roger entertained, and I analyzed her every move, wondering about her life. She manipulated with the finesse of a stealth fighter. The Czech prostitute ran around the store, convincing Roger to buy everything, from clothes to shoes to handbags. We exited Harrods, me carrying a mini shopping bag containing a Lancôme lip gloss, she juggling six massive shopping bags and a promise to reconnect with us later.

The genius took the booty and hightailed it with no intention of ever returning.

"I'm impressed!" I texted her later, hammering out my message with angry fingers. "A real pro. You scored a shitload of gifts and took off."

Her return text made me laugh. "I'll leave the gifts at the front desk."

I'll be waiting a lifetime for that.

Roger feigned indifference about being dumped and continued his cocky show, dragging me to dinner at another fancy restaurant. We hit the bar while we waited for a table and he ordered us two dirty martinis.

A well-dressed gentleman sidled up to the bar to my left, and I got my flirt on. Unsolicited, Roger made his grand statement about us being friends. During dinner, the waiter delivered champagne.

"Excuse me, madam," the waiter said, "this is from the gentleman over there." His arm swept toward a table of men. "He would like to take you to out on the town tomorrow night."

"No," Roger said. "Going out with other men is not allowed. You are here with me and will stay with me."

Defeated, he grew tired of London and flew us to Italy. "The best brothel is in Milan," he said. "You're going to love it."

A gentleman working the unmarked door ushered us in. The maître d', decked in a tuxedo, greeted us like royalty. "Ciao, ciao! Who might be this lovely lady be?"

"Little P," Roger said with disdain.

I felt confident in my micro mini silver-sequined number and sky-high heels. A rare but welcomed sensation. Scarlet velvet walls warmed the bustling bar. Elegant ladies mingled with "johns" in jewel-toned gowns. Masculine leather banquettes surrounded a small dance floor. Every corner dripped with women—chiseled, adorned, and tousled to perfection. A few girls flashed icy glares, but I avoided them in favor of watching a fabulous redhead take center stage and straddle a bistro chair. The way she taunted the prop, I believed her life depended on winning the hearts and wallets of every man in the room. Roger perused the ladies and took a seat at a banquette to order the mandatory champagne and caviar. I lingered near the bar and let my date enjoy a moment with his new trophy.

Never seen such thin women eat with such abandon.

I struck up a conversation with a sculpted beauty in a glistening, yellow bias-cut evening gown. The neckline plunge revealed most of her breasts, her nipples concealed by a thin layer of satin. With her every move, my eyes performed constant nipple-monitoring.

"How you know him?" she asked. Her accent was distinctly Eastern Bloc.

"Roger? We're only friends."

They all know him. Now I know the reason for all the icy glares.

"We know each other from home," I added, wondering if she bought what I was selling.

"I am Katarina," she said. "We all know him long time." Her glossed cherry-red lips left no stain on the rim of her glass. "Your friend saw Claudia for many years." She pointed to a corner table packed with beauties. "The one with short hair. She cut hair when Mister Roger didn't want her anymore."

"What do you mean? Didn't want her?"

"He always pick her when he visits Milano, give her money for her flat. One day, he chooses someone else, stop paying and never say why." A martini olive was pinched between her teeth. She sucked it into her mouth. "Advice for you, take what you can because you don't know when the river runs out."

After I extended a smile toward Claudia, whom I considered my equal, I dipped over to the banquet. A petite woman with platinum hair, a color not found in nature, partook of Roger's generosity. Her delicate finger scooped up caviar while he reached between her legs.

"This is Vania," he said. "She will be coming home with us."

Back at the Four Seasons, I failed to lock the bathroom, and Vania slinked in and turned the lock.

"You see, men are not my preference," she said. "I am here for you."

"Well, we're all here for that guy." I pointed toward the bedroom. "A bad idea to make him mad."

"Why don't we make him happy?" Vania nuzzled me.

Buddha Bar house music blasted from the sound system. We swayed, and in one motion she peeled off my sequined number. The two of us danced, caressed, and licked while the creeper leered from a corner chair.

The lion grows impatient, yearning to pounce.

"Join me," he said, patting the bed with a fiery stare.

Vania laid down, her legs spread. With tentative motions, I removed her panties. She writhed and arched. His hairy hand reached for her creamy breast, and she recoiled. After a momentary sulk, he returned to his penis.

When daylight streamed in through the windows, I escorted my nymph to the lobby.

"Give me your number, Little P," Vania said, pushing her phone into my hand.

"Sure."

I want to lose that godforsaken nickname.

The bellman hailed her a cab. The car drove away, and she turned and blew me a kiss. My head throbbed, and nausea surged in waves. The asshole mocked me with dramatic reenactments of the previous evening's activities.

"Get out," I said.

An hour later, he returned with a Chanel handbag. "Sorry," he said. "You and Vania put on a wild show."

The next trip landed us in Mexico; a five-star resort where the employees touched their hearts and bowed to every passerby. Flowers in the shape of a heart adorned the bed in the evening, which I swept to the floor. With blank eyes, Roger gazed through my body as I showered in the exotic open bathroom. The voices in my head told the truth: I was nothing more than a filthy slut.

A month later, we attended a wine auction in Aspen with Roger's brother and his guest, Susie. At her encouragement, we went on a pee-break together. She confessed to me her situation and told me she was on the dole.

"Ditto," I said with relief. We swapped lipsticks and compliments. Susie carried street sense, and I displayed more wrinkles. The outer armor signified a traumatic life.

Roger treated Susie like an ugly stray dog, which pissed me off. The only explanation I could think of was he wanted her and got rejected. Or maybe he was jealous his brother had snatched her up first. A redheaded wine snob, freckled from head to toe with almost no chin, tagged along at Roger's elbow, his wife left back home.

What kind of woman would marry him?

One afternoon, the asshole, the redhead, and I went for a gondola ride. Susie and Roger's brother rode behind us. I appreciated the mountain view through the scratched glass, pretending to be anywhere but there.

"Suck my dick," the redheaded guy said to me with beady eyes.

The color drained from my face. "Excuse me?"

"What the fuck?" Roger said, feigning shock. "She's going to suck you off right here in front of me? Why are you such an idiot?"

I can't spend time with this prick anymore.

Chapter Twenty-Nine

I had built up Family Week in my head since Nick confirmed he was attending with Christian. Today marked the first day of this dreaded week, and I was riddled with anxiety and nerves. Mike said to take the worst-case scenario and work backward from there: what was the worst that could happen? Nick might tell me off; Christian would figure out I was a bad mother. I took a deep breath.

It will all turn out as it should.

The shower healed. I lingered longer than usual. My pelvis ached with desire, but I had no handheld to place between my legs. My reflection gazed back at me. I willed myself not to criticize. My inner child rested on my shoulder.

Treat her with compassion.

White Chuck Taylors laced, ready as I would ever be. From the farthest corner table, my baby leaped up and ran toward me.

He loves me.

"Did you grow taller?" I asked, inching next to him.

"I miss you," Christian said. "My life sucks when you're gone." Boyish eyes searched for answers; answers I couldn't find for myself.

"I'll be home before you know it." After sniffing his hair, I smoothed a cowlick.

Nick stood with sad eyes and a half-smile. A golden tan couldn't camouflage the dark circles parked below each eye.

"Hi," I said with open arms. He gave me a cold, stiff pat on the back.

Today will be rough. He's hurting too.

"We are both not happy," Nick said. "There is homework."

"Sorry."

He hides feelings with sarcasm.

The lights dimmed and brightened.

"Welcome everyone," someone said over the racket. "This is an important week for our residents, and your presence shows you are supporting the changes your family members are making in their lives. We'll reconvene in the auditorium in ten minutes."

"Do you want something? Tea, water, lemonade?" Hopeless thoughts ran through my mind.

"Lemonade, please," Christian said. My little nugget wore an old t-shirt with a permanent stain from a dripping chocolate ice cream cone, placed in the back of his drawer for a reason.

"No, thanks," Nick said, his erect posture seemingly intended to intimidate the strongest of humans.

Christian followed me to the drink table. "Can you take lemonade anytime you want?" he asked, wiggling with a sour-taste shudder.

"Yes, lemonade all day, every day," I said.

Kim came up beside us and pulled a glass from the rack. "This is my son," I said. "And over there is Nick."

"Your mom talks about you all the time," Kim said, then turned to me. "I saw your hubby in the corner." She wanted to say more but refrained from doing so in front of Christian. "Talk later."

⚮

It wasn't easy scoring three seats in a row in the main auditorium, but we managed. Just as we sat, Rhoda waved me over. "Be right back," I said. "Got to say hello to a friend."

"This," Rhoda said, introducing me to her husband with bold hand motions, "is Prudence."

Her husband, a burly man with a doughy face and a pea-green polyester polo, smiled at me. "Thank you for being kind to Rhoda," he said.

"My pleasure."

Rhoda's nose crinkled when she smiled, but her face fell when she gestured to where Gloria sat, alone. My heart ached, and I walked over to her.

"No one showed up," Gloria said, a stoic expression countering her wilted posture.

"You are loved by me and so many others," I told her. "Sorry, I'm sad for you. Let's talk later."

What could I say to make her feel better? I was torn between my own problems and concern for Gloria, frustrated by my lack of solutions. The group leader moved to the podium, and I scurried to my seat.

"My name is Samantha Whitlock, and I have been sober for twelve years. My expertise is codependence and alcoholism. Please introduce yourself, then choose three words from the chart on the wall to best describe your emotions." She motioned to the chart, then pointed directly at Nick. "Let's start with you."

Someplace deep inside, I snapped, brittle as an icicle. My earlobes swelled and heated, and I clutched my hands together.

Nick cleared a frog from his throat. "My name is Nick," he said. Then, looking at the chart, he said, "Love . . . for my son. Joy . . . to spend time with him. And fear . . . over what I will find out about my wife in the next few days."

Something happened then. My body twitched, and all I could think about was running away. I stood and bolted from the auditorium, straight to the lobby. There was a huge planter with a scrappy palm in the corner of the room. I ducked behind it and hid.

"What's going on?" someone said. It was Mike. I looked up to see him standing beside me, seemingly not surprised to find me there.

My words came out in heaving sobs. "Nick said he . . . he . . . he's happy to be here with my s-son . . . and *nothing* about me."

Mike's boxer hands pulled me gently to my feet. "Go back in with a loving heart," he said. "Do not allow him to affect your self-esteem."

The pep talk from my cheerleader.

"Heaps of regret crashed down on me," I said. "Not getting a scrap of encouragement caused a panic attack." Weak, I pushed a palm frond to the side. The humor of my location struck me, and I started laughing so hard I got the hiccups.

"Keep your sense of humor in times like these," Mike said, his blue-gray eyes twinkling. "Now, when you're ready, walk back into the room."

No words came. I cupped my palms in prayer and bowed.

"The release of emotion is a sign you're moving toward recovery." My hero paused before exiting. "I'll be in my office if you need me." The bright sunshine blinded my eyes as he walked through the heavenly gates.

I took a deep breath and strolled back in the direction of the auditorium.

"Welcome back," Samantha said. "Please introduce yourself."

"I'm Prudence, sex addict." I gazed at the chart of words on the wall, not really needing them—I had memorized them from day one. "Love, for my husband and my son. That's all I have."

I take the high road.

The main session ended, and we split into small groups. Mrs. Yamamoto greeted us, an apron cinched around her small waist. Her head nodded as everyone chose their seats. Anxious expressions riddled the face of every patient. Five recovering addicts, and twice as many visitors.

"A sheet of paper is being distributed, which describes the different forms of child abuse," Mrs. Yamamoto said. "After we review the document, I will allow fifteen minutes for you to sketch a scene from your childhood, where you feel you may have experienced abuse in some form. For example, when I misbehaved as a child, my father made me stand facing the wall for hours on end. I might draw a scene showing myself standing against the wall. Any questions?"

Nick jotted down notes in his half-uppercase, half-lowercase chicken scrawl. After one of his community college professors had diagnosed him with dyslexia, he'd advised Nick to write things down to help him better process what was being said. "An academic star in the making," Nick said in a mocking, self-deprecating voice.

"Excellent, Dad."

I rubbed my ear nervously.

"This is not an art competition," Mrs. Yamamoto said. "Don't concern yourself with what your neighbor is sketching. This is your story, and no one else's. You may begin."

We retrieved our paper and crayons from under our seats. The color brown called out to me. My stomach churned with sickness.

I'm ready to put Richard behind me, close the door, and lock the key.

I sketched furiously. The fifteen minutes passed in what felt like seconds.

"Please put your crayons down and give your attention to me," Mrs. Yamamoto said, breaking the concentration of the amateur artists. This petite, soft-spoken woman presented herself with such power.

Mental note to work on the tone of my voice.

"Let's start to my right and go clockwise to learn about everyone's story."

A box of Kleenex moved its way across the chairs. None for me. My horrific past had walled up those emotions long ago.

Nick's vulnerable side, the one I yearned for, peeked out from beneath the disguise he wore for the world. He held the crumpled paper in his hand. "I was about ten," Nick said, head bowed, looking down at his crude drawing and speaking in an almost childlike tone. "I found out my girlfriend made out with someone, and I ran home to tell my mother. Friends were gathered on our patio, having martinis. My mother glared at me and told me to stop crying." His jaw pulsed. "I told her what happened, and she burst out laughing and encouraged her friends to laugh, too." A red flush flowed up his neck. "Don't be such a baby. Go play with your friends."

He associates emotions with ridicule.

Mrs. Yamamoto strolled across the room. "Most everyone experiences trauma in some form. The lesson here is to accept what happened, learn, and go forward with your life." People walked past the classroom window.

Life continues.

"One can't close the door on the past," she said, "but we can accept it."

Christian held up his paper. "This is me, holding a report card," he said. "My parents are screaming at me."

Self-flogging won't work anymore. Got to dig in, acknowledge the mistakes, and vow to do better.

The same scene replayed in my mind, my mother yelling at me over my grades. My cherub crinkled his nose; freckles dotted the bridge. The stubborn cowlick stood on end.

"I am sorry," I said.

∞

My golden ticket came by way of an off-site pass issued by my shaman. Starchy cravings called for Italian. Classic red-checkered tablecloths gave the place a cheery atmosphere. The server draped a sheet of paper over the tabletop and set out a box of crayons.

"A little too much of that today," Christian said dryly. His sense of humor was the only trait he pulled from his father. "Want to play hangman?" He prepped the game while I perused the menu, savoring the tingly high before gorging myself to fill the void.

When the food came, I slathered crusty bread with butter and shoved it into my mouth. Greasy goodness shot pleasure signals through my body. The restaurant door opened, and Ryan and his parents strolled in. The three of them looked like movie stars. Ryan tipped his head; his mother shot me an icy glare.

No matter how hard I tried, I could never appear as pulled together as Ryan's mother in her snazzy slacks, crisp top, and smart navy blazer. A Hermes scarf was tied to the handle of her coveted Birkin bag. Rumor had it, one couldn't walk into Hermes and purchase a Birkin; one had to know someone and prove their commitment to the Hermes lifestyle.

The parmesan-coated pasta twirled around my fork, I stabbed a few tomatoes on the way. Salty, tangy, cheesy pasta never disappointed.

No wonder they don't serve grease and gluten in treatment centers. Far too pleasurable.

My foot tapped to the seventies beat piping through the air, all senses on overload.

"How's the food been there so far?" Nick asked between veal parmesan bites. We had fought many times over the years about my disdain for eating baby lambs raised in a box. The crease above his eye deepened when he smiled—a battle scar from his epic teens. He nursed a Chianti; I longed for a sip, but liquor breath upon my return, I deduced, might not be well received.

"Not bad," I said. "I keep my eating to the minimum since I still can't use the gym." I felt a sense of immediate regret upon exposing my weaknesses.

Did I show all my cards? Men don't notice a woman's flaws when they're naked.

"Cheers," he said. "Stressful day."

My body drained with the effort it took not to say "I'm sorry" yet again. Nick's lips were flecked with burgundy stains, a haunting reminder of the bad times.

"Hangman!" Christian slapped his crayon on the paper. "Can you come back to the hotel with us for a little while?"

The agony of not knowing when he would see me again was setting in. I glanced at Nick and caught a glimpse of his vulnerable smile. This was all the encouragement I needed to say yes to a visit to the hotel.

"My curfew is at nine," I said.

We piled into the rental car and drove to the hotel as I warded off a panic attack. Once in the hotel suite, I felt a stranger. We settled onto the couch, and Nick flicked on the television. His veiny hand rested on my thigh. I wedged my palm underneath his, scraping weightlifting callouses along the way.

Buff Nick works out for Naomi, not me.

I feigned relaxation and lay my head on his broad shoulder. His t-shirt smelled different.

Must be her detergent of choice.

"Let's prepare the bed," I said, shifting the boys to the perimeter and disassembling the pullout sofa bed. Once the bed was made, Nick and I sandwiched Christian. When Christian was asleep, Nick tapped my shoulder and winked.

I followed him to the bedroom, and he locked the door. Self-conscious negativity strained my mind. Nick stared as I unhitched my plain-Jane bra, my nipples erect and vulnerable. Familiar sensations crawled over my skin. All but his touch; it had changed. My body reached for an orgasm but could not let go.

Nick thrived on sexual intimacy the way a plant needed water. I was riddled with paranoid delusions my extended absence had driven him to cheat. I succumbed to the understanding he had fucked Naomi the day before.

Serenity Hills lingo ran on reel-to-reel: focus on the present, live in the moment. We lay entangled afterward for as long as I could stand it. I was anxious to return to my sanctuary. A blackness engulfed me, the same blackness that had come over me when I had cheated on Nick.

I closed my eyes . . . *Alistair.*

"We better get going, I can't be late for curfew."

The convict goes back to jail.

Silence filled the car. Christian nodded off.

"Catch you tomorrow for some more barrels of laughs," Nick said, pulling to the curb in front of the main entrance.

Christian woke up the moment I made a move. "I'll walk you in," he said. Our hands glued together up to the entrance.

"Night, Momma."

"Goodnight, my love."

He turned and waved as they pulled away.

"Hope you enjoyed your evening," Nurse Ratched said in a pleasant tone, her infamous clipboard snapped in position.

I turned and faced the words on the wall, all of them memorized, yet still, I pondered them. "Guilt, shame, and pain."

Guilt for eating bread and pasta. Oh, and for fucking.

"Anything else?"

"Love and joy."

"Wonderful to hear." She smiled.

Like a robot, I performed my nightly routine: floss, wash face, analyze blubber rolls, put on pajamas, and pray.

Lord, I don't deserve this child, but I am grateful and will do my best to be a better mother. Amen.

Piles of homework loomed, yet my body ached for sleep. Every lesson returned to the same thing: healthy boundaries. No one made a person feel a certain way. My boundary-less life with a walled up, estranged husband. I laughed. How the hell did such different people end up together? I closed my workbook. A warmth gushed in my panties. Short on underwear, I blotted it with toilet paper and checked my skin in the poorly lit bathroom mirror. My eyebrows needed plucking. No tweezers.

Fiddledeedee! A new day begins tomorrow.

∞

We connected early so we could eat breakfast together. The bags under Nick's eyes had doubled overnight.

"Hi," I said, and immediately set about rearranging Christian's hair.

Nick scowled his not-a-morning-person greeting. The eggshell walk grew old.

His exhaustion or bad mood is not my problem.

"I ended up sleeping with Dad," Christian said. His darling face drove away my negative thoughts.

"An old-fashioned slumber party," Nick said with an eye roll. The ultimate form of degrading another human.

"You must be starving," I said, ushering them along, avoiding eye contact with the assistant chef who always gave me twangs between the legs. I rubbernecked around the room as we ate—the telltale sign of my obsession with other people's lives—and caught sight of two backlit figures standing by the door. One was tall, the other short and petite.

"Hey, Uncle Henry!" Christian called. He bolted to the door, and I abandoned my tray. Next to Henry stood my ray of sunshine.

"Chickie!" Lily said, beaming. "You didn't think I could miss Family Week, did you?" Her teensy arms wrapped around me.

My eyes welled with tears. A part of me still believed I didn't deserve goodness in my life. "You came all this way for me?"

"You're family," she said, and it was all I needed to hear.

I threw my arms around her again and reeled Henry in. After breakfast, we headed to a small meeting room where handouts had been set atop every chair.

Samantha moved to the podium as the last few stragglers took their seats. "Hello again, and welcome. For those of you who weren't here yesterday, my name is Samantha, and I am a recovered alcoholic. This morning, I'll be guiding you through a portion of the Family Week activities."

She motioned to the chart of words on the wall. "For those of you who are new, as a part of the healing process here at Serenity Hills, we routinely refer to the words on this chart to describe our feelings, which in turn helps us to better understand ourselves. For this exercise, I'm going to ask you each to choose up to three words from the chart that best describe how you feel. As we go around the room, please state your name and tell us what words best describe your current mood."

Butterflies scrimmaged in my stomach with visions of Nick and Lily duking it out, resembling the pressure cooker Gram had used for her famous pot roast.

Samantha waved her hand to Henry, who sat at the end of the row.

"I'm Henry, here for my sister, Prue." He stared at the chart. "Love and fear," he said, and his voice cracked when he said the word "fear." The unworthy lump in my throat grew.

"My name is Lily, and I am here for my best friend, Prue. Love and pain." Lily was draped in conservative clothes for this adventure: moss-green trousers cropped above her ladylike ankles; an airy blouse in a soft floral pattern, outlining her shoulders; around her neck, a string of pearls, a gift from her father for her sixteenth birthday.

When everyone had finished introducing themselves, all eyes turned back to Samantha. "Please fill out the questionnaire resting on your chair," she said. Her presence radiated a combination of femininity and power. "There are extra pens should anyone need one."

Nick raised his hand, and Lily sighed, "Loser."

When the pens stopped moving, Samantha once again commanded our attention. "Who responded 'yes' to eight or more questions?"

A few people lifted their hands, including the man I'd married.

"Every single question," Nick said.

"This test measures how well we express and handle conflict," Samantha said. "Anger is important, and when expressed in an appropriate way, it can be quite positive." She hung on her words, and the rest of us did too. "Misdirected rage can be dangerous."

One gentleman spoke up. "What should I do about my temper? I want to fix the problem."

"Consider attending a temper management program. There are information pamphlets on the table you can take afterward."

Nick clenched his jaw. I hated the thought of him being uncomfortable.

"The next lesson outlines the characters we played as children." Samantha drew a list of phrases on the whiteboard: *Class Clown, Peacekeeper, Scapegoat.* "My childhood role was the troublemaker," she said. "I figured negative attention must be better than no attention."

A dagger twisted between my scapulas.

Disgusting Richard, my absent mother, and a sick, drug-addicted father.

"Please circle a phrase that best describes your family role. Feel free to come up with your own."

"Which one am I?" Christian asked, licking his chapped lips.

I passed my water bottle in his direction. "Peacekeeper," I said.

I thought about my own family role: I ran the house; I didn't want to upset my mother.

Caretaker.

"I was definitely the troublemaker," Nick said, pantomiming a gun to his head. I laughed out loud.

I looked at Henry. The words he'd written were scrawled in ominous black ink: *The Lost Child.*

I had no words.

Samantha moved around the room. "Do any of you see similarities with your childhood roles and how you deal with your adult relationships? Personal growth happens when we let go of the roles."

Panic pounded through my chest when I thought about how I'd monitored Nick's alcohol consumption.

Dammit. Still the caretaker.

∽

The electric clock buzzed in the otherwise silent, hot, stuffy room. Terror filled me at the thought I'd failed in my vow to be different from my mother. Doubt flooded in. My son's boyish hands trembled, and I squashed the urge to tug my ear.

"This is Christian's time to talk," Mike said. "Do not comment or react. The child of an addict must speak without judgment."

My shaman gives instructions with an open heart.

"Please don't yell at me," Christian said. "Try not freak when the house is messy." He referred to his notes. "Please don't leave me alone all night."

How could I leave him and come home at five in the morning?

"I want to spend more time with you, doing something I want to do. Or even nothing. But not always the stuff you want to do." He cracked a smile.

I kept my hands folded on my lap, willing them to be still.

"Try to understand me, and not the image you want me to be," he said. "I need a mom, not a friend."

I am the worst mother in the world.

"Now is your opportunity to respond," Mike said to me. "Please refrain from judgment or justifying."

I wiped my damp fingers on my shirt. "I'm sorry," I said. "What you said is true."

My actions are the test.

∽

Nick laid on the plot of grass where my indiscretion with Alistair had occurred.

It's unfair for me to compare the two, but inevitable.

The tally checks: pros and cons.

Dark aviators blocked his eyes, hands propped under his head. It was admirable the way he could appear so laid back while a storm raged inside.

My body blocked the sun from beating on his face. "Any idea where Lil and Henry might be?"

"Couldn't take the heat," he said, supine and unmoving. "They're sitting in the restaurant." He turned to Christian. "Why don't you go get some ice cream, buddy."

"Okay," Christian said. "I'll go find Uncle Henry."

Nick's demeanor exuded aristocratic elegance. Worn flip-flops graced his bony toes, and a small tattoo peeked out from the edge of his sleeve. There were moments when he was the most handsome man and other times when he was downright ugly.

Is his attractiveness based on my mood, or his?

"How'd everything go?" He sat up, leaving a mold of his body in the grass.

"I'm taking everything he said to heart," I said. Judgment and cynicism slathered his face at my words. "Sorry, I want to do better, to be a better person." A wall of words calmed my nerves.

He crossed his legs. The sun beat against my back, and I dropped to the grass, desperate for a cold air pocket near the ground.

"I love you, but I'm not *in* love with you," Nick said. "It's hard to picture how we can go on from here."

Bright sunlight illuminated him. Small pits scattered his incisors. Oil and sweat moved his glasses down the bridge of his nose. Negative visuals of Richard's greasy nose crept into my mind. My heart pounded like a stampede of horses.

"We need to work hard and communicate better," I said. "Let go of the past and try to move forward. It won't be easy, but our love will strengthen us." I wanted to believe every word.

He appeared unconvinced. "The situation with Naomi is real, and I want to continue the relationship. At the same time, I'm not ready to end things with you."

I'm too quick to comment. Think before you open my mouth.

I unfurled from the grass and reached out a hand. An ominous cloud blocked the sun, casting shadows over Nick's face. "Sorry I hurt you," I said, fighting off emotion.

Keep my head in reality and leave my favorite place, fantasy, behind.

Christian came back, ice cream in hand. Lily and Henry followed. Their arrival was a blessing. It prevented us from getting into a real knock-down, drag-out fight right there on the quad.

"Hi, Dad." Christian scooped ice cream into his mouth. "What's next?" Our fearless commander came in a small package.

"We have a grownups-only meeting," I said. Poison riddled my insides. "Can you wait inside with your book?"

"Fine," Christian said.

"I'll walk him over to the dining room," Henry said, wrapping an arm around Christian's shoulder.

"Shouldn't take more than an hour," I added as they walked away. Lily waited on the sidewalk with her hands on her hips. I turned to her. "You look pensive. Is everything alright?"

"I'm afraid I might say something I'll regret," Lily said. "Makes me anxious."

"Rigorous honesty is the only way this program works," I said. "And for the record, I'm terrified too."

Nick, Lily, and I met Henry outside the dining room and headed to the Purple Group meeting room. Mike was sitting at his desk when we ushered ourselves in. Lily instinctively chose the seat beside my regular spot.

"Welcome, everyone." Mike snapped into professional mediator mode. "Prudence is working hard, and I'm pleased to see her solid support system. Each of you plays a significant role in Prue's life." He pressed the button on the boom box. "Let's take a moment of silence before we begin."

Chimes pinged, and I closed my eyes and focused on calming my mind. Letting go. The Purple Group room I had visited every day since my arrival felt strangely off-kilter with Nick present. None of us had done this before, which comforted me. We were all standing on unsteady ground.

"Today is about making amends," Mike said. "Nick, you will go first. Do you want to make amends to Prudence?" He held his arms at his sides in an open, neutral stance. His barrel chest lifted and lowered with each breath.

"Yes." Nick's voice sounded shattered, and it pained me.

"Begin when you are ready," Mike said. Our mediator sat at the edge of the circle of chairs, guarding, gatekeeping.

My body floated above the room. A tickle of uncontrollable laughter crept in; I bit my cheek.

"I closed you off from my heart and wasn't sensitive to your needs," Nick said. I wondered about the authentic man, and if I would like him. "Sorry I forgot your thirtieth birthday."

In my desperation to ease his suffering, I smiled.

"For not being supportive when you lost the baby . . ."

A box of tissues was passed over to Henry. Still, my agony refused to surface.

"I apologize for not taking you to doctor appointments or surgeries," Nick said. "My alcoholism causing you embarrassment. The betrayal of our wedding vows and acting like a boy when you needed a man."

Pale, sad eyes. The apology, contrived and disingenuous. Nothing has changed.

He finished. Mike stood, radiating positivity across the room, strengthening me. "Whenever you're ready, Prudence."

"I apologize for betraying you and our marriage vows," I said. There was no point in mincing words. "Sorry for lying." My apology was as flat as my pancake ass. "It was wrong of me to put my friendships before you."

Nick's patented wounded-animal expression crushed me to my core.

"This is a positive step toward healing and forgiveness," Mike said. "Comments?"

"This whole process is not changing anything," Lily said, composed and confident. "I appreciate what Nick said, but he isn't addressing the real issue." Her voice strengthened. "This guy is an alcoholic, and until he gets sober, how are they going to continue?"

Time stood still.

"Thank you." There was a pause as Mike found himself at a loss for words. "Nick, do you want to respond?"

"None of this is Lily's fucking business." Veins popped in his arms. "I can quit whenever I want. I tried the meetings and don't relate to those people and their stories. I'm going to stop my way." His neck twitched, and his face turned into a fireball. I mapped the fastest path to the exit.

"The program has a saying," Mike said. "'Terminally unique' is a common phrase to those in recovery. Many join AA believing their story is different from the rest. I'm not saying yours isn't."

The twelve steps stared out from the wall. Step one: admit we were powerless over our addiction.

"The decision to quit is yours and only yours," Mike continued, "but I guarantee you, your story is in the book."

Henry cleared his throat. "All I want is for my sister to be happy and move past the horrors of our childhood." The frailties he carried were invisible to the naked eye. "In my opinion, this couple thrives in an unhealthy way. Why would she go back into the same lion's den? Significant changes need to happen."

I chewed my cuticles, swallowing the dry skin, and rubbed my ear. Lily reached for my hand. "Nothing bad is going to happen," she said.

"There is no way I can decide this on the spot," I said. Impulse got the best of me. "I love him, but he doesn't love me."

The poisonous secret decayed my insides; a naïve belief he would grow fond of me. I made the most of a bad situation and lived by my mother's elastic walls theory.

"The person sitting in this chair is not the broken woman who checked in here," I said, shocked by the forthright words stumbling from my mouth. "For now, we should remain apart until you choose sobriety. Try to date, fall in love again. Can we discuss the money situation and this sense of abandonment?"

"Remember," Mike interjected, "children are abandoned, not adults."

"Right, sorry. I am angry at him for not being upfront about the severity our failing business." The lump throbbed and expanded. "The other woman needs to be out of the picture and off Nick's radar."

"The friend I know and love," Lily said admiringly.

"You are both hurting," Mike said, "and although it seems like we regressed, in actuality, the only way to move forward is to talk about the real issues. The painful ones." He cracked his boxer knuckles. "To recap, Nick stated he will stop alcohol when he is ready. Prue stated she would like to live apart until he quits and leaves the other woman."

"Why am I the bad guy here?" Nick exclaimed. "The bitch fucked every guy in town." He crossed his arms over his chest. Henry flinched. A dagger plunged into my heart.

"Refrain from name-calling." Mike towered over us, his legs braced in a fight stance. No man had ever defended me. Mike's eyes danced around Nick's stare.

"You're right," I said. "I did horrible, hurtful things, and you aren't the enemy. The demise of our relationship is both our faults."

"Time is up," Mike said. "Let's gather for the Serenity Prayer." He opened his hands. Lily grabbed one and Henry the other. I offered mine to Nick.

"I will always love you," I whispered.

Lunch went well. It seemed everyone's tension had defused, except for mine. So I faked it. We entered our last assignment refreshed. The toxins needed to get out.

"You will tell your spouse what you like or love about them." Chimes rang outside in the hot, unfulfilling breeze. "This exercise is done with an audience. In five minutes, others will be coming in to listen."

Just like clockwork, after five minutes, eight people entered the room—a combination of patients and family members. Our group sat together on one end of the rainbow shape. At the front of the room, Nick and I faced each other.

He smoothed the crinkled homework paper. "I admire your creativity, your fantastic sense of humor, your loving heart, your beautiful aura."

That eye-sparkle from Belize. The beginning.

"I love your adventurous spirit, the way you lift people up, your vulnerability, your selfless kindness, your devotion, and strength."

Could this be the new and improved version? The words bounced off like arrows hitting metal.

A few people dabbed their eyes. One woman asked to comment. "I dream of having this kind of love during my lifetime," she said.

Fools believe us, a relationship built on sand, crashing into the sea.

"Thank you for sharing," the group leader said, unsure of where to place her false image of us.

"I love your sense of humor," I said. "How you stay calm under pressure, your intelligence, your physical and emotional strength." It was not a perfect love story, but the story belonged to us. "Your patience, your gift with uplifting and motivating people, your tenderness, and loyalty."

"Awesome!" Christian said, elated by hearing his parents get along. "Family hug."

He offered to speak at graduation, and the group agreed.

"I'm here to support my mom," Christian said into the microphone, peppering his speech with perfectly timed pauses, the kind you'd hear in a presidential address. "I'm proud of her. She checked in to deal with her pain. I'm lucky to be her son. Thank you."

The audience applauded and stood in ovation. Family Week had come to an end, and I was still alive.

When everyone's rental cars had pulled away from the entrance to Serenity Hills and I was alone again, I ran to Mike's office to get my name on his private counseling list.

CHAPTER THIRTY

*A*t couple's therapy, Sheryl described intimacy: "Couples experience an extreme high in the beginning. Endorphins prevent us from seeing the true self. We are blinded by love." She drew an upward line in black marker on a whiteboard. It resembled the first rise of a roller coaster ride. "This high can last a month, six months, or a year—but never longer." The marker dragged back down.

"The drop," she said. "Reality. The person's flaws appear, and the blinders lift. We must choose to stay or go." The page resembled a stock report more than an intimacy description. "Let's say the couple stays together. What follows represents a series of bumps depicting the life of the relationship. You fight, make up, you love, hate, and love again."

Old enough to be my mother, vanilla-dressed Sheryl turned back to the whiteboard. She drew one last line straight up, past the original line. "After this stage is something beautiful, perfect, and alluring called intimacy."

I pictured her at a Dead concert in the seventies, intelligent and free-spirited, on the outside edge of hippie-dom.

If I stay with him, I will never know what intimacy is.

"Couples live like this for years. Some may never achieve the greatest height. This is the strongest love."

I wish I could bottle it and give to him for Christmas.

Nick moved to a two-bedroom apartment overlooking the marina. I imagined it to be a complex swarming with hot, single ladies. Child visitation happened every other weekend, but Christian's chronic stomachaches stalled the routine. Signs of the other woman in Nick's bachelor pad messed with my head. The obsessive thoughts got the best of me. We never again discussed the possibility of my getting help. My sickness festered under the skin and poisoned my insides.

The parents' magazine at the doctor's office said kids craved routine during times of strife. On Sundays, ours became a bike ride. Christian careened ahead. A man opened his patio gate, and Christian screeched his brakes, skidding to a stop.

"Got a rubber burn with those tires," I said, easing up next to him.

"Gorgeous lady, stop and say hello," the man said. His deep tan matched the surf attire, all the way to the flat-brimmed hat with an intact under-the-brim sticker.

"Hello," I said, straddling my bike like a human kickstand.

"Never seen you before." He motioned for us to pull our bikes closer to his gate. "Stan," he said. "This is my house."

"You were on the patio," I said. "I assumed it was your place. This is my son, Christian, and I'm Prue."

Male attention always elated me, sending joy signals to my brain equal to that of my father on cocaine. Christian reached out for a handshake.

"What a gentleman," Stan said, displaying a row of Chiclet teeth. "How about dinner Saturday night?"

"Sure," I said.

"Come by here at seven, and we'll grab some food." He winked, triggering a creeper vibe.

∞

Stan motioned for me to park in front his Porsche. "How about I give you a tour of my house?" he said.

Chipped-oak cabinets with missing handles and stained Formica screamed for a remodel. The plastic in the drop-down ceiling was yellowed from years of use. One long neon bulb sputtered and blinked. Matted beige carpet emitted a faint urine odor.

"The place could use some updating," he said. "I've been waiting for the right girl to come along. Got plenty of room for your son."

Red flag.

A surfboard leaned against the entry wall as I followed him up a curved staircase. Plastic framed posters of palms and sunsets covered the walls. Three distinct pillow mounds were piled on one side of the king bed.

"For propping up my legs," he said.

Sexy.

Pitted-gold fixtures and moldy grout in the bath; moisturizer, mouthwash, pill bottles, Advil, nail clippers, and deodorant on the counter.

Why doesn't he put this stuff in the cabinet?

The restaurant door smacked me as he failed to hold it. I was undeterred by his poor manners due to my enthusiasm for a free meal.

"I got a deal on the Porsche," he said as we were seated. He picked up the menu and looked it over. "An entire entrée is an awful lot of food." He lifted the brim of his hat and scratched his forehead. "Why don't we split?"

My mouth dropped open.

"The chicken," he said to the waiter. "Split between two plates."

An attractive enough face and decent personality. But the cheap part: a death sentence.

Back at his place, we fooled around on the grimy couch. He lowered his shorts, and his penis popped out like a clown from a wind-up box. "Grade-A meat," he said. Loose skin dangled from his stomach.

Enough to make a fine handbag.

"Impressive," I lied.

He wedged in beside me and stroked himself. Decent enough kissing got my head and body in the game.

"Let's get more comfortable," he said.

Indecision coursed through me. My legs spread over the king bed, he fumbled around, lost in the mud flaps. I emitted the obligatory moan.

"You make me so fucking horny." His skin flap swung as he pinned my legs in the air. All the while, I planned my exit strategy.

"Oh, you're going to make me come, baby . . . you move so sweet . . . here comes the cream. Oh, yeah . . . I'm coming . . . Oh, God!" Facial contortions I'd seen in pornos. I bit my cheek to squash the urge to laugh. "Wow, baby." He moved to the pillow pile. "Want to watch a little TV?"

"I need to get home," I said, searching for my clothes. "Thanks for a fun night."

"Wish you could stay. I'll call next week, make a plan."

Mr. Leather Handbag seemed perfect for the occasional screw. He fell in my mix when I needed to fill the void with a triple.

After losing Roger's cash wads, my struggles worsened. Stress hit me hardest at night. Alone in bed, my mind raced while I ground my veneers. The last of my inheritance was taking its final breath. Month after month, an eviction notice hung on the knob. The water, electricity, and cable were shut off until I could scrape enough together to turn it back on. Intense pride stopped me from asking Henry for a loan. Or maybe I feared he would say no.

∞

"Prue, it's Lenny. How are you?"

Lenny was a friend of Mom's who I'd seen at the various social gatherings she'd dragged me to over the years. Lenny had never been married, and Mom claimed he had a thing for me—which was laughable, since he was old enough to be my father. It amused me how perfectly matched Lenny was with his name: short and thin, with patchy hair and an eager personality. He was a real doofus.

"Wow. Are you in LA?" I asked, sinking into a club chair.

"En route. Listen, I'm in a jam. Any chance you can be my date for a gala this evening?" Airplane noises clouded the background.

"I think so," I said, hoping I could find an overnight sitter. "What's the attire?"

"Wear a fancy dress. Don't worry, you'll be the most beautiful woman there."

I was pissed my lack of means prevented me from picking up a new dress. "What time?"

"I'll send a car to pick you up at six. Heard about your mom," he said. "I'm sorry."

Lenny owned a jewelry store in a strip mall. My nickname for him was Jewels. He stood shorter than me by two inches. He had a small, wiry body and a toilet bowl rim of hair. Inflicted with OCD, Jewels repeated actions: cash counting, opening and closing the hotel room safe, plugging and unplugging his phone. He performed each routine with frenetic energy. I had no clue whether he still found me attractive. He talked about his ex-girlfriend in excess.

"Jesus, Prue, I can't believe your hubby left you destitute," he said. I lay in silence, waiting for the bell in his head to ring. "Let me cover six months of your rent."

I'd waited for the optimum moment to reveal my fiscal situation: post-coitus. The right decision, even if intercourse with Jewels was the grossest experience of my life. He didn't do foreplay. He simply pummeled me and was done.

"Wow, amazing. Could you believe I stayed hard so long and didn't use Viagra? Damn, I'm such a stud." Black hair swirled over the white skin peeking through.

"Prop up on all fours," he said. "Let's turn your rear ruby red." Glazed eyes watched me move into position—the spankings repeated while he instructed me to bark like a dog.

At home, piles of credit card bills arrived in the mail. Multiple three hundred-dollar dinners, combined with single nights in swanky hotels, sent me reeling.

"Why don't you fuck your girlfriend at your apartment?" I snapped at Nick over the phone. "Why at a hotel?" It took every bit of strength I had to not go batshit crazy on him. "How are you affording these expensive dinners? By the way, I heard Naomi is married."

Little did Nick know, I had asked a friend to do a background check.

"Naomi is separated but not divorced for personal reasons, Prudense. The hotels are halfway between our homes, but we don't stay the night together. This is not your concern."

How does their encounter unfold?

✆

An associate introduced me to the architect. His conservative clothes stood in stark contrast to his dirty mouth. With a fat ass and bulky thighs, his body had a womanly shape. Crusty psoriasis and lumpy moles riddled his legs. An oversized forehead exposed a receding hairline, but when he revealed his recent separation from a sexless, twenty-year marriage, I knew I could help.

He waved from the hotel balcony. I tugged my ear and attempted to give myself a pep talk. Roger had paid me, but not for intercourse. I justified giving him blowjobs as a way of returning the favor for helping me out. But meeting up with the architect was different. This was point-blank doing it for money. No denying or skirting the issue.

When I got into the hotel room, he popped the cork on a bottle of expensive champagne. "To us," he said.

Pull off my panties and get to the finish line.

"Cheers." I forced a smile.

"You're a hell of a sexy woman," he said, tearing off my shirt with his eyes. "For you." He pointed to a wad of cash, which I promptly jammed into my purse.

The second glass of champagne calmed me. I unbuttoned his no-iron khakis and mentally listed the things the money would cover: electric bill, groceries, rest of the rent, a sweatshirt for Christian.

To finish, he crouched over my face and jerked off. Sweat and lube splattered everywhere with his rigorous hand motions. Red-faced and beady-eyed, with one last grunt, he released.

After a few more obligatory sips from my glass, I checked the clock. "I need to go. My son gets out of school at two."

"Can't wait to see you again."

In my car, I calculated how much I had earned per second, weighing the repulsion with the reward.

"You aren't seeing me just for the money, are you?" he said the next time we met up. "Because I get the feeling you are into me, and I want to help you."

"Of course not," I lied.

"Let me cook for you, babe. We can listen to music and drink red wine. Do you like steak?"

"No, I'm a vegetarian."

Anything to avoid dinner at his place.

"No matter. I'll make all the vegetables you want."

We rendezvoused at his old house when his ex-wife was out of town. I laid on the family room oriental, and he kneeled over me. A fat roll blocked his face; his balls swung as he stroked his tiny penis.

"Touch my ass, baby, I think I'm falling in love with you."

CHAPTER THIRTY-ONE

"**O**ne slot left," Kim said, handing me a pencil. "You must need therapy after getting through Family Week."

"An understatement," I said. "Lots of highs and lows."

Kim followed me down the stairs and out into the quad. "Did you score a hall pass?" she asked. "I was afraid you got punished for the kiss."

"No punishment, not sure why. We ate Italian. Damn tasty. Afterwards, we went to the hotel and screwed."

"My next question!" We stopped between two buildings. Kim nibbled on a chunk of her hair. "Well? Details, please."

"All it did was add to my confused state," I said. "Guilty and lonely feelings afterward. There was a sense of obligation, yet something ate away at me." I hesitated; Kim remained locked on my every word. "There was this sensation I was betraying Alistair. Hell, I can't articulate what I'm trying to say."

"Holy crap. This sounds like a shitstorm. But then again, it might mean you're getting over him. Nick, I mean."

"Want to draw?" I asked. "Kill a little time."

We went to the art room and grabbed paper and colored pencils from the bin.

"It sucks you're leaving at the end of next week and I'll be here without you," Kim said. "Somehow, you keep me calm."

"Enjoy it, because next thing you know, you'll be headed home. Boom. Back to reality."

She wiggled in her chair. "Now that you told me you did the nasty, I can't shake it from my mind. Perhaps you no longer need the relationship, since figuring out you deserve happiness." Her root-beer colored eyes dug into my soul. "You want to know the truth? I didn't think Nick was handsome. He wasn't anything like I thought he would be. He came across like a dick."

Shattered pieces of my old self clung with all their might. "He changes from handsome to ugly, depending on his mood."

"Forgive me for playing amateur therapist, but you aren't the picture of happiness since seeing your hubby." She smoothed Eos lip balm over her mouth.

"The past few days brought some clarity," I said. "So much went down between us, yet we hold this bonding history. Our love story is not what I had hoped for myself."

Kim's expression softened. "Love shouldn't be this hard."

"Most everyone gets the same reaction when they meet him. Not sure why he can't be warmer and friendlier." I drew a few unfulfilling lines on my paper.

"The last puzzle piece of your addiction. His cold demeanor left you a stranger in your own home all these years. No wonder you snapped."

I looked down at my sketch: a crude house, with palm trees and a dog.

A dark tendril moved off Kim's forehead. "I wish I had more understanding of why I started banging everyone in sight. Some people think this addiction is a bunch of bullshit. I can't even use not having a positive father figure as an excuse. My dad was awesome. When I was little, I'd fall asleep in the car and he would carry me into the house." She licked the balm from her lips. "The funny part was, I was pretending to be asleep, and he knew it."

"That's so sweet," I said, wishing I'd had someone to carry me. "Your trauma timeline showed some of the telltale signs of someone who'd endured child abuse. Like a mentally ill mother who made you be a grownup at five years old. That's as bad as being molested. At least your husband will be there when you check out of this place." I cursed my luck and bad choices. "It's hard to imagine mine supporting me and not judging."

Kim stared out the window. "You know what? You still exude a sexual vibe."

I scratched my foot, stalling. "Not sure what I'm doing or how to stop."

"Well, you're going to have to accept it. It's in your DNA."

I wondered whether a woman's sensuality was a learned behavior or her birthright. "I used my sexuality to get what I wanted when I was little and, some would say I still do. A small voice tells me I deserved to be molested because I asked for it."

"*This* voice says no child deserves or asks for something as sick as that. Get it out of your mind." She spoke with such a commanding tone that it occurred to me I must have triggered a memory within her. She turned her eyes back to her drawing. "How was coming clean? Did you tell him everything? I'm freaking about confessing."

"He knew about the infidelities. No point in causing him agony with every last detail. If I were in Nick's shoes, I might not take me back. He told me that I used my diagnosis as a sex addict to justify my bad behavior." I balled up my sketch and threw it in the wastebasket. "Mike wants me to do aftercare."

"I sure am," Kim said. "There's no way I could be fixed in five weeks." She checked the clock. "I better go to my appointment."

I wandered outside to see if anyone was around.

"Princess," Mitch called out from the smoking area. He lit a cigarette from the burning ember of Gloria's lipstick-rimmed filter. "Come sit with us."

I slumped down beside a ghostly-pale Gloria. "I need my Prue fix," she said, pouting. Her dirt-streaked doll dangled between her knees.

"Been in the thinking place," I said.

"Sounds like me. Wish I could turn it off, but I can't." She blew a ring of smoke, the circles disappearing into the sky. "I mean, does anyone really care if I live or die?"

I moved closer and let her lay her head on my shoulder. "I care," I said. "We all do." Her sense of aloneness was understandable. The loss of my mother and grandmother had left a crevasse in my heart.

My heaviness rose past the latticework and shot toward the stars.

"We're all going to make it," I said.

My lifeline: hope.

"I'll swing back later," I said, rising from my seat. "Love you guys." Before I left, I leaned in and whispered into Mitch's ear. "Keep an eye on Gloria."

❧

I dropped down onto Mike's sofa and crossed my legs beneath me. "Gloria is depressed. I'm worried about her."

"No one in her family showed up," Mike said. "It's natural for her to be upset. I'll talk to her. You can't save the world, you can only save you."

"Family Week reopened wounds. After breaking us down, we got sewn back together, but not in the same way."

"The week is meant to tear down walls so everyone is quite vulnerable, and build each person back up before sending them on their way." He had a smart new haircut: two-three, velvet sides, and bristled on top. "How do you feel about Nick?"

I laughed. "That's the million-dollar question. Less desperate, I guess. The sense of urgency for immediate answers has diminished. I'm more hopeful than I was before I checked in. I love him, but am toying with the concept of letting him go. We're toxic together."

The fearful words, spoken aloud and put out to the universe.

"Enormous strides were made this week," Mike said, sounding like a parent who just watched his child hit a home run. "It's unlikely Nick will move to a place of healing or forgiveness anytime soon."

My chest tightened; the constant reminder I had no power over Nick's decision. "Most of my stress is over how I'll cover my bills. The anger over trusting someone with my money is pointless. It's all gone, and I have to start over."

"Trust it will all work out. You're a survivor."

I caught myself tugging on my earlobe and set my hands on my lap. "The unknown puts me on edge. It's a struggle. Concern about going back to my old coping mechanisms, men . . . and you know." Horror swallowed me and spit me back out on the floor.

Filthy, dirty slut.

"Practice consciousness and put into action all you learned here. Self-sabotaging would be unproductive and a risk. I'm confident you won't go back to your old survival techniques."

I wished I was as certain about it as Mike sounded. "What should I do about my marriage?"

"Put you first. Let go of whether he judges or accepts you. You cannot change his alcohol consumption, nor can you make him love you. What you *can* control is you—your actions, thoughts, and reactions. Live one day at a time." He locked on my eyes, and I melted. "You brought many blessings to your relationship. Celebrate the blessings each day."

I want to wrap him up and take him home.

∽

The door flying open startled me. It was long past lights-out. It was Deirdre.

"Have you seen Gloria?" she asked. She looked wild-eyed and frantic.

"Earlier, with you." I slipped on my shoes.

"They can't find her." She paced the room nervously.

We moved outside. "Did you check the veranda?"

"Yup, and the dining room, meeting rooms, her room. Everyone is looking for her."

"Did anyone call Tom?"

Maybe Tom left his wife and picked up Gloria because he couldn't live without her.

"Rumor has it she got a letter from him today. He broke it off. Tom and his wife both signed it."

I gasped. "That's horrible."

Deirdre's fingers dug into the flesh of my arm as we walked to the nurses' station. A heaviness enveloped me. We stepped through the door and into the sterile room. Gloria's baby doll lay on the counter. I pulled it into my arms.

"Oh, no," I said. "Please, no."

I pressed the baby's smoky clothes to my face. Nurse Ratched inched over, her eyes like two black holes sucking me into permanent darkness. With each passing moment, the battle to fight my feelings crumbled. The salty taste of tears touched my tongue.

"Gloria took her life this evening," Nurse Ratched said.

Deirdre sobbed. A backlit figure walked through the door. Mike wrapped his arms around Deirdre, then pulled me in.

"Group meeting in five," he said, his voice cracking. "We are going to deal with this together."

Who will take care of Gloria's baby?

CHAPTER THIRTY-TWO

The last week of rehab; the week where we put it all behind us, accepted our pasts, and vowed to never go back again.

The week I might snap.

Gloria visited me in my dreams. She sat in my room wearing her favorite pink flamingo t-shirt, a cigarette in one hand, her baby doll in the other.

Her mouth moved, but I couldn't understand what she was saying.

The only available computer had a crying girl seated next to it. She sniffled and snorted with my every mouse click. It took all my might not to console her. There were two emails of any interest in my inbox. I read Lily's first; I needed time to muster up the guts to read Nick's.

Hi Chickie,

It was an honor to be there and witness your hard work and personal growth. You inspire me. My broker recommended I diversify my portfolio with real estate. I'm going to invest in a property in Los Angeles. After you're released from the padded room, we can check out open houses. The "landlord" will rent it to you cheap if you promise to free up the guest bedroom when I visit. Think about it. Love you. –Lil

My magical soul sister.

I clicked on Nick's email next.

Prue—I'm over it. F-Week, too brutal for words. Ready to call it quits. We can hash out the custody details later.

The rest of the email was written in regurgitated rehab lingo he'd learned during his one-week visit to Serenity Hills. As if he was some sort of expert or something now. I hoped he was just venting. No one ends a marriage by email. I kicked myself for fucking him during Family Week.

Stop acting like a tramp.

My therapist would not be going home with me. I had to figure this out on my own. My situation changed moment by moment; overreacting would not be wise. I logged out and denied Nick the satisfaction of a response.

Week five took place in the farthest building on campus. A part I had not seen.

I am hopeful.

Half of the group was comprised of patients. The other half were visitors who believed they could clean out their past in five days. The part I feared most about survivors was hearing everyone else's abuse stories.

An overweight woman with soft features and rosacea greeted us. She reminded me of a woman one might see in an old Dutch painting.

"Welcome," she said. Her hands were clasped together and she smiled, rocking in her chocolate-brown therapeutic shoes. Her fashion sense meant nothing; her ability to heal my past meant everything. "Please choose a seat, and we will begin."

A kindergarten teacher on the first day of school.

"You all have moved toward happiness and freedom," she said. "Freedom from the chains of your past." She stated her name, but instead of it registering in my brain, it splattered on the wall behind me.

She wrote on the easel. "This week is about facing your abuser." The words *shame* and *abuse* were displayed in bold letters. She uncapped a pen with her mouth, circled the words, and marked an X straight through the middle of each one. "Confronting your abuser will help you get rid of the horrific shame you carry because of their actions. Any questions?"

My knees flexed together. The man beside me spoke up.

"What if our abuser didn't come, or is dead?"

Did he really ask that?

Green ink bled over the group leader's thumb and index finger. "An excellent question. This is for catharsis and healing. It's not necessary to bring in the person and make things more traumatizing."

A storm brewed inside me — my stepfather's greasy face, his hand beating me.

I paid closer attention on the third day. I didn't want to be one of the losers who fell too far behind, assuming they could erase their entire past in a single week. Dressed in a floral frock and the same brown shoes, the group counselor held a plastic baseball bat. Two empty chairs and a small table holding a lifetime supply of tissues had been added to the room.

"Today, we confront our abusers. Donald offered to go first."

Donald was a big guy; I figured he must have weighed at least a deuce and a half. He wore his steel-gray hair in a clip and a different Tommy Bahama shirt every day. The exterior did not match his quiet demeanor.

"I want to put it behind me," he said meekly as he settled into the chair and held the bat, which seemed to shrink in his grip.

"Are you ready to face your abuser?"

Donald emitted a feeble grunt.

"We are going to walk him in." She transformed into a snake speaking in tongues, a language only she knew. The clap of her hands startled me. "Sit down!" she yelled to the imaginary abuser.

Donald squeezed his eyes shut. His skin turned dark red as he screamed and smacked the empty chair. Panic-stricken, I clasped my hands over my head and folded in half. Little Prue could not sit still because she might be the next one hit. I whimpered and moved without permission. The floor grew closer. Hand over hand, I crawled to the corner.

The rational adult, gone.

Donald continued to pound his abuser. "Motherfucker!" The chair held its ground, taking the beating it deserved. "You robbed me of my innocence and put your sickness on a child!"

The chair bobbed and weaved and finally toppled with one last blow. Silence filled the room—all but the moans coming me. The bat slid from Donald's hands, snot dripping into his mouth.

At the end of the session, I exited the room with the rest, sick with embarrassment over how I'd reacted.

"Can I have a word with you?" the counselor asked. I nodded. "Your file shows the unbearable abuse you endured. Listen to your body. Trust it!"

Again, the next day, I fled to the same spot in the corner. This time, a blanket awaited me. I hid underneath it, in a ball.

My donkeyskin of protection.

On the last day, it was my turn to face the Devil. My mother invaded my thoughts. Rage bubbled below the surface. I placed her in my heart and forced the person I had buried in the crypts of Hell to come alive.

"You no longer need to carry the horrors put on you by this sick man," the counselor said. "Are you ready for us to bring Richard in?"

With violent trembling, I pulled my legs to my chest. Shark-infested waters flowed beneath my chair. "Please, don't bring him in!"

"Would it be helpful if two of the bigger men assisted with escorting him in?"

The same, unidentifiable sound spewed from my mouth as my imaginary perpetrator stepped through the door. My mouth opened. I tried to speak; no words came, only hyperventilating. The counselor pressed the harmless plastic bat into my hands, but it grew heavy, far too heavy for me to hold.

"I can't," I whimpered, turning my head.

The box of tissues was shoved in my lap. "Throw them at him!"

Slowly, my inner power strengthened. The first tissue floated like a feather, but they began to fly harder and faster as I summoned all the rage within me.

The snake spoke for me, yelling into the vacant space where my imaginary abuser sat, as the tissues flew from my hands. "You are a sick and twisted man," she said. "You molested me and put your hands on me." The snake spoke in tongues, but I understood. "I give you back your shame!"

Three empty boxes. I opened my eyes to a mound of tissues. I breathed in; the group cheered. My vision cleared.

An emptiness inside left my healing incomplete. There was one more person I needed to forgive: Mom. The truth was, she had never protected me, and her affair with Mr. Sutton had displayed her true character. I vowed to write Mrs. Sutton and apologize for holding the secret all these years.

The walk back to the campus got me thinking about the road ahead of me—the road back to reality. Rather than counting my steps, I listed the things I missed: my phone, music, Twizzlers, bread, bubble baths . . . my freedom. With Nick's email looming over me and my newfound strength, I decided to call him.

The next phase has begun.

The line wait gave me unwanted time. My mouth grew parched, the water bottle lost in the chaos. The previous caller had left the receiver warm and sweaty.

Why does he inflict terror in me?

The timer dinged. The line on the other end rang twice, then Nick picked up.

I smiled with intent. "Well, I finished," I said. "I graduated." I fought the urge to fill the void of silence. "After a lot of thinking, I realized I want you to be happy. And if you don't see a future in us, then I understand. You need to move on."

Why do I put his happiness before mine? Someone who sucks the life out of me.

"I'm not ready to say goodbye to Naomi," Nick said. My hand went numb. "Too much has happened. How can we move forward when the past is so painful? I'm not sure I was ever happy with you."

He stole my line.

"Not ever?"

"Nope, never."

I could die alone.

"Nick?"

"Yeah."

"The timer is about to go off. Let's discuss this more when I get home. For now, I'll stay in the house until the lease is up."

"Fair warning," he said, "I won't be giving you money. You can make your own."

My head started spinning. "Christian needs his home, and I don't want to move him with all these changes."

"One last thing," Nick said, ignoring my words. "I'm going to fight you for custody."

"Goodbye, Nick." My hand stuck to the phone. I dragged a sleeve across my sweaty forehead. He was calling my bluff.

This man cannot be a fulltime father, nor does he want to be. He is rattling me. He can't take my child.

Back in my room, I began packing my belongings. Kim banged on the window and mouthed, "Let me help you."

"Come on in," I yelled. "The door's open."

"Fuck, I'm going to miss you!" She wore a tight, white tank top that exposed floral bra straps. A long bohemian skirt outlined her legs with each step.

"Cute outfit," I said with admiration.

"I can only wear it from my room to yours since it's not Serenity friendly."

"True."

"So, how was it?" She emptied a drawer onto my bed and began folding clothes.

"Different, yet healing. I don't want to say too much and spoil it for you." I yanked a mini denim skirt from a hanger. "Half of these clothes, I couldn't wear!"

"Same here. My whole wardrobe is unwearable."

"Dress sexy when you get home," I told her. "You'll be ready to spring out of your Catholic schoolgirl uniform."

"You know I will! Let's plan a visit when all this is over. Put my number in your favorites. Shit, I almost forgot! Mitch said to come by before you go." I bent over, and she smacked my ass. "Got to go, love you!"

The last personal item to be packed was the stuffed pony Nick had given me on the way to the airport—an item so small, yet it symbolized the goodness in my marriage.

I left my bags outside the door of my room for the orderly to take to the nurses' station, then walked to the smoking veranda.

"Prue!" Mitch leaned against the railing. "My Princess is leaving."

"It'll be difficult for me to keep up that status after I check out," I laughed.

"Here is everyone's phone numbers and addresses. I assume you'll get Alistair's on your own." He winked. "Sadly, one number is missing, and we're all devastated by it."

The darkness Gloria left behind.

"I think Tom snuck in here and killed her," Mitch added.

"The same thought crossed my mind," I said. "A defenseless bird with a broken wing." Mitch teared up, and it broke me. The gate opened, and I sobbed into his clean white shirt. "Sorry."

He wiped a tear from my cheek. "Oh, how I will miss my Princess." He bowed and walked away, down the path. A sob echoed through the trees.

Rhoda wandered toward the veranda. An unlit cigarette dangled from her lips. "Damn, I hate goodbyes." She lit the cigarette in defiance of the rule against smoking outside the designated area. "I've been wanting to break a rule since I got here," she said, blowing smoke in the direction of the nurses' station. "Never forget, you are a goddess." Her rosy lenses fogged. "Dammit, I promised myself I wouldn't cry."

"Friends for life." We hooked our pinkies together.

"One of my all-time favorite humans," she said, sucking in a long, deep drag. "One more thing." Smoke puffed from her mouth with each word. "Ditch that husband of yours. He's all wrong for you. The group predicts you and Alistair will end up together." With an impish grin on her face, she stamped out her cigarette.

"Hilarious." I kicked a pebble from the path. "Who knows what the future holds?" I began to walk, but after two steps, I turned back. "I love you so much!"

CHAPTER THIRTY-THREE

"You did it," Nurse Ratched said.

I went for the hug I had yearned to give her. "Sorry if I was a bitch or anything."

"Never apologize for being a strong woman," she said.

The office door opened and Mike walked in. "I've been looking for you."

With gentle hands, he guided me to the lobby where I'd had my breakdown during Family Week. The palm tree in the corner appeared healthier, greener—a living trophy of my growth.

"There were moments of doubt," he said. "I was wrong. You shined, did the work, and inspired others with your resilience." It was the final boost I needed to step out into the world alone. "Never forget, you deserve love."

"You changed my life." Sadness burned in my heart. My hands covered my face; the last remaining piece of the shell I'd wrapped around me like a suit of armor crumbled to the floor. I sobbed, and he reached for me.

"It will all work out the way it should," Mike said. "I have a gift for you." He handed me a book: *Twelve Steps and Twelve Traditions*. "Your side of the street is clean. It is your job to keep it that way. Go to meetings, work the program."

"Thank you seems too small to express my gratitude," I said.

Mike performed this job week after week, day after day, whether he connected with a patient or thought they were a total mess. A spiritual guide with all the compassion one man could give. "Well, I guess this is goodbye."

I held his face in my eyes, embedded in my mind and heart forever. And then he walked away—back to his job of changing lives.

"I'm going to miss this place," I said to no one in particular. The bin containing my belongings rested on the counter. I reached for my phone. It was a physical representation of my inappropriate past, and I was tempted to smash it to pieces. "A lot of numbers need to be deleted from this thing."

Nurse Ratched stood stoically behind the counter, hearing not a word. "Initial here," she said and handed me a clipboard. I signed my name one last time at Serenity Hills.

Arms came from behind and wrapped themselves around my waist. The voice that spoke into my ear was smooth and comforting. "The thought of goodbye is unbearable," Alistair said, "yet not seeing you off felt downright wrong."

I turned. All paperwork completed, I was a free agent. I laid my head against his chest; closed my eyes and breathed him in. He handed me a folded piece of paper.

"These are all the numbers and addresses you will ever need to find me." His eyes turned glassy but remained focused on mine. "Read the note when you get home, and promise me we will see each other again."

"Promise." Every inch of his face burned in my corneas. I unbuckled my mother's watch and pressed it into his hands. "This is for you. Keep it until the next time we see each other again."

"I will cherish this." He tucked the delicate timepiece into his pocket, then held my hands and pulled me close. "You inspire me. Your story and strong spirit make me want to do better for myself and my future."

We moved in slow motion. His pillowed lips met mine. I held the moment with my whole heart. Our hands remained intertwined as he backed away, until we couldn't hold on any longer.

By the exit, Jimmy the driver waited.

Full circle.

"Ready?" he said.

"Yes."

Scared, excited, and exhilarated, I slid into the back seat. Serenity Hills disappeared in the rear window. Saguaro cacti rolled by, but their arms no longer reached out to me.

"You know what I'm craving?" I said.

Jimmy flinched. "What's that?" Through the rearview mirror, concerned eyes watched me.

"Twizzlers." I laughed, and the tension left his shoulders. "My all-time favorite candy. The strawberry flavor. Damn, I love those things."

"What about red vines?"

"Hate them with a fiery passion."

We rode the rest of the way in silence. The tragic loss of my dear friend, Gloria, sunk into my heart, giving me permission to cry, to let the salt flow down my face.

God bless you, my sweet angel.

Eyes peered at me through the rearview. Perhaps Jimmy had grown accustomed to people breaking down on the ride back to reality.

What I wanted was a dress the color of the sky, but a donkeyskin would protect me. Was I wrong to crave the magnificent blue dress?

What I need is not beautiful to the naked eye. The donkeyskin represents my new life.

"You alright?" Jimmy asked.

"Yes, I think so," I said, and for possibly the first time in my life, I believed it. "I might even be better than I was before."

The car pulled to the curb at the airport terminal. I walked inside, all alone, my head held high. At one with my donkeyskin, she blanketed me with everything I needed.

ABOUT the AUTHOR

A native New Yorker and captivating storyteller with a flair for embellishment, Jennifer Irwin currently resides in Los Angeles with two cats, a dog, and her boyfriend. After earning her BA in Cinema from Denison University, she worked in advertising and marketing, raised three boys, and ultimately became a certified Pilates instructor. While she has written screenplays and short stories since her college days, *A Dress the Color of the Sky* is her first novel. For more information, visit www.jenniferirwinauthor.com.

ABOUT the PUBLISHER

Glass Spider Publishing is a hybrid micropublisher located in Ogden, Utah. The company was founded in 2016 by writer Vince Font to help authors get their works into shape, into print, and into distribution. Visit www.glassspiderpublishing.com to learn more.

A Glass Spider Publishing Reading Group Guide
A Dress the Color of the Sky
by Jennifer Irwin

The questions and discussion topics that follow are intended to enhance your reading group's discussion of *A Dress the Color of the Sky*, the poignant, eagerly awaited debut novel by Jennifer Irwin.

1. The title appears in the story when Mrs. Sutton reads the fairytale *Donkeyskin* to Prue. How does the title fit into Prue's journey? What is the significance of the donkeyskin?

2. The theme of the book pertains to how the events of one's childhood can mold and shape who we become as adults. How did the experiences Prue had as a young girl affect the woman she became? What underlying themes was the author trying to get across to the reader? Was there redemption in the book? Were you surprised by the complications Prue encountered and the twists and turns of the plot?

3. How does the cover reflect the themes of the book? What do the three horses in the background represent?

4. What was unique about the setting of the book, and how did it enhance the story?

5. The book has many difficult and painful scenes. Did reading any of them make you uncomfortable? If so, why? Did this lead to a greater understanding of some aspect of your life?

6. Were the problems/decisions/relationships in Prue's adult life believable or relatable? Which character did you relate to the most and why?

7. What is the significance of the nicknames Prue used for the men in her life? Can you identify a nickname someone has given you that is either degrading or endearing?

8. How did the author's use of moving back and forth in time create empathy for Prudence? What was the significance of adding Prue's inner thoughts? How did this enhance the story?

9. "Dad offered to drag me along on his vacation to Belize with Virginia, his new flame. Her physique matched his requirements, but she was disheveled and careless in her attire and hygiene. She schlepped around her degree in clinical psychology like it was enough to keep my drug-addicted dad in check. I had to live with the unanswered questions and unresolved ache buried in my heart and my mother's grave. With Mom gone and Thatcher out of the picture, I needed a getaway." How does this passage set up the meeting of Prue and Nick? What do you think Prue's state of mind is before meeting Nick?

10. What role did Mike play in healing Prue? How was he able to get close to her without any physical contact?

11. Would you like Prue if you met her in real life? What characteristics did you find appealing or repulsive, and why? What do you think was her turning point to finding self-love?

12. In your opinion, what were the pivotal scenes? How did the author create a sense of chaos in both Prue's inner and outer world?

13. How did you like the author's writing style and word usage? Do you have any favorite passages?

14. If you were to break apart the book into two sections, Prue's childhood and adult life, which part did you find to be the most interesting, and why?

15. The author was very careful with the sex scenes in the book. Why do you think she wrote a book about a sex addict without including a lot of gratuitous sex?

16. If the author were to write a sequel to this book, what would you like to see happen?

17. Why do you think some women are skilled at listening to their guts and some aren't? Have you ever dated someone you knew was wrong for you, but stayed in the relationship anyway? Has a friend ever warned you not to date someone? Did you accept their advice?

18. What events in the book stand out as memorable?

19. Describe the main character's personality traits. Did any of the characters remind you of someone you know? Were the characters believable? Did you approve or disapprove of Prue's behavior? Why do you think her friends were not aware of her behavior? Do you think they enabled her?

20. This book is being made into a feature film. Who would you cast for the roles of the main characters?

21. If you had to choose one lesson the author was trying to teach, what would it be?

22. What was the significance of Prudence giving Alistair her mother's watch?

23. In several passages of the narrative, it was indicated that sexual addiction, like all other addictions, is not so much a choice as it is the result of childhood trauma and life experience. Do you believe this to be true? Why?

CPSIA information can be obtained
at www.ICGtesting.com
Printed in the USA
LVOW07*0252101017
551788LV00001B/1/P